WHERE WERE
YOU
ON THE
DAY

To Bill,
Thanks So Very Much!
I hope you enjoy the story.

R.T. HAYTON

PAGE PUBLISHING, INC.
New York, NY

First originally published by Page Publishing, Inc. 2016

ISBN 978-1-68409-083-9 (Paperback)
ISBN 978-1-68409-084-6 (Digital)

Printed in the United States of America

For love lost along the way...I think of you often.

Russian Steppes, Winter, 2002

Gregori Ilyanovich Stassiski had been a colonel in the Soviet Strategic Rocket Forces. At the moment, he was waiting at an abandoned air base alongside an empty runway in Eastern Siberia. He scanned the skies to the west, the direction from which the cargo plane should be appearing at any moment. Seeing nothing, he dropped the binoculars back to his chest. He sighed, glancing at the shivering man next to him. Mentally he grinned, enjoying the discomfiture of the overly coated, ex-KGB agent standing there. He had needed Sergei in the beginning; whether he would need him much longer remained to be seen. The little ferret had almost outlived his usefulness, and his constant nasal whining could be a little abrasive at times. With all the fur he was wearing, he resembled a ferret indeed. A red-snouted, runny-nosed ferret.

"Gregori, just who are we waiting for again?" Sergei asked, stamping his feet against the cold.

Grinding his teeth slightly at the interruption of his train of thought, he decided to answer.

"Sergei, you know very well who we are waiting for," he replied. "The man who is going to make us obscenely rich for the rest of our lives. The buyer of our treasure. Please be quiet and patient. We need to be focused and composed when he lands. Concentrate!"

Dismissing his friend for the moment, Gregori once again began to scan the skies. His ears had detected a faint drone to the southwest, almost too faint to be detected above the wind. Turning in that direction, he saw a large ex-soviet transport plane beginning its final descent into the valley that held the air base. He watched for a few seconds and lowered the binoculars again.

"Here he comes now!" he whispered excitedly.

They were so close. Years had gone into preparing for this moment right now, or one very similar to it. He had grabbed this opportunity with both hands when it was presented to him almost twelve years ago. He had been in his prime then when the USSR had begun to fall apart. That traitor Gorbachev, that weakling, had betrayed them all and given up their country to gangs, and mobsters and thugs had caved in to the West.

All the satellites had begun to break away, and Mother Russia had done *nothing*. His whole life had been committed to a military career. His had been a rising star along with many other fine young officers. The first *real* generation of people born in the Soviet Union, they were going to spread the peoples' will all over the world and . . . nothing. The Reset button had been pushed. Eighty years' worth of struggle and history amounted to nothing, and his country had virtually ceased to exist overnight. Gangsters, pimps, capitalists, anarchy, and wage slavery returned, and the Americans were right at the heart of it all.

How he hated them.

They crawled all over Russia, sniffing out secrets, winkling away documents, files, people, and research. They had assigned *liaison officers* to their Soviet counterparts to oversee the *safe dismantling* of Russia's nuclear arsenal. Gregori remembered the complete disdain and condescension of the officer assigned to him and sniffed hard through his nostrils. 1991 had been the year that Sergei approached him. He had told him of a secret research facility of some files withheld from the Americans, full of secret missiles that even he, Gregori Stassiski, had not known about. The missiles weren't even listed in the Soviet's database yet—they were that new. They were the very finest weapons *ever* manufactured in the Soviet Union. Small six-megaton warheads, twenty to a missile. They were multiple-reentry warheads, or MIRVs. One missile, on its reentry to the atmosphere, could fire on twenty individual targets or hit one target twenty times. He had secured twenty of those fine weapons, *four hundred* individual, six-megaton weapons, enough to destroy almost every major city in the world. No one even knew he or they existed.

He had made extracertain of that after the fact. That facility, all the research it had contained, all the people working there with that knowledge in their heads had died in a freak accident. An industrial accident followed by a tremendously large explosion. On that June day in 1991, Gregori Stassiski had become the second strongest nuclear power in the world, and no one really even knew who he was.

He fulfilled his obligations, was cooperative, and was open with the orders he was given. He assisted the Americans in dismantling much of his country's excessive nuclear ordnance, signed the papers, discharged his men, and collected his pension. He retired to teach, of all things, history. For years, he had felt them watching him, watching all of them. A click on the line before he began dialing a number, his personal effects rearranged slightly in his apartment while he was at work, files replaced in his office, the tips of pages sticking out slightly. Gregori kept his nose clean and ignored it all. The perfect worker, he had left the military life far behind, buried in the ashes of the old Soviet Union. He assumed the mantel of a slightly foggy intellectual, deliberately perpetrating the image of an oblivious airhead.

One by one, though, the people watching him grew bored. He could feel them slipping away, almost a sixth sense informing him that they had chosen new targets, that they had new problems to keep track of, people that were far more dangerous than a fuddy-duddy professor teaching history. He began to relax, to breathe easier. Gradually, he began to contact his people, individually, at reunions, at casual encounters on the street, until he had reassembled his entire command, everyone that had willingly participated in the events of June 15, 1991. All would share in today's payoff, and then they would scatter to the winds.

"Here he comes," he said, louder, for Sergei's benefit.

The transport plane circled the runway for a few minutes and then came in for a landing. The engines screamed in reverse as it touched down in an effort to compensate for the ice-caked landing

7

strip. Shards of broken ice crackled and spun away across the runway as the plane turned slowly and began to taxi back near to where the two men stood. The engines cycled lower, and a small hatch opened in the side, followed by a stairwell that folded down. Two armed men appeared first, followed by another figure carrying a briefcase. He was also heavily swathed in furs to keep the subzero chill at bay.

"Yusef, my friend!" called out the colonel. "It is great that you made it here under such trying conditions! Welcome! Welcome! Can I offer you something hot to drink? Let us get you inside, where it is warmer!"

"Praise Allah, it is *cold here*," the heavily bundled figure replied in flawless Russian. "Let us go somewhere *much* warmer, or at least out of this wind, to discuss things! You are looking well, old friend!"

"*Da da*," Gregori replied. "Teaching seems to agree with me for some reason."

The two men laughed, walking toward the hangar. Their entourage followed as they approached rusty large doors. The doors themselves, once meticulously kept clean of rust, squealed in protest as the men inside forced them open, large flakes of orange iron oxide raining down. Gregori noted absently that they, like his homeland, had weathered the years in bad form.

Inside, temporary floodlights had been installed and rigged to illuminate the hangar. On twenty tables lay the contents of twenty missiles that had been designed to decimate the United States and the West. Gregori smiled grimly, considering the "affiliations" of his friend, and realized with a sense of irony that they would most likely serve their original purpose very well indeed. Yusef's eyes had grown perceptibly wider as he took in the contents of the hangar.

"You . . . were not exaggerating, my friend, were you?" he asked softly.

"No, Yusef, I was not," he replied somberly. "Come! Let me show you what you have been seeking!"

He steered his friend to the closest table. A few custom-made briefcases stood there, open for inspection. Inside each sat four equally-sized hemispheres, each nestled in its own hollow. Each hemisphere was half the critical mass needed for a nuclear detonation.

Another suitcase nearby held the fruits of Soviet research, chemical compounds necessary to exponentially boost the fissile material into the six-megaton range required of each warhead. Yet a third briefcase held the assembly necessary to put it all together into a lethal, city-leveling device. All over the hangar, the rest of the warheads were being disassembled and fitted into their own custom cases as well.

"These weapons," Gregori said quietly, laying a hand reverently upon one of the cases, "are the results of forty-five years of research done by the very best minds that my country could produce. No expense was spared, no corners were cut. The deployment methods planned for these were truly elegant."

"I can see that, my friend," Yusef replied. "How many"—his throat caught, and he cleared it quickly—"how many are here?"

"There is enough here to level approximately four hundred cities," Gregori replied.

"Allah be praised!" he exulted, his eyes shining and very near to tears. "They will pay and pay and pay!"

"Yes."

The two men gazed across the hangar, each lost in his own thoughts for a moment.

"Do you also have what I have been seeking?" Gregori asked.

Yusef shook himself for a moment. "*Yes!* Yes, my friend, I do, although the way my bosses moaned like old women, you would have thought that your asking price was too high! Now that I truly *see* with these old eyes, I am thinking perhaps that you did not ask for enough! Is there an office or someplace a little more private that we can go over everything?"

"Right this way," Gregori gestured, and the two men walked into a warm little office, where a heater had been set up.

Four men entered behind, carrying suitcases. Gregori noted that the coffee was ready as well. After the two men were alone, he gestured toward the pot.

"May I? Would you care for some?"

Yusef nodded, an affirmative. He unsnapped briefcases while Gregori poured for them both.

"Here you are, Gregori"—he gestured to the briefcase—"ten billion euros in gold certificates, twenty billion euros in currency, and another seventy billion in Swiss numbered accounts being transferred to you, now."

He tapped a few keys on his laptop, and hundreds of covert accounts around the world spewed data, which translated to money, appearing instantly in a private account in Switzerland.

"One hundred billion euros as requested," Yusef said.

The two men sat sipping coffee for a moment.

"This last briefcase for you," Gregori said, "holds all the technical data we harvested from the facility. All the schematics, the yields of each weapon, and the research files to get there."

He handed it over. The two men finished their coffee, speaking of other things. Finally, they stood, shook hands, and exited the office. Gregori gestured off to the side of the hangar, where a Gulfstream IV was parked.

"The final piece of my retirement, Yusef. Is she not lovely?"

"May she carry you to a place far warmer than this!" he said, nodding and smiling. "Where will you go now?"

"Someplace far out of the coming fallout, I suppose," he replied.

"Good luck to you, then, Gregori!"

"Good luck, Yusef!"

They each saw to their respective teams, and a flurry of loading began.

"Allah be praised," Yusef murmured, walking up the cargo ramp. He caressed the pallets of warheads like favored children as he walked past.

CHAPTER 1

The Martyr

February 2006
Al-Qaeda Training Camp, Somewhere in El Salvador

Asif al Amani was engrossed in the technical manual that he had been studying on the Soviet SS-21 Satan 3.3 missile. His short-cropped hair was plastered to his forehead from the heat of the Central American rain forest. He had been reading for hours, studying for the mission. In fact, the previous five years had been nothing *but* studying for the mission. Studying technical manuals was only part of the job. He had been living the life of a Spanish-speaking migrant worker as well. He dressed as they did, had his hair cut the same way, ate the same food, spoke in Spanish, thought in Spanish, worked and played and read in Spanish. In fact, he didn't even really think of himself as Asif anymore; he would only answer to the name of Miguel these days. Miguel Hernandez. Any other name or reaction to anything but this adopted culture would lead to a serious breach of security. In fact, it was unthinkable to even consider it. There was so much at stake. The entire plan could come unraveled. He just hoped that the others were as disciplined as he had forced himself to become.

For a moment, he reflected on his training so far. He grinned slightly. After a year of being here and totally immersed in the language and culture, his handlers had ordered him—*ordered* him—to get drunk. Not just a little bit either, *borracho*! Then they had grilled him while his head spun and he felt like vomiting, yelling at him in Arabic and Spanish, seeing if he would slip up and give anything away. To his shame, he had, sadly. The hangover was punishment enough. A few weeks later, they had done the same, and he had almost passed. After a few dozen times of that, though, he had managed to stay in character, and they were pleased. At first, he had been outraged, but it gradually dawned on him that if he were to pass in the West as what he was pretending to be, then he needed to *be* it. He made a habit of having a few cervezas daily now, just to stay in practice.

He knew there had to be others like him, even though they had never met, studying, practicing to become something they were not, living the simple lives of people that had never heard of jihad or the constant war with America and the West. Like himself, they believed in what they were doing, so much so, in fact, that they had already become martyrs. They had sacrificed family, friends, sense of self and future for the opportunity to strike back at the pigs who had already taken so much from them. Miguel knew he was a cog in a much larger machine, an important piece, but still a small part of what ultimately would be a very large, very deadly machine. He knew his part well at this point and was starting to feel a little anxiety about getting on with it. Asif had been chosen for his looks, his intelligence, his facial features, his height, and his exemplary performance as the leader of a terror cell in the West Bank.

His calm demeanor and placid-seeming eyes matched those of many migrant workers slipping across the border to the north and into the United States, looking for work. Total immersion in this migrant culture was going to be the key to success. Miguel rolled his head around so that his neck cracked, and he stretched, hearing a few small pops. He glanced out the window to the small town beyond. Children were kicking a partially deflated soccer ball down the street, in the dust and dirt, and were yelling happily. He wondered what would happen to them all once this phase of the project was over. Shrugging, he went back to the manuals.

It had been five years since 9/11, and the Americans, in typical American fashion, were already beginning to forget the lessons learned on that day. They were chafing under harsher security measures at home, tired of the *war on terrorism*, tired of the status quo, tired of the inward-focusing eye of their government, tired of all of it. As long as they had cheap gasoline and fancy cars, big-screen televisions, sports, shopping, and the unbelievable luxuries that drove their consumer-driven culture, they would continue to focus on things that were largely unimportant to the rest of the world.

America was like a giant, strong-willed, schizophrenic, bipolar child he had often thought. It was a country that made no sense. They would go out of their way to destroy something, often with spectacular and devastating results, the whole time spouting rhetoric and a desire for victory only to turn around once "victory" was achieved and build back what they had destroyed. Then while they were rebuilding, they would profess friendship and goodwill. They spoke of freedom while supporting tyranny, funded terror even, if it met with their approval, stomping around the globe like a giant child unaware of the beautiful things being trampled underfoot in the garden.

People here in El Salvador spoke of the United States as the promised land, where all their dreams would come true. They wanted to go there for a while and make enough money to come back and live a good life here. Those that went sent back exotic, beautiful luxuries to share with their family. Americans had no idea what was really important; they treated the world as a vacation destination, almost like a museum, where they could travel and see where they had come from, all the while never realizing that other people actually lived there. While a poor family in a war-torn country celebrated the occasional quiet meal together, a housewife in San Francisco was having a hissy fit because she couldn't get her latte a certain way. They were all spoiled children there who needed constant reminders of why they should be afraid.

It was puzzling to Miguel. Paranoid about security, yet they left their entire borders wide open. People slipped across and back daily, running drugs, weapons, people, and other things. They made laws and then did not enforce them. They demonstrated against war and then blew up entire countries. They said one thing and did another.

The hypocrisy was a stench in the nostrils of Allah. It was a puzzling, interesting situation indeed. His benefactors were preparing to take full advantage of it as well. This next lesson would not be forgotten so easily. There would be no warning this time. No aircraft to prevent from flying, no way to prepare, no sirens announcing the end. It would simply happen. Hopefully, it would be the end of them and their constant meddling in the world.

He was lost in his thoughts again, going over the plan in his mind, and so he did not hear the door behind him open quietly. He did not hear the five men that came in, pushing a wheelchair in front of them. The first indication that he was no longer alone was a polite throat clearing. Miguel turned in his chair and looked back. The man in the wheelchair was a surprise and a pleasant interruption. He had been tall once, well over six feet. His short beard was completely gray now, and there were lines around his eyes and across his forehead that made him appear much older than he really was. The toll of being the most wanted man in the world for the last five years showed on his face. Even so, he was a regal figure, for he was dressed in fine cream-colored robes. Compared to him, Miguel felt small and dirty.

Smiling, he rose from his chair, walked over, and knelt at his mentor's feet. The man in the wheelchair put a hand on his head and asked him to stand so that he could look at him. He rose, meeting his eyes with a sense of love. The eyes were the same as they had always been; regardless of how much he had changed on the outside, the man before him was still the same. The eyes gave him away. Right now they were warm with affection, sparkling with humor. They could, and did occasionally, go as flat and dead as a shark's eyes when he was angry. Those calm brown eyes had casually, brilliantly planned the events on 9/11, had seen to the smashing of the Soviet invasion of Afghanistan, and had caused untold problems for the Americans to the north. They had seen too much. Miguel admired him more than any other man he had ever met. In spite of the pain he must be in, today he had a smile for Miguel.

"Outstanding! I wouldn't have even recognized you if I passed you on the street! All of you are doing such good work here. How are your studies progressing?" he asked.

"They go well, sir," Miguel replied in Spanish.

"What did he say?" the man asked.

"He said," one of the men replied, flashing Miguel a grin, "that his studies go well. In *Spanish*, sir."

"Of course. How thoughtless of me. Will you translate for me?" he asked. "How soon do you think you will be ready, Miguel?"

"I could leave tomorrow, sir," he replied.

"Very well. If you are ready to go into the lion's den, it shall be as Allah wills it. All arrangements have been made. Your handlers agree with you. You are ready, and so you will depart for America in three days."

"Yes, sir," Miguel replied, his pulse quickening.

The man in the wheelchair straightened. Palsied hands pushed him to his feet. He shook off the offers of help from his minders with an irritated grimace and embraced Miguel. Right next to his ear, he whispered in Arabic, "Go with Allah to guide you, my friend."

Osama bin Laden collapsed back into the wheelchair, and he motioned for the others to take him out of the room. At the doorway they paused, and he studied Miguel for a long moment, as if memorizing his features. Then he nodded and said very quietly, "You will do well."

* * *

November 2016
Bellam Boulevard, San Rafael, California

Miguel blew on his hands, trying to keep them warm. Northern California was much warmer than other parts of the United States in November, but it could still get pretty chilly, especially at dawn, on Bellam Boulevard. He was looking for work, and all up and down the street, other like-minded souls were doing the same. The migrant workers and the construction contractors that hired them flagrantly disregarded the signs posted every fifty feet threatening to report them to the IRS. Hundreds of migrants flagged down trucks daily and any other vehicle with a driver offering a day's worth of employment. San Francisco contractors paid the best, hiring them by the truckload to build things. Others looking for lawn care or other odd jobs hired them as well. It was under-the-table work, and therefore illegal, but they paid in cash; you didn't have to pay taxes on it or deduct for union wages, so one still came out ahead in the end. The street was usually empty by noon.

As the sun peeked over the nearby rooftops, Miguel closed his eyes and tried to remember what the call to prayer had sounded like at dawn. In his imagination, he walked to the mosque, unrolled his mat, and faced east, toward Mecca. Then he prayed. He could do things like that in his mind, he had found, where no one was watching. Inside, he could still be Asif!

He only had one small part left to play in the drama that would *hopefully* unfold soon. It had been ten long, lonely years since he had come to this place. It had been fifteen years since he had left Palestine. The Americans were more divided and oblivious than ever. *Please, Allah, let it be soon!* The large, scary part of the operation was long over. Smuggling the nuclear device into the country had been remarkably easy. Transporting it to the construction site and building it into the elevator shaft had been a piece of cake as well. The bomb now lived in a lead-lined alcove within the Bank of America's twenty-third-floor vestibule. Its wiring meshed into the building's power grid, it took a small trickle to keep the batteries charged. There was a second device that powered up and powered down the disposable cell phone that was the trigger. The phone was kept powered off until needed—no sense in having a wrong number set things in motion early. Asif shuddered at the thought.

No, it was the waiting that gnawed at him. It was hard. He could only hope that the others had been as successful in their efforts as his cell had been. He assumed it was so, for surely, if the Americans suspected anything, it would be front-page news all over the country. He wondered how many others waited as he did upon cold streets, trying to pass the time until they were activated. He hoped that they remained patient, that they stayed in character until it was time.

How he hated this place. These smug, sophisticated, arrogant people. They were so sure of themselves, so sure of their place in the world, so superior in their attitudes and opinions, so . . . entitled. They looked right through him as if he did not even exist. He was a nonperson, a thing to be used, neither welcomed nor unwelcome, just another *Mexican*! Many of these people waiting on the street, looking for jobs, did their yard work, cleaned their pools, cleaned up after them, and took out their trash. They raised their children, did their laundry, bought their food for them, and were more involved in running their lives than they were, yet they might have been invisible. Remarkable. Shocking.

How could anyone live that way? Constantly surrounded by strangers and totally dependent upon them.

Miguel shook his head slightly. They were so *weak*. How could these stupid, dependent, ridiculous, petty people do the things that ruined countries? How did they find the *will* to hurt anyone? How could it even be possible? They, their children, their *pets* lived better than the people looking for jobs on this street. They couldn't go a day without a grocery store, or a Starbucks, or a shopping mall, and those weaknesses alone were enough to make Miguel hate them. The real reason he hated them, though, was their indifference, their casual disregard for life, and their total obliviousness to the world around them. The lack of knowledge of history, of current events, of the things that they neither took responsibility for nor cared about was astonishing. He doubted if many of them could even locate his part of the world on a map. On the inside, he was a devout follower of the Prophet. He worshipped Allah. He had surrendered to his will. He cringed to hear the ignorant things that these people repeated, that they took as the gospel truth about his people and their religion. Even the well-meaning ones, the—what was the word? *Liberals*, that was it. Even they knew nothing.

They didn't see the poverty or the hunger or the terror of a cruise missile striking down both innocent and guilty alike. If they didn't see it, it wasn't real, apparently. They didn't smell the sewage running down the middle of the street. They didn't jerk awake at night hearing small arms fire in the distance, or the heavier reports of a tank as it leveled a city block. They couldn't understand the terror as the screaming engines of fighter jets banked overhead, unleashing hell and incinerating those that crawled the ruins beneath. They simply did not know, and did not want to know, or even care about what happened daily with their silent consent. *By* remaining silent, by not caring, they allowed people like him to die by the thousands. *Every. Single. Day.* Hatred, at least, open hostility, he could have understood and lived with (it is natural to hate the person who is your enemy); indifference, however, it infuriated him. It stoked his rage in the night, and it kept him focused.

Soon, they would burn. They would know fear and terror and pain. He would finally be able to die, to put an end to this life and rejoin those that had been taken from him. If he had had his own way, like the rest of his cell, he would have been long gone from this place, but someone needed to be here. Someone needed to bear witness, and that was to be his burden. Someone needed to stay and activate the bomb. Someone needed to call the number that only he knew. All he had to do was wait for the day and decide where he wanted to be when it happened.

He was waiting for the word.

Miguel sighed, silencing the eternal litany of hostility deep within himself. Let it all go for the moment. In the meantime, he needed to find work for this day so that he might eat this night. He waved at a guy in a beat-up Volkswagen Jetta that was turning into Marin Square. The guy didn't even notice him.

Oh well, he's probably late for work, Miguel thought, waving at another passing pickup truck.

CHAPTER 2

Living the Dream

Tuesday, November 17, 2016
Interstate 101, North of San Rafael, California

Harvey Rayton Townsend drove his Jetta rather carelessly through his morning commute. It was Tuesday, the seventeenth of November, and Thanksgiving was in nine days. It couldn't come soon enough, in his honest opinion. It was one of three days in the entire year where the store was closed for the day. He hated the name Harvey, and so to his friends, coworkers, and acquaintances, he had shortened his middle name and simply went by Ray. So yeah, in a week, he would be off totally and completely for one glorious day, no phone ringing with employees asking questions, no calls from his boss, no calls from angry customers wondering why their artwork wasn't finished and in its frame yet. He was a bit tired because he was overworked, understaffed, and underpaid for all the crap he had to put up with daily. He *needed* that upcoming day off. He would just be able to be Ray on that day. A normal guy who could hang out, drink a beer or two, maybe see a movie, or watch a little football. He couldn't honestly remember what it felt like to be "just Ray." In fact, it felt like what he did for a living was becoming more and more who he was, and it wasn't fair. He was so much more than his job.

Ray managed a custom-framing store for a national arts-and-crafts chain. Being a manager was a pain in the ass, and it carried over into his personal life. When you are salaried, apparently, it meant that you were always working. So when he was working, he was the manager, and when he wasn't working and someone called him, he had to be the manager. So the reality of it was, he was always working, whether he was working or not. His company had cut payroll hours again, which meant that someone somewhere needed to pick up the slack, and because he was salaried, that usually meant himself. There were no boundaries anymore. The economy still sucked, and it was *expensive* to live in the Bay Area. That, of course, meant that he needed this job to stay here. Failure was simply not an option. It was a hard pill to swallow, though.

Because he had no personal life to speak of, he had no time for the people that should have been involved in his personal life. Cheryl, his latest girlfriend, had dumped him a few weeks before. They had been living together for the last year, and because he spent so much time at work, he had missed the signs that she was going to be out of the picture soon. The one sign he hadn't missed was the one taped to the front door, which he saw after coming home from a seventeen-hour day at the store.

I'M LEAVING YOU, ASSHOLE! was kind of hard to miss. Ray grinned mirthlessly—at least she had had a sense of humor. Just one more failed relationship in a whole string of them.

Anyway, Thanksgiving was next week, and the spoiled elite of Marin County were out in force, driving their sports cars, wearing trendy clothing, and dropping obscene amounts of money on things that neither they nor their families really needed. The upside, though, was that Ray had a job based on that useless spending, and they charged through the nose for custom framing. He'd probably even bonus this year because of it. At the moment, he was late for work. Again. Traffic was a heartless bitch. Again. With all the people on the road, presumably going to work somewhere, you wouldn't think that the country was still suffering from the worst economy since the Great Depression, but it was.

Southbound 101 was its usual parking lot. People inched toward the Golden Gate Bridge and the city beyond. Snarling, Ray swore and laid on the horn. He flipped off the lady in the Mercedes that had just tried driving into him. He watched as she overcompensated and jerked back the other way. He managed to get into the far right lane and inched toward his goal. His exit was *right there*, but at this rate, it would be another ten minutes until he got there. If he were any judge of things, he might make it to work by eight fifteen, maybe. If he was lucky. Maybe.

Morning talk radio was abuzz with the last ditch executive orders issued by the Obama administration, still trying to establish some kind of legacy before Bowman took office in the spring. Executive orders that would no doubt be reversed as soon as possible by the new administration. Republicans had swept the elections earlier in the month, and both houses now had a supermajority. They also held the Oval Office, so once again, one party held the Senate, the House, and the Executive office. Ray was curious to see if anything would really change in the country. Conservative pundits were still crowing about it, of course, how Americans had spoken, that they had chosen the Republicans and sent a message out to the world. *Blah blah! Rah-rah!*

Ray still felt like they didn't even get it. It wasn't so much that Americans were conservative or liberal; they just were *anti-incumbent.* They hated the establishment and were pissed. He wondered yet again where the voice for the middle class was, if it even existed anymore. The 80 percent of the country that was in the middle politically, economically, and socially. Where were the good, normal people with good ideas that could fix things? He wondered why extremists always got the most attention when they composed the smallest segment of the population. How were people supposed to internalize all the information that seemed to fly at them?

"It's that 20 percent that's going to get us all killed someday," he muttered. "I guess normal, rational problem-solving is out of fashion."

People in the Bay Area were pissed about the elections, of course. He couldn't count the number of gray ponytails bobbing as their owners angrily discussed the results in shopping lines and at cocktail parties. Ray was actually secretly pleased, because anything that offended them made him happy. He secretly wished that someone would have drowned Nancy Pelosi at birth or that a safe would fall and crush Sean Hannity straight-up Looney Tunes style. Pissed off by politics, he savagely switched stations and started listening to a metal station. The angry, animalistic sounds of Disturbed flooded his car with bliss. "Do you feel that . . . ? Oh shit . . ."

He was finally able to get over, and he narrowly missed side-swiping a van as he jumped onto the 580 merge and exited 101 into San Rafael.

Turning right onto Bellam Boulevard, he saw the usual hundreds of migrant workers waving at every passing vehicle for work.

"Will you give it to me?"

Ray waved back and pulled into Marin Square, where the store was. It would be another futile day of trying to please the unpleasable. Living the dream. The fact of the matter was, if he could get away with it, he wished he could hire some of those guys out there on the street. They'd probably do a better job than most of the kids he had to employ, but without documentation, there was just no way. He sat in the car for a few more minutes until the song ended, and then, switching off the ignition, he climbed out and stretched. The muscles on his lower back snapped and popped and fell back into place. Yawning, he climbed the steps to the front door, feeling like a condemned man. His stomach growled, and he looked longingly at the family-owned Taqueria across the parking lot, wondering if he had enough time for a breakfast quesadilla. They did a booming business with all the workers out there.

Sighing, he instead turned back to the front door, unlocked it, and entered the building. He heard the high-pitched whine of the alarm.

"I need a vacation."

As he keyed off the alarm, the sound of the system was replaced by the ringing of a phone. He hadn't even turned on the lights yet. *Really?* Sighing again and suppressing another yawn, he answered it.

"Thank you for calling Hollywood Framing, San Rafael. This is Ray speaking. How may I help you?" he said in his cheeriest, fakest "I am just *so* interested in what you have to say!" voice. He glanced at the wall clock—8:20. *Oh well,* he thought.

There was a woman on the line, whining, not getting to the point, talking about everything except the reason she was calling so early. They didn't open until nine.

Get the fuck to the point! he thought while making sympathetic sounds. Finally she did.

"Yes, ma'am, we are currently working on that order. The frames were delayed shipping here because of the hurricane in Texas."

He held the phone away from his ear slightly and could still hear every word. He screwed around with the volume control a little, and it lowered to a comfortable level. Much better.

"I assure you it will be done today, ma'am," he started to say. A pause.

"I realize it's two days late, ma'am, but when you place the order, we tell you that it's an *estimated* completion date—"

Another pause.

"I am sorry about that, ma'am, but we have no control over the shipping. All our frames are cut in Texas—"

Another batch of yelling.

"Yes. We're working on it right now . . . we're doing the best . . . I said, we're doing—"

More yelling. More inane storytelling. Heart-wrenching sob stories. Ray was getting bored quickly. And irritated, yes. He was becoming irritated. This did not bode well. He was *still* standing in the dark, being yelled at by a woman with no clue that they weren't even open yet. Apparently, she had started trying to call at 6:00 a.m. He was doing his absolute best to stay calm, and finally, he snapped at her, raising his own voice and cutting her off midsentence.

"Have you ever considered the fact, ma'am, that if I weren't standing here in the dark, talking to you *right now*, maybe, just maybe, I could get my store open for business and start to work on completing your order? That the sooner I can hang up, the sooner I can get it done?"

Apologetic noises were coming through the phone now. Ray didn't even know what she was saying; he had stopped listening.

"Yes, ma'am, it will be done by this afternoon, and I will personally call you when it's finished. Thank you. Have a great day."

He resisted the urge to slam the receiver back into the cradle on the wall. As he was walking into the frame shop to turn on the lights, the phone began ringing again. It was really going to be a bad day. He just knew it.

* * *

Miguel glanced at his watch as the guy in the green Jetta drove by in a hurry, but at least he waved today. He grinned to himself. *Late again!* A large panel truck came booming up the street and pulled to a halt nearby.

"I need seven!"

Miguel and six other guys were clambering aboard when his cell phone rang. He answered it and promptly jumped down, waving another guy in to take his place.

"Is this Miguel?" a voice asked in Spanish.

"Yes, it is," he replied.

The voice whispered one word in his ear and then hung up.

His heart rate skyrocketed. Today. Today was the day. Finally. After all the waiting, studying, preparing, and playacting. After all the menial jobs, the degrading work under hard-eyed foremen, the day had come. The time had come. No more Americans looking straight through him as if he didn't exist. Today he could *finally* do his duty. Today, he could have his vengeance, and today, Allah willing, he could finally die and rejoin his family.

He walked back to the Canal District, to the two-bedroom apartment he shared with twenty other people. The space was divided up with hanging curtains. Miguel's little cubby consisted of a couch with storage beneath it. It was pushed up against the wall behind a hanging sheet. He walked quickly to gather a few small personal effects and his duffel bag. When he arrived, he found two of his roommates there. Cesar and Julio were already drinking Tecate.

"Hola, 'migos!" he said.

"Como 'stas, Miguel! Quieres cerveza?"

"No, 'migos, gracias," he replied, hurriedly packing his small bag. "I am going home today!"

"Que bueno! Vaya con Dios, Miguel!"

"Y tu, tambien," he replied, heading for the doorway.

As he approached the door, he considered warning them to leave. To run far, far away somewhere. He decided against it, though. Too much was at stake. He felt badly about it. They were good fellows, and they had had some good times together. But too much was riding on what he did in the next ten hours. Several weeks ago, he had decided where he wanted to be on The Day. When the time finally came. He wanted to be on the Marin Headlands, right above the Golden Gate Bridge. There he would make the most important phone call of his life.

The view of the city this evening would be extraordinary.

* * *

Ray glanced at the wall clock with a sense of relief. It was 4:45 p.m. Finally, time to go. He was ready to get out of there. He had gotten a lot done today. Two planograms set for art supplies, sixteen orders framed and wrapped, the store more or less recovered and reset, paperwork and payroll completed. The deposit was dropped at the bank, and he had taken five more huge orders that would undoubtedly end up being late because he was down a framer, and the store was hopping with customers.

Brushing a few people off, he walked to the front office to grab his windbreaker, issued a few final instructions to his assistant manager, and finally stepped outside to see late-afternoon sunshine and smell the salt breeze coming from the Bay. He took his first deep breath in what felt like hours and shrugged to loosen the tension around his shoulders.

'Tis the season, he thought, *for greed, selfishness, whining, and complaining.*

In the parking lot, two people were fighting over the same parking spot, neither granting the other an inch. Ray wondered if it would come to blows, Lexus versus Mercedes.

Every year at this time, people got more ridiculous, more desperate, more demanding. Every year, the expectations from the corporate office got more authoritarian, more time-consuming, more confused, and more contradictory. Do more with less. He wondered at what point would he be the only person working in the store, maybe even sleeping there. They cut and cut and cut, and his days got longer and longer and longer. Today was the exception—he was leaving on time. But most days, he worked almost sixteen hours, with an hour commute on each end of it. Tonight, though, he was actually leaving a few minutes early, and he grinned. Tomorrow was going to be a day off. He consciously switched his cell phone off in his pocket. It was time to start establishing some boundaries again. Tonight he would be "just Ray." And tomorrow too.

Ray wondered where the stupid corporate-office types got off. What the disconnect was. He wondered if they even knew where the money came from while they were working their Monday-through-Friday, nine-to-five jobs. Heaven forbid there should be a crisis on a weekend! Not one phone was *ever* answered in their offices on those days. He hadn't had a full weekend off in four months, and he hadn't had a vacation in two years. Vacations simply weren't worth it if you spent the entire time away worrying about whether you'd have a job when you came back. Not to mention all the extra workload for the things that *didn't* get taken care of while you were gone. Ray was tired of the holidays being for, presumably, everyone except himself and his fellow salaried slaves. They did the job every single day, 362 days out of the year, rain or shine, most holidays or not. He was simply getting tired of being a spectator in his own life and really, really wanted to be a participant again.

"Hell of a day!" he whispered, walking to his Jetta, "*But* it's over now. I'm off tomorrow, gonna grab me a six-pack of Red Tail on the way and order a pizza when I get home."

He got in the car, turned up the stereo, and mentally prepared himself for the highway gladiatorial combat that involved getting home. There was more bad news on the talk stations—insurgents, Wall Street woes, gas prices. Now that gas was cheap again, they wanted to tax it back to five bucks a gallon. *Bastards!* Unemployment, health care, holiday sales not up to snuff, immigration, blah, blah, blah. Tonight, the president was going to be addressing a joint session of Congress.

"I can't believe I voted for that guy the first time." Ray laughed. "I guess I'm the idiot for even wasting my time voting in the first place, right?" he asked his reflection in the rearview mirror.

Switching back over to a metal station, he settled in for the drive home.

* * *

November 17, 5:25 p.m.
Marin Headlands

Miguel climbed the final few feet to the spot that he had chosen. This was where his life would end. It was a pretty place with a bench. The view was of the Golden Gate Bridge and San Francisco. Small yellow wildflowers were curling their petals for the evening, and the sea grass waved in a chilly breeze blowing in from the Pacific Ocean. He was all alone on the jagged cliffs tonight. His rental car sat lonely and alone now in the parking lot below, down by the old battery. To the west, the sun was a sliver on the edge of the world, and the light clouds above looked like strands of beaten copper and gold laid out on a painfully blue display surface. Overhead, a jetliner climbed into the sky, bearing people home for the holiday.

He set his duffel on the park bench and stretched, taking deep breaths of the salt-laced air. He licked his lips, tasting it on his tongue. Looking past the Golden Gate, he noticed the city was already lit like an expensive jewel for the evening. Miguel took it all in, the tiny white triangular sails on the bay, a cargo ship rumbling past beneath him, out to sea and exotic locations. The quiet serenity of sunset and the beauty of this place had always entranced him.

He breathed deeply again and glanced at his watch. Twenty minutes to go.

The instructions had been clear. At exactly six, he was to detonate. He had a little time left. He unzipped his duffel bag to change into more appropriate clothing and had a glimpse of his prayer mat inside. His grandfather had given it to him long ago, and he cherished it. He was just reaching in to pull out his garments when he realized he was no longer alone.

"Hey, Paco!" a voice called to him. "The park is closing in a few minutes. You have to go!"

Miguel ignored it, and instead of pulling out clothing, his hand tightened around the butt of a 9mm.

"Did you hear me, man? I said we're closing! I need to lock the gate to the parking lot!"

Putting on his best "No hablo Ingles" act, Miguel turned slowly to see a park ranger walking toward him.

"Que?" he asked.

The ranger sighed.

"Go? Me? Now?"

"Yes! Go! You! Now!" the ranger replied, gesturing toward the path to the parking lot.

Miguel smiled, laughing inside. They always did that. Like increasing the volume of your voice and speaking slower, emphasizing the words in English, would actually make a non-native speaker understand.

"Que?" he asked again.

"I said," the ranger began, "you need to leave *now!*"

"How about you leave now, bitch?" Miguel replied evenly and in perfect English.

"What?"

Miguel pulled the 9mm the rest of the way out of his duffel and shot the ranger in the face.

"I guess you don't understand English," he said with a laugh.

Pulling his smartphone from his pocket, he quickly dialed the number for the bomb and set it on the bench while he changed into flowing white robes. He unrolled his prayer rug and knelt to pray. He would do this one last time. As himself. As Asif al Amani. A lot was going through his mind at the moment, his thoughts flickering through the last fifteen years. The long road that had led to this place, this time, this moment. He hadn't lied to the others earlier; today he was going home.

Asif truly reflected upon his life and this act of martyrdom he was about to commit. Never had he imagined doing something like this. His had been a good life. He had worked hard, studied hard.

He had married a beautiful woman named Aziza. Together they had produced a beautiful child. A son. He had owned a little house on the Palestinian side of the Jordan River. His grandfather had lived with them. He thought of all the reasons this was necessary. He had never been a particularly religious young man. He had never understood the zealotry of his friends. Their hatred of that far-off place called America. They were always trying to get him to go to some demonstration, to hear someone speak, to act.

Asif had wanted none of that. Times were hard but happy at the same time. He was loved, and he loved in return. He was a lover, not a fighter. He believed in hard work and the rewards that it gave. He did not have time for the radicals. He respected them, but he also needed to provide for the ones who depended on him. He was doing his best. A memory surfaced, of tying his two-year-old's little shoes. His wife hugging him warmly before he went out the door in the morning. His grandfather smiling approvingly from the other room, missing a few teeth from chewing khat. The sun shining on his shoulders as he closed the door, inundated suddenly by the sounds of the streets. A few blocks away, rhythmic chanting, another funeral procession going past. Vendors selling everything and anything under the sun. The smell of green hidden gardens mixed with dust, the tang of sewage. The sounds of bicycle tires and bells ringing, the bleat of a goat, and people everywhere moving. Asif had been leaving to find work on the day that he lost it all.

The crowds had been surging that day, the chanting louder at times and then fading away. He kept getting pushed farther and farther from home, going with the flow. Trying different shortcuts, going through convenient alleys, always farther away. The chanting had become very loud now, and suddenly, rockets flew up and to the west.

Moments later, two fighter jets banked overhead, their engines screaming. Loud explosions rolled through the canyon-like streets of town, and in the distance, a huge fireball rolled skyward, the concussion eventually reaching him. He felt as if his insides were lifted up and put back down again. Asif began to run toward home. (His mind skittered away from the memory, trying to go elsewhere, but he needed to finish this sequence.) The run back had been a blur; he had been knocked down, fighting his way through the crowds, and his nose was bleeding. Everyone was trying to go the other way, and he was pummeled, forcing his way against them, pushing against the throngs. Finally, he emerged onto his street, confused, wondering if he had lost his way in all the excitement. He was lost in his own town. Wait until he told Aziza—she would laugh at him! He did not recognize this neighborhood at all. The sound of wailing filled the air, and helicopters circled overhead. The air was full of dust and the smell of things not meant to be burned. He had walked like an invalid to where his house should have been and instead found a crater. Glancing down at the pavement, he bent down and picked up a little red shoe. It was still tied. He held it in his hand.

His beautiful life had been over at that point. There was nothing of them left to bury. Asif had tried to kill himself. For days, he lay on a friend's couch. Not eating, not drinking. He wanted to die. Eventually, his path had led to the mosques, to surrender. He had learned to hate. Revenge became his mantra. He did everything in his power to hurt those that had hurt him so deeply. Asif had accepted missions that would have killed other men, and sometimes, he wondered how he had lived when so many others had died. It was as if Allah was punishing him for his prior disbelief, his lack of faith. Prolonging his life and not rewarding him with his own death.

So he became a killer.

He thought back to his training for this mission. The brutal roundabout trip to the jungles of El Salvador. The eventual trip to the United States from there. He had been packed into the back of a white van with people smelling of fear, marijuana, and unwashed bodies. Their eyes shone in the darkness with hope. He thought of the weapons smuggling and the relief of *finally* having built the bomb into the building that he had helped construct and would now destroy with a single phone call. All these things had led to today. Today he was going home to be with his family in paradise. Today he would end the pain.

Eventually he stood back up. At peace now, he rerolled the prayer mat and replaced it in his duffel bag. He picked up his cell phone from the bench and glanced at the clock. Two minutes to go.

"Son of a bitch! You killed Hal!"

Asif turned to see another ranger confronting him with his weapon drawn. He carefully put his hands over his head, his thumb on the Send button.

"I should fucking just waste you right here, you goddamn sand nigger! Get down on your knees!"

"It's Asif," he replied quietly.

"What?"

"My name," he said, kneeling, "it's Asif. Not Miguel, or Paco, or Hey, You, Beaner, Wetback, or Spic. Definitely not Sand Nigger. Asif al Amani. That's my name."

"I honestly don't give a shit!" the ranger replied. "Whoever the fuck you are, the police are on their way, and you and I are going to wait here quietly just like this until they get here."

"Too late," Asif said lightly, pressing Send with his thumb. Behind him the world went white.

"Oh fuck me!" the ranger screamed out.

* * *

Jerry McGowen was a janitor at the Bank of America building across the bay. He was damn grateful for the job too. It was a pretty easy gig. Just sweep up, take out the trash, buff the floors occasionally, and call it a night. He was mopping the twenty-third-floor vestibule right by the elevator doors and watching a hot piece of ass walking down the hallway. He could have sworn he just heard a phone ring from inside the wall.

That's weird, he started to think.

He didn't have long to wonder, though, because in the time it took him to notice the ringing, he simply ceased to exist.

The whole process, really, only took a few seconds. A small explosive device hurled one-half of the critical mass at the other. The two combined, and a fission explosion occurred. That activated the booster packs of deuterium and tritium that were part of the package. As the chain reaction spread outward from the Bank of America building, all the oxygen atoms were stripped out of the air, igniting the hydrogen left behind. It went from fission to fusion in a heartbeat—the very air *burned!* A six-megaton explosion seared San Francisco off the face of the earth, almost as if God had taken a giant melon ball scoop and removed it. For microseconds, everything instantly burned and melted inside a fireball ten times hotter than the sun. Everything ceased to exist within a three-mile hemispheric crater, then the air and the water of the bay rushed back in to fill it with a titanic thunderclap. A fiery debris cloud raced away in all directions, destroying everything that it touched.

On the Headlands, Asif's eyes boiled in their sockets, and he felt his skin stripped away one atom at a time. He would have screamed, except he had no lungs to draw breath, no tongue to form words, no face. It burned.

Allah, it burned! It—

Letters to the Lost

Brian Weber was ten years old. He and his sister Tricia attended Olive Elementary School in Novato, California, a suburb north of San Francisco, in Marin County. They were walking home from a late band practice. Thanksgiving was next week, and Mr. Fiskjung wanted them to all be ready for the annual Christmas choir and band concert that would be coming up the week after. It was about five minutes to six, and it was starting to get dark out. Long shadows from the surrounding hills had swallowed the town in darkness some time ago, but the sky in the west was still pink and rosy. Tonight was lasagna night for dinner, his favorite. They were walking along, and Tricia was skipping. The streetlights had just come on for the evening, and that was when it happened.

The entire southern horizon lit up like the sun was rising again. The sky turned from a deep-rose color to bright daylight blue for about ten seconds. He and Trish squinted their eyes against the sudden brightness. Brian looked up in amazement as rings of clouds blew by overhead in perfect circles. The streetlights winked out, and a passing car rolled to a stop a few feet away, the engine just dying suddenly. As the light faded, he saw a cloud in the distance, over the hilltops. It was shaped like a giant mushroom, blacker than the approaching darkness and glowing in the center with an incandescent heat. It was larger than anything he had ever seen. The streetlights remained off, and a rumbling *Boom!* was echoing through the hills. The pavement lurched beneath his feet. Beside him, Trish was sobbing hysterically. She had wet her pants.

Brian felt that she was crying more from discomfort than any realization of what that cloud signified. What it meant to them both. Brian was just old enough to know what a giant mushroom-shaped cloud meant. He didn't think his parents were ever coming home again. He felt the tears welling up, about to spill over onto his cheeks, but he *could not* cry right now—his little sister *needed* him. Tricia was six. She had just started first grade this year, and the two of them walked to and from school together every day. His mother reminded him constantly to look out for her. "Take care of your little sister, Brian. Be careful. She looks up to you. You are her hero." It was a responsibility that he took very seriously. He grabbed Trish's hand, and the two of them began to run home swiftly.

They lived about six blocks from the school, on Cherry Street. Brian was praying that they would see his mother's BMW in the driveway when they got home. But it wasn't. The driveway remained empty as they turned the final corner. Taking his house key from the lanyard around his neck, Brian unlocked the door, and they ran inside the dark, silent house. Dagwood, their golden retriever, looked up from his squeaky newspaper as they entered, and he wagged his tail. Other than a few licks from the dog, no one was there to greet them. Brian tried the light switches, but the power was out.

While Trish went upstairs to change clothes, Brian went into the kitchen, lit a few candles, and tried to find the flashlights, but all the batteries were dead in the ones he could find. Shrugging, he began to make two peanut-butter-and-jelly sandwiches. A peanut butter sandwich always made things better. The two of them always beat their parents home by a few hours. His mother was in real estate and worked out of Sausalito, the town just north of the Golden Gate Bridge. His father owned and managed a software-development company on Market Street in San Francisco. Dad always got home a lot later than Mom did, it seemed. He was a very busy man. He always seemed to be on his cell phone when he was at home, usually yelling at someone. Even on family day, his father was very rarely there even when he was.

Mom and Dad. Brian froze for a moment, his thoughts racing and his eyes darting around, then he slowly smoothed the peanut butter across the bread. He felt a wave of dizziness sweep across him. His whole reality seemed to turn on some kind of invisible axis for a moment.

"Just makin' some peanut butter sandwiches," he whispered, "in the dark. Everything is just *fine*. Sure, the lights are off, but they *will* come back on. Mom and Dad will be coming home soon. It'll be okay."

Outside, Brian could hear shouts and screams and people running around. Off in the distance, a siren started up weakly, and then just as suddenly, it cut off. Wind buffeted the house in strong gusts, making the frame creak. Dagwood came padding into the kitchen, his toenails clicking on the tiles, right behind Trish, who was now wearing dry pants.

Dagwood looked hopefully at Brian for a moment, hoping for a handout. When one was not forthcoming, he curled up under the table with his nose on his paws. The candles flickered, and Brian got Trish settled in at the table with a peanut butter sandwich and a glass of milk from the fridge. She had a coloring book too. That was good.

"I'll be right back, Trish. I'm gonna peek outside for a minute. You okay?"

Trish nodded, humming a little.

Brian slipped out to the porch for a moment and just stared south at the cloud that seemed to have gotten bigger since they got home. The wind was lashing the trees outside, and brown leaves spun through the air to join their brethren lying in drifts along the street. Mr. Friedman, who lived a few doors down, was jogging past in the direction of his own home. Friedman's son Josh was a year older than Brian, and he was kind of a capital T, *tool*, most of the time, but occasionally, they would hang out and play video games together.

"Mr. Friedman!" Brian shouted. "What's happening?"

Brian hated the sound of his own voice as soon as the words left his lips. That "I am about to start crying, and there is *nothing* I can do about it!" edge that was beginning to creep in.

Friedman came to a halt for a moment, looking at Brian up on the porch.

"Brian, are your parents home by any chance?" he asked.

Brian shook his head. "Not yet," he whispered.

Friedman began to pace in circles, thinking, and his lips moved as if he were arguing with himself. Then he rubbed both hands through his hair and looked at Brian as if coming to some kind of conclusion. Brian thought he heard Friedman say "They're small, we can take two more" before he turned to face him again.

"Okay!" he said. "Brian, I want you and Trish to come over to our house in a few minutes. Do you understand? It's very, *very* important. Pack a small bag, like for a sleepover. A change of clothing, extra underwear, socks, that kind of thing. Bring a warm jacket too. You guys can stay with us until your parents get home, all right?"

Friedman waited for a moment, looking at Brian to make sure he understood. Brian nodded.

"I need to go now, Brian. Ten minutes, okay?"

Brian nodded again as Friedman turned and began jogging toward his own home.

Slipping back inside, Brian closed the door firmly behind him. He walked back into the kitchen and caught Dagwood up on the chair, eating Brian's peanut butter sandwich with absolutely no remorse.

"Look, Brian!" Trish said, holding up her coloring book. "I finished the ponies!"

"Awesome, Trish. They look great!" Brian replied. "Hey, how would you like to sleep over at the Friedmans' tonight? Mr. Friedman said it would be okay. What do you think?"

Trish thought it over for a moment, her small face pensive. Then a tiny smile lit her face. Abby Friedman was sixteen and babysat them occasionally. Trish absolutely idolized her.

"Will Abby be there?" she asked.

"I'm pretty sure she will be, Trish," Brian replied, nodding seriously.

That seemed to satisfy her, because she agreed. Brian hurried upstairs to pack a small bag, and he wolfed down a candy bar and a glass of milk while he grabbed what he needed. Then he ran into Trish's room as well to help her finish packing. He stuffed lots of snacks, some sodas from the fridge, as well as a few coloring books into his own bag. When they were ready to go, Brian grabbed a yellow legal pad from the counter and hurriedly wrote a quick note for his parents.

Dear Mom and Dad,

Mr. Friedman asked us to spend the night at his house, so we will be there when you guys get home, okay? I'm sorry we didn't ask permission to sleep over, but I don't think we should be alone right now. Please don't be mad. I love you. See you tonight!

Brian and Trish

Brian grabbed some scotch tape from the drawer and taped the note firmly to the front door. Then after he grabbed Trish's hand, the two children ran for the Friedmans'. When they got there, the whole family was hurriedly stuffing an old Bronco, and Mr. Friedman was wearing a holstered .45 on his hip. That alone made Brian stare for a moment. You just didn't see that kind of open display in California very often. Mrs. Friedman got the children situated in the back of the vehicle, between large piles of camping gear, and within moments, the entire family, plus two more, were out of the driveway and gone.

All up and down Cherry Street, all over Novato, the San Francisco suburbs, the state of California—in fact, across the entire country—similar dramas were unfolding. Notes on front doors, under windshield wipers, the fronts of businesses, and in apartment buildings rustled and flapped in the deadly winds exhaled by America's dying cities. As people fled, the notes stayed behind, waiting for people that would never receive them. Letters to the lost.

The Day

Excerpt from the Journal of H. Rayton Townsend
November 17, 2016

Today. What can I possibly say about today? All I wanted was a six-pack of beer and a piping-hot pizza after work. Not too much to ask for in the grand scheme of things, is it? Would the world have really stopped turning for something that minor? Apparently so, because it did. What can I say about today to truly sum up all of its parts? Today was a day full of ridiculously petty people with ridiculously little, unimportant, petty needs? Of course I could, but then again, I am/was in retail, and that would be a day just like any other. No, today was profoundly different from that. It was a day unlike any other in history, for me and everyone else. Today took a serious right turn from reality and dumped me into The Outer Limits, or The Twilight Zone. How about we just call today The Day and move on? I like that. It's not trite or presumptuous; it doesn't deviate from its meaning. It just simply is The Day. Years from now, if any of us survive this, those of this generation will be able to look at one another and ask, "Where were you on The Day?" And we will all know what we are talking about. That being said, dear reader, let me tell you about The Day. First, I want to apologize. It has been years since I have done something as archaic as putting pen to paper to express my thoughts, you know, social media and all, right? Well, maybe you don't. Anyway, I need to get this down, and going forward, this will be my record—my testament, if you will—of what happened, what happens next, and someday perhaps, if any of us live, it will be something to look back upon and contemplate.

My sanity depends on this, I think, and it's cheaper than therapy. So here goes. It was 6:02 p.m., and I was almost home from work when it happened . . .

* * *

Ray was snarling in traffic again. He was fantasizing about just ramming his Jetta into the ass end of another vehicle. It seemed that he was angry all the time lately. *Why couldn't people just drive? You have a road, and you have a car and a gas pedal. You just go!*

"Fucking holidays! Fucking retail! I need a vacation *and* a new line of work! *And* a shorter commute!"

They were crawling along at a ridiculously slow pace. A huge yellow arrow was blinking once a second, informing the drivers in the left lane that they needed to get over into the right lane. It was visible for at least a mile back up the road behind them. He was already in the right lane, but the left lane was moving faster because everyone was merging at the last possible second, and as a result, the right lane—the right, *right* lane—wasn't moving at all.

"Apparently, all of you dumb fucks in the left lane are blind! Did you miss the giant fucking arrow?" he yelled out the window.

Taillights winked as people crawled along, heading for home or holiday parties or their families. He changed stations again and let his head fall back against the seat rest. *Hurry up and stop!* Nothing on the air was really capturing his attention at the moment, and for a brief second or two, he was tempted to listen to the president's speech. Maybe he'd just plug in his digipod instead. There were thousands of songs on there.

"What song would you like to hear, Ray?" a woman's voice asked him in an Australian accent.

"Will you marry me, Joanna?" he asked.

"I can't seem to find that song, Ray," she replied.

"Oh well, can't blame a guy for trying, right? Joanna, play 'Ænema' by Tool, please."

"Playing 'Ænema.'"

Nice! Ray began singing along with the song, convinced at the moment that it was written about his fellow Californians in general. The guitar solo in the beginning helped his mood immensely.

"Fret for your latte . . ."

Singing along helped him unwind a bit. He had stopped at an ATM on the way out of Marin and withdrawn a few hundred bucks then gone to Best Buy to see if anything new had come out. He might even do a little holiday shopping tomorrow on his day off. He had picked up a couple of new DVDs, so it would be pizza, beer, and a movie when he got home.

"Fret for your lawsuit . . ."

Looking around, he took in the countryside and resolved, not for the first time, to enjoy the scenery at least. No matter how horrible the commute was or how horrible the people driving in the road were, he would at least enjoy that while he drove. It was pretty. The sun had just sunk below the ridgeline to his left, and the sky and the clouds were phenomenal tonight.

"Circus sideshow . . ."

A self-entitled bitch in a BMW tried to cut him off from the left lane just as he was passing the *huge* fucking arrow. One of these days, he was going to let one of them just hit him. It probably happened four times a day. She probably expected him to move out of the way. It would be their insurance that went up, not his. Tonight, though, he just didn't want to deal with it, so instead he lay on the horn and held it for a few seconds longer than it was polite to do, and she flinched back, flipping him off. Ray laughed and returned the gesture. As he inched forward, there was no way he was going to let her in. He was almost through the gap. He glanced in the rearview mirror and saw her starting the same routine with the guy behind him. The same damn thing. The speedometer crept upward. Five, ten, fifteen miles an hour, and then there was room to move. Traffic began to loosen up by the landfill, and he was driving almost forty-five now.

"Mom's gonna fix it all soon . . ."

The same BMW went whipping around him, and she slammed on her brakes, almost rear-ending the car in front of him.

"Well"—he laughed—"I guess you showed *me*!"

As he was driving on the down slope along the Marin–Sonoma County line, the entire roadway in front of him whited out for a second. The sky turned a bright daylight blue for about ten seconds, and the shadows of the trees just sort of *moved*. Behind him, it was as if the sun had risen again to the south.

"Millions of dumbfounded dipshits—"

Screech!

The stereo gave a death wail, and the car died at the exact same moment. Swearing in earnest now, his power steering gone, Ray forced his still-coasting vehicle to a halt off to the side of the road and braked to a hard stop. Pulling the emergency brake up with a ratcheting sound, he looked around. The strange sky, the chaos all around him, all of it was surreal but was happening nonetheless. In the southbound lanes, a pickup lost control and smashed into the rear end of a semi. Another tractor trailer was crashing downhill, plowing into stopped vehicles in the roadway, and went through the guardrail at the bottom of the hill with a rending crash right into the creek bed. Broken glass was swirling around it in a blizzard.

Everywhere, drivers were coasting to a stop and off the road. The light had been so bright. Bars of purple danced in his peripheral vision, and his eyes slowly adjusted to the twilight again. He blinked away involuntary tears. That had hurt. He glanced at his watch, and it was stopped at 6:02 p.m. A wind gust rocked the car, dust billowed past him and the other vehicles stopped on the 101. The sky behind the hills to the south glowed with an ominous orangey red. Thunderclaps came from the distance and echoed, rebounding among the hills and canyons that made up this part of the state.

He watched other people getting out of their vehicles, and unfastening his seat belt, he got out himself. Glancing up, he noted a series of circular vapor rings racing overhead. He knew deep down inside what had just happened. His stopped watch, the stalled vehicles, the flash, but he needed the validation of *seeing* it. He had to *know*. Ray staggered as the ground lurched beneath him, the car rocking on its springs as the tremor passed. An earthquake too? Great. He opened the trunk and grabbed his first aid kit and a tire iron.

Ray hopped the guardrail and ran across the southbound lanes to the wrecked truck listing into the creek bed, its back broken. The front of the vehicle was dangling over the edge, while the rear half seemed to be having trouble deciding whether to follow the front all the way in. The rear tires were still spinning. From the crumpled cab, he could hear the driver screaming.

"My eyes! My eyes! OH MY GOD!!! I can't SEE! ....no....no... no, no, no, no......HELP! PLEeeeeaaaase..........!"

It took Ray three tries with the tire iron to pry the door open. With a tortured screech, it finally banged back and fell against the cab. The entire vehicle lurched for a moment, balancing, and Ray danced back. It settled for a moment with a groan, and fuel was gushing out of it into the creek bed. Ray unbuckled the man's seat belt and began to pull him from the now-smoking vehicle.

"It's all right. It's all right, man! Everything is going to be okay!" he said, hating himself for the lie. Because everything was definitely *not* all right. And things probably *weren't* going to be fucking okay.

"Hey! Where are you from? Do you have kids? A wife?"

The man mumbled something in response, still sobbing.

"Come on, we need to get you out of here. We have to go right now!"

He noticed a bottle of water on the seat and grabbed it. Ray helped the man climb down and led him, with his hands over his eyes, out of the gully and back up to the roadway. He helped him sit down for a moment, past where the wreck had occurred, and with another tearing, protesting, squealing sound, the semi went the rest of the way over and into the dry creek bed.

"What's your name, man?" Ray asked him when he was seated.

"Brad," he responded.

"Brad, let me take a look at your eyes for a second. Can we do that?"

Hesitantly, Brad lowered his hands, and Ray winced. The skin around Brad's eyes was scorched with easily second- or third-degree burns. It was bad. Ray quickly ripped off a part of his dress shirt and soaked it with the water bottle. He very gingerly tied it around Brad's forehead, the wet fabric, lightly touching the skin. He wasn't even sure if that was the right thing to do with a severe burn, but Brad sighed with a little relief. He dug into his first aid kit and pulled out some of the generic pain pills. Brad was a big guy, so Ray doubled the dosage. It wasn't much, but he hoped it would help him in some ways.

"Here, Brad, take these and a few sips of water, okay?"

"Okay."

"Can you stand up?" he asked him.

"Yeah."

"Here, take my hand. We're going to find you some help, if we can. Anything else hurt?"

"I don't think so," Brad replied, standing up with a little help. "Did I . . . did I kill anyone? After the light, I couldn't see. I know I hit people."

"I don't know, Brad," Ray replied, looking at the trail of devastation down to the creek. "Take my hand. I'll help you. We need to walk, okay?"

"Okay."

Stumbling behind, counting on the kindness of a stranger, the man fell into step with Ray, and they began to walk uphill toward Petaluma. All along the road, people were asking one another, "What happened?" People were trying to get signals on cell phones, trying to start dead vehicles, pulling other people from wrecks. Ray paused for a moment to take it all in. Absolute chaos surrounded him. Flashes and snapshots of people coping in different ways. A well-dressed man standing next to a Buick and mopping hot coffee out of his slacks with a napkin and cursing. Two stoner kids near a VW Bus straight out of the sixties trying to light a bong with shaking hands and laughing about it. Two completely overwhelmed EMTs next to a stalled ambulance tending to a growing number of wounded and frightened people. The sky boiling with fire and the ground trembling occasionally as something in the far-off distance exploded. *Madness.*

Ray had always considered himself to be a resourceful guy. In charge. In management. A problem solver. There was nothing that couldn't be solved with a little thought and ingenuity. He was a member of the NRA, an experienced hunter and backpacker. He was good with people and comfortable in his own skin. This, however, was simply too much, just way, way too much. How was he supposed to deal with something like this?

They were approaching the ambulance, and Ray helped Brad lower himself down until he was sitting with his back to the tire near the front cab. He approached one of the EMTs and tapped him on the shoulder. The man spun with such a savage look on his face that Ray stepped back.

"You have to *wait* your turn!" he spat out. "We can't help everyone all at once, all right? You got it?"

Ray held up the first aid kit so that it was dangling at eye level between them, the white cross visible, and the EMT deflated a little bit.

"I brought this for you," he replied evenly. "It's not much, but it might help someone. Band-Aids, burn cream, some generic pain meds, antibiotic ointment, and gauze. Do you want it?" Ray asked, holding it out by the strap.

"Yeah. Thanks, man. We're just so busy, ya know?"

Behind him, someone was crying out for help.

"There's a guy named Brad leaning against your front tires. He's blinded. I'd appreciate it if you could look at him soon."

The EMT nodded.

"You need some help, right?"

"Yeah."

"All right, then. Do your thing, and we'll figure this out."

Ray spent the next five minutes trying to help get people organized. He put on his manager hat one last time and just started telling people what to do, and they did it. He didn't even know these people, and they were following directions. He had three people getting people organized shortly so that the paramedics could do their jobs, fielding the wounded before they arrived so that the guys who knew what to do could do what they did. The guy from the Buick was a doctor, it turned out, and Ray hooked him up with the paramedics. He asked everyone he came in contact with if they had a first aid kit in the car, and soon, people were running back to their vehicles to get them along with bottled water and snacks. Shortly, everything was going as it should, people were calming down a little, and Ray nodded to the first EMT as he walked past up the hill. The guy gave him a thumbs-up, and he laughed.

"Probably the first important thing I actually did today," he muttered.

Ray left Brad with the EMTs and continued up the hill. There was a small crowd gathering there, staring over his head. South. Back toward the city. Eventually, he got there, puffing a little, and taking a deep breath, he turned and saw it. What child of the Cold War wouldn't recognize its distinct features? It looked just like the Nevada test site pictures. Mushroom cloud.

"Wow," he whispered, unable to say more.

Ray stared, entranced. He was completely mesmerized by the evil, pornographic beauty of it. A deadly flower had sprouted over the City by the Bay. It was seductive. Thin tornadoes danced to the sides of it, strobe lightning and fires rippling through it. A column of smoke and fire and the ashes of people's dreams rose up impossibly high, the top of it blowing away in the stratosphere. It's top was limned red by the last rays of the dying sun. It was horrible. It was awe-inspiring. It was indescribable, and it would be indelibly stamped on his consciousness for the rest of his life. Some people were as entranced as he was; still others took a glance and ran screaming to wherever it was they thought they could go.

He didn't know how long he had stood there with his mouth open. Eventually, Ray became aware that someone was speaking to him, and it took him a moment to comprehend what was being said, as if English no longer made sense. He had to force himself to understand.

"What?" he finally stammered out.

A motorcycle cop had been shaking him by the shoulder.

"Keep moving, sir! You have to keep moving! Away from that! Get to shelter!"

"Okay," Ray replied, feeling dazed. It was like a dream.

With a last glance at the cloud, he turned and began to shuffle toward Petaluma, where he lived. Ray shook his head, trying to wake up. Every once in a while, he turned and looked back the way he had come, walking backward for a moment, then he would continue. That guy didn't know it, but he wasn't even a cop anymore. Ray wasn't a manager anymore. Nobody was anything anymore except a survivor. Nothing would ever be the same again. The Day had changed everything.

"That's fucked up, man. It's just, like . . ."

"I know, dude. It's just . . . trippy."

There was laughter.

Ray glanced to the side and saw the two stoner kids from the VW Bus earlier. They were well and truly baked and were passing a joint back and forth between them as they walked.

"Mind if I hit that, guys?" he asked.

"Whaaaaaaat?" one of them asked with a grin.

"Are you cool, man?" the other one asked.

"Well," Ray replied, "I used to be, but it's been quite a while. Today kind of changes things, huh?"

"Totally, man, totally," they said, passing it over.

Ray took a long drag and held it in his lungs. Then he breathed out a huge cloud of smoke, coughing. "Thanks," he wheezed out, handing the joint back. "That's some good shit there. If you don't cough . . ."

"You don't get off!" they replied in unison.

"All right!"

Ray laughed with them and took another hit a little later, thanking them again. He declined a third.

"I'm a two-hit quitter, guys, but thanks," he said, feeling kind of baked himself. But it had calmed him down substantially.

People helped one another that first day. The blind literally led the blind in a long shuffling column northward, away from the desolation behind them. It took Ray four hours to walk a distance that he would have normally driven in ten minutes. Many quiet, scared people walked near him. Their conversations were hushed in the darkness as they plodded onward. Ray left that column of people when he got to his off-ramp, and he walked down the freeway into Petaluma. Lucky's, the grocery store nearest the off-ramp, was being looted. For a moment, he paused, wondering if it was worth it to try to get anything he might need. The chance of being hurt seemed too great, though, too much of a chance to take, so with a sigh, he turned the other direction, toward his apartment complex. Shots and screams echoed in the distance. He just wanted to get home.

An older Bronco from the seventies went barreling past him while he was walking on Lakeville Highway. It was packed with household goods and two little kids staring at him with wide eyes. Ray wished them luck wherever they were heading. At the intersection with McDowell, a police cruiser was lying on its side. An officer was nearby, facedown in the street, his head a bloody ruin. His sidearm was missing. Behind him, back toward the center of town, an orange glow was beginning to flicker against the night sky, but it was miles away and of no concern at the moment. He was passing the 7-Eleven where he had planned on buying a six-pack on the way home. The windows were smashed out, and it was dark, with no one around. The pot from earlier had made him thirsty, so he decided to risk it. Ray sprinted toward the darkened store, his senses jangling. Outside, he paused, listening. There was still no sound close by, so he entered through one of the smashed windows. Crunching across broken glass, he saw that the store was trashed. Ruined goods were everywhere. He walked to the coolers and found a few bottles of water that were still cold. He drank them right there. He walked to the checkout counter and grabbed a plastic bag and picked up a few loose cans of beer to put in it. Then he stopped again and listened. Still silent. *This just feels so wrong to do!* He stepped behind the counter and found the elderly Sikh man that had run the place for as long as he had lived here. Someone had smashed his head in, and the eyes bulged with outrage.

"Goddamnit!" Ray breathed out. "They didn't have to *do* that."

He looked around for something to cover the old man's face and found a towel.

"Sorry, guy," he whispered, putting the towel over him.

Ray found half a carton of cigarettes back there and slipped them into the bag with the beer. Then he got out of there.

Once he was back on Lakeville Highway, things seemed a lot more dangerous, and he stuck to the shadows on the north side of the road. He even picked up the pace a little, jogging for a few blocks and then walking fast. An idea was beginning to form in his head. He wanted to go *home*. Not just to his apartment in Petaluma, but all the way. Back to his family in Illinois. He had been on the West Coast for close to fifteen years now, and it was way past time to leave. There was nothing for him in California now, no job, no relationship, no reason to stay, so he started thinking about details and how he was going to pull it off. He would get there, though, even if he had to walk the entire distance alone and on foot.

Now that he was thinking again, he started to analyze the situation. After all, this was probably just a localized emergency, right? San Francisco got nuked. Boom. Gone. Somewhere, however, outside the blast and EMP zone, there had to be more. Transportation, help, emergency people, medical services, FEMA, and all that good stuff. All Ray had to do was get outside the disaster area, and he could probably use a credit card to buy a bus ticket home. Poof! He'd be gone and on his way back to Illinois, where he belonged.

Exhausted, he finally made his way into the apartment complex, climbed the three flights of stairs to his unit, and got inside fast. He searched a few kitchen drawers and found some candles. Experimentally, he tried the gas burners on the stove, and they lit up. The gas was still on for the moment, it seemed. He lit a few candles from them, and placed them around the kitchen, lighting up the place. The next thing he did was fill every vessel and container, sinks, and tub with water while it was still flowing. That done, he walked into the bedroom, with two cats twining around his ankles and purring. He stripped out of his now-dirty work clothes and scrubbed off with some water from the sink. That helped wake him up.

He changed into hiking clothes, pulling on a base layer, cargo pants, and a flannel shirt. He dug his good hiking boots out of the closet and put them on. Then he began to rummage in the desk, looking for something, and finally found it. Carrying the object and a lit candle to the dining room, he set them down on the table. He made himself a roast-beef sandwich from the fridge and cracked open one of the salvaged beers. Then Ray did something that he hadn't done for years; he opened up his journal and began to write. He had given it up years before, but today was journal-worthy, no matter how you cut it.

Eventually, he moved to the couch to continue writing. One of the cats pressed against his thigh, sleeping. Troubled, he occasionally looked out the windows that faced south, to the glow on the horizon that used to be San Francisco.

Every hour or so, he would take a break from writing to do a quick task. He would pack his backpack, locate another camping item, eat some food, or use the bathroom. Gunshots and voices yelling nearby made him wedge a chair under the doorknob and load his 9mm at one point. He snuffed the candles and peered out the windows. Below, a Latino gang stalked by in the darkness. He kept the handgun beside him on the couch after that.

Yep, going home suddenly seems like a really swell idea. Finally, he fell asleep around 3:00 a.m., the journal open on his lap, and the pen slipping unnoticed from his fingers.

CHAPTER 5

The Elected

President elect James Bowman was on vacation. It had been a grueling campaign, with primaries that had started almost two years before the election. The primary fighting had been more savage than the general election. It had been a relief when all he had to worry about was running against one opponent. He was a conservative from Texas and had run as such, speaking his mind, appealing to the nation's values and common sense. He was a fiscally conservative, "help people that help themselves" kind of candidate. Something about his demeanor had appealed to the American people, and he grinned inside when he thought of the political cartoons poking fun at him for his *Mr. Smith Goes to Washington* routine. What those elitist cartoonists didn't realize was that that very image they tried to pin on him as a hokey, dumb ass ultimately was what had gotten him elected. The American people were tired of the smartest guy in the room trying to lecture them like some Ivy League twit. So the election was won, and he was on vacation. Him, his wife, their two kids, a Secret Service contingent, their aides, the petitioners, the media, the political cronies, the paparazzi, a Supreme Court justice by the name of Sam Clark, their maids, the PR types, and the White House staffers that were prepping his people for the transition in February.

"Some vacation," he muttered.

There was even an adopted mutt around there somewhere that they had rescued as part of a campaign promise. For all outward purposes, to the world it looked like the president elect had gone on vacation to Catalina Island.

Bowman had decided that as soon as the numbers came in, if he was the guy still standing after election day, he was going to be getting right to work. The truth of the matter was that he was inheriting a mess, a mess that had been added to, compounded, and exacerbated by the last two presidents before him. A mess that got bigger by the day, compounded with interest hanging like a millstone around the necks of future Americans. The housing bubble had burst again, and those dickless POS bankers were to blame again. The stock market had imploded, again, out of nowhere, launching a new recession. The Fed had given him no help there, not to mention all the numbers that had been cooked to make it look like the economy had been improving—employment, housing, etc.—when there were so many variables left out. The fact was that things were actually worse than 2008, and a lot of the outgoing president's friends had made a whole lot of money over the last eight years. If something wasn't done to stabilize things and soon, it was all going to come crashing down.

"Well, that's why you get paid the big bucks now, Jimbo," he said, looking out the window at the kids playing with the dog.

So by day, he played golf and schmoozed the press, took advantage of the photo ops, got an occasional massage, played with the dog, and walked the beaches of Catalina, holding his wife's hand. At night, well, nighttime was a whole other issue altogether. He studied at night with financial analysts, read documents, picked out his codes for the arming and launching of nuclear weapons, and read the occasional piece of fan mail that actually made it to his desk. An Air Force aide with his football waited in the other room to go live in February. He was briefed on current global situations, filled in on ongoing special ops, and interviewed people for jobs. His clear-cut picks for his cabinet were on the island with him as well, even before being sworn in and vetted by Congress. They, in turn, were being briefed by the outgoing administration people. The Obama staffers were on loan to brief his folks, to share information, and to generally pass the ball onward. Bowman reflected on the cycle of transition a little bit and shook his head. So many of these folks were party people, and if it wouldn't have been a *huge* political faux pas, he wouldn't have minded keeping a few of them around. Well, they would land on their feet, involved in the campaign of the next rising star from the opposition party, and in eight years, or four, if he was very unlucky, they would be working for a different president.

Bowman had a few friends along as well. They were friend-ish anyway, people that had taken an interest in his career, a few Washington insiders: two senior senators, one from Kentucky and the other from, of all places, California. Her constituents would have kittens if they knew she was here and being consulted with. He was looking forward to change and trying to guide the country back on the right track. The road ahead was going to be rocky and full of pitfalls, but somehow, America was going to survive and, if he had anything to say about it, to prosper as well.

The curtains billowed gently in the evening breeze, bringing the smells of beach and flowers wafting inside. A wind chime tin-kled softly somewhere. Bowman stood up and stretched, feeling his back pop and crackle a bit, and sighed. He was about to sit back down again, to continue going over the contents of the folder in front of him, when there was a bright flash off to the east. Curious, he walked to the veranda, pulling the gauzy curtains aside. His eyes squinted against the extremely bright light, and as it faded, a large mushroom-shaped cloud took its place. Out on the lawn, people were pointing and yelling and, unfortunately, panicking.

That was Los Angeles, he thought. *Son of a bitch!*

Farther down the coast, another city-sized flashbulb went off, and he gaped, unable to internalize it.

The suite doors banged open behind him suddenly, and Secret Service agents swarmed inside.

"Mr. President, we have to evacuate you immediately," Bill Thompson, the head of his detail, said.

"I know," he replied. "Give me a moment, okay, Bill?"

Bill nodded as Bowman turned back to the view for a moment, then squaring his shoulders, he walked back to his chair and sat down to put his shoes on.

* * *

The next forty-eight hours were a whirlwind of activity. The first family was airlifted to the nuclear destroyer POE and transported to Hawaii. There the initial extent of the catastrophe was made clear. DC was gone, the entire chain of succession wiped out, reports coming in of city after city destroyed, the devastation mounting by the day. Millions were dead, displaced, homeless, and without water, health care, power, or social services, and communications, where they weren't down altogether, were spotty. There had been conventional attacks on power substations, bridges, and police facilities. Panic was sweeping the country from coast to coast. The president had been addressing a joint session of Congress, the Supreme Court, and foreign dignitaries with a comprehensive terrorism-response plan. The last part had almost made Bowman laugh out loud, but he managed, barely, to remain solemn and to look presidential. Irony. Go figure.

Sam Clark had shuttered himself in the University of Hawaii law school for three days and finally emerged to tell Bowman that even though it was unprecedented, he could find nothing that said in the event of such a catastrophe that he couldn't be sworn in early. So at dawn on the fourth day after The Day, James Bowman was sworn in to be the next president of the United States by the last Supreme Court justice alive, with the last two senators alive in attendance.

Quirking an eyebrow, he whispered just so they could hear, "Between the four of us, we have all three branches of government present. How about that?"

His football went live, and with the help of the United States Navy, he was able to procure some senior-branch commanders to work in the temporary offices of the Joint Chiefs of Staff. He was prepared. He had spent the last few weeks learning what he needed to know to bring the country back. America would survive; it would probably be very radically different, but it would survive.

"What are your orders, Mr. President?"

"We need to go to California, so if you can, please try to raise Sacramento and get the governor for me. We need to get in touch with what's happening on the ground and fix this."

"Yes, sir."

CHAPTER 6

The Armageddon Plan

The president, the man who had been vice president of an outgoing administration just a few minutes ago, lay gasping and dying in the other room. His skin was a sickly, ghastly gray color. He had decided not to run for president, yet here he was. His health, failing for years, had finally betrayed him. The stress of the last twenty minutes had pushed him over the brink. He had been in a car just outside the DC metro area when the first bomb had detonated. His detail had recovered and gotten out of there, flooring the gas pedal on the hardened limousine streaking through the countryside to Mount Weather, Maryland. The second bomb had detonated moments later, and the realization of what was happening had hit him hard. He had suffered a massive heart attack after the second flash, and his Secret Service detail rushed him to the closest medical center to seek assistance.

The doctor, straightening from his examination, looked at the aides and agents clustered near the door and shook his head silently. He left the room, mumbling about finding a good, stiff drink. President Biden motioned for one of the aides to get closer, regaining consciousness for a few brief moments. He knew what had to be done. He whispered, straining in the aide's ear, to launch the Armageddon Plan. Operation Ghost was to be implemented immediately. The government had been decapitated, and the sad thing was, he would never know who had done it, never be able to strike back. As the only remaining senior elected official, he had the responsibility of assuring the survival of the United States of America. *Scion* would set this to rights. He had to. He prayed it was only DC, but this had a much bigger feel to it; this might have been all of America. He would never know.

Except for his strained whispers to the aide, the room was silent. The sky boiled in all directions, and it was bad. He tried again to sit up, managed to gasp out a few more words to the aide, fell back, and died.

The United States had lost two presidents in twenty minutes, all the constitutionally acceptable replacements, the Supreme Court, and both houses of Congress. The plan Operation Ghost was their only option.

"What did he say at the end?" whispered a junior aide.

"He said, 'God help us all,'" replied a Secret Service agent.

* * *

Scion

Ted Hotchkiss was awakened shortly after midnight by a shielded, military-grade mobile phone that he always had with him. It was a secure line that incorporated the latest scrambling, antihacking/counterhacking technology in existence. There were only a few like it in the entire world, and he had one. Only four people had this number, and if it was ringing, it meant that a world of shit was about to get dumped on him from somewhere. He swiped his thumbprint for verification and answered with one word.

"Scion."

There was a pause as voice analysis and additional encryption protocols cycled.

A voice began speaking at the other end of the line. The conversation began with the code word *ghost* inserted randomly in the beginning of what sounded like a non sequitur.

"Do you believe in *ghost* stories?"

"My favorite one was the 'Golden Arm' by Robert Service," Hotchkiss replied.

"Very well."

Pickup instructions followed after Hotchkiss had verified his chipped location, and the agent signed off. He yawned, shaking his head. This cloak-and-dagger bullshit had been fun when he signed up for the program as a favor to an old friend. It had been something to do once every few months. He would be whisked away to an undisclosed location to practice running the country and stepping into the shoes of the president of the United States. Kind of fun, actually, sort of like camping at a survivalist resort, it beat the hell out of sitting through another board meeting or riding herd on a bunch of squeamish, clucking bankers or lobbyists or whomever his day was filled with. In time, though, the novelty had worn off, and he had seen it for the commitment it was, the responsibility that it was. Ted Hotchkiss had never really wanted to be the president of the United States of America. Too public, too much criticism, too many . . . constraints.

He was familiar with power, though. He had it, he had been raised to it, and then he had multiplied it exponentially once he reached adulthood. Hotchkiss was maybe the wealthiest man in the world. He had stopped keeping track some time ago. Bill Gates and Warren Buffett were amateurs compared to what he did. They only ran corporations; he ran countries, stock markets, governments and managed the people that managed everything else. His was a silent wealth. Prestige and influence shaped his life, and those were the only things that mattered.

It was not an advertised fact that he pulled so many strings, moved so many pieces on the game board of the world. His was not a lifestyle to be reported on in crass news rags, social columns, or paparazzi. He held much of that world in contempt. It was much more exciting to bend a finger and watch a government fall, a market collapse, or to shape an entire people to his will. He had lost interest in that as well. At forty-nine, he had pretty much accomplished everything he had ever wanted to accomplish, and so for the hell of it, he had enlisted in the program at the behest of one of his father's friends.

Marie and the kids were in New York City for Thanksgiving at her parents' place. A posh, well-appointed address off Central Park.

He had wanted to be in a more rustic setting in the Adirondacks. As he got a little older, he had gotten bored with her as well. His children were disappointing. Marie had become more silly as time had gone on, so fixated on what she perceived her place to be and completely uncomprehending of why he didn't show any interest in the social games that she seemed to delight in. She had a lover these days, and he had been trying to decide if he cared enough to do anything about it. His eldest, Jack, was going to be attending Harvard next fall and was spouting liberal garbage, which, if he really thought about it, would get him tarred and feathered by the masses. His youngest, a girl, Jessica, was turning out to be just as silly as her mother.

Ted sighed again, dressing hurriedly in the dark. The power was out.

He walked downstairs to the kitchen. There was a pot of coffee that was still warm, and he poured himself a cup to wake up. The staff had all left for the evening, but he smiled to himself when he saw the plate of holiday cookies on the counter. Mrs. Johnson, his housekeeper, had left them for him with a little red bow on top of the Saran Wrap. He would need to make sure that she was taken care of when she retired.

Sipping the coffee and nibbling on a cookie, he looked out the large windows toward the mountains and thought about the coming weeks. Operation Ghost. He shook his head slowly. Who would have thought that in his lifetime, he would see something like this initiated? The Armageddon Plan. Wow.

The plan had come about as a direct result of the Reagan administration. It was created by secret executive order as part of a continuity of government program that was secret as well. Reagan had feared at that time that if a nuclear showdown with the Soviets occurred, the entire command structure of the US government could very well be decapitated, the possibility existing that every single person in the chain of succession might be killed or incapacitated in a way that all effective government would fall apart, resulting in complete chaos and anarchy and the end of the United States of America. Maybe even the whole world. Someone needed to be around to shut it off.

The Russians knew the locations of every hardened facility in the continental United States. Multiple ICBMS were aimed at each of those locations. Likewise, the Americans knew the same thing about the Soviets. The odds of any leadership surviving were close to zero. A plan needed to be implemented that would allow a government to resurface in the United States to meet the needs of people and interact with foreign governments in the wake of a total or limited nuclear exchange.

The plan worked. Initially, it had involved men like Dick Cheney, Donald Rumsfeld, Oliver North, and Ed Meese. These men, among others, had drilled constantly during the Reagan years and even the Bush years that had followed. Before they had ever really gotten involved in politics, they were trained to run the nation on a moment's notice. During the Clinton years, the plan had been discontinued as a waste of money and resources. After all, the Iron Curtain had fallen, the Soviets bankrupted, and the threat of nuclear war faded away. Eight years passed, and even though officially the program was cut, the participants retained all their training, codes, and contacts as well as their privileges. It was black budgeted, without congressional oversight or approval, and it disappeared from the books.

Suddenly, another Bush was in office, 9/11 happened, and it just so happened that Dick Cheney, one of the original participants of Operation Ghost, was the vice president. The plan was immediately put back into play. Cheney vanished for almost a year after the attacks, and there were mutters in the press of a shadow government being formed. It had existed all along. New members were drafted, and that was where Ted Hotchkiss had come into the picture.

The plan called for and got alternates to actual official government positions. Heads of corporations, military people, experts on various subjects and fields were drafted to step into those positions at a moment's notice to fill up and reconstitute the executive branch of the federal government. For example, the alternate president was given daily briefings that matched that of the actual president of the United States, his staff the same, his alternate Joint Chiefs the same. It was a shadow government, in truth, but without any kind of official responsibility except as a last resort. An elaborate series of exercises, drills, and secret procedures were implemented. Safe locations were set up, additional hardened facilities developed, mobile communications put into play. Stockpiles of weapons, food, gear, and other assets to maintain and fulfill the needs of a functioning government were duplicated and hidden for The Day, when they would be needed to come out of hiding and resurrect the United States.

Hotchkiss went over his own role again in his head. He unlocked the hidden safe in his first-floor office, handcuffed his briefcase to his wrist, and gathered additional documents and other things sealed in plastic. He stepped to the front door just as the knocker sounded upon the oak. When he opened the door, he noticed there were three men in dark suits awaiting him.

"Are you Scion?" the man asked.

"I was the Scion. Now I am the Ghost," he replied.

The man nodded.

"Right this way, Mr. President. My name is Al Michaels, and I am the head of your Secret Service detachment. We are ETA twenty minutes to a helicopter putting you on a direct flight to Mount Weather."

Hotchkiss nodded, got into the limousine, and in moments, they were lost to the night. It had begun.

The Mark of Cain

Big John Cain was a man with no scruples, very few principles, and even less conscience. He lived in a world that didn't give a shit about him, so he made it a point to return the favor whenever he could. He lived his life one day at a time, one town at a time, and one bitch at a time. He worked on his hog and floated from town to town to pay for it. The open road had been his longest lover. He had taken her to bed with him the summer he turned eighteen, leaving behind a shit job and an even worse, abusive, alcoholic father. He had never looked back. John felt that God had cursed him, because everything he had ever loved had been taken from him. Everything except the road and his bike. So the best way to make it through life was to not love anything at all.

John was the roughest bar bouncer in Nebraska. He cracked heads without a single qualm and got paid well to do it. He was twenty eight, and stood six feet five inches. He was all ropy muscle and rock-star long hair. His beard hung halfway down his chest, and he braided it when he was out riding.

On The Day, he was getting another tattoo when his cell phone rang. Looking at the caller ID for a moment, he answered it.

"Yeah?" he said.

There was a lot of yelling on the other end of the line, and the tattoo artist gave him a strange look.

"Well, that's not *my* fuckin' problem!" he yelled back.

The artist sat back and waited.

"Jesus! They are *your* fucking dogs, for Chrissakes!"

The tattoo artist looked like he wanted to be somewhere else.

"Fine! Motherfucker, I am coming over there right now!" he roared.

Cain glared at the tattoo artist for a second and then apologized.

"Sorry about that," he mumbled, putting the phone away. "I'll have to come back later to get it finished."

"Take your time," the artist replied.

Cain stalked out to his bike and felt an almost sexual tightening in his groin as the engine throbbed to life. Gunning it, he pulled away from the curb, cutting off a minivan that swerved and honked. Cain flipped him off and laughed.

It was a long ride out to Charlie Mack's in the country, and the cool air, mixed with small pockets of warm air, improved his mood as he rode. In fact, by the time he was almost there, he felt great. He and Mack had been running a dogfighting ring there for some time, and it paid the bills, in addition to selling pot and bouncing.

Pulling into the dooryard, Cain revved the engine a few times to let Mack know he was there and then cut it off. It was quiet for a moment, and he could hear the engine ticking in the November air as it cooled. From the barn came the incessant barking of the dogs.

Cain stepped off the bike and stretched, his breath frosting the air in front of him as he exhaled. Turning around, he saw Mack exiting the barn and walking toward him.

"What's up, Mack?"

"Somethin' wrong with the dogs," he said, gesturing over his shoulder at the barn.

"Let's take a look then," Cain replied.

The two men strolled into the barn, and once they were inside, the barking redoubled in intensity. A row of shabby cages stood alongside one wall, holding an assortment of pit bulls, rottweilers, and large mutts. One of the mutts, Charlie swore up and down, was a half-breed wolf. He was a big bastard, whatever he was, with mismatched eyes—one yellow and one blue—and long shaggy fur. He was the only dog in the room that wasn't howling, barking, or raising some kind of a ruckus. He was a killer too. The week before, he had killed two dogs in the ring and hadn't gotten so much as a scratch. His upper lip curled in contempt as the two men approached the row of cages. Cain had never liked the look of this particular animal and held his gaze, the dog staring calmly back at him.

"Fucker is too damn smart," he told Mackinson. "He'd most likely kill us both in a heartbeat if he had the chance."

Mack studied the dog for a moment and sighed.

"Yep, he probably would," he replied.

"Stop looking at me like that, you bastard!" Cain yelled, whacking the front of the pen with a baseball bat that had been leaning against the wall nearby.

The dog broke eye contact and curled up on the floor of his pen, ostentatiously ignoring the two men.

"So what's wrong with the rest of them?" Cain asked, sparing a look for the only quiet dog in the room.

"Not sure," Mack replied. "When I got up this morning, they were howling and whining and acting crazy. I heard dogs behave like that right before an earthquake or some shit. Almost like they can sense something we can't. It's been really spooky out here today, John, and in all honesty, they are creeping me out."

Cain shook his head, looking at Mack in disbelief.

"Pussy. So the dogs are spooked. So the fuck what? Now you are spooked too? *This* is what you called me out here for? Jesus, Mack!" Cain said contemptuously. "Get your shit together. They gonna be able to fight tonight or what?"

"Should be able to. That one can for sure," Mack said, pointing at the dog, now calmly asleep. "As for the rest of them, not sure."

"Well, maybe he'll die in the ring tonight. I heard those guys coming tonight have a real ass kicker in their kennel. Big ole Blue Nose pit named Hercules. We'll match that wolf mutt with him. Gonna be a good show regardless. We still on for seven thirty?"

Mack nodded.

"I'll see you, then," Cain said, strolling out the barn. Behind him, the dogs continued to howl and snarl. Cain shrugged. He planned on betting against that mutt tonight. "Hercules," he said with a grin. "Got a good sound to it."

* * *

The Dog knew only three things in life. The cage, the arena, and the bloodthirsty rage of the crowd when he killed. There were vague memories of a small blond-haired boy throwing a ball for him when he was small himself, but those memories were fading. The people who had taken him away from that life were bad, the dog knew that, and they smelled wrong, broken somehow. He hadn't smelled good people since the boy.

The Dog didn't kill because he liked to kill. The Dog killed because he *had* to kill. It kept him from being killed himself. He did not like the men who were his masters, though—he knew that too. Shaking himself after a long afternoon nap, he scratched at an itch behind one ear and calmly watched the people shuffling into the barn with his ears pricked. They were loud as usual. Obnoxious, stupid, and drunk already, some had a skunky smell as well. That meant one thing: tonight, he would have to fight. He would have to try to stay alive again. He yawned, showing long white teeth and a long purple tongue. He stretched, front paws in front of him, his rear legs and tail rising up in the air behind him.

The others were howling again, and he knew why. The air crackled with the intensity of some huge *thing* waiting to happen. The air was charged with feeling today, a feeling that things were not as they should be, out of balance, lopsided, dangling over a vast space. *Change* was in the air, and the world held its breath, waiting. He couldn't resist anymore. He felt the same anxiety as the others did; he just hid it better. The Dog sat down, raised his head, his muzzle almost touching the roof of his cage, and took a deep breath and howled. One crystal clear, deep-timbered primal wail to acknowledge whatever it was just for himself. The entire barn fell silent as people and dogs turned to look at him, the moment stretching out as man and beast alike felt the hair rise all along the backs of their necks. The moment stretched and shattered as the other dogs commenced their clamor once again, the drunken people howling back at him and one another. *Fools!* The Dog narrowed his eyes and growled.

He laid his ears back against his head and sniffed in the scent of evening air beyond the double doors of the barn. There was something different about tonight, yes. The air didn't lie. He would need to try to live through it.

The barn warmed quickly as people packed in, and it quickly smelled of greed, bloodlust, arousal, and beer being spilled into the sawdust. The debris kicked up by shuffling feet sparkled in the air and drifted toward his cage, the desperate scents and mixture of smells almost too much to bear for his sensitive nose. The Dog sneezed once, twice, a third time. He yawned again.

Whump whump! was the sound the floodlights made as they came on over the ring. There was feedback from large speakers wired to a microphone as the other bad man began roaring at the crowd. The crowd roared back. Cain was approaching his cage with a length of chain leash in his hands, and The Dog stood up, stretching again and growling deep within his chest. He locked eyes with the man, and the man looked away first. If The Dog had had the capacity for human speech, he would have thought *Coward* to himself. His attention was riveted now to the large pit bull being brought in through the doors of the barn. He knew instinctively that this would be his adversary tonight.

The cage door opened, the man looped the chain around his neck, and the dog jumped down without being pulled or forced.

He entered the arena with a regal air. Proud, defiant, his head up, but utterly indifferent to all around him at the same time. Almost as if he were leading the man rather than the other way around. Across the ring, the pit strained at his leash, locking eyes with The Dog, who coolly looked back. The loud-voiced man was screaming through the speakers again, the crowd screaming back, and suddenly, the leash was gone from his neck.

The pit lost his own leash a second later, and both men leaped out the ring as his adversary charged. The other dog was fast, his jaws gaping and blowing foam as he closed on The Dog. The Dog answered with a charge of his own, snarling, and at the last instant before contact, he turned so that his shoulder came up under the other dog's muzzle, slamming the jaws shut with an audible clack. Sidestepping, he hamstrung the other dog, his jaws closing with a crunch on the pit's left hind leg. The bone broke loudly, and The Dog could taste his enemy's blood. The crowd roared in approval. He leapt backward nimbly, avoiding the other dog's bite, jaws closing on air where The Dog had been microseconds before. The Dog kept his distance, and the pit struggled to stay with him, circling, circling until he saw the opportunity to strike again. He charged and hit the pit on the side, knocking him completely over, and he savaged the pit's other hind leg, teeth slashing, bones crunching.

And then he was clear!

The pit was in trouble now. Both hind legs dragged in the dust right through the filth of the ring. Horrible, whining, growling sounds came from his throat. He struggled to reach The Dog, to kill this creature that had hurt him so badly. The Dog charged in again, utterly focused now. The crowd was roaring its approval as dust flew through the air, billowing. The Dog sank his jaws into the pit's neck, behind the back of his head. Blood jetted into The Dog's mouth. Warm, coppery fluid ran from his jaws as he bit deeper, flying like crimson jewels to splash into the dust of the ring. He bit deeper, feeling the other dog struggle beneath him, and he began to shake his head. The other dog bit his foreleg, but he did not relinquish his hold, shaking the other even harder. He bit deeper, harder, shaking his enemy until he heard the spine snap, and still he savaged the corpse. Rising suddenly, he stood, the pit hanging mostly limp from his jaws. Death spasms kicking legs that would no longer run or claw or kill. The Dog, all 185 pounds of him, stood victorious and defiant in the ring, glaring at the now-silent crowd. His enemy held in his jaws, he was a vision of death, and that was the last vision anyone had of him as the lights suddenly snapped off without warning.

He did not waste his opportunity when the light stopped. Dropping the adversary in the dirt, he began to run toward the edge of the ring. His eyes adjusted to the dimness quickly, and he was focused on the glimmer of fresh, clean snow now lightly falling outside the barn doors. Cain was in his way as he leapt over the barrier of the arena. He planted both front paws solidly in the man's chest as they fell together. Hind legs already bunched to kick off, he heard a whoosh of exhaled breath, caught a glimpse of a bearded, startled face, and was gone out the doors to freedom and whatever that might entail.

To the west and south, a new sun was rising, making the snowflakes shine as they drifted down, and the barn was erupting into pandemonium.

Postapocalyptic Radio

CHAPTER 8

Air date: November 18, 2016
Time: 20:57
Transmission Duration: 1:59
Somewhere in Nebraska

"Ohhhhhhh, man! I saw this coming down some time ago! Yes, indeed, I did! People have always told me that I was a little off, a little crazy, and a little paranoid. Even said I was unique, in a really offensive and condescending way. You know the way, right? The way that know-it-alls and wannabe intellectuals adopt when they have nothing of any real substance to say. You know what, people? For a while, there I was, starting to think they were right. The fact of the matter, though, is that right now is the best time in history to be an introverted, socially absent hermit living under the radar. All those pricks are dead now, so their 'informed opinion' doesn't really add up to dried shit at the moment. I've always been a nonconformist, doing things my own way, living an alternative lifestyle, hanging out with freaks and hippies and musicians, mostly digging the underground music scene. Just finding my own way, you know?

"At any rate, I am coming to you live this evening from an undisclosed location somewhere in Nebraska. Boy, I am really glad to be in here rather than out there—that's for sure. It has been one helluva day for the USA. The old girl took a beating today. Like DV/DA, interactive-porn kind of beating. Preliminary reports coming in from overseas are showing several American cities are just gone, man! A series of unexplained nuclear detonations have wiped at least twenty-six cities right off the map. The list so far is as follows: San Francisco, LA, San Diego, Portland, Seattle, Las Vegas, Albuquerque, Denver, Atlanta, Chicago, St. Louis, New Orleans, New York, Philadelphia, Washington, DC [subject laughs at some length here before continuing]—the sick fucks hit DC twice! As an aside, they could have just blown DC away and left everyone else alone, ya know? That would have done us all a favor! Boston, Dallas, Miami, Charlotte, and possibly a few more. Hang in there, folks! It's going to be a wild ride, and no one knows if it is over yet! Looks like a coast-to-coast epidemic of terrorism is on the menu. I will update later as more details become available.

"In the meantime, for those of you that can still hear me, keep your heads down. Duck and cover and all that shit and keep those requests coming in for more music by heliograph, carrier pigeon, Morse code, or Pony Express! Today I put together a kick-ass list of Armageddon tunes just for you! We're going to keep spinning the hits for you crazy kids right here at KPAR, Postapocalyptic Radio! First up, and don't groan, you know it is inappropriately appropriate. It may even be in bad taste, but if you aren't humming this little gem already, you should be. Here's R.E.M.!"

"That's great! It starts with an earthquake . . ."

* * *

Harley Earl was an unusual fellow. In fact, most people would consider him to be downright odd. He had obsessions about things, jumping from one hobby to the next, one phobia to the next, with an enthusiasm that was downright manic. You could say that he was a social hypochondriac. He was OCD about playing the lottery and a lot of other things as well. His whole life had been a case study of adult ADD, and in a single word, Harley was a *mess*. So let's start with the lottery. Harley had to buy exactly one ticket for every drawing, every time, or he'd kinda go a little nuts. He played the exact same numbers every time, even writing them out on the form the same way in a superstitious fear that any deviation from that would result in him not winning. He *had* to, because if he ever forgot to buy a ticket, he was convinced that that would be the day that his numbers won. He would miss out on the big Cashola payout!

Every drawing, he would watch television with nail-biting apprehension, only breathing easy after his numbers didn't come up. He could relax then and get some sleep. He bought his tickets one at a time, and then he would buy a ticket for the next drawing. Harley was the eternal optimist, and he never deviated from the pattern. The cycle went on for years, and then one night, his numbers were drawn. He had known at some point that they would be.

Oh, he didn't win the "super, duper I have more money than most third world countries" kind of jackpot; he won the "I have enough money to live comfortably for the rest of my life and pursue my dreams and fantasies" kind of jackpot. In fact, the local paper even ran a story about him. It was on the back page, right under the grocery store coupons: LOCAL MAN WINS LOTTERY.

When Harley finally won, he had enough cash to do *nothing*, which was okay with him, because he did a lot of nothing anyway. Mostly, he collected unemployment between jobs, and Harley always seemed to be between jobs. He listened to a lot of music, played a lot of video games, watched a lot of television, and surfed the Internet at odd times during the night. Harley did a lot of reading too. He was that guy at the bar that everyone knew. Now, don't get me wrong; they didn't know his name or anything like that or even really knew him. They just knew that he was "that guy at the bar" that they nodded to every Friday and Saturday night. Harley didn't really drink a lot. He was mostly there just for the live music and to chat with the band when they were done playing for the evening.

You see, Harley never really wanted to take a chance on life. It was just way too messy. He was a loner, not necessarily by choice; he was a loner because he was *afraid* to *not* be alone. Harley didn't like getting his feelings hurt, and most people sucked. It was easier to just not have relationships with anyone, and it was one less thing to worry about. Harley wanted to do what *Harley* wanted to do. He didn't trust people, he didn't trust his coworkers, he didn't trust himself, and he didn't trust the government. *Especially* the government. Anyone, really. And as a result, Harley didn't have a whole lot of friends. So when Harley won all that money, it was okay. He had a whole lot of "one less thing to worry about." Harley was alone, but he was very rarely lonely. He never really realized that he was the way he was; he was just sailing through life, oblivious to everything except what happened to grab his attention at the moment. He wasn't stuck-up or snooty. He wasn't mean. He just wasn't connected to anyone or anything, because that was how he liked it. He avoided responsibility and making decisions that affected other people. He dismissed anything that made him remotely uncomfortable as one less thing to worry about, whatever *it* happened to be at that time. Winning that money was a godsend.

So now that Harley had several "one less thing to worry about"—i.e., working, paying bills, eating, and interacting with people that he would rather not have anything to do with—he started thinking about just exactly *what* he was gonna do with all that money.

Harley was idly reading the paper one morning, having his coffee and a civilized breakfast, and he was reading up on what was happening in the world. He read articles about the West Nile virus, avian flu, swine flu, droughts, food shortages, oil, climate change, rising sea levels, killer storms, terrorism, politics, misuse of antibiotics and mutating viruses coming about because of their casual misuse, crashing economy, and real estate bubble. Essentially, he was coming to the conclusion that the world was fucked.

He was shaking his head over the wholesale higgledy-piggledy in the world when a small ad, along with a small article, caught his eye. The article was on how people were taking decommissioned missile bases and government sites and turning them into lavish luxury homes. The taxes were cheap, the government was selling them dirt cheap, and a man by the name of Ed Peden was acting as the real estate broker to sell them. *Hmmmmm.* They were nasty, dark holes in the ground mostly, junk-filled, covered in graffiti, and littered with cigarette butts and empty beer bottles. Some were taking on groundwater after thirty years of neglect, yet the pictures of the rehabbed ones looked quite nice. Fixing one up would have to be a millionaire's hobby, and Harley just happened to be a millionaire. He mulled it over for a day or two, thinking that a rehabilitated missile silo might just be a keen place to weather the coming end of civilization. He did some online research, bought a video walk-through of some of the properties for sale, took the tours, and eventually called his broker and bought one.

Harley purchased a two-hundred-acre Titan 1 missile base for just under a quarter of a million dollars. (Only eighteen were ever built.) It had a little over two miles of underground tunnels that linked the control dome, the power house, three launch silos, antenna silos, support silos, offices, and many features that he didn't know about yet. The place was filled with asbestos insulation, two of the three silos were filling with water, and there were all kinds of rusted junk lying around that would have to be removed. Altogether, though, Harley saw a lot of potential in the place. The lift still worked, he would have eighty-eight thousand square feet to lie around in, and the two hundred acres topside could be farmed or leased out or whatever. There were also two deep wells tapping the aquifer and working sewage-disposal systems. The government had low taxation expectations for the property and would even provide financial assistance for the cleanup.

He brought in a double-wide trailer where he would live while the project progressed, which he would also use as his command post and a base of operations. First things were first, though. He had large construction-grade dumpsters delivered to the site—all the rusting junk just *had* to go. He called in a few contractors and had them bid on the job and finally awarded the contract to a guy he liked. All the old surface debris went into the recycle bins, along with the inoperable hatches on the silos. Once the silos were opened up, he had some cranes brought in to haul more junk out of the deep, stripped launch tubes. Miles of old electrical conduit were cut out and hauled away, including decaying framework and dead animals that had wandered in and never found their way out. Harley sold all the metal to a steel-recycling place and made almost enough money back to pay the contractors for removing it.

The next step was the asbestos. That old nasty insulation had to go. He hired another specialist contractor to do the job, and it took weeks, but finally, every shred of it had been removed. The government had helped pay for it, which was even better. The third and final step was to get someone in to sandblast the place and seal the concrete to prevent seepage. All the graffiti was sandblasted away, along with lead paint and other nastiness. He had essentially stripped the entire complex down to the walls. It was a massive concrete underground shell with a *lot* of possibilities now.

While the place was being gutted, Harley hadn't been idle. They had pumped all the groundwater out of the flooded silos and sealed them. Large circular glass skylights had been installed, with custom titanium hatches that irised open and close to let in the daylight when he felt like it. Harley had gone for the biggest solar power package he could find and got a tax credit for buying it. The deep wells had been flushed out, and cold, icy, rocky mountain water was the prize. Basically, the whole place was cleaned up now and prepped for construction, and Harley was really excited about it. He had a nice elevator shaft installed to replace the open-air lift and built a large two-car garage around the opening at the top. Then he brought in a landscaping company to do an earth overprocess for the garage. Essentially, it looked like a hill from three sides, and the fourth opened up on the long lane that went out to the main highway.

He spent three months with an architect, designing and working on plans to make the place into a loner's paradise. Sometimes, Harley would walk the empty hallways with a flashlight and a hard hat on and just think about what it would all be like when he got it done. This was his biggest obsession to date, and the coolest project ever. Aside from his solar systems up topside, Harley had a few ideas for power on the inside as well. That was his next project. The original base had been powered by water-driven turbines. They were designed to keep things running in the event of a catastrophic power failure. The Army Corps of Engineers had excavated a landing that overlooked an underground river nearby, and the gushing, flowing water would totally power some generators. The originals had been removed when the base was scrapped, but all the work had been done to make it possible, so he brought in a few generators and had them bolted down and wired into the new lighting-and-power system he was having installed. The amount of power generated was frightening.

Eventually, after he hooked up to the grid again, Harley would end up selling power back to the power company. That was one less thing to worry about.

A few more weeks went by, and Harley had, by this time, installed tasteful fiber-optic lighting for use during the daytime and an intricate system of new power conduits to supply light and heat during the night and to power massive dehumidifiers. Every tunnel, every office, every silo was lit well and brightly and made ready for more building. Harley had acres of carpeting installed, hardwood floors, drywall, wood paneling, and additional lighting. Carpenters and plumbers built bathrooms, bedrooms, a library, a gourmet kitchen, dining room, and family room. He built a movie theater and storerooms with lots of shelves. That took care of the old command dome and powerhouse, where the original batteries had been stored. He even had a large fireplace in the living room.

Harley converted the base of one of the missile launch silos into a swimming pool with a Jacuzzi and sauna area, bar and cabana, and a large winding staircase that went around and around the silo up to about twelve feet beneath the skylight. There he built a nice deck out of oak beams and iron. Across the deck he scattered old-world, luxury-liner-style deck chairs to lounge in and take in some sun if he felt like it. The support areas off the pool silo, he turned into a luxury condominium, where he could rest, nap, read, and enjoy the pool access. The entire inside of the silo was done in a Mediterranean style. Stucco and red roof tiles topped the condo that stuck out slightly over the pool, with civilized balconies sporting wrought iron railings. He had the walls painted a sky blue to lighten things up. Recessed niches in the wall had soft lamps on timers that would illuminate as dusk approached, giving an otherworldly effect to the shimmering water of the pool below. Overall, it was a large, open, well-lit area that didn't really feel as if it were underground. Harley would eventually end up spending a lot of time in there.

The second silo, Harley turned into a greenhouse. The *ultimate* greenhouse, actually. He had installed angled mirrors to reflect the sun down inside, both on the walls and outside. One of the two deep wells had been tapped to power a waterfall from the very top of the silo. Harley had had stonemasons in to create realistic cliffs in this room. The waterfall tumbled over jagged rocks, planted with hardy, growing plants, and plunged two hundred feet into a small trout-filled pond ringed with rocks, grasses, and vegetation. At different levels around the silo, ledges filled with good black Midwestern topsoil supported a variety of fruits, vegetables, and edible greens. The pond fed a small stream studded with boulders that meandered its way across the floor and eventually ended against a stone cliff that pumped water back to the top to begin the cycle again. Small conifers were planted on the waterfall side, which would eventually fill out and grow, and for the final touch, Harley brought in some brightly colored native songbirds to fly around and make the place feel like it were outside. The planted terraces were accessible by climbing cunningly designed ramps that gradually spiraled upward, taking him from one level to the next.

Harley converted the support areas for this silo into a processing center, where he could freeze, can, or store his constant bounteous harvest. Mason jars lined one wall, where he could keep his heirloom garden seeds. All in all, when it was complete, Harley was immensely satisfied with this silo as well. He would often sit for short periods, listening to the falling water and meditating. Of course, fresh tomatoes were a bonus too.

WHERE WERE YOU ON THE DAY

Harley had just one more silo to finish, and he wasn't sure what to do with it yet. So he had the contractors come in and build the framework, install the drywall, and paint it a generic white. The empty rooms looked a little sad, but they were clean and dry and ready to go. Harley just had to find a purpose for them. He was satisfied. Eventually, they would find a use. He was sure. He spent two more months buying furniture and artwork, televisions, movies, and video games. He had a state-of-the-art communications-and-security system installed, and he did his best to fill the place up. They did a little more landscaping topside, and eventually, he was ready to move in.

When he was done with the plumbers and electricians, painters, and contractors, the trailer went away, and Harley moved in permanently. After sleeping the first night in his new bedroom, Harley took a long hot shower, slipped on a plush white bathrobe and fuzzy slippers, and went into his gourmet custom kitchen to fix breakfast. Opening the refrigerator, he was shocked to discover that he barely had any food in there. He needed to go grocery shopping.

Harley hated grocery shopping. Too many people.

Harley had just thought of a use for the empty silo.

He grabbed his tablet and ran into town to the local diner. He ordered a huge breakfast. As he sat there, drinking his coffee, he sketched out what he wanted to do with the third and final silo. Two floors would hold walk-in freezers for frozen meats and other goodies, three floors would be for dry goods, and two floors would be for maintenance supplies and cleaning stuff, all the miscellaneous minutiae that went into running a large household. So rather than having to go to the grocery store, he could have the grocery store come to him. While doodling, he even decided he needed a wine cellar and a beer-and-alcohol pantry.

So workmen went back in again, and he had large freezers and shelving installed, and that was it. The silo 3 grocery store was ready for business. He ordered four semis' worth of stuff to stock it and probably wouldn't need to go shopping again for a year or two. Pallets of canned goods were delivered. Flocks of frozen turkeys and chickens, sides of beef and pork, cases of frozen pizza, and ice cream. Sacks of coffee beans, grains, and vintages of wine were delivered, and he had fun putting it all away. Not to mention paper towels, Kleenex, toilet paper, toothpaste, glass cleaner, furniture polish, mopping solution, brooms, dustpans, lightbulbs, etc. The list had gone on forever, but once it was all in, Harley was *set*. He had a whole mountain of "one less thing to worry about." He had dropped a ton of money on everything to make sure he was comfortable.

So Harley settled in, well supplied and in good spirits. He would sleep late in the morning, power up the antenna array for his satellites, and watch European news if he so desired. He'd surf the net, play video games, read, listen to music, exercise, cook, and garden or meditate, or watch movies. Essentially, Harley did *nothing* on a grand scale for almost six months. Then he got bored. He had spent millions, built a dream pad, loaded it up with tons of things to do, had cleaned out whole sections of specialty stores, stocking up on stuff, with more on order, but there are only so many movies a guy can watch, so many video games a guy can play, so many books a guy can read before a guy gets bored. Every day was starting to feel the same: he'd wake up, brush his teeth, take the elevator upstairs, jog down to the main highway to get his mail and his newspaper, and jog back inside, and back down the rabbit hole he would go. Just like Bugs Bunny. Harley needed a hobby.

His property was loaded with wild game, turkeys, deer, and other varmints, and although he'd never been much of a hunter, Harley decided to give it a try. So for the next few months, he got really into shooting sports. He turned one of his vacant rooms into an armory with a big locked door. Inside he had reloading equipment and empty brass for cartridges, and he invested in rifles, shotguns, pistols, and black-powder guns, even antique guns, to hang on the wall for decoration. He bought gun oil and cleaning equipment and wiping rags, bore brushes, and scopes and lasers. Lasers were cool.

While he was doing guns, he figured he'd do bows as well, so he bought an awesome crossbow, an awesome compound bow, and a few nice English longbows, both traditional and composite, and a ton of arrows and bolts to go with them. He purchased thousands of rounds of ammunition in all calibers, and just for the hell of it, he studied gunsmithing and got himself an FFL license. Topside, he built a rifle-and-pistol range and got a few archery butts set up. He lined the edges of the shooting lane with poplar trees, and it looked really nice and would look even better when the trees filled out.

So Harley practiced. He plinked gophers with his .22 and taught himself the mysteries of becoming a hunter. Finally, the day arrived for *the great deer hunt*, and Harley was excited. He had been watching a ton of deer on the property for weeks and had set up a blind near where they gathered in the morning. He set out with his .30-06, all scoped in, and some deer antlers to clack to draw in the bigger bucks. Everything went exactly as he had planned, and around 7:00 a.m., a huge twelve-point buck walked right into his crosshairs. His finger tightened on the trigger, and Harley paused. He suddenly realized that if he pulled the trigger, something special would be taken out of the world. He really didn't *need* to take this deer.

His freezers were full of meat down below. Harley loved shooting and had had a great time learning to do so, but he had a hard time killing for something he didn't need. He didn't need this deer's head over his fireplace. He could buy venison if he wanted to eat it. So he set the rifle aside and watched the deer instead. *Let them be fruitful and multiply.* Maybe at some point, he could lease out the hunting rights for people who really needed the food.

At the end of the day, Harley went home, unloaded his rifle, cleaned it, and then locked it away in the armory.

His next obsession was tropical fish, both freshwater and saltwater varieties. Harley found aquascaping to his liking and very soothing to create natural-looking habitats for his little fishy friends. He drove hundreds of miles in search of tanks, equipment, pumps, heaters, and custom systems. Once it was up and running, lit, and aquascaped, he drove hundreds more in search of fish, corals, live plants, and creatures to stock them with. He really got into it; he even set up a shop where he could design and build his own tanks with sheets of plexiglass and real glass, drill presses, sanders, and saws. Like everything else, if he was going to do it, he was going big. He had tanks that held thousands of gallons of water built tastefully into the decor of the main living area, with computer-controlled water-testing equipment to monitor them. Finally, all that was left to do was leave it alone and watch how big everything got. He had whole eco-systems in play, and the light and swirl of life was everywhere. Harley really enjoyed watching the fish.

He decided he needed to get out of the silo for a while, so he got some camping and backpacking gear, packed the Range Rover full, and set off on a year-long trip to see America. He saw a lot of beautiful places, slept outside every night, went fishing for trout, and cooked his meals over an open campfire. He saw the beauty of the outdoors and made himself at home there. He hiked the quiet, misty trails of the Pacific Northwest, meandering along the ocean, breathing in the scent of redwoods and eucalyptus trees. He hiked the ridgelines of the Rocky Mountain Trail through Glacier National Park and got into the backcountry of Yellowstone, much farther from the asphalt than most tourists ever got to see. He took up photography on his trip and looked forward to developing pictures when he got home. He camped along the edges of alpine lakes, catching his dinner to prepare with onions and lemon, pepper, and potatoes. Harley walked the somber Civil War battlefields of the East Coast and camped in the Everglades, where the alligators barked at night like dogs. He tried to find every back road, every forgotten hamlet, every vista that he could find, and in the end, feeling refreshed in both mind and body, he went home.

Harley's hobbies came and went. He tied flies for fly-fishing. He went to school for a while to study things that he was interested in, just for fun. He did photography and collected coins and stamps. He did art and writing and sculpture and model railroading. He collected fossils and artifacts. Nothing really held his attention for more than a few months, though. Harley didn't mind. There was always something more to learn about, to see and do, and he had all the time in the world to do it.

One day, he drove into town to pick up his latest book order, and just for the heck of it, he popped into a new hobby store that had opened. There were a few neat drones that he had to have, and while browsing, he found a ham radio set up, so he grabbed that too.

He dropped the drones in his hobby room and commenced to set up his ham radio. Over the next few months, he kept expanding it until he had quite the setup. He soundproofed a spare room to be his studio and commenced broadcasting. Harley talked to people overseas, and he talked to people locally. He learned Spanish, Russian, and Chinese just by talking to people on his radio. The man who really didn't want to be around people found enormous joy in talking to them from a distance. He had finally found an interactive outlet that would let him express himself. Harley had found a hobby worth hanging on to.

Until one day, in late November of 2016, he turned on his radio and found that some terrible things had happened. A lot of his buddies had gone off the air.

Curious and feeling cut off from the world again, he powered up the satellite dishes and tried to catch the news. Most of his domestic stations were off the air or simply had the words "Please Stand By" hanging motionless across the screen. Finally, he locked onto a newsfeed from the BBC, and what Harley saw made his blood run cold.

Apparently, many, many American cities had been destroyed at dusk the previous evening, and a few more had been destroyed today. A map on the wall behind the news anchor showed the continental United States and a storm of mushroom cloud icons hanging above just about every major American city. This was very, very bad indeed. So bad, in fact, that Harley's knees wouldn't support him, and he kind of half-collapsed on the couch behind him. The British couldn't decide yet whether this was an act of terror or some kind of preemptive nuclear strike by a foreign power.

Harley was *terrified* of nuclear war, and being in a converted bunker in an *undisclosed location* suddenly seemed like a swell idea. In fact, it had probably saved his life, and that was definitely "one less thing to worry about!" Harley hadn't realized at that time what all his hobbies were; he was an antisocial hermit that liked being alone, but everything leading up to this day had ultimately made him the ultimate prepper. In fact, he was probably the most prepared person on the entire North American continent to ride out the coming chaos.

So now we come to the point of all this. The crux of it all. Since domestic news seemed to be off the air, Harley came to the conclusion that at the very least, it was his civic duty to gather information and broadcast it to the people that were out there. Folks deserved to know what was going on in the world. He could relay things via Postapocalyptic Radio. News, weather, sports, fallout patterns, and those groovy tunes, every hour on the hour, until he heard back from someone. And if he didn't hear back, that was okay too; it would simply be one less thing to worry about.

CHAPTER 9

On the Road with the Friedmans

Brian woke up from a dream of playing his trombone. He had been soloing during the holiday concert, and people had been applauding wildly. As he blinked awake, he realized reality was starkly different. For one thing, it was very dark, and he was covered over by all manner of things, blankets, bags of clothing, and he was literally stuffed into the back of the Bronco with a still-sleeping Trish.

He had to pee too. He rubbed his eyes, and everything came crashing back on him. He put his face to the rear window and saw Mr. Friedman talking to three guys in the road outside. Abby and Mrs. Friedman were out there too.

They were on a back road somewhere near the Sierras, by the looks of things, moonlight glowing from snow-covered peaks. One of the young men said something, and Friedman frowned, casually resting his hand on the butt of the holstered .45. They backed toward their own vehicle slowly, got in, and drove away. Talking in soft voices, the three of them got back in the Bronco, and they kept driving east, away from everything. Brian worried about it for a few minutes and then eventually dropped back off to sleep, the tire's rhythmic lullaby pulling him under.

The next time he woke up, it was morning. They were in a campground somewhere in the mountains, and Mrs. Friedman was cooking breakfast on a propane camping stove. Looking through the window, he could see Abby and Mr. Friedman setting up a tent. Brian woke Trish up, and the two children wormed their way through luggage and camping gear to finally exit the vehicle. The smell of bacon caused his mouth to be flooded with saliva, and he realized, when the alpine air hit him, that he *really* needed to pee now. Mrs. Friedman pointed them toward the bathroom, and the two children ran in that direction.

Brian was looking forward to breakfast. He was zipping his fly when he was shoved from behind into the urinal. He just managed to stop himself from going in, and he spun around to see Josh Friedman grinning at him wickedly.

"Pudwhacker!" he shouted as Josh ran away.

Brian chased Josh out of the bathroom all the way back to the campsite, and Mrs. Friedman corralled them and got them settled in for breakfast at the picnic table. They all ate, and then Mr. Friedman went into the tent to get some sleep. He had driven all night and was exhausted. Mrs. Friedman assigned camp chores to the children. They washed all the dishes up and got everything put away. Then they went exploring. Abby went with them to keep all three of the young ones in line.

There was snow on the ground here, and the children had the novelty of a snowball fight. It rarely snowed in the Bay Area, so this was a rare treat, and they had a good time. Other people were pulling in now as well. Campers stacked high with household goods, overloaded SUVs, and smaller vehicles. Tents were going up in other sites, and other children joined them to run around and blow off some steam.

In spite of the novelty of the situation, Brian only had eyes for the adults coming in. Their faces were taut with tension, frown lines permanently etched between their eyes. Quiet, hushed, tense conversations with warning glances were directed at any children nearby. This made Brian thoughtful, and he paid attention to things. In fact, he was honestly starting to get a little worried about stuff and was thinking about going back to camp with Trish when he was smacked from behind by a snowball. Instead, he turned, laughing, and ran to rejoin the fun.

"Should I go round them up?" Abby asked her mother as she watched the children play.

Gail Friedman thought about it for a moment.

"No," she said, shaking her head. "Let them play for a little while longer. They won't have a chance like this again for a long time, if ever. No one knows what is going to happen next. Let 'em be kids for just a little while longer."

Gail closed her eyes and breathed in the cold, crisp alpine air scented liberally with sun-warmed pine and held it for a moment. Under normal circumstances, she loved it up here. For now it seemed moderately safe, but she knew deep down inside that this couldn't last, that they would need to be moving soon. They had to get to Nebraska before the government shut everything down. Taking another deep breath, she smiled reassuringly at Abby then went to talk to the new neighbors.

The Friedmans camped in the Sierras for a few days as they weighed their options. Mr. Friedman and a few of the other adults had talked it over, and it seemed that the best thing to do was to get *out* of California. Others that had arrived at the campground had brought word from other places. LA, Seattle, Portland. The news had flown from CB radio to CB radio. It seemed even Las Vegas had been hit. Nowhere seemed safe, but they couldn't stay here long either, not with the snow starting to pile up. The most recent arrivals talked about huge camps being built outside the Bay Area, outside Sacramento and other places. Apparently, they were rounding people up and sending them there by the thousands until the crisis had passed.

After three days of talking and listening to others and getting the occasional news report, they decided on Friedman's brother's ranch in Nebraska. It was located just outside Stockville. The Rockies might be hairy, but it would only get worse the longer they waited. Nebraska seemed like the best option, and it would be important to have family close.

Three days after the bombs, they packed up camp and prepared to leave. The Bronco had been repacked in an organized fashion this time, and everyone had a little more room to move around. A few other couples with young kids had decided to caravan with them as far as Nebraska. There would be two more SUVs and three campers. Altogether, about thirty people would be in their group. Gas was going to be their biggest concern. They figured they might be able to siphon from stalled vehicles if necessary or buy it while they could. Other folks were headed out as well, and people waved good-bye as they passed one another.

The next three days went by uneventfully. They passed through Nevada and over the Rockies. They swung pretty far north to go around the remains of Denver, but things were kind of a chaotic mess and no one bothered them. By sticking to back roads and camping, they were able to avoid the worst of it, and there were many others on the road as well. They arrived at the ranch on Thanksgiving Day and waved good-bye to the rest of their little caravan as they passed by on their way to other places and other families. Brian wished them luck from deep down inside. The Bronco rutched over the cattle guard out by the highway and took the long rock driveway up into the hills, where the main house was located.

Pulling into the large turnaround in front of the house, Mr. Friedman cut the engine and got out, knuckling his back. He sighed, and a lot of tension seemed to drain out of him. Smoke was coming from the fireplace chimney, and everything seemed . . . well, normal. When he looked back across the driver's seat at Mrs. Friedman, a smile creased his face.

"Well, guys, we made it."

The screen door opened, and a big weathered-looking man went outside.

"Well, well," he said, laughing, "look what the cat dragged in!"

"Good to see you, Josh," Friedman replied. "I brought the whole clan with me and a few extra little ones as well."

"We'll put 'em to work, then," he said with a wink. "Damn, glad to see you, brother!"

The two men hugged.

"So let's get everyone inside, and maybe you can fill me in on what is going on out there. We lost power about a week ago, and a few folks running through Stockville were babbling on about Denver being nuked. No one knows anything, and I have been staying close to the ranch, taking care of things, ya know?"

"Yeah," Mr. Friedman replied. "I imagine that you've been a little busy."

"We have turkey for dinner, with all the trimmings. It *is* Thanksgiving, even with everything else going to hell. Might as well make the best of it, right?"

Friedman motioned for everyone else to go inside and smiled as the kids raced for the bathroom. The two men walked slowly, talking and comparing notes as they heard everyone inside greeting one another.

Friedman's son, Josh, had been named for his brother, and even though they had been separated by distance, they remained close. That was important, Friedman reflected, because he had a feeling they were really going to need people around that they *knew* they could count on until this crisis passed. Josh's ranch was large. His grandfather had started it back in the twenties, their father had added on to it during his tenure of ranching, and Josh had taken over a few years before when their old man had decided on a permanent vacation that involved deep-sea fishing, warmer climates, and shuffleboard. He hoped his folks were okay in Florida and was trying to figure out how to get word to them.

Josh was currently running about two hundred heads of black Angus cattle with the rest of the ranch in hay. He had just finished baling it all two weeks before, which was lucky. They might be able to trade the fodder for things they needed. He would need the extra hands this winter for sure. Everything was going to be just fine.

As they gathered around the large dining room table a few minutes later, Friedman began to fill his brother and wife, Angela, in on what they knew. Their faces fell as they realized just how bad things might get.

"Basically, it breaks down like this, guys," Friedman began, turning his coffee mug in his hands. "Seattle, Portland, San Francisco, LA, Vegas, and Denver are gone. We don't know about things farther east, but Salt Lake City made it through. And those Mormons may be a lot of things, but they are organized and already out and about, doing their thing, what they can do to help. We were able to gas up in Utah and fill the jerricans, but that was the only place to fill up between here and the Sierras. Basically, the whole West Coast is fucked, under martial law, or burning. There are armed gangs shooting it out with the Army and National Guard in some areas, and no one in authority is talking. Everything we heard was secondhand rumors or from people who saw it go down with their own eyes. That little campground was quite a crossroads for a few days, people going east and west. We heard enough, though, to get the hell out while we could."

"Smart," Josh replied. "We knew about Denver here, but nothing else. There has been a fair amount of military traffic on the road, but again, like you said, no one is talking. Kinda makes me think we should head into Stockville tomorrow and talk to some of the other folks about this. Might not hurt to load up on some stuff we can use as well, do a few deals before there's a serious gas shortage, before it all disappears for good."

"Isn't that hoarding?" Angela asked. "We don't want to become a target by having *too* much, you know."

"I'd call it strategic planning, dear," Josh replied. "At any rate, we can't solve the world's problems by sitting here discussing them, but we can solve our own. Here's what I think we should do."

The adults talked the morning away while the kids played and got a tour of the ranch by their cousins. It was Thanksgiving, after all, and the place had a definite holiday feel to it now that more people were around.

Freedom

CHAPTER 10

The Dog did not know the word, but he knew what it meant. He ran and ran into the darkness, downy snowflakes falling all around him, into a darkness so complete it boggled the mind. No more cage. No more killing. No more bad people smelling of rage and cruelty, cigarette smoke, and alcohol. Running was good. At one point, he stopped, looking all around him at the dark countryside, and realized that this was what was meant to be. He sat down, tilted his head back, and howled to the darkness, then with his ears pricked he listened. Far away in the distance, he heard his brothers and sisters reply. He howled again for the sheer joy of it, and the few travelers on the road in the darkness that heard him hurried on their way, anxious to be inside and safe on this night of nights.

The Dog howled for a third time, satisfied, and then continued onward. He did not know where he was going, but he had all the time in the world to get there. He ran and crashed through snowdrifts, steam rising from his hot, wet fur. He buried his nose in the scents loose on the evening wind. He smelled cooking far away and earth and other things that he did not know but that deep down inside he felt he *should* know them, for they seemed natural and right as well. He drank from pools of water and marked his scent for all to smell and know. He slept when he was tired, amazed anew each time that he awoke that he wasn't in the cage. He was hungry, and he did not know what to do about it.

The third day that he was loose, he was sniffing around some bushes, and a scared furry running *thing* ran quickly, zigzagging through the snow. It was brown and small and smelled *different*, and it was running, and before he thought of it, he had chased it down and pinned it with a paw. It struggled to escape, and it slipped from beneath his grip and darted away. The Dog had never seen such a thing, and he whined deep in his chest, sniffing it out. A few minutes later, he found it again. And it ran again. This time, he pinned it and bit it. Warm blood went into his mouth, and The Dog realized that these small brown things were *good* to eat. They were everywhere too. So The Dog was no longer hungry.

After a week of running from the Bad Place, and Cain, The Dog found something interesting. It was like a house and not a house, and it fascinated The Dog. There was another kind of man there, a Lonely Man, but he didn't know that he was lonely. People seemed to need other peoples, but this Lonely Man did not seem to realize it. Maybe he was like The Dog and all the other dogs, except in his case, it would be that people had gone away and left him. Maybe. The Lonely Man also smelled different from other people he had been around with. He smelled of Underground, and The Dog wasn't sure why. He smelled of green places, but the world was not green right now; it was white.

The lonely man puzzled The Dog, and he decided to keep an eye on him. Once a day, the Lonely Man would go for a walk, and The Dog would walk with him, but at a distance, watching. The Dog would follow him from the house that wasn't a house, down the road, past the big tree, and back again. He did it at the same time every day, but once he went back inside, he didn't come out again. So it became routine for The Dog to shadow the Lonely Man and keep him safe from the Bad People. Once he was back inside, The Dog ran a long ways to a town he had found.

There was an older female *people* who was leaving out for him a dish full of good food. She would sit on her back porch inside the windows and watch for him. It had taken him a few days to trust enough to approach, but what she put in the bowl smelled delicious, and eventually, with a wary eye, he had approached and taken his fill. She never tried to grab The Dog, and he appreciated that.

One day, after walking with the Lonely Man for a while, he had run to the town, and there was a fuzzy round green thing next to the dish. The Dog paused, staring at it. He remembered this from before. Before the Bad Place and the Cain, there had been a boy. *His* boy. And they had played with . . . a ball. That was what it had been called, a *ball*. The Dog gingerly picked it up in his mouth, squeezing it with his jaws, and then he threw his head back. It flew into the air. Delightful. He batted it with his paws and chewed it. He heard a laugh and spun around with the ball in his mouth to see the old woman standing there. He crouched down, unsure of what to do. Then he bolted.

"Oh well," she said, "maybe tomorrow."

The next day, after his walk with the Lonely Man, he arrived at the old woman's house just as she was filling the bowl. He whined from the edge of her backyard, and she turned to look at him.

"There you are! You're later than usual. I was starting to worry. Now wait right there. I have something special today."

The Dog approached the dish and began to eat ravenously. The screen door closed, and he looked up. She was standing there with a delicious huge bone.

"You're going to have to come get it," she said with a smile.

The Dog approached cautiously and gradually extended his head out to sniff the beef bone. It still had little scraps of meat on it. He licked it, but she hadn't let go yet, and very cautiously, he wrapped his huge teeth around it. Then he snatched it, growling, and ran out of the yard.

"You silly thing!" she called out behind him. "I just want to pet you!"

The Dog hunkered down in his bushes, where he had made a nest of sorts, and began to gnaw the bone. It was full of marrow, and he crunched and slobbered on it all afternoon, worrying out every delicious bite.

The next morning, The Dog awoke at his usual time, stretching and yawning hugely. He shook the snow from his fur and paced around for a bit, marking his domain. As he was raising his leg a last time, a small furry thing ran out of the bushes, and he chased it down and bit it. He almost devoured it on the spot, and then he thought of the old woman. Fair was fair. He went into her backyard and laid it on the steps. Then he turned and ran in order to get to the Lonely Man's in time for the walk.

He arrived back in the early afternoon, and the woman was putting out a warm dish of something for him that steamed.

"Thank you for the rabbit," she said. "I cooked him for you!"

Rabbit. He cocked his head and looked at her. That was a new word.

He smelled the dish and tried a bite. The . . . rabbit was delicious. That was what you called the small furry things.

He licked the dish clean and looked up at the old woman, cocking his head.

"You're a smart one, aren't you? I can tell," she said. "Will you let me pet you today?"

The Dog whined.

She slowly extended her hand, and he went forward to sniff at it. Her fingers still smelled like rabbit. He licked her hand and then danced away, disappearing into the bushes.

The days blended together, and The Dog had his routine, and gradually, he came to trust the old woman. She would sit on the steps and talk to him while he ate, occasionally running a small warm hand down his back. She was the best people he had met so far. And she threw the ball for him occasionally. Maybe the world wasn't such a lonely place after all.

Between the old woman and the Lonely Man, The Dog was entertained and busy. His routine was nice, and he got plenty of exercise.

One afternoon, he heard the sounds of two wheels coming down the road to the town. He remembered that sound from the Bad Place, and he ran to look and see. Yes, Cain was coming. He had found him. Now there were loud sounds and fire. Smoke and *booms* hurt The Dog's ears. And blood. People blood. The scents and the sounds and Cain, scared The Dog. The old woman! She was on the other side of town. He must make her safe. The Dog ran through the smoke and fire, always having to turn to avoid the loud two wheels. He was running up the street to her house when he saw two other people drag her from her home into the front grassy place. The Dog growled and tensed up to attack.

And then they killed her.

He whined, laying his ears back, dancing in place, unsure of what to do.

The other people got on their two wheels and drove away, laughing. The Dog ran to the old woman and nosed her, but she wouldn't move, and he whined again. He pawed at her, and she stayed still. More two wheels were coming, and The Dog ran away. He wanted his ball, and he wanted to leave this place. Now.

Pandemonium

The night of the dogfights had changed everything for Big John Cain. Pandemonium had erupted in the barn at the end of the first fight when the lights went out. Forty or so drunk and stoned, blood-thirsty fanatics in a dark barn was *not* a good thing. A couple of fistfights had broken out, and that bastard of a dog had knocked him over while he was escaping, which, Cain reflected, might not be such a bad thing, all things considered. He had never liked that particular animal. With him gone, it was probably for the best.

Charlie had been unable to get the lights back on, and after they checked the fuses for the third time, they had canceled the evening's fights. They had piled out into the dooryard of the farm. It was completely dark and snowing. The power seemed to be out everywhere. Everyone kind of hung out until the beer was gone, then they drifted off to their own places. Cain was restless. The incessant howling of the other caged dogs was getting on his nerves, so he decided a midnight stealth mission back into town was in order.

He felt the same thrill he always did as the engine kicked to life. It was cold outside, and the snow was falling heavier as he pulled out of Charlie Mack's place. He drove the seven miles back into town slowly and noticed that things were pretty dark there as well. All the streetlights were out, no homes were lit up, and with the engine rumbling, he pulled up in front of Sparky's Bar, the place that he had been bouncing at lately. It was quiet outside, and he sat there for a moment in the snow, the engine warm between his legs. Up the street, a few police cruisers were sitting, their lights flashing, near the courthouse. He wondered what that was all about. Shrugging, he stepped off the hog and entered the bar.

Gino, the bartender, looked up as Cain came in shaking the snow off his jacket.

"We're closed," he said abruptly before recognizing Cain. "Hey, John," he said, "we've had no juice for about five hours now, so I figured I'd make it an early night and close up the place. How were the fights tonight?"

"Shitty. Mind if I grab a brew?"

Gino motioned toward the fridge as Cain went behind the bar. He was up to his elbows in soapy water, washing glasses one at a time.

"Why shitty? If I had known the power was gonna be out, I would have gone out there tonight myself."

Cain sighed. "Well, first off, I lost a hundred bucks on the first fight—the *only* fight, actually. We lost power too. Secondly, people were pissing me off, and that bastard dog escaped, the one I hate. I think I told you about him, right?"

"Yeah, the wolf dog?" Gino shook his head. "He was a money-maker, though. He's won like, what, eleven fights so far this year?"

"Yeah. Fucker," Cain agreed. "Then a couple of the boys got into it, had a few fistfights, smacking one another around, and we had to break those up. All in the dark, too. What's going on up the street at the courthouse?" Cain asked, taking a pull on his beer.

"Beats me," Gino replied. "Cops have been over there since seven. No one's talking."

Cain mulled it over while he finished his beer, then he helped Gino swamp the place out and lock up for the night.

Central Nebraska sucked, and Cain thought, not for the first time, that maybe it was time to move on someplace warmer, maybe Fort Lauderdale or Key West. The police cruisers were still up the street when he left, their lights circling in the darkness.

He rode the six blocks to the crappy little house he had been renting, shrugging off power outages, unexplained police cruisers, and missing dogs. He was ready to call it a night. Cain had had a rough night and was just bored. When he got there, his current girl-friend, Gina, was waiting for him. He was getting a little tired of her too.

"Where have you been?" came a voice from the darkness. "It's about fucking time you got here! I was getting tired of waiting for your dumb ass." Gina lit a candle and set it on the shitty coffee table in front of her for dramatic effect. She was on one, it seemed, and wanted to fight.

"Shut up, bitch!" Cain snarled back, going to the fridge for another beer. He slammed the door shut and cracked the tab.

"What are you going to do if I don't? I'm *sick* of this shit, John! You just bail when you want to and leave me here waiting for you to come back. We had *plans* tonight!"

Cain laughed. "Oh yeah? Like what?"

"Well, my sister and her boyfriend were gonna meet us for dinner, and we were supposed to hang out and watch some TV afterward. Then the power went out. They already left."

"Your sister, huh? And now she's trapped another dumb sucker into taking care of her, right? She's almost as worthless as you are! Besides, when did you even tell me they were going to be coming over?" Cain asked, starting to get pissed. "You *know* we have the fights this night every week!"

"That's another thing! Those goddamn dogs—"

"Those goddamn dogs are what pay the bills around here, bitch!"

"That's it!" she screamed. "I'm leaving!"

"Fine! Go! There's the fucking door!"

This was par for the course, too. Cain knew what usually came next. A bitter fight, rough sex, and reconciliation of a sort. Gina always had the same modus operandi when she'd had a line or two of coke.

Gina glared at him, grabbed her purse off the coffee table, and was walking toward the door when she hit him with a ringing slap across the face. *That was new!* Cain thought, rubbing his jaw, and he slapped her back, knocking her sprawling.

Gina was off the floor and at him like a tiger, going for his eyes with her nails.

Cain wrestled her arms away from his face and held her from behind, his arms pinioning hers to her sides.

"Let me *go*! Goddamn you!" Gina screamed. "Somebody help!"

"Shut up!" Cain roared back, his face scored and bleeding where she had scratched him.

"You are hurting me!" she yelled, scraping a heel down the front of his shin.

Cain had had it. He knew what came next and was slightly aroused. He wrestled her over to the back of the couch, and holding her arms behind her, he bent her over it.

"Stop it!"

Cain ripped her jeans off, bending her over further, and unzipping his fly with his free hand, he pulled his cock out.

"John! Goddamn you! Stop!" She struggled.

"This is what you want, isn't it? Well, you're going to get it now!"

Cain penetrated her with a lot of friction, and she screamed and then rapidly got wet.

He fucked her hard. Savage, deep thrusts. He held her arms behind her with one hand at the wrists as she began to moan. He knotted his other hand into her hair as she began to push back into him in rhythm.

"You love that, don't you?" he asked.

"No," she whimpered.

"Huh?" he said, pounding deeper.

"I . . . don't . . . ," she moaned out.

Cain released her hair and slapped her on the ass hard a few times.

Gina moaned some more, and then she came. Cain continued to fuck her, releasing her arms, and she gripped the couch as he slammed into her from behind.

"You love this!" he hissed. "You love being treated like a whore. I know you do!" He slapped her ass again.

She cried out again as he came. "Oh my god . . ."

Cain kissed the back of her neck, pulled out of her, and rezipped his fly. He smacked that ass one final time and then walked over to the table to grab his smokes. She was still bent over the back of the couch, panting, as he lit two then walked back to give her one.

"You can be a real bastard sometimes, John," she said, taking the cigarette and inhaling deeply.

"Still leaving?" he asked with a smirk.

"Maybe tomorrow," she replied. "I haven't decided."

"Let's smoke some pot, then," he said.

All in all, Cain reflected later, lying in bed with one of Gina's legs over him and the relaxed muscles that came from smoking the chronic, that the night hadn't turned out too badly. He yawned. Hopefully, tomorrow would be much, much better.

CHAPTER 12

Eviction Notice

A loud banging on the door early the next morning roused Cain from a fuzzy dream. He always had vivid dreams after smoking too much weed. The banging continued, and his head was threatening to explode. What time was it anyway, 7:00 am? Pulling his jeans on, he yelled at whomever was banging on the door.

"Christ! All right already! I'm coming!"

The banging continued regardless.

"Shut the fuck up with the banging!" he roared out, jerking the door open.

Two sheriff's deputies were standing on the front porch, looking inordinately pleased with themselves.

Now what? he thought.

"Well, well," Officer Paulson said, "Mr. Dogfight himself! Up and around and about at an early hour, I see."

"Can I help you guys with something?" Cain replied, politely he felt, all things considered.

"Yeah, you can, Big John," the other deputy said. "Chief wants to see you down at the station, pronto."

"I'll come down in a bit, then," Cain replied.

"Nah, son, you'll come right now," Paulson said, pointing at the cruiser on the street. "Let's go."

"Let me get a shirt on at least," he said, turning back inside.

The two deputies followed him into the living room. The bong was sitting on the coffee table from the night before, and beer cans littered just about every other available surface.

"Wow, Jake!" Paulson said to the other deputy. "Looks like reasonable cause to me."

"Did you have a party last night, Johnny boy?" Jake, the deputy, asked.

"Something like that," Cain muttered, unconcerned and pulling a shirt over his head.

"We should charge you with possession, smart guy."

"Well, you'll have to charge your kid, then, too," Cain shot back. "I sold him a quarter ounce last week." Cain grabbed his jacket.

"Let's go, tough guy."

The three men walked out to the cruiser sitting at the curb. The power was still out. They got in—Cain in the back, of course—and drove the few blocks to the sheriff's office.

"Am I being charged with something?" Cain asked.

"At the moment, no. But time will tell, of course."

Cain reflected on that for a moment. *This* day was starting off being a bigger pain in the ass than the day before. Sighing, he got out and walked up the steps and into the sheriff's office.

He was led down the hallway and into the office of the sheriff himself. Tom Briggs. Jake the deputy knocked on the door, and a voice called out, telling them to enter.

Going in, the two deputies took up spots by the door and gestured for John to step forward to the desk.

Briggs looked up and grinned. "Well, as I live and breathe, it's the notorious Big John Cain."

Cain had a distinctly uneasy feeling in his gut looking at that grin.

"Have a seat, John. I wanted to have a little chat with you."

Cain sat down.

"Now, John, as you know, you and I have tangled in the past. Things haven't always worked out between us, and you know I don't approve of most of your activities and, shall we say, hobbies, since you have lived here. That being said, I am giving you until sunset to get out of town. I don't care where you go now, and I don't care what you do, but if you come back here, well, let's just say things might get a little unpleasant."

Cain smiled and leaned back in his chair. "And why exactly would I leave town, Sheriff Briggs, just on your say-so? You don't have the authority to just kick people out of town because you feel like it. Please. If you are gonna charge me with something, then do it, throw me in jail. I'll be out in a week and back to my hobbies. You'll still be a prick, and life will go on in this little Nebraska shithole. In all honesty, I was kinda kicking around leaving soon anyways, but now I think I'll stay and hang around a little longer just to piss you off."

Briggs just grinned at him. "No, son, you ain't, and here's why. We just simply don't have to put up with your white trash ass anymore, or anyone like you, for that matter. Nope, Dobson is taking out the trash right now, today. No more bullshit, no more trials, no more misdemeanors, no more appeals. You are persona non grata here, John. Going forward, if I see you in my town, or if my deputies see you in town, we're going to blow you away, throw your body in a hole, and forget about you. Clear?"

Cain just gaped at him as he smiled again.

"You have until sunset, and then the trashman comes."

Cain rose to leave, and as he put his hand on the doorknob, Briggs spoke behind him. "Don't come back here. Cain. I mean it."

Shouldering past the deputies, he stalked out of the sheriff's office.

Walking quickly down the steps, he looked over his shoulder and saw the two sheriff's deputies smirking at him. Cain memorized their faces for later. This wasn't over. Then he turned and started walking back to his shitty rented house for the final time.

By the time he got there, he was furious. More so at being intimidated by that prick sheriff than anything else. He had to go. That was crystal clear. For some reason, he got the impression that if he defied the order to leave, he was going to die. Cain strode in the front door, letting the screen bang shut behind him. The power was *still* out. That irritated him too. He walked into the bedroom and noticed Gina was still passed out, one bare leg sticking out from under the comforter. He grabbed his saddlebags from the closet and began stuffing them with things he was going to need. He packed his .44 Colt Python and grabbed a sawed-off Mossberg 12-gauge from the closet, stuffing in ammunition for both. He packed about a pound of weed, a carton of smokes, and a fat wad of cash. Going to the kitchen, he put in a bottle of Johnny Walker Black, some spare boxers and socks, and a couple of T-shirts, and he was done packing and ready to ride.

Cain reentered the bedroom and changed into riding clothes. He layered it because he wasn't sure how long he'd be out on the road. He pulled on some base-layer stuff, cargo pants, and a heavy wool overshirt. He pulled on his leather outers, and his WWI German infantry helmet with the spike. As an afterthought, he grabbed the samurai sword from the back of the closet, too. It was a souvenir from the Second World War courtesy of his grandfather, who had fought in the Pacific. Cain had had it restored at one point, and it was the real deal. He slid it out of the scabbard about an inch and looked at the ripples in the metal, and it was sharp as hell too. Looking around, he realized that was it, everything he really cared about.

He left the unconscious Gina in bed; he was done with her too. When he got outside, he pulled out his cell and saw that he had service and placed a call to Mack. Mack answered on the third ring.

"Mack, I'm on my way out there, man. Something weird going on here. We have to talk."

"Sure, John. I have a lot to tell you as well."

"I'll see you in a few, then," he said, ending the call.

His bike gleamed solid silver from the driveway, and affixing the saddlebags and holstering the 12-gauge, he fired it up. He took a long last look at the shitty little house and then pulled away, engine snarling.

Cain pulled into the farmyard at Mack's place and cut the engine. He was pleased to see a few other bikes there, and he mentally checked a few names off the list. Fred Kneller, Bill Olson, Keith and Tony Faught, a few others. Good guys to have in a fight, and if he didn't miss his guess, they had also gotten wake-up calls from the good sheriff.

Opening the kitchen door, Cain walked in and found everyone gathered there around a little radio.

"What's up, guys?" he asked.

Mack looked up from the table and grimaced.

"It's all gone, John," he said.

Cain frowned. "What's all gone?"

"The whole damn country."

"What . . . ?"

Mack sighed. "It breaks down like this: Yesterday, last night, about the time we lost power here, a bunch of nukes went off. There are reports coming in, patchy and sloppy, but so far, sixteen American cities are just gone. Boom! Nuked."

Mack gestured to a map on the table with all the cities circled in red. Cain stood very still, the wheels in his head spinning. "Shit! That explains it, then . . ." he trailed off. "Those sons of bitches knew about it and haven't told anyone in town yet." Cain looked at the other guys in the kitchen. Blank faces stared back at him.

"How many of you guys had a chat with the sheriff this morning?"

There were nods.

"I thought so. They think they can do whatever they want to now." Cain took a deep breath, an idea rattling around in his head as it went off like a flashbulb.

"Well," he added musingly, "if they think they can do what they want, you guys realize, of course, that the opposite is true as well, right?"

"What's that, John?" Mack asked.

"It means," Cain continued with a sense of growing excitement, "that *we* can too!"

He looked around the table with a grin as one by one, the others grasped the concept as well.

"*That* is why they wanted us out of town. Do you all realize what an *opportunity* this is? We can finally *do* what we want! There are no rules anymore! We can ride this whole state and do what we want to do! We will be like modern-day Visigoths at the fall of the Roman Empire, the Vandals, the motherfucking Huns!"

"Huns?" Mack asked.

"Never mind, Mack," Cain said, shaking his head. "We'll have to test the waters at first and see what happens, but if I am right, we're going to be kings! We will build an Army, and then we will *rule* here! We'll need more guys, of course . . ."

Everyone hunkered down over the table to discuss the future. Things were going to be great!

The Evacuation

From the Journal of H. Rayton Townsend
November 18, 2016
Petaluma, California

I was awakened shortly after dawn today, and as I struggled awake (I hadn't even realized that I had fallen asleep!), there was a truck rolling slowly through the apartment complex. It had a loudspeaker on the roof, blaring the same message over and over:

> **Residents of this community! The Federal Emergency Management Agency has declared in conjunction with the president of the United States a state of national emergency. You must evacuate this area immediately. Proceed to the nearest curb and wait. Trucks have been dispatched to relocate you. Martial law is in effect. Looting will be dealt with swiftly and harshly, and a daylight curfew is in effect.**
> **Residents of this community! The Federal Emer . . ."**

* * *

Ray jerked awake as the truck rolled past downstairs, right past his deck area. The day was overcast, the sun a deep-red, blood-orange color behind swirling clouds. To the south, the entire horizon was a sinister, inky black of smoke, dust, and debris. Flashes of light from deep within told of more things burning and exploding. Or maybe it was lightning. Ray wasn't sure. A fine ash was falling from the sky and coating everything outside, and he shivered. The power was still out, and the cats were looking at him, stretching and yawning.

He stood up from the couch, wincing, and stretched himself. He realized then that yesterday had really happened. San Francisco was gone, and his future was drastically uncertain at the moment. The unreal, dreamlike feeling was gone, and he was now faced with the stark, sobering reality that he was alone, and frightened, and he did not know what to do. At least his head was clearer now. Maybe being evacuated would put him closer to that Greyhound ticket home.

He ran into the bathroom and emptied his bladder, wishing he could grab a quick shower, but the water was well and truly off now along with the gas. It was a good thing that he had filled up so much the night before. He was already dressed for traveling, and he went over everything again in his head as he brushed his teeth. He filled a few Nalgene bottles with water and attached them to his pack by the door. Lifting the flap, he stuffed his Beretta inside along with two boxes of shells. He wanted to be discreetly armed, should anything go south. He also grabbed his documents, passport, social security card, bank statements, and insurance information. For good measure, he stuck two rolls of Morgan silver dollars into the pack and took a few minutes to sew three ten-dollar gold coins into the waistband of his pants.

The cats were meowing at him that their dishes were empty. *The cats!* What was he going to do about the cats?

"Well, ladies," he said, "I guess you're going to be on your own for a while."

He grabbed the fifty-pound bag of cat food and dumped it all over the kitchen floor. He had filled every pot, pan and dish, and sink and tub with water the night before, so they had plenty to drink as well. Sliding the large glass door open on the third floor deck, he felt that they should be able to escape when the food and water ran out. That was all he had time for. Picking them up one at a time, he loved on them for a few seconds, petting and talking to them. He made sure all their toys were out, and then shouldering his pack, he locked the door behind him and made his way down curbside, where his other neighbors were gathering.

"They're cats," he murmured to himself, "they'll go feral, but they'll live."

He glanced up to the window and saw them watching him leave. *Good luck, kitty critters!* he thought.

Trucks came through fifteen minutes later and gathered those that were ready to leave. Ray sat in the back, near the tailgate, next to a scared-looking kid in a National Guard uniform. As the truck was exiting the complex to the main road, Ray glanced out the back and saw five young Hispanic men kneeling by the side of the road, their hands up and fingers laced behind their heads. They were guarded by four or five soldiers. As the truck began to accelerate, shots rang out, and they fell face forward into the dirt.

"Holy shit!" he exclaimed. "What the fuck was that about?"

"Looters," the young soldier said with a grimace. "Rapists, murderers, thugs, bad people. Don't worry about it."

Ray blinked.

Within minutes, they were on 101, heading north, away from the bruised and destructive sky behind them. Everyone was quiet for a little while.

"Does anyone know anything yet? Who did it?" he asked the soldier.

"Nah, man." The kid took a long drag on a cigarette, his eyes red from lack of sleep. "No one tells us shit."

Ray watched as he blew the smoke out of the rear of the vehicle. Some of the more prissy passengers were muttering about it, but one look from the kid with the M16 shut that down fast.

"Where are we headed?" Ray finally asked.

"Our orders are to pick people up as we find 'em, willingly or not, and take 'em to the FEMA camp north of Santa Rosa. It's going to be another long day," he replied.

That was all Ray could get out of him.

The drive to the camp was uneventful. Dead cars were pushed to the side of the freeway for as far as Ray could see. Here and there were a few people walking, always north, always away from the city. Occasionally, the trucks would stop and pick up a few more.

When they got to the camp, Ray was relieved to see big tents set up, with Red Cross emblems on the roofs. Helicopters were taking off and landing in a purposeful way, delivering supplies, and ahead, people were being processed into the camp in an orderly fashion. Two Marine Corps jets flashed by in the distance as he jumped down from the tailgate. Another soldier with a bullhorn was bellowing instructions as the trucks came to a halt.

"Men to the left! Women and small children to the right! Let's go! Let's go!"

People began to line up accordingly, and for a split second, Ray had visions of places like Bergen-Belsen, Dachau, and Auschwitz flashing through his mind. Then he shrugged it off. This was America, after all. Things like that simply didn't happen here. These people were here to help. They wouldn't let it happen.

Ray approached a table where a harried-looking man with a clipboard waited. He asked for his name, his age, his social security number, his address, and if he had any immediate medical needs, etc. He was checked off one list and put on another, issued an ID bracelet, and sent to another area where a man with a Geiger counter swept him from head to foot. The man winced a little, and suddenly, Ray was pretty alarmed.

"Is it bad?" he asked hesitantly.

"Not as bad as some coming through here, but you definitely got dosed. Everything you have on is slightly hot, and it's borderline safe. Where were you when it happened?" he asked.

"Just north of Novato, along the Marin–Sonoma county line," he replied.

"Minimum safe distance," he muttered, making a note. "If you had been south of Novato, you'd already be losing your hair."

Ray glanced ironically up at his shaved head, and the man laughed.

Ray nodded at his pack.

"None of this stuff was with me on the road yesterday, and it took years of constant upgrading and expense to build up my back-packing gear. It should be okay, right?" he asked.

"Well, let's see. You mind opening it up so I can sweep it?"

He unpacked everything, and the guy swept it all. He took Ray's Beretta away, but other than that, he let him keep everything else. He went into showers, where he was given a special soap. He scrubbed and scrubbed, rinsed, scrubbed, and finally emerged with his skin feeling a bit raw. He was swept again for radiation, issued new clothing, and sent to the next tent. There he received a physical and potassium iodide tablets. After that, he was assigned to a tent with three other guys and left to his own devices. Once there, he took a nap, wrote in his journal for a bit, and eventually drifted over to a community tent where he found himself playing cards with a guy named Mike and eating dinner.

Mike was from Novato and was already losing his hair. His skin had a jaundiced cast to it, and he didn't look too healthy to Ray. He had a good attitude about things, though. The two men talked about the day before, swapping stories. They talked about people they had known and recalled fun things to do in a city that no longer existed. Ray mourned the fact that he would never again go to the pier and watch the sea lions. Every trip he had ever made to San Fran, he had spent at least an hour watching them, fascinated.

Eventually, topics shifted to more personal details, like they always do.

"So what do you do for a living, Ray?" Mike asked.

That was when Ray's throat closed up a little, and it all hit him. Hard. Such a simple question to ask, really, and up until that point, he had been just getting by, dealing with what he had to do. Up until yesterday, it would have been an easy question to answer. Sucker punch. He had been on autopilot, reacting, doing what was necessary without really *thinking* about what it all meant, and pondering the implications.

"What do you do?"

He thought back to leaving work the day before, the pettiness and duration of his drive home, the good natured, can-do attitude of his staff. His assistant manager, who worked so hard for him to get the job done. She had had three kids and a husband that she loved very, very much. Gone. He thought individually about some of his part-time employees, college kids for the most part, always getting into trouble and laughing it off. Cocky with their own immortality and youth. Gone. All gone now. There was no way they had survived just a few miles outside the city. He hoped it had been fast for them. He reflected for a moment, all these images and thoughts racing through his brain. No job. No home. No pets. No meaning. Just himself at the moment.

He opened and closed his mouth a few times to respond, not even sure of what to say.

"I guess I am unemployed, Mike," he finally replied, kind of laugh-crying it out.

Both men howled with laughter, and the guy sitting to Ray's left choked on his meal a little and joined them. They laughed and cried then laughed some more. They played cards and talked, and eventually, the meal was done and they moved on.

As Ray was walking back to his tent, he noticed his first suicide. A man had hanged himself. Soldiers were cutting down the body as he passed by. There were a lot of priests and ministers, shrinks, and grief counselors here, and although the man on the pole was the first that Ray had seen, Mike and a few other guys at dinner had told him about more people that had done the same. A crowd ahead of him caught his attention, and in the middle of it, there was a man of Middle Eastern descent getting the living shit kicked out of him. He stopped to watch for a moment until soldiers finally waded into the fray and took him out.

Looking around in the twilight and starting to see things *clearly*, Ray realized that there were things about this situation that he didn't like. Already, there was a shift in the atmosphere, a palpable sense of menace. Many more people had been brought in throughout the day, and they had all brought their problems with them. A place that this morning had seemed so full of hope and purpose was starting to look a little off to him. Smoke was rising from a quarter of a mile away. They were burning body bags. There were a lot of them.

Ray felt pity for all the people that were from here. The natives. He had a place to go, a way out, and family waiting for him there. No matter what it took, he was going to get there too. They had no place to go; theirs had vanished in one incendiary heartbeat. Feeling moody, he went back to his tent to write a little more in his journal and get some sleep.

* * *

From the Journal of H. Rayton Townsend
November 19, 2016
FEMA Camp, North of Santa Rosa, California

I am numb. Whoever said "No man is an island" obviously never spent time in a FEMA camp. I feel so alone here, yet I am surrounded by half a million strangers. Northern California sucked for meeting people before The Day—I mean, it was hard enough to meet people that you connected with before all this went down, and now it is virtually impossible. Forty-eight hours after the attack, and things are beginning to break down. People are still arriving here by the thousands! Around the clock, a never-ending tide of humanity is coming in. Scared, hurt, pathetic victims. There are wolves on the loose too. Predators sizing up the new arrivals, large parties of angry, disenfranchised young men, their eyes hot with calculated hate. Racial tensions are about to boil over, and the camp has self-segregated into sections. Black, white, Hispanic, Asian, Mayan Indians from the Yucatan, and others. Sanitation is becoming an issue, even arson. I have to get out of here.

* * *

The trucks continued to roll in day and night, and more and more people arrived. The next few days went by in a blur for Ray. He stood in the drizzle near the processing center and watched the buses roll in and unload. People being sorted and cleaned up. Now the badly injured, the burned, and the sick were being brought to camp. Blind, burned, crippled things, missing hair and eyes and teeth. He wondered when the Army was going to run out of body bags and shivered. They were taken off the trucks in stretchers. Ray didn't think they'd be able to help most of those people. The doctors in the surgical units were overwhelmed, asleep on their feet. The body bags outside those tents piled up faster than they could be burned, and the mood was turning ugly. Rations had already been cut, and the meals in the dining tents had decreased in size by a third.

Looking around, he estimated that there must have already been half a million people in the camp north of Santa Rosa. This was horrible, and there was no end in sight. No one knew anything. There had still been no announcements, no news. There seemed to be no plans or strategy beyond bringing people here and dumping them off. Everything was starting to run out.

He wanted to go home so badly, back to his roots in Illinois, but the prospect of traveling alone terrified him, and winter was almost here in full force. He mulled it over again: stay here and die with the wolves, or become one, or take his chances on the road and try to get out. Try and make it someplace unaffected by the chaos that seemed to be compounded daily. It was obvious, in retrospect, to see the chain of events that had led up to this very situation, and everyone should have seen it coming. Hindsight was twenty-twenty, though, and it had been willful blindness. The federal government didn't exactly have the best track record for handling a crisis. Now it was too late.

Gangs prowled the camp now, melting away whenever a patrol appeared. The impromptu streets had turned to mud, sucking at one's boots, as the fall rains descended on Northern California. Rapes were on the rise, along with murder, revenge murder, executions, and barely restrained panic were at the corner of people's eyes and on the tips of their tongues when they gathered in small groups to discuss it. A sense of desperation and fear was everywhere.

Ray started laying plans to get out of there. Someone had stolen most of the contents of his backpack just the day before. He had foolishly left it stuffed under his cot when going to lunch at the mess tent. He had returned from the meal to find the contents that weren't stolen strewn all over the tent. His journal, a few small personal items, and his socks and boxers were all that really remained to him. His camping food, water purifier, along with his buck knife, hatchet, and sleeping bag were gone, along with his stove and other necessities for hiking a long trail. That really pissed him off, and he carried what was left everywhere with him now. Stupid. He should have carried it everywhere with him from the get-go. Live and learn. He wouldn't be making that mistake again. He'd actually been surprised to find a few things left behind, including the pack. It was an Arc'teryx, and it was top-of-the-line, but apparently, they had just wanted his stuff. It had taken him an hour to get it all back together and to take inventory of what he had lost.

The next day, he saw a gang member wearing his extra shirt, but alone against thirty or so guys, he simply ducked his head and walked past, not even bothering to confront the thief. He started to feel some of that desperate rage himself and wished he still had his 9mm.

Ray hadn't been idle; he had made a few new friends in the last few days. People like himself that wanted out and had a place to go. Many had been laying their own plans to get out of here. As the population surged and surged, it began to feel like someone had taken a maximum security prison and blown it up to encompass the entire world. Factions were forming along racial, political, and economic lines, and the pressure to join one or another or be crushed between was lying heavily on everyone's shoulders. One couple had a place in the Sierras they were going to probably make a run for, and they had hinted that he might be welcome to join them in getting there. He was considering it. Everyone agreed they would have to leave, and soon.

Even the soldiers guarding the camp were getting twitchy, and that was something that set off alarm bells in Ray's head. Their numbers had swelled the last few days. He didn't want to be anywhere near here when the lid blew off the pressure cooker. He really started to wonder who was in charge, if anyone. He listened to their conversations if he could without appearing to do so. He would kneel down to tighten a bootlace, act like he was looking for someone in particular, linger near a trash can for a few moments longer than necessary. Or he would sit against a wall where soldiers gathered, pretending to read a paperback book. Always near a group of three or four soldiers who just happened to be discussing or bitching about what was going on. All he could glean, though, was that they were shooting looters near and inside the border of Marin County and that there were more refugees on the way.

He started stashing food to leave. The MRE packets were really useful for that, with everything inside the big envelope packaged for individual consumption. A packaged side dish, a dessert pouch, snacks, the accessory packs with coffee and creamer and sugar, gum, napkins, and toilet paper. He had taken to scanning the mess tent after meals for uneaten, unopened items. There was always something left over that no one wanted. He even used the rest of his cash to buy a bunch of choice meals from the guy who distributed them in the dining tent.

On The Day, he had withdrawn two hundred in cash from an ATM on the way home. He had bought his DVDs at Best Buy and browsed, but he hadn't spent most of it. Now he spent it on more tangible things. The guy had taken the money and looked the other way while he helped himself. Ray had loaded up on the best meals there were, breakfasts, and some choice entrees. He had scored chemical heaters to warm the meals, and those would compensate for his lost stove, plus they were lighter. He got the beverages too and condiments. He stole a nice stainless steel mug to replace the one he had lost and palmed a few unopened cans of Sterno from the chafing dishes.

Oh, it was on! Once he had been robbed, the gloves came off. He hated feeling like a thief, but he felt completely justified in doing what he needed to do to get out of here. He just didn't give a shit anymore. He hadn't wanted to come here, hadn't asked to be disarmed, and didn't deserve to be robbed. He would do whatever it took. Duct tape went in the pack, an extra towel from the shower tent, soap. A replacement infantry knife and the webbing to wear it. A flashlight. He scored a tarp and an extra blanket. He kept trying to get his hands on a firearm, but all those were closely accounted for, and none of the soldiers were that careless.

All of a sudden, his backpack was full of supplies again, and he felt like he was ready to leave. If he could just make it out of the Bay Area and over the Sierras, he was convinced he would find that bus ticket home. The lack of information was maddening, though. Nothing was being announced or reported, and it gritted on his nerves like sand.

Ray decided to go scrounge up some dinner.

Behind him, the buses continued to disgorge the sick, the weak, the injured, and the dying. The drizzle continued to fall and began to turn to snow.

Bowman

CHAPTER 14

"How bad is it?" Bowman asked.

Carl Burns took a deep breath before responding. "It's bad, Mr. President," he said. "At our latest estimate, we have lost twenty-seven major cities. There were two additional detonations yesterday and one more this morning. We have had NEST teams in the air since the initial event, sweeping for signs of radiation over our remaining metro areas, but they have been unable to really get any ground assets in due to the widespread panic. People have been fleeing what's left, not waiting around to see if there will be a delayed blast in their location. We're pretty sure Sacramento is secure at the moment, but then again, we thought the same thing about Columbus yesterday. It was a ghost town when it finally blew. So many people had fled. The blast probably got a few looters, and that was it."

Bowman mulled it over for a few moments. NEST teams, nuclear emergency search teams, flew in special helicopters equipped with state-of-the-art sensor arrays designed to pick up just a trickle of radiation. A hospital x-ray machine could pull in a NEST array for a closer look.

"Did we lose people over Columbus, Carl?"

Carl nodded.

"Goddamnit," he breathed out. "The data they gathered. Anything?"

"Nope," he replied. "Not a single blip, and then boom. No warning, no indicators, nothing. They never knew what hit them, sir."

"All right, get me their info later. I want to write their families. So this may not be over yet is what you're telling me."

"We think that maybe it is, sir. The major remaining metro areas are mostly empty, and this had all the hallmarks of being a surprise attack, designed to catch people with their pants down. Our analysts feel that if they had more, they would have used them. They hit DC twice, I guess, just to make sure they got everyone there worth getting."

Bowman winced, trying to imagine what that had looked like. Not good.

"Do we have any idea who did this to us and just how the hell it happened?"

"Initial patchy reports are saying it was Al-Qaeda, IS, Hamas. This was such a big hit. It seems that everyone wants to claim responsibility and get their finger in the pie. Our military analysts are estimating that the yield on each device was between four and six megatons. They were hydrogen weapons, sir. Only the Russians and the Chinese and a few of our allies have the capability of producing a yield like that. There were no launches made anywhere in the world. NORAD and USSC have no data on any of the other powers' silos being prepped or any unusual activity that would have led us to believe that there was a launch imminent. This was coordinated internally. The bombs were placed and then detonated at a designated time."

"I'll bet they're hopping now, right?" Bowman asked with a grim smile.

"Yes, sir. Pretty much every nation in the world is mobilizing and going to their highest military readiness levels."

"Jesus!" Bowman rubbed his hands over his face, and eyes, he hadn't slept more than three hours since The Day, and it was beginning to show. "What are we doing for the people? It's been four days. What are our current options?"

"At the moment, sir, not much. FEMA was, of course, activated immediately. In the areas where we still have limited communications, the EAS was activated. Robocalls were made, activating all National Guard units and federalizing them for the duration of the emergency. That's it. We wanted to make sure it was over before committing more assets to large metro and other population areas."

Bowman was seething, beyond furious. He took a deep breath, then another, and then finally looked up at his staff, his aides, his transition people, and he let the silence stretch uncomfortably. And then he began to speak in a quiet, icy voice so that almost everyone in the room had to lean forward to hear him.

"That is unacceptable, Carl. Four days. Millions dead, wounded, scared, and out of touch. There are people dying out there without even knowing why. We have to do something. We need to do something. They need to know that someone is in charge, that someone cares, and that someone is doing something, for God's sake!"

Bowman took another deep breath and centered himself. He had to calm down.

"What about the VP? Did Tony make it out of Atlanta?"

"Atlanta was one of the first places to go up, sir."

Bowman massaged his temples and rubbed his eyes again.

"All right," he finally said in a normal voice, clearing his throat, "someone put some coffee on and get it in here. It's going to be a long time before we stop people, so you have twenty minutes to take care of stuff, then I want you back in here. Find as many people to help you as you need. Draft more if necessary. I want a list of affected cities in my hands when we reconvene, assets, liabilities, options. Got it? I also want a list of *unaffected* cities that we can house people in. I want domestic military assets, civilian, rolling stock, power generation, food-distribution warehouses, anything and everything that we can use to get this country moving. Make it happen, Carl. The longer we wait, the more people are gonna die. I want the closest military base on the mainland on the phone or in contact with us ASAP. I want the Canadian prime minister, the president of Mexico, and basically all the leaders in the Western Hemisphere on a conference call."

In the governor's mansion, things began to happen. People began to move and coordinate with other people. President Bowman's people got *on* it.

Carl Burns watched people exit the conference room with haste, nodding approval as their steps firmed, and they began to move with purpose. James had picked some good people there.

"How about you, sir? Can I get you anything while you wait?"

"Just hit the lights on the way out and let me get a twenty-minute nap or so, Carl. And, Carl?"

"Yes, Mr. President?"

"Make sure they stay focused, okay?"

"Yes, sir."

CHAPTER 15

Mount Weather, Maryland

The guards snapped to attention as the president of the United States, Ted Hotchkiss—a very rumpled, pissed-off, and bedraggled Ted Hotchkiss—exited his armored limousine at Mount Weather, Maryland. He cast a baleful look around before entering the hardened complex. Four freaking days, it had taken that long to get here from his house in the Adirondacks. The helos had been downed by weather and blast debris almost as soon as they had launched to reach his rendezvous location. They had had to go with a plan B to reach Mount Weather overland, through roads choked with refugees, looters, and survivalists, his Secret Service detail trading fire with a smaller group that had seen the limousine and thought it would be an easy target. His people had disabused them rather quickly of the notion before they could continue on.

He showered and shaved and then convened a meeting with his cabinet. Looking around the room, he saw a general, an Air Force colonel, his working group, and a minor DC undersecretary of defense analyst. It looked like the majority of them had made it here, and there were, at the most, three missing faces. Not bad for a quick response to an unexpected situation.

"All right," he said, clearing his throat, "congratulations on your safe arrivals. We have drilled for this for years. You all know what to do. Give it to me. How bad is this situation? This is the real deal, so don't pull any punches. We are now the government of the United States of America. What do we know?"

Hotchkiss essentially got all the details: twenty-seven major metro areas burned from the earth so far, domestic sabotage on highways, power interlink stations, and trains, at least thirty international terror organizations taking responsibility. FEMA deployed. The National Guard federalized for the duration. Remaining domestic assets, military and civilian, listed, itemized, and in his hands. Contact made with state and local governments. And he was just about to issue instructions to contact foreign governments when something an aide had said penetrated his consciousness.

"I'm sorry, what was that? You are . . . ?"

"Sue, Sue Stevens, Mr. President. Department of Homeland Security."

"What did you just say, Sue? I apologize, I was reading one of these reports and just caught the end of it."

Sue looked at him wide-eyed for a moment, the blood draining from her face.

"It's okay, Sue, I don't bite. Just tell me."

"Well, Mr. President, we just had word from the West Coast. James Bowman is alive. The president elect, sir. He was sworn in early by Supreme Court Justice Sam Clark and has apparently taken command of the situation."

"What do you mean he 'has taken command of the situation'?"

"Well, sir, he is coordinating all domestic and foreign assets of the United States, contacting foreign heads of state, pulling the military together, coordinating with FEMA, state governors—essentially all the same stuff that we are trying to do—and they just contacted us here at Mount Weather to get a status update on how we are and if we had any further information on the East Coast, sir." She ended with a gulp.

Hotchkiss thought about it for a minute, hands folded across his chest, staring at the dimmed ceiling high above with his head tilted back, and shook his head back and forth. Interesting. This was interesting. Funny. Bizarre. And completely not taken into consideration when the plans were made. He dismissed James Bowman with a snort. There was no way that Boy Scout was going to be able to handle the largest restoration operation in human history. The very idea was ridiculous.

"Ridiculous!" he said with conviction. "The inauguration isn't until February. He has taken charge, has he? I think not. No, ladies and gentlemen, like it or not, I am the president at the moment, and as such, I am declaring a state of emergency effective as of right now. There will be no elections, changes of office, or other shenanigans for the duration of this crisis. I am also declaring martial law. Get our domestic and foreign military assets on the horn and pass the orders. I want this country locked down. And, Sue?"

She looked at him with absolutely no expression, calm.

There's good material there, he thought. "Get James Bowman's presidential ass on the phone. We need to have a conversation."

CHAPTER 16

A Difference of Opinion

James Bowman was going over a few summaries being presented by his secretary of defense, Marc Adams. Marc had done an excellent job in a short time. He had been coordinating with all hardened facilities throughout the continental United States, starting with Cheyenne Mountain, Offutt AFB in Omaha. (Omaha had survived unscathed, and that was a bonus; it was centrally located and was at its highest state of readiness.) Looking Glass was aloft and helping with communications and asset management and working his way through all other military and civilian government facilities.

"Great job, Marc! Keep it coming in. Let's make sure we stay on the leadership in the affected states. I want those National Guard troops deployed and keeping order in any town with a population over five thousand. The smaller towns are going to be rural, and most of those folks already do a good job of keeping their houses in order. Everyone knows everyone usually and can figure a way out on how to get stuff done. How are we doing with the power grid? Do we have enough security at our generating—"

"Excuse me, Mr. President?"

Bowman broke off what he was saying and glanced down the table.

"Yes, Carl?" he replied.

"Sorry to interrupt, sir, but we have a situation that may need addressing right now."

"Go on."

"Well, it's kind of weird, sir. I'm not sure if it's . . . well, it's weird, sir."

Bowman grunted a laugh.

"Has anything for the last four days been normal, Carl?"

Carl shook his head.

"Spill it."

"We have a phone call, sir, for you, from someone claiming to be the president of the United States."

"You're joking."

"No, sir, I am afraid I am not. It's a secure line direct from Mount Weather, Maryland." Carl consulted his notes. "President Hotchkiss?" He shrugged. "I don't know, sir. I've never heard of him. He wasn't in the chain of succession, but apparently, he has Mount Weather, has just started contacting all the people we have been contacting, has declared a national state of emergency and martial law, and is having his people demanding to speak to you immediately."

Bowman thought about it for a minute. Hotchkiss. The name was familiar for some reason. Why? Something he had read when he was a freshman senator on the Senate Armed Services Committee. But what? A name in reference to what? It hadn't been a report they had spent a lot of time on. It was tied to a spending bill.

Bowman couldn't remember. The name was familiar, but this was ridiculous. The president and vice president were dead, Congress and the Supreme Court and most of DC were ashes blowing out over the Atlantic Ocean, he had a country to put back together again, and now this nonsense.

"Carl, do me a favor and get Sam Clark and our senators in here, and let's get this guy on speakerphone. Can we do that? He has Mount Weather, you say?"

Carl nodded and then added, "On lockdown, with authentication codes and everything."

"Who the fuck is this guy?" he muttered. There had better be a damn good explanation for this waste of time.

Sam wandered in and took a seat. He was followed shortly later by Senator Johns and Senator Paulson. Bowman quickly filled them in on the situation and saw a flicker of recognition in Paulson's eyes at the name.

"Do you know him?" Bowman asked.

Paulson hesitated a moment and nodded.

"He's richer than God, owns everything, and has his finger on more strings than you can possibly imagine. In fact, I think I saw that he donated to your campaign."

"Have I met him?" Bowman asked.

"I don't think anyone has ever met him," Paulson replied.

"Sam, what do you think?" Bowman asked.

"Take the call. What can it hurt?"

Bowman nodded to Carl. "Connect us, please, Carl."

"Mr. Hotchkiss, this is President James Bowman. I understand that you needed to speak to me urgently." Bowman tried to keep the exasperation out of his voice.

There was a long pause as Hotchkiss came on the line.

"James Bowman." A cultured voice came out of the speaker in the middle of the conference room table. "This is President Ted Hotchkiss. Congratulations on the recent election. I voted for you and contributed to your campaign. I was glad to hear that you are well and are trying to get things together out there on the West Coast. I appreciate all your help, and it shows that your heart is in the right place, but I am afraid that I am going to have to ask you to stand down, sir. Unfortunately, you are not the president yet, and I am not sure when we can get you installed in that office, but until such time as this crisis passes, I am going to need to be in charge. Perhaps I can find a place for you in my administration during reconstruction efforts, and when I step down, we can make sure that we get you into things as the legally elected president of the United States. It will just muddy the waters if we both try to do the same job."

Bowman raised his eyebrow and looked at Sam Clark. Clark made a circular motion near his temple and gestured at the speakerphone.

"I'm sorry, Ted," Bowman replied, "but you are out of your mind if you think that I'm going to step down from the position that the American people elected me to hold. I was sworn in yesterday by the only living member of the US Supreme Court, in the presence of two United States senators! Who swore you into office? Who elected you to serve this nation? A guy I just heard of five minutes ago is telling me to abandon my position during the greatest storm this country has ever endured? You're nuts! I don't know how you managed to get Mount Weather under your thumb, but that's US government property, sir, and one of *my* assets on the East Coast! I'd recommend that you stand down in turn, surrender yourself to arrest to the commanding military officer present, and when I have time to deal with you, I will."

Slow clapping emerged from the speakerphone on the table. And laughter.

"Bravo! There's my favorite modern orator from the last two years! I liked that one speech you made about finding out if sand glows in the dark. Gave me shivers! Now, James, do you know what one of the signs of a president having control of the United States government is?"

"Why don't you enlighten me, Ted?" Bowman replied calmly.

"Is the POE still on station off the Bay Area? Never mind, I know she's there. I recommend you have one of your people get her on a secure channel."

"Do it," Bowman mouthed to an aide who ran out of the room.

"I'll wait while you get Captain Jennings on the horn," Hotchkiss said.

Bowman felt the hairs on his neck beginning to stand as the flat screens of the situation room came to life. There was a pause, and Captain Jennings came to attention on one of them.

A live video link connected them both ways, and the captain was able to see Bowman and his cabinet arrayed around the conference table.

"Mr. President. Sir!"

"Do you have him yet, James?" the voice asked from the speakerphone.

"Yes, I do, Ted," Bowman replied, feeling a little uneasy. He had a feeling he knew what was coming.

"One of the signs an acting president has that he is indeed the president is a display that he has control of the military assets of the United States of America. That he is indeed the commander in chief. Correct?"

"Go on," Bowman replied.

"Have Captain Jennings look out his port window off the bridge. You see, Ted, one of the most difficult things to do is to get a boomer that has gone dark to surface within sight of a sovereign nation's coastline, in front of rival military assets. Why don't you ask what Captain Jennings is seeing?"

"Captain, if you would please look out the port window," Bowman said courteously. "Enlighten us as to what you are seeing."

"Sir!" he replied as he moved out of sight for a moment, the camera on the bridge panning to follow his movement. There was a long pause.

There was a flurry of activity on the bridge, and Jennings turned back to the camera.

"Report, Captain."

"Sir, a United States nuclear submarine is surfacing off our portside bow. It is the USS *Revenge* sir."

Bowman sighed.

"Does he see it, James?"

"Yes, he does, Ted," Bowman replied wearily. "So what is this, treason? A coup of some kind? Did you coopt one of Obama's people? With all due respect, Mr. Hotchkiss, did you cause this mess for personal power or gain? Your little display changes nothing. It shows you have some military assets under your control, but not all of them. I've got my own football, after all. We just had a nuclear disaster in this country, and now you want to get in a pissing match that involves more threats using a nuclear deterrent reserved for the president of the United States?"

"No, James. I just wanted you to be aware that my claims to this office are legitimate. That I have all the powers of the POTUS and that I have been doing this job a lot longer than you have. Do yourself a favor, step down, and let me fix this mess. It can, and probably will, get ugly if you don't."

"I can't, in good conscience, do that, Ted. I took an oath to protect and defend the Constitution of the United States. There is nothing in there that says I have to yield that office to a billionaire self-proclaimed false president that thinks he should be in charge. I was elected. You weren't. End of discussion. The people need a leader that they know right now. End this madness now, or you are right, it's gonna get ugly."

"Now you listen to me, you self-righteous little shit! You don't know what you're doing, and I do—"

Bowman made a chopping gesture across his throat, and Carl hung up the call in a most satisfactory way.

Bowman looked at his shocked cabinet for a moment. He really needed some sleep, his temper was completely frayed, and he was still a little unnerved and disturbed that he had a rival on the East Coast capable of making a nuclear submarine surface. In fact, it almost gave him the shits. At the same time, it firmed his resolve. He had a job to do against threats that were both foreign and, it seemed, domestic as well.

"Get in touch with every base commander in the United States and inform them of the situation. They need to know that there is a coup attempt being routed out of Mount Weather, Maryland. They are to disregard any orders being issued from that location on pain of court-martial. Admiral Robbins," he said.

"Yes, sir."

"I want a boomer on standby off the East Coast. We may have to take out Mount Weather."

"Sir!"

"Jim!" Clark exclaimed.

"We may have to do it, Sam," Bowman replied. "We can only have one government right now. I'm not going to allow some dictator appointed by a dead president or whomever to take over the country. We don't need this, we really don't. The way I see it, the East Coast is already heavily fucked, right? Fallout, chaos, and the rest of it? What's one more nuke?"

James Bowman looked at his cabinet for a long searching moment, pale faces looking back.

"Does anyone want out of this? You can go, no hard feelings, back to your families and get out of this. You can do it with my blessing. Anyone?"

One by one, he met their eyes around the table.

"Anyone?"

They all decided to stay.

Getting Out

CHAPTER 17

From the Journal of H. Rayton Townsend
November 21, 2016
FEMA Camp, Santa Rosa, California

We are getting out tonight. The military presence here has swelled beyond belief! Conditions have deteriorated in just four days. Too many people, not enough resources. It's as simple as that. I think the camp has tripled in size since I first arrived. They are bringing everyone here now regardless of the risk of contamination. I spoke to a guy today who was nowhere near the city. They rousted him out of his home. There was no risk of fallout, etc. What is happening? Where will this place be in six weeks? No news yet, just local stuff. Lots of questions and no answers. Today we watched trucks roll in with bales of barbed wire on the back. Not sure if it's to keep people out or to keep us in, but we're not hanging around to find out. We'll be leaving when it gets dark.

* * *

"Did you see that?" Ray whispered to Kyle Meyer.

The two men were walking the perimeter of the camp and had struck up an almost instant friendship. That was rare. He was referring to the large flatbed trucks that had just rolled in and parked nearby.

"What was that?" Kyle replied absently. "Sorry, I was thinking about something else."

"There is barbed wire on those trucks," Ray replied, breathing out quietly. "Tons of it."

Kyle paused and took a long look at the tarpaulin-covered flatbeds nearby. A few soldiers were making an effort to tie the tarps back down where they had come loose in the wind.

"*You two!* Move along now!" a nearby corporal ordered them.

The two men kept walking.

"Interesting," Kyle said a few steps later. "I wonder why they were so nervous that people might see that."

"I don't know. I don't like it, though. We need to tell the others and get the fuck out of here, Kyle," Ray said. "I think we should go tonight."

Kyle nodded, thinking.

"The scary part is, is it to keep us in or other people out?"

"I don't care what it's for," Ray said. "Once that fence goes up, that's it. We're here for the duration whether we want to be or not. Do you wanna get stuck here, man?"

"Absolutely not," he replied. "I'm gonna grab Carly and get things together. Will you find the Webbs? We can meet at our tent right after dinner."

Ray nodded. "Sounds good."

He took a few breaths as he watched Kyle walk away. *Focus!* he thought to himself as he went to find Ben and Becky Webb.

Ray found the Webbs in their tent with Ben's brother Brian. They had had the misfortune to be in the Bay Area on The Day. They had taken an early vacation for Thanksgiving, picked up Brian in Humboldt, and had been on their way to San Francisco to spend the holiday with Becky's mom. All three were from the area of Tacoma, Washington. Ben was an independent contractor, doing general construction, and Becky had been the office manager for the firm before they got married. Brian had been in school. They had gotten as far as Santa Rosa when the bomb had gone off and had gone no farther since.

"Hey, guys, we gotta talk," he said, making an imaginary knocking motion near the support post.

He quickly filled them in on the barbed wire situation, and he saw their resolve firm up as the implications set in.

"We can't stay here in this . . . place," Becky said.

"I know, Beck," Ben replied. "What time do you want to meet up, Ray?"

"Right after dinner in their tent," he replied. "You may want to start packing."

He left behind a flurry of activity as stuff was quickly stowed in bags. Brian looked worried for a moment before diving in to help. Ray hurried to his own tent to grab a few things that he didn't carry everywhere in his pack.

Since he had been robbed, he carried it everywhere now. All that was really left to grab were a couple of olive drab Army blankets, but he rolled them together tightly and strapped them to the top of his pack. He spent the next four hours wandering the camp, seeing if there was anything else he could pick up, but everyone was just as wary as he was now, and the gleanings were scarce. He thought as he walked. Kyle and Carly's cabin sounded like just the right place to head for in an emergency, and that was what they were planning on doing. Ray and Kyle had had a few friends in common down in Marin County, and they had only met a few times before this, but you grabbed at anything in a flood to stay alive and undrowned.

Ray liked what he had seen from the Meyers so far. Carly was solid. She was a paramedic and had a straight no-nonsense approach to life that didn't put up with too much bullshit. Kyle was quiet and slow to speak sometimes, but when he opened his mouth, a lot of people were surprised at how meaningful and apt his comments could be. They had a one-year-old daughter named Lena, and she was a cute little kid. Smart as a whip, too. Just like her folks.

Time in the camp seemed to drag as dinner approached, but suddenly, food was being served, and Ray jumped in line quickly. He grimaced a little at what was being served up, but it was hot and filling, and he had no idea when the next hot meal would come along. He snagged a few packages of crackers off a table and an uneaten apple and went to find the Meyers.

He found everyone in the Meyers's tent, Kyle, Carly, and the baby sitting on one cot, Ben and Becky sitting on the other facing them, with Brian standing in the back. Everyone looked up as Ray ducked in and sat cross-legged on the floor near the opening. Then they went back to discussing the whens and hows of leaving. No one was sure which direction they should travel. The terrain got a little rugged north of Santa Rosa, and it wasn't like they could head directly east. They would either need to go north and then swing to the east, or they would need to go south for a bit before they could do the same. Both directions offered dangers, but the south seemed to offer more, with the looting and risk of recontamination from radiation. They finally settled on the way north as their best bet. Just after dark, they would slip out, following 101 north through Healdsburg, and go from there. There was nothing to do until then except wait, so Ray took another nap.

They slipped out of the north end of camp a little after 8:00 p.m., avoiding a foot patrol and circumventing the temporary plastic fencing that designated the edge of camp. Then they traveled sort of cross-country for a bit. A light drizzle was coming down, and Ray wasn't sure if it was just heavy coastal fog or a light rain. Either way, it was in their favor for their escape. Escape. That was how Ray had started to think of it anyways.

They eventually made their way back to the highway well north of the camp and began trudging along, everyone lost in their own thoughts. Three hours into their trek, Ray estimated, they'd made about five miles at that point. There was a roar behind them. Like a home run hit in a stadium that held millions of people. The sounds of small arms fired crackled over the hills and ridges, echoing along with a heavier report of something larger, every once in a while.

Armed convoys began to use the interstate, flashing southward at reckless speeds, and the little group hid to the side whenever one was approaching them. Apparently, the barbed wire had been designed to keep people in. As they stepped up their pace from fear and time went by, the sounds of conflict faded into the distance behind them. There were a lot of abandoned vehicles to the sides of the road as they walked. EMP from the bomb had killed some of them, and it looked as if others had simply run out of gas. The abandoned vehicles began to bother Ray for some reason, and he thought about it for a few minutes while they walked. Then it hit him; all the vehicles they were passing were locked, with their windows up. No one had checked on any of these cars and trucks since The Day. There might be stuff in them they could use.

Ray was at the back of the line, so he stopped by an abandoned Mercedes, picked up a chunk of concrete that had come loose from the pavement, and smashed out the passenger-side window. The sound was so loud in the darkness that it scared Carly half to death. She was walking in front of him at that time. The baby woke up and began to cry, and shooting him a frustrated, accusatory look, she took the little one off to the side to calm her down. Kyle and the Webbs went back to see what the commotion was all about. They were all shocked, he could tell. He was a little shocked himself at how loud it had been.

"Ray!" Kyle hissed in the darkness. "Why did you do that?"

"Well, I have a mostly full pack of food, but that's about it, guys. What do you have? There might be stuff in these cars we can use, clothing, flashlights, maybe a weapon, drugs, first aid kits. No one has gone through these cars yet, and if it's not us now, it probably *will* be someone else in the future. Better us getting it than them, right?"

Everyone stared at him for a moment, wrapping their heads around it, and then they began to nod. Ray was appearing calmer than he felt. Respect for personal property was ingrained in all of them. Up until this point, they all had been pretty much law-abiding citizens.

The idea caught on quickly, though. Carly walked far enough ahead to keep the baby quiet, and the rest of them soon refined their technique for breaking into vehicles without making too much noise. It paid off tremendously. There were hundreds of cars along the way. Their very first car yielded up a United States Rand McNally road atlas, and Ray stuffed that into his pack immediately. He also found detailed local maps of Northern California that showed roads that the main atlas didn't. Other cars yielded up small scissors, pocket-knives, nail clippers, lip balm, snacks, and bottled water. People had been going about their business on The Day and hadn't expected their vehicles to crap out on them. So there were groceries in some vehicles, diapers, tampons, playing cards, lighters, cigarettes, and a ton of small first aid kits. They took every one of those they could find and flashlights. In another vehicle, Ray found a store's bank deposit bag with about six thousand bucks in cash. He took that for sure and didn't mention it to the others.

They walked for eight more hours that night, vandalizing every vehicle that crossed their path, and that was how they ended up outside Healdsburg in the early-morning hours. There was a yellow school bus to the side of the road that they broke into to get some sleep. Ray settled in to take inventory. Altogether, they were in a much better place supply-wise than they had been before leaving the camp. Everyone else was doing the same. A lot of things went into individual packs and bags, but everyone agreed to pool their first aid and pharmaceuticals together and put them in Carly's care, she being the closest thing they had to a doctor at the moment. Ray was pleased that he had a substantial number of trade goods now.

Everyone settled in to get some sleep.

CHAPTER 18

Hitchin'

From the Journal of H. Rayton Townsend
November 22, 2016
Healdsburg, California

I awoke this morning sore, tired, and confused, in the
back of a yellow school bus we broke into last night.
It took a few moments to realize why I was awake. A
pickup truck was making its way slowly north on 101.

* * *

The truck was making its way slowly through the stalled traffic on 101 when Ray awoke. It was the only thing moving for quite a ways in any direction. Wiping the sleep from his eyes, Ray quickly threw his blankets off and moved to the front of the bus, where Kyle had fallen asleep. Ray quietly shook his shoulder, and he snapped awake.

"Truck coming," he mouthed, jerking his head toward the outside. Ray pointed at the battered red Ford pickup making its way toward them and raised an eyebrow. Everyone else was still asleep.

Descending the steps into the roadway, the two men waved the truck down, and it came to a stop about fifty feet away with a squeal of brakes. A bluff square-shouldered man in his early fifties got out and looked them over. He had his hand casually at his waist, resting on the butt of a holstered semiautomatic handgun.

"I don't want any trouble," he said.

Ray and Kyle glanced at each other.

"Neither do we!" Kyle replied.

"Where are you guys headed?" he asked.

"East," Ray replied.

"That's the first working vehicle, besides Army, that we've seen all week," Kyle said.

"Yep. She's an old girl, doesn't have all the electronic, computerized shit they put in cars these days. My name is Frank Rogers."

"Kyle Meyer and Rayton Townsend," Ray replied, extending his hand for a shake. "Where are you headed?"

"Calistoga," Frank replied. "I was out at the coast, camping and photographing sea lions, on The Day. I thought I should wait a few days for things to settle down before heading back home, and I'm glad I did."

Ray liked him immediately. Frank was a retired cop from Marin County and had signed out of the job permanently the previous year. He and his wife had built their dream home in Calistoga. Ray and Kyle filled him in on their backgrounds and how they had gotten where they were. Frank pointed back at the truck and showed them the police scanner he had been listening to all night.

"Things are an absolute mess south of here, guys. That camp north of Santa Rosa?"

Ray nodded.

"Well, everyone just sort of went apeshit last night around midnight. Rioting, fighting, all kinds of madness. The troops there were trying to keep everything under control—rubber bullets, beanbags, tear gas, that kind of thing—but eventually, they had to resort to lethal force. A lot of people got killed last night. The soldiers just got overwhelmed. A lot of folks broke out of that place and headed south into Santa Rosa, burning, looting, and fighting it out. City residents, National Guard, evacuees, and local law enforcement are tangling there right now. It's total chaos."

"I'm glad we got out in time," Kyle muttered.

Frank gave him a considering look.

"How far east are you headed?" he finally asked.

"Illinois," Ray said right on top of Kyle's "The Sierras."

"Well, I can probably give you a lift as far as Calistoga, you and your folks, if some of you don't mind riding in the back."

"That would be just fine, Frank!" Ray said with a grin.

Kyle ran back into the bus to wake everyone up and gather their gear. Ray stayed outside, talking to Frank and explaining about escaping the camp the previous night. In ten minutes, they were on the road to Calistoga. Ray rode in the back with Kyle and the Webbs. He caught up on his journal and did some writing while the others watched the countryside go by. Carly and the baby were in the cab with Frank, out of the wind and drizzle. The road they were on was rugged, hills and valleys, and the sky remained gray and threatening. It was miserable out, and Ray only wrote for a short time before putting the book back into his pack. He would need to get some Ziploc bags for it soon so it would stay dry. He didn't want the ink from his words to run.

Ray had always associated the name Calistoga with the bottled water he saw for sale in the grocery store. He thought for a time about how a place and a product name could become linked and one and the same in someone's mind. Ray was kind of hoping they had some of that water around. A guy could get pretty thirsty worrying about everything all the time. Now that he had beaten his first objective by getting out of the camp and was casually riding in the back of a pickup truck, he had time to think and to plan ahead. He was worried about his physical condition more than anything at that moment. The walk the previous night had been long, and even though he was a casual outdoorsman, he had the feeling that there would be many more days of walking ahead of them. He had kidded himself for a while now, saying things to himself like, "I'm still in pretty good shape for being thirty-eight years old. Not too bad for an old guy."

But there was no kidding now; this was the real deal.

He had to be brutally honest with himself. His shoulders ached, his pack was almost too heavy, his knees and ankles and feet were sore, and he needed to get back in shape as soon as possible. The next few months were likely to be some of the most physically challenging work that he had ever attempted. Being a weekend warrior and being a professional backpacker through hiker were two entirely different things. A few more months of this, and he would either be dead in a ditch somewhere or he would be a total badass. He also had to factor in their rate of travel, thinking—always thinking—about the needs and capabilities of his traveling companions. Everyone was introspective on the ride, and no one really spoke, but looking around, Ray could see that everyone's thoughts were just as dark as his own, and so he let it rest. He felt much better when they were driving into the city limits of Calistoga. Maybe there would be information here and a chance to acquire more supplies.

Frank offered to put them up for the night after dropping them off downtown, and he gave them his address and directions on how to find the place. Then he waved and drove off down the street. The town looked pretty much untouched. There were no refugees here yet, and it didn't look as if the place had suffered like Petaluma or Santa Rosa or parts of the south had from the effects of The Day. Ray felt like they were out ahead of it. Oh, people knew that things were bad, and the locals looked at them curiously as they had jumped down from the truck. But the looting hadn't happened here. Yet. Ray felt that this was a good sign and they could get some things they needed. If they could stay ahead of it, they might have a chance.

He saw an outdoors store down the street and made a beeline for it. When he walked through the door, the little bell jingled above his head, and a storekeeper was sitting by his cash register, going over a few receipts. He looked up as Ray went in, who noted with some relief that the power was still on here. Ray took in everything with a glance. There was a hand-lettered sign hanging from the front of the register that said No Checks. No Credit. No Debit Accepted. Cash or Trade Only. It had only been five days since the bomb, and Ray was pleasantly surprised to see that they were accepting cash. He expected to get gouged here, but material supplies were worth way more than cash at this point. He had six thousand dollars in his pocket and was more than willing to hand it all over. He smiled at the storekeeper.

"How ya doing?" he asked.

"Not too bad considering," he replied. "Can I help you find anything today?"

Ray had an entire list, but he figured he'd better start small and work his way up.

"A hat with a wide brim to keep the sun off my balding head," he replied.

"We have a whole outdoor-clothing section, if you want to take a look back there," the shopkeeper said, pointing.

"Can I leave my pack up here by the register?" Ray asked politely.

The man nodded.

Ray grabbed a basket and started shopping. He found a nice floppy-brimmed Columbia Sportswear hat with a stampede string. Looking at the price, he winced. *Seventy-five bucks! Highway robbery!* But it went in the basket anyway. Everything was drastically marked up, but he did what he could, focusing on the important things. Ray settled on the floppy-brimmed hat, a fleece hat, and a nice pair of gloves, boot socks, compression boxers, a few sets of Under Armour thermal wear, a pair of sunglasses, a pair of cargo pants, two T-shirts, and a really nice jacket with a removable fleece liner. He also found a Snugpak sleeping bag with a temp rating that went down to 0 degrees, along with a bivvy sack. All that cost him almost nine hundred bucks.

His clothing shopping done, he started cleaning out the freeze-dried food section, and he grabbed a Kelly Kettle, a water purifier, extra cartridges, sunscreen, bug repellant, small tools, and a compass. He essentially went through the entire store, front to back, reequipping himself with all the things that had been stolen in the camp. Up front, in front of the register, was a glass case holding an assortment of knives and hatchets, and he settled on a nice, lightweight Gerber hatchet to add to his pack.

"We accept cash, sir, or any items you may want to trade."

Ray settled in to dicker with the guy. His goal was to bring the weight of his pack down and not increase it, so he was able to unload all the MREs he had acquired in camp—they were heavy—all the spare pocketknives from the cars they had looted, along with some other stuff. He had almost a carton's worth of smokes in his pack but decided to hang on to them for when they would really be needed for trade. What he unloaded knocked five hundred bucks off the total. What he was buying cost around five grand, so he had almost a thousand left to spend here.

He went back through the store and grabbed luxury items, power bars, drink mixes, extra Nalgene bottles, snacks, another camp stove, and the fuel for it. Maps and a few small books designed for backpacking and wilderness survival. He had twenty-five bucks left and nothing to spend it on. Ray felt much better than he had when he went in. The owner had let him repack everything there, and he walked out with his pack lighter but carrying more stuff. It was on his back, ready to go, but he had four large plastic bags of stuff besides that. He figured that what was left in the bags could be distributed to the rest of his group. But *he* was completely reequipped and ready to go. There hadn't been a gun or ammunition available in any store for any price. When he had left, he had seen the storekeeper marking up his prices again.

Meeting back at Frank's house, they all compared notes. Prices had been way higher than anyone expected, and the gouging looked to continue for a good long while. Everyone had something more than what they had come in with, though. Food cost a lot, and luxury goods even more. There were some hard stares when he had come in carrying the extra bags of stuff. When Ray had said that everything in the bags was for them, though, people had broken out into smiles. Ray filed that tense moment away for later, though. He hadn't liked the Webbs' reaction *at all*, especially Becky. They would bear watching.

Frank's wife cooked them a small but nice meal, and since the power was still on, everyone took advantage of a hot shower and laundry. Before they left in the morning, Ray pulled two of the mixed packs of smokes out and gave them to Frank.

"Thanks, Ray, but I don't—"

"For trade. For later when it gets worse," Ray interrupted. "Smoke 'em, trade 'em, give 'em away if you want. I just wanted to say thank you for the ride and the meal and a warm place to sleep last night."

Frank blinked at that and looked thoughtful for a moment. Then he slipped them into his pockets.

"Good luck, Ray," he said quietly. "I hope you make it to Illinois."

Ray shook his hand and nodded.

"I'll send you a postcard when I do."

Snapping the waist belt of his pack snugly around his hips and with a smile and a wave, Ray took his first step, then another, and followed the rest of his group into the dawn.

A Coup Attempt

"I want orders to go out to every military installation in the Lower 48 that we have been in contact with, understand?"

General Dobbs nodded. "Yes, Mr. President."

"They are to disregard any and all directives issued from Sacramento or command-and-control facilities besides Mount Weather. You are to continue trying to get our boomers in line and responsive to Atlantic Command. That four days on the road getting here cost us."

"Yes, sir."

Hotchkiss steepled his fingers in front of his face, thinking. Who would have thought that Bowman would be so organized, so fast, and that he'd have the balls to do what he had done already? Ted was half-tempted to let him have the civil authority as he was doing a good job there, getting assets and people in line. Half the FEMA people had simply blown off his attempts to contact them, stating that they already had instructions from the president and were following through for the good of the people. There was no way Hotchkiss could let him control the military assets, though; they were in a war for sure, even if no one had formally declared it, against the United States. This was what he had trained for in the last decade, sacrificing personal time, running through endless scenarios.

Unfortunately, good job or not, James Bowman was going to have to have an accident. Operation Ghost had minor political functionaries and military attaches pretty much all over the country. He was going to have to activate a few of them close to Bowman and probably orchestrate a coup for real. He could not allow for there to be another president. Not if he was going to save this country and undertake the monumental effort of reconstruction. Splitting the job was out of the question.

"Can you get me Sue Stevens from the Department of Homeland Security, please?"

Hotchkiss waited for a few moments, sipping his coffee and thinking.

"Mr. President?" she asked, entering his office. "You needed to see me, sir?"

"Have a seat, Sue. You look tired. I think we all do. I wanted to chat with you for a minute."

Sue took a chair in front of his desk.

"Sue, if I recall correctly from training, the DHS has lists of our actives and our auxiliary inactive members from all over the country. Correct? There's a database, right?"

"Yes, Mr. President. They are located on a secure server here at Mount Weather and other secure servers for fallback positions. Classified, encrypted, biometric, password-protected data files."

Hotchkiss thought for a few more moments.

"Where else is the info stored?" he asked.

"We have a data site at Offutt AFB, Cheyenne Mountain, a few of the larger AT&T comm sites scattered through the Midwest, and one in red, blue, and green team mobile command centers. Do you need access, sir?"

"I think we do, Sue," Hotchkiss replied with a smile. "How dedicated would you say most of our people are to the program?"

"Well, they are career people, heavily vetted, above top secret clearances most of them, and the rest have need-to-know access should it become necessary if the chain is broken."

Hotchkiss grinned. It was purely Machiavellian, plots within plots within plots. Redundancy was the whole reason why Operation Ghost should have gone off without a hitch, just no one had planned on a catastrophe happening in an election year.

"How loyal do you think they would be to this presidency? My presidency, that is."

Sue blinked. "Well, sir, their loyalty is to the program, and since you are the head of the program at the moment, their loyalty is to you."

"Excellent. Do we currently have people on the ground in Sacramento?"

"We do, sir. I took the liberty of ascertaining that detail as soon as it became apparent that President Bowman was operating out of there."

"Military and civilian?"

"Yes, sir. Both. Would you like me to print you a copy of our ground assets there?"

"If you would, yes. We are going to need to contact those assets as well, Sue. Figure out a way to get me in touch with them, okay?"

"Yes, Mr. President."

* * *

Bowman, Sacramento, California

The first coup attempt came that night while Bowman was sleeping. The last five days had pushed him past exhaustion, and he almost collapsed on the way to his bedroom. His Secret Service detail helped him into bed. He was awakened just past 4:00 a.m. by shots and screams in the hallway outside his door, and throwing on a bed robe, his wife's, he noticed with a rueful grimace, he tore the door open to see just what the hell was going on and stepped into a pool of blood.

"The fuck?" he muttered sleepily, wondering if he was still sleeping.

His detail were down, all of them. So were an Army captain and four privates. James felt a hand on his ankle and glanced down. It was Bill. He had been with him on Catalina.

"Bill," he whispered, stooping down, "what happened here?"

Bill grunted, putting pressure on an abdominal wound, and he slid his piece over to Bowman.

"Take it, sir. One . . . in the chamber . . . safety is off . . ."

Bowman picked up the .45, turned the safety on, and dropped it into the robe's pocket.

He helped Bill put more pressure on the wound.

"They were going to . . . try and take you . . . under arrest—*shit*! That hurts!" he said, flinching back.

"Jim, what's happening?" his wife asked from just inside the doorway.

"Tammy, call for help, please," Bowman replied calmly. "We have hurt people here."

His wife turned into the bedroom. He heard her urgently calling for help on her cell phone, and a few minutes later—it felt like hours—he heard running footsteps approaching from down the corridor.

Across the hallway from the bedroom, the Army captain was beginning to stir, and Bowman pulled the gun out of the robe's pocket and flicked off the safety. Another security detail was coming fast along with a medic and a full squad of US Marines. The captain came to and met Bowman's eyes, raising his own pistol. Two steps had James across the hall, kicking the gun out of his assailant's hand and putting his own to the captain's head.

"Nope. Not today. You're gonna have a lot of explaining to do, son."

An hour later, having seen that Bill was being taken care of along with the Army captain, Bowman was back in the situation room with his cabinet. He was in sweats, and he still had Bill's .45 in his pocket. He wasn't going to be far from a handgun after this.

"What do we know?" he asked.

"Well, sir," Carl began, "obviously, it was an attempt on your life by people that we have inside here. I would assume our friend out east had something to do with it."

Bowman grunted. This sucked. It really, really sucked.

"I think we should double down on your security detail until we know—"

Bowman raised his hand, and Carl trailed off.

"How would we know that the next attempt doesn't come from them? I was lucky tonight, guys. If they would have had someone on my team, I would be dead now, right?" he sighed heavily. "How's Bill doing?"

"He's going to pull through, Mr. President."

"Good. Glad to hear that. Now. The elephant in the room. How do we respond?"

"I think we should contact Hotchkiss and let him know his plan failed, and then I think we need to switch up your location more and keep you on the move until we can root out the moles."

"That would probably be a good idea," Bowman agreed. "How soon can that Army captain talk?"

"Probably gonna be tomorrow at the earliest, Mr. President."

"We still need to figure out how Hotchkiss has the authority that he does and discover just what the hell is going on as well, right? Do we have any info on that yet?"

There was a long, embarrassed silence.

"All right, let's make that a priority. I want all pertinent teams working on figuring out some answers, because, guys, right now, I am struggling with a serious urge to shove a thermonuclear missile right up Hotchkiss's ass. I don't want it to come to that, but just one more excuse like this morning, and we may have to consider that."

There was a commotion at the doorway and a short heated exchange, and then an Air Force aide came running into the room and snapped a quick salute. Everyone was on their feet, still jumpy, and Bowman told everyone to sit down again.

"Yes, Airman?"

"Mr. President, sir, we have another situation. I have some reports that you need to see right now, sir. There are more coming in as well. Something is happening all over the country, sir."

Bowman extended his hand for the dispatches and began to read. Then he sighed. More bad news. He handed the reports he had already skimmed to his chief of staff, and Carl began to read as well, his eyebrows rising.

"Mr. President, if this is true . . ."

"Yep," Bowman replied. "On top of being in the middle of the greatest crisis in American history, we now officially have a civil war."

The reports were of coup attempts in nearly all the military installations with which they had reestablished contact. Some had succeeded, and others had failed. Hotchkiss was trying to remove base commanders that were resistant to the orders being issued from Mount Weather. Cheyenne Mountain had been one that they had lost. Offutt Air Base was now under the command of a Colonel Johns. He had relieved General Surrey of command when he began issuing orders that originated from Mount Weather. Fort Bragg was theirs. Pearl had undergone a serious brawl, with forty-two dead and twice that amount wounded, but it was still in Bowman's pocket. Every installation in the Lower 48 was going through some sort of minor or major upheaval and either defecting or staying loyal. Even some federalized National Guard units were moving away from their assigned areas of operation and speeding east, presumably to Maryland. It was madness on top of madness.

"So," Bowman began, "the military-industrial complex rears its ugly head." He laughed bitterly.

The dispatches continued to come in, some good and some bad.

"Do we still have a secure line to Mount Weather?"

"Yes, Mr. President," Carl replied.

"Let's talk to Mr. Hotchkiss again. Afterward, I want a conference call with all loyal base commanders. We need to get to the bottom of this."

* * *

"So now he wants to talk, does he?" Hotchkiss said with a grin. "Very well. Let's get him on the line."

Hotchkiss looked around the table at his cabinet. More reports were flooding in, and the news was good. A lot of the domestic power was shifting his way, and pretty soon, he'd have Bowman isolated and cut off out in California. He could deal with that later; for the moment, though, securing assets was of vital importance. The US military was a pretty big stick to wield, and the more of it he had, the faster he could move on to other projects.

* * *

"Sir, we have retaken Cheyenne Mountain," Carl whispered to him just as the call was about to go through.

"That's good news," Bowman replied quietly. "What happened?"

"It was another mutiny led by midgrade commissioned officers. They pretended to go along with it and then arrested all the top brass at once."

"I think I am going to be handing out a lot of medals soon," Bowman muttered.

Carl winked at him.

"Do we have him yet?" Bowman asked, the speakers clicking and encrypting and then settling into a steady silence.

"James!" Hotchkiss's voice boomed from the speakers, and one of the techs adjusted the volume slightly. "Is that you? Still alive to trouble me, I see. Have you reconsidered? Planning to surrender with terms?"

Bowman took a deep breath to calm down and center himself.

"Ted," he replied in a voice a lot calmer than he felt, "I can't decide yet just what you are and what you think you are doing out there in Maryland, but I think we need to talk."

"Absolutely! What can I do for you today?"

"Well, I need to understand something. Our conversation yesterday was a little startling, and now that I have had time to think about things, I need to know how it is that you came to be where you are. I want to know why you consider yourself to be the president of the United States. I would also like to know why you are starting a civil war on top of the events that we have all been dealing with for the last week. If you can explain it to me sufficiently, I might be willing to entertain the offer that you made."

There was a collective gasp from around the table, and Bowman made a placating gesture to keep everyone quiet.

"Maybe we could start with why you tried to have me killed this morning."

"That's an easy one," Hotchkiss replied. "The country simply *cannot* have two presidents right now. Like I said yesterday, it will simply muddy the waters and confuse people, and I need to be in charge. I have the experience, the people, and the program in place to build this country back from the brink. You are simply too new at this, and to be honest, they hadn't even briefed you on *the program* yet. Without all the information at your fingertips, you cannot make informed choices, cannot command, diplomatic, strategic, or otherwise. I can."

"So why not *help* me?" Bowman replied, frustrated.

"And be the power behind the throne?" Hotchkiss replied. "It's tempting. I've done it before. Made the people happy by having a friendly face in the White House and pulled the strings behind closed doors. But not this time, James. Nope. You see, this will be the greatest challenge of my career. It *excites* me to consider rebuilding America. I haven't had a sandbox like this to play in for quite some time, and I'd really like to be the guy that builds a better America. The problem is, if I am going to do it, I need to have all the authority to make it so. I can't have a puppet president getting cold feet and trying to make changes behind my back, James."

"So you would stoop to murder? Kill loyal Americans, kill their president, to play in your sandbox? Ted, this morning's actions are morally incompatible with who we are as a people. Good men and women that didn't have to have died today. Are you some kind of self-styled Bond villain or a sociopath? I mean, who *does* that?"

Hotchkiss sighed and was quiet for a moment.

"Look, James, there are no easy answers here. I have taken a substantial amount of resources from you in the last twenty-four hours. People, assets, tools. I will take more if I have to, because I have to. It's a job that I have to take seriously. This country isn't going to be a democracy again for years. It needs one vision, one goal, and one set of hands molding it into what it needs to be. There's no room for a committee. The program was only designed to reconstitute the executive branch of the government. I and my people, we are it. I like you. I do, really. I am proud of what you have accomplished out there. I mean that. Your heart is in the right place. Tell you what, why don't we meet face-to-face somewhere? Have a . . . summit, perhaps? That way, together, maybe we can figure out who is going to run the country."

"We should probably get on that as soon as possible, Ted. People are dying out there. The entire upper Midwest is without light, heat, water, power, or social services, and it's buried under seven feet of snow right now. The longer we wait, the higher the body count is going to be."

"I know that, James. That's why I need you to stand down. Oh, by the way, I have that sub you ordered in off the East Coast now. Naughty, naughty. A suspicious fellow might think you were planning on taking out Mount Weather. What's one more nuke more or less, right?" Hotchkiss laughed and cut the connection.

Bowman felt a distinct chill in the room. There was apparently a mole in his cabinet.

Standing very slowly, he looked at his people.

"I want every one of you working on setting up a summit meeting with Hotchkiss's people. Make the arrangements."

He had a feeling he knew who it was, but it had to seem that he was making the effort of reconciliation. Bowman needed time to think.

Follow Your Gut

CHAPTER **20**

Colonel Johns was a very tired, very capable officer in the United States Air Force. He was also very worried, but he had learned to trust his gut a long time ago. It had kept him out of trouble his entire life. It had helped him make the right career choices and the right personal ones, in combat and in the political realm of the armed forces. He had been flying a desk for the last eight years, something that was more difficult and challenging than flying jets over the Middle East. At the moment, he was stalking down a hallway, accompanied by his staff and a mixed bag of elite forces officers that he had inherited overall command of just four hours earlier. His gut had told him that he was doing the right thing, but convincing his head was taking all his effort. The men were confused, but they trusted him implicitly. He was a born leader, and he never put someone in harm's way without good reason.

"Major, call a general staff meeting for 1100 hours. Please have the gentlemen from the Eighty-Second Airborne, our complement of Navy SEALSs and all base commissioned officers present. It will save time if I address everyone at once."

"Yes, sir," Major Donaldson replied. "Any further orders, sir?"

"That will be all for now, Major. But come find me when you have finished with that."

"Yes, sir." The major snapped a salute, which Johns returned.

The entourage continued down the hallway for a moment in silence. Johns was pissed too. He had never ever considered that his career would take a turn into the twilight zone, but here he was, and now he had to do something about it. In his right hand, he clutched a folder with a death grip, and the contents had his lips compressed to a thin white line.

"Lieutenant Evans," he said, "are you sure we got all of them?"

Lieutenant Evans was an intelligence officer with the Eighty-Second Airborne, most recently out of Fort Bragg. He was twenty-six, and if Johns was any judge of character, and he seemed to have a talent there, he could pick them; this young man had a spectacular military career ahead of him.

"Well, sir, we got everyone on the local list, everyone on this base, but we are still coordinating with local authorities to round up some of the civilian contacts."

"The shooting for the moment is over, though, right?"

"The last combat operations ended about twenty minutes ago, sir."

"Casualties?"

"We had four dead and twenty-one wounded, sir. All enemy combatants are either in custody or KIA, sir."

"I will see to them shortly."

"Sir."

The moment he had been dreading was rapidly approaching. At the end of the hallway, in the detention section, two air policemen from special services came to attention in front of a locked door.

"At ease," Johns said quietly, and both men relaxed.

From inside, he could hear yelling and someone banging on the door.

"Has he been like this the whole time?" Johns asked.

"Well, sir, his voice gave out about an hour ago, but he seems to be getting frisky again," the sergeant replied.

Johns's lips compressed again into a thin line, a bad sign for anyone that knew him really well. "We'll just see about that," he replied quietly. "Lieutenant, would you accompany me, please? The rest of you gentlemen, please remain close by but feel free to take a quick break. This may take a while."

"Yes, sir!"

"Oh, and, gentlemen? As soon as you get a chance, I want you to see to your men. Make sure they have everything they need. As of four hours ago, we are on an immediate response, threat imminent, wartime footing. Winter gear, rations, ammunition, the whole nine yards. I don't want any more surprises, understand?"

"Sir!"

Johns took a deep breath and opened the door.

General Mike Surrey had done quite a number on the interrogation room. The table was flipped over, one of the chairs was smashed and dented, and the other sparse furnishings were in disarray. Evans took up a position by the door, his hand resting casually on the butt of a holstered .45. Johns casually walked into the room, set one of the flipped-over chairs upright, and took a seat without saying anything.

"Johns!" Surrey exclaimed. "It's about fucking time, mister! I am. Going. To. Have. You. Shot!"

"Sit down, Mike," Johns said quietly.

Surrey's face was beet red, his uniform in disarray, his chest heaving with emotion and fury. Johns just looked at him.

"Lieutenant, if you please." Johns gestured at the upended table, and Evans set it back upright.

Finally, Surrey grabbed one of the intact chairs and slammed it down on the other side of the table. He took his seat, glaring at Johns, and Johns sighed unobtrusively.

"Now, General, you and I are going to have a quiet conversation about what just transpired on this military installation."

"I don't think so, Johns. I can't think of anything that I want to discuss with you at the moment other than your court-martial and pending execution for treason!"

Johns's lips thinned again for a moment.

Then he laughed.

"Really? You can't think of anything you want to discuss, General? I can. I can think of a whole bunch of things to discuss. Let's start with the fifty or so young men and women who are dead or injured on this base. Would you like to talk about them? Your . . . *associates* are all in detention or dead, and we are currently rounding up the civilian cadre of your little cabal as we speak. What I am trying to understand is, what was going through that teeny, tiny little Mike Surrey brain of yours to think that you were going to get away with it?" Johns spat out.

Surrey's eyes had gone to slits, and Johns reflected on how he had never noticed how porcine the man's expression could be at times. He shrugged.

"See, General, this is your opportunity to explain your actions over the last eight hours, and in large part, what you say here is going to determine whether or not I'll have *you* shot. You have been relieved of command and placed in detention for a reason. For the last five days, we have been taking orders from the lawfully elected, *constitutionally empowered* president of the United States of America in Sacramento. The United States of America was attacked, wounded, and is in crisis at the moment. I am trying to understand why as of 0200 this morning, you began taking orders from an unauthorized source in Mount Weather, Maryland, when you specifically had orders to disregard said instructions. *Your* president gave you a direct order, General, and you disregarded it! Now," Johns said very quietly, "I want to know why."

Surrey laughed in his face.

"You have no idea what you are doing, Johns. You are in such deep shit right now. I never realized what an idealist you are, but boy, you really took it in hook, line, and sinker, didn't you? He's not *my* president! *Our* president! He's a fool! The real president is in Mount Weather! Do you really think that novice politician on the West Coast has the first fucking clue of how to fix this? Please."

"Or we can talk about Operation Ghost if you prefer," Johns interjected smoothly, sliding the folder across the table at Surrey.

Johns watched as the man's face went white, the blood literally draining from his features. Then he nodded.

"So I was right. You really are a piece of shit, Surrey, you know that?" Johns said. "I took the same oaths you did to protect and defend the Constitution against all enemies, foreign and domestic.

This little *program* of yours is so far outside that oath. I now consider you to be an enemy combatant. You as good as turned your back on legitimate civilian authority over the military, stripping all power from the people and trying to put it directly into the hands of a dictator. How dare you! Who gave you the *right* to do that? We *have* a president! An elected representative of the people, you son of a bitch! I could understand this decision if Hotchkiss were the only command authority available, but he's not. You know he's not. And you decided to throw everything over to someone who what? Had a lot of money before everything went down? Well, guess what, Mike? Without a fucking country, how much do you think that money is worth?" Johns was screaming and half out of his chair at the end, and Surrey was staring across the table, trembling.

Johns stood up to leave, but before he did, he turned back to General Mike Surrey and addressed him in a cold voice. "I have to go explain to the men what happened here today, General. They deserve to know the truth. I hope it inspires them to fight for the right reasons. We are still a republic and not a dictatorship. We cannot allow people like you to be in charge. Tomorrow, we will convene a military tribunal for a courts-martial."

Johns walked out of the room.

Four hours later, Mike Surrey hanged himself.

Offutt Air Force Base, Omaha, Nebraska, 1100 Hours

The assembled officers rose and came to attention as Colonel Johns entered the briefing room.

"As you were," he said calmly, and everyone sat down again. Johns looked out over the room and nodded in satisfaction. Arrayed by service branch, he had officers from the Eighty-Second Airborne, a contingent of Navy SEALs, his own base staff, pilots, National Guard officers, and a sizeable government contingent from the local area along with FEMA chiefs.

"Ladies and gentlemen, this morning, I was made aware of a situation that affects us both directly and indirectly. It made me reexamine my oaths as an officer in the United States Air Force in a way that made me distinctly uncomfortable. It made me order actions that were unpleasant and that ultimately resulted in fatalities, both civilian and in our command structure, here on the base."

Johns paused a moment to let that sink in.

"As you are all aware, martial law has been declared in the wake of the catastrophic attacks that we suffered just last week. The military in this area, along with civilian agencies, as represented by all of you here, is in charge of the situation. In the last week, we have seen a complete breakdown of civil order in this region. People are dying. We have suffered disruption in communications, power, social services, and now, unfortunately, government."

Johns cleared his throat and took a sip of a glass of water on the lectern.

"Up until this point, the commander of this base and those stationed on it have been taking direct orders from the president of the United States, who has made his temporary base of operations out of Sacramento, California. James Bowman was lawfully sworn in by the only remaining chief justice, Sam Clark, in the presence of two United States senators. Does any of this deviate from what all of you understand to be true? Does anyone have any comments or questions?"

Johns looked around the room. No one responded, their eyes rapt with attention on what he had to say next. He nodded decisively. Good.

"Early this morning, the commander of this base, General Michael Surrey, began taking orders from a usurper to the presidency. A man by the name of Ted Hotchkiss has set himself up as a dictator on the East Coast, out of Mount Weather, Maryland. He is an appointed president with all the powers of the real president that, up until this point, we have been taking direct orders from. Last night, Michael Surrey attempted a coup against the lawful government of the United States. I took the liberty of relieving him of command of this base and have placed him under arrest pending a court-martial. When I took that action, other elements of this military cabal that we recently became aware of tried to free him and reestablish control of the base. It resulted in a bloodbath. We had fifty-two KIA and forty-seven wounded, mostly on the side of those launching the coup attempt."

There were a few murmurs now and a shuffling of feet. It was sinking in. He spared a glance toward the civilian contingent.

"Are there any questions so far?" he asked, looking around the room again. "No? Then I shall continue. The implications of having a rival government are dire. Reports coming in seem to indicate that this coup attempt was successful on other military reservations throughout the continental United States. In others, as here, it was successfully repulsed and had failed. It was brought to my attention after the fighting ended this morning that this base was the repository of restricted databases containing the name of all conspirators in this *program*, which led to last night's bloodshed. We have successfully arrested or neutralized all local threats to the status quo. Civilian leadership was highly supportive and helpful to the elimination of these subversive elements," John said, nodding at the local leaders.

"We have, since this information came to light, been distributing it via secure web link to other installations and undamaged government facilities so that those in charge may purge their leadership of any other coup attempts. This breakdown in order has cost us. It has cost us time, it has cost us leadership, but more importantly, it has cost us *lives*—American lives—and in the wake of the attacks last week, I find this to be completely unacceptable. The rot of this program was ingrained in every group represented in this room. FEMA had to purge its leadership, our local governments had to do the same, and the branches of our armed forces seated here now had to do so as well. I don't think I need to emphasize that we simply cannot afford to do this again. So I want you to all look deep within yourselves, examine your conscience, examine your fears and your resolve, and I want you to make a decision right now, today, about what kind of country we are going to be. I, for one, want to live in a representative democracy where the military answers to a civilian authority elected by the people, of the people, and for the people. General Surrey opted for tyranny and a dictatorship. I could not accept that, and I am grateful to God that the rest of you couldn't either. Otherwise, we wouldn't be sitting here, having this discussion at all. If anyone feels that they cannot perform their duty going forward, out of fear or a lack of commitment, then now is the time to make it known."

No one resigned or got up and left. Johns let the silence drag out. He had a few more things to say yet.

"Excellent. There's a few more points that I would like to bring up. There is a very real possibility that the United States is in a civil war as of this morning. What else can a decisive break between regions and peoples and leadership be called? So as of this morning, this base will be on a wartime footing. We will continue with our original missions, which are to restore order and help repair and preserve essential infrastructure to our area of operations. Violations of the law of the land will be dealt with strictly and harshly, and a nighttime curfew will remain in effect until such point as the president deems otherwise. Armed forces personnel will operate with reasonable restraint where possible, will provide security, and will continue to administrate relief supplies, erect shelter, restore power, water, medical and social services to the Midwest region. Continued cooperation with civil authorities is deemed essential, and I am looking forward to interacting with each and every one of you to hear and implement your ideas. Thank you for your time. You are dismissed."

* * *

The information war went on throughout the day. Individual ships, foreign military assets, small units, larger domestic installations at times sat on the fence and waited to see which way things were going. A lot of people were hesitant to openly engage in hostilities with fellow Americans. At other times, violence ruled the situation, with one side or the other losing out. The program hadn't been as deeply embedded in many sites as the originators would have wished, the reason being that they would have been written off in a full-scale nuclear attack. It was solely a need-to-know operation, and that was its downfall. Bowman had been a wildly popular presidential candidate, faring well with millennials and with the military in general. Obama had had a 15 percent approval rating among the armed forces at the end of his presidency, and as a result, many of the younger officers viewed the establishment choice of an appointed president with suspicion. There were holdouts, unfortunately, especially on the East Coast. By sunset, America's domestic assets leaned toward the Bowman administration in a 70-30 split.

Bowman had read the reports coming in with a rising sense of optimism. It seemed that people were on the right track in supporting him, and he felt that he would be able to push his domestic agenda for reconstruction forward. He wasn't surprised when another call came through from Hotchkiss late the evening of December 4. Bowman had been waiting for something like this, and he eagerly approached the situation room, hoping that they could put the madness behind them and finally start with getting America back on her feet again. Relief shipments were coming in from Europe and Asia, and he had established cordial relations with many foreign powers. The Middle Eastern situation was deteriorating rapidly, but European leaders and Putin and the Chinese assured him that they could handle things with a minimum of US input. The domestic split had been taking up a majority of his time, and he briefly considered the international situation with a mental shrug. The United States was still strong enough to defend herself, but she needed to heal herself first. He had to get rid of Hotchkiss, though; that went without saying.

As he and his staff entered the conference room, Bowman whispered to an aide to go in search of Sam Clark, Senator Paulson, and Senator Johns. He wanted them present as well. Bowman's opinion of Johns had risen a notch when he found out that she and Colonel Johns were siblings, and it was a happy coincidence that the two of them had been able to converse for a short time after the change in leadership at Offutt. He still had Bill's .45 in his pocket, and he wondered if he was going to need it today. Johns' release of the program information had been enlightening, and they had quietly purged all program assets from Sacramento, save one. Bowman had been ordering a strategic withdrawal of all US assets overseas; he wanted the military home. They would be needed in the coming months and years. US allies were far from helpless, and it was time that those that were take responsibility for their own security and future. There would be no more free rides or handouts from the United States for a long time, if ever.

Bowman took his seat and fiddled with a pen, nodding his thanks as a cup of coffee, black, was placed on a napkin by his right elbow. He waited while everyone came in and got situated around the table. Finally, a technician nodded quietly at Carl.

"Do we have him?" Carl asked, and the tech gave a thumbs-up.

"Put him on," Bowman said.

The flat screens flickered to life, showing the view of a command center in Mount Weather, and Bowman got his first look at Hotchkiss. *Well, he's a smooth-looking son of a bitch,* Bowman thought with a raised eyebrow.

"Mr. Hotchkiss, I understand that you wanted to speak with me," he said.

"I did at that, James," he replied. "You have been a very busy guy lately, and I wanted to congratulate you on a job well done. It seems that while you are consolidating your assets nicely, you haven't quite managed to get everything lined up, and after a few days of considering, I wanted to put an offer on the table. I think we *should* meet somewhere for a summit."

"Is that so?" Bowman replied. "Where and when? We'll be there. I want this over with, Ted."

"How about we meet in one week in Omaha? December 11. I'd like to make you an offer on a way to resolve this situation and still do the jobs that we were paid to do."

"Fine," Bowman replied. "I'll have my people talk to your people to hammer out the details. Is there anything else?"

"As a matter of fact, James, there is." Hotchkiss's eyes moved around the room. "Ah, I see Senator Paulson there with you. How are you, Ed?"

"I'm fine, Mr. Hotchkiss. Been a little busy lately. But then again, haven't we all?"

"Isn't that the truth?" Hotchkiss replied.

Hotchkiss continued to look around the room, memorizing faces, it seemed to Bowman, or maybe it was just a trick of the camera.

"And Senator Johns! You look to be in good health as well. You know, that stunt your brother pulled in Omaha a few days ago rather irritated me, but you win some and you lose some. As you know, a political opponent is never out until they are out, right?"

"Agreed, Mr. Hotchkiss, so when do you plan on resigning so that we can move forward with healing the country?" she replied.

Hotchkiss acted like he hadn't heard her.

"You know, there would be a place here for both of you at Mount Weather, should the need arise. It might help to prop up your positions with your constituencies once they find out that you are supporting rebellion. It would provide a certain legitimacy that would allow you to retain your positions. I will only offer once."

"That's all right, Mr. Hotchkiss," Paulson drawled in his best back-country Kentucky twang. "We all's are used to rebels where I come from. Don't matta' much no how, what fellas like ya'll from th' big city say. But thank ya kindly, suh."

Bowman almost laughed outright at the response but schooled his features just as Hotchkiss looked at him again.

"I would assume that you feel the same, Ms. Johns?" Hotchkiss asked with a chill in his voice.

"Well, sir, I am in my home state of California at the moment, and folks seem to like me being here just fine, so that would be a polite refusal from me as well."

"Very well," Hotchkiss said. "I would like to meet with you and your administration in one week, in Omaha, James. I will make arrangements to fly in that evening. I think there's a way we can both do our jobs without interfering with each other. Good day to you all."

Hotchkiss cut the link from his end.

"All right, guys," Bowman said, "what were your thoughts on *that* little bizarre conversation?"

"He's running scared, Jim," Clark said immediately. "And I think maybe at the moment, he's more dangerous than ever. Trying to plant seeds and sow dissent would be my guess."

"That was my impression as well," Bowman replied.

"He is still sitting on Atlantic Fleet assets, sir," Admiral Finkston said from the end of the table. "We have had a few defections from there as well to our side, but his people are doing a fantastic job of jamming up comms, so we're not even sure if most of our people realize there is a second more legitimate option."

"Keep trying, Admiral," Bowman replied. "Locking down California was lucky for us. We have some of the best tech people in the world out here, and if anyone can hack through, I'd put my money on them."

"General Scott, any more updates?" he added.

"We managed to pick up the Marine Corps training bases and a few assets we thought were lost in Florida. We also got through to Guantanamo Bay, sir. I told the base commander there to start packing up. We may want to move them back at rather short notice."

"That's good work, General. On a touchy subject, did you inquire about the remaining detainees there?"

"I did, Mr. President. We still have 116 of the most dangerous enemy combatants on lockdown there."

Bowman fiddled with his pen for a few moments, going back and forth on any number of issues regarding the prisoners. Then he sighed.

"We can't afford to send them back into the field, and I will not bring them here with things as they are. Give the order to liquidate them, General."

"Um . . ." Scott blinked, then shook it off. "Yes, Mr. President."

"General Scott, if you have a problem with the order, I can ring the base commander and give it myself. I have no problem with taking full responsibility for such a thing. Do you want me to do that?" Bowman asked. "These are the same people that just fucked us six ways to Sunday, and in all honesty, I am not going to lose sleep over executing a few terrorists."

"No, sir, that wasn't it."

"Well, Scott, then what was it?"

"I was just reflecting on what a rare, precious thing it is to finally have a commander in chief who is willing to do what is necessary to keep the American people safe, sir."

Bowman snorted in amusement and shook his head.

"Any other thoughts, opinions, or gossip?" Bowman asked, looking around the conference room. "Anyone? All right, keep going, keep plugging away on the projects that you have been assigned so far, and, Carl, please get your people on arranging transportation and hammering out meeting details with Hotchkiss's people for next week. I think we'll fly in on the evening of the eleventh as well. Arrange for security, for both of us. Remember, if one of us ends up dead, the other guy may end up running the whole show. If that is going to happen, I want Ted Hotchkiss's body to be the one lying lifeless on the tarmac."

Bowman nodded, shuffled a few papers into a folder, stood up, and left the room.

A Shit Job

CHAPTER 22

Levant, Kansas

It had been nine days since The Day. Officer Jennings was with the Kansas State Police. He had a shit job to do. In fact, he had told his boss and anyone else who would listen that this was a shit job. Except, no one was listening. On The Day, he and his partner had busted the guy in the back of his cruiser with multiple pounds of pot, cocaine, heroin, and hallucinogenic drugs coming across the state line from Colorado. He was a midlevel dealer, and in more normal times, they would have turned him over to the legal system to prosecute for possession with intent to distribute. He had rotted in a holding cell for the last nine days as they had bigger concerns now.

Jennings shook his head. His boss had told him to take him to the other side of the state line and let him go, get him out of Kansas, and let Colorado deal with him.

"What a fuckin' waste of time," he muttered. The evidence bags in the back trunk would have set this clown up for a number of years, and it was one of the bigger busts of Jennings's career. Then The Day had come along, and there were simply more things to worry about than drug dealers.

"So you are just going to take me to Colorado and let me go?" the guy in the back asked.

"Yep," Jennings replied. "And it's way better than you deserve, too. I'm frankly surprised that they are wasting the gas on this, and you'd be better off with two in the back of the head."

"That's a threat, man! When do I get to talk to a lawyer? I'm going to sue you and your whole department, man! You won't be in charge of a garage sale when we get done with you, pig!"

"Almost to Colorado," Jennings sighed.

Up ahead, Levant, Kansas, was just coming into view, and the air was smoky. Jennings slowed the cruiser way down and almost stopped on the deserted two-lane highway.

"What are you doing, pig? We ain't in Colorado yet, man! Why are we stopping here?"

"Shut up," Jennings replied tightly.

Jennings peered ahead up the road and saw about three dozens bikers tearing down the road right at them. A house in Levant exploded at that point, and he felt the *thump* of it shudder up through the car.

"Shit," he breathed out, whipping the car into a U-turn. He began accelerating away from Levant.

"Hey, man! What the fuck? Why are we turning back? You're supposed to take me to Colorado, pig!"

"I said *shut up*!" Jennings replied.

"I can't wait to get a lawyer, man. I am going to sue your ass, man. You are going to pay and pay—"

The bikers were coming up fast now, and Jennings could see them whooping it up and waving chains around their heads.

They were flails. Maces.

Jennings glanced at the speedometer. He was going 110.

Four of them pulled up on either side of the cruiser then fell back then pulled forward. Jennings did his best to keep it straight and level while they smacked the sides of the vehicle with their maces. One broke the windshield and the driver's side window.

Jennings slammed on the brakes, and the bikes flew past. The perp in the back slammed forward against the metal divider between the front seat and the backseat and was spitting out blood and gibberish.

Well, that shut the little fucker up, Jennings thought with a grin.

The bikers were gathering together on the roadway to the front, and glancing in the rearview mirror, he saw more approaching from the direction of Levant. *Think!*

He floored it at the bikers ahead of him, and he thought he was going to break free of them when a tire blew. Jennings lost control of the vehicle, and they flipped and rolled into a deep depression to the side of the road. When it finally came to a halt, they were upside down in the ditch.

He heard shouts and whoops from the roadway above and the fading sounds of bikes disappearing into the distance. Jennings hung helplessly upside down in the driver's seat. His back was broken. He could feel nothing from the neck down.

"Hey, man, let me out of here!" The guy in the back was yelling and pounding on the divider.

Jennings began to laugh. The bikers were gone, his back was broken, and neither one of them was going anywhere. It was funny, really.

"Hey, pig! What's so fuckin' funny? When I get out of here, man, just wait! You won't be laughing then!"

"I'm pretty sure I'm going to be dead soon," Jennings replied, "but you, you're going to be in for life, you little bitch!"

"Yeah right, man, we'll see. What do you know?"

"I know the keys to let you out are in the ignition, and I can't move anything below my neck. I know that's pretty heavy-gauge steel between you and me, and the odds of you getting out of the back are pretty slim. That's what I know. So will you die of thirst? Of hunger? Or will you be keeping me company for a while after I die? All you have to do is get out of the back, and you are free. I don't think you can, and that's what's so funny to me."

The perp continued to beat against the divider while Jennings laughed. Eventually, he lost consciousness and died.

The guy in the orange jumpsuit lasted almost five days before dying of thirst.

CHAPTER 23

Winters

From the Journal of H. Rayton Townsend
December 2, 2016
Winters, California

We left Calistoga nine days ago on foot and have had to stop here in Winters, California, for a bit. So I thought I might use this break to catch things up in the journal a little. A lot has happened in the last few days. The Meyers's daughter, Lena, is sick. It's some kind of respiratory infection. The pediatrician here feels that he can handle it, but if left untreated, it can get a lot worse. Kyle and Carly are really worried, and I heard a few nurses at the clinic talking when they thought that no one else was around. Apparently, they are already running out of antibiotics. I haven't said anything to Carly and Kyle yet, but this can be bad. Very, very bad.

* * *

They had stopped for a few days in Winters, California. The night before arriving, they had camped near a back road in some brush, and Lena, the baby, had developed a horrible cough. She was inconsolable, crying all night, and terribly congested. Carly couldn't do anything to help her. It was amazing to Ray how quickly, in just nine days' time, how fast people could go through food and supplies. The food he had shared out was almost gone, and he had no intentions of sharing any more of what was in his pack. The rest of the group had continued to eat three squares a day, just like nothing was going on. He, in comparison, had been limiting himself to one large meal when they stopped at night, along with brief snacks of trail mix or a power bar for breakfast and lunch.

Maybe it was selfish of him, but he had much farther to go than the rest of them. So he needed to watch what he consumed. He was already losing weight, but he felt stronger, converting fat into muscle and burning the spare calories he had around his waistline. He had decided early on to only eat what was needed to keep from getting shaky. The Webbs, so far, had only really contributed an inordinate amount of complaining and a general surliness that was contagious. Ray stayed away from them for the most part now, frustrated by the selfishness and the sense of entitlement. Ben by himself wasn't too bad, but Becky was an entirely different piece of work.

They weren't outdoors people. Ray got that, he really did. Camping wasn't for everyone, but Becky felt that the world should conform to her wishes instead of the other way around. She was awful. One more comment on the cold or the quality of his gear compared to theirs or the fact that he seemed to have plenty to eat and they didn't, and he was about to scream.

It was a relief when they arrived in Winters after nine days on the road. All of them had found accommodations in a gymnasium of the local Catholic school/church in town. It was doubling as a Red Cross shelter at the moment.

As soon as they were settled in, Carly and Kyle had gone to find a doctor for the baby, and Ray had decided to go with them to have a look around. The Webbs had collapsed on their cots in the gym and shut down for the moment. Good. He needed a break. Looking around town as they walked, Ray noticed once again that getting away from the immediate surroundings of San Francisco had pulled a lot of the tension out of the air. They were still out ahead of things, but refugees had begun to trickle into Winters, thus the Red Cross shelter in the gym. Still and all, there was a sense of normalcy here, and so far, they hadn't seen much.

Winters was located about twenty miles from Sacramento. They had gotten there mostly by walking, but occasionally, someone had stopped to offer a ride. Even if it was only a few miles, every little bit helped and added up. No one really had any additional information for them. It was a bit unnerving, to say the least. Ray planned on scouting around a little more once the Meyers were situated at the clinic. They had walked to Winters Community Hospital first, but they had had no room for more patients, and so the people at WCH had sent them to the clinic. So now they were walking there.

When they got there, Ray was a little taken aback at seeing how many people were waiting to see a doctor. There were about thirty folks in the waiting room that was designed at most to comfortably accommodate six to eight people max. When the Meyers finally got to the desk to take a number, the haggard receptionist gave them some forms to fill out. Looking around, Ray realized that most of the folks waiting were really, really sick. Diabetics, the elderly, many people with very small children like Lena. It made his skin crawl. He turned his attention back to the receptionist, who was talking to Kyle and Carly at the moment.

"… say, you were planning to pay for this?" she was asking.

Kyle and Carly looked dumbfounded.

"What do you mean you won't accept our insurance?" Kyle was beginning to say angrily, and Ray put a hand on his shoulder to calm him a little.

The receptionist sighed.

"We can't take your insurance at the moment because we are offline with *all* our insurance providers. We cannot provide service at a private clinic without compensation, so unless you have a way to handle this transaction, you will have to instead go across town, to WCH, to the emergency room there."

"That is completely fucking ridiculous!" Kyle shouted. "My little girl is sick, and they just *told* us at WCH to come *here*!"

"Excuse me," Ray cut in smoothly, looking directly at the receptionist. "Is everyone here, your entire staff, as worn out and exhausted-looking as you are?"

"I haven't had a day off since *The* Day!" she snapped back. "And neither have the two doctors, four nurses, and six orderlies that we have working in the clinic. We have been *sleeping* here, in between shifts, 24-7, and it's a private clinic! So either pay up or go to the hospital! I don't imagine they are in any better shape than we are, but they *have* to take you. *We* don't! And if you think for—"

"*She* is a paramedic!" Ray snapped, pointing at Carly. "And a damn good one too! Maybe if you took a moment to pull your head out of your ass, you guys can work something out. Maybe she can even *help you* get a day off here. I'm sure she can do at least as much as your nurses here, and maybe even more. Right, Carly?"

Carly nodded, her jaw set tightly. "I will do anything to help get my little girl healthy again. We have a long way to go yet. I can help you guys out here."

The receptionist seemed to deflate a little bit.

"I'll go ask the doctor about it," she muttered and left without meeting their eyes.

Kyle looked at Ray and grinned. Carly's smile was absolutely dazzling.

"How in the world did you think of *that* so quickly? *I* didn't even think of that, Ray."

"You just gotta work it, girl," Ray said with a wink. "Is that gonna work out okay? I don't want to get you into more than you're willing to do, but staying a few days to work the clinic won't hurt us too much, and if it helps out Lena . . ." He shrugged.

"It's going to have to," she replied. "I'll do what I can."

"In that case, I'm going to see what I can find out. Gather any information, that sort of thing," Ray replied. "I'll see you guys later."

As Ray walked out of the reception area, the doctor was being introduced to Carly, and they were shaking hands, working out a deal. Ray was walking around the side of the clinic when he saw two nurses smoking and chatting. They hadn't seen him yet, but he overheard what they were talking about.

"Almost out of antibiotics. There's been no shipment! How long can we keep doing what we have to—" she cut off as the other nurse nudged her.

Ray nodded and walked on past.

He was introspective as he walked the streets of Winters. Medical supplies running out already in a mostly unaffected town. Antibiotics, insulin, antidepressants, pain killers. People needed a lot of different meds just to stay alive, and sane, in some cases. Winter was coming, and there was not a lot of traffic moving on any roads that he had seen so far. There were the occasional locals running into town, but that was it. Where was FEMA? Probably in the camps around San Francisco, he guessed. Maybe a lot of these smaller places were considered secondary due to the attack there.

He found what he was looking for soon enough. Bars and barbershops always had the good gossip.

Walking into Crab's Korner, Ray looked around. There were a bartender, a few locals, and a few strangers perched at the bar. Ray walked to the bar, plunked his pack down, and took a stool as the bartender approached.

"How's it going?" he asked.

"Okay, I guess. What'll you have?"

"What do you have on tap?" Ray asked.

"Anchor Steam, Guinness, Red Tail, and Sam Adams," the bartender replied.

"I'll have a Red Tail," Ray said. "What'll the damage be for that?"

"That's $17.50," the bartender replied.

Ray whistled appreciatively. "That much, huh?"

The bartender shrugged.

"Tell you what, I have five bucks and some smokes. Wanna trade?"

"Cigs are going for $45 a pack right now. How about six smokes and your five bucks?"

"How about the beer, seven smokes, a free refill, and some information?" Ray asked.

"Sounds good! Deal!" he said, slapping the countertop. "People keep trying to buy individual cigarettes anyways, and this way, I don't have to crack open any packs to supply them."

Ray handed over his fiver and seven cigarettes. The bartender handed him a cold Red Tail in a pint glass. He took a long pull on the beer and sighed. That hit the spot.

"What have you heard?" he asked.

"Nothing good. Lots of rumors. I heard from one guy with a shortwave radio that LA got hit too, and maybe even Seattle and Portland. One thing is sure. It's a lot bigger than we originally thought. Maybe the whole West Coast."

Ray sat very still for a moment and then took another sip of his beer.

"You okay, man?" the bartender asked.

"Yeah," Ray said finally. "How reliable would you say the short-wave guy is?"

"Pretty reliable. He's a survivalist type, a little off, but he's okay. Quiet. Doesn't cause any trouble, pays his tab, and tips well too."

Ray nodded.

"The thing is," he continued, "I heard about LA from a few other people too. One guy was on his cell on The Day, right here in the bar. He was talking to his wife in LA at the time. At the same time we saw the cloud off to the southwest, his signal cut off to her. Maybe the bomb in San Fran fucked up the signal, but he couldn't get through to her again. He was able to call other people in other places, but no one in LA was answering their phones. You do the math."

Ray nodded again.

"The president elect, Bowman, was in Sacramento a few days ago as well. Might still be there for all I know. Probably out here to see the damage for himself. They say he had his whole cabinet with him. Secret Service guys were everywhere. It was an even bigger clusterfuck than the camps being set up outside of Sac."

"More camps?" Ray asked casually, raising his eyebrows.

"What do you mean *more camps*?" the bartender asked. "Hey, where are you from anyways?"

Ray finished his second beer and smacked his lips. Good stuff.

"Thanks for the beer and the gossip," he said, shouldering his pack. "San Fran was well and truly fucked when I left there. I wouldn't go south anytime soon if I were you."

He nodded again and left.

The stories were the same in every bar that Ray visited. The president elect. Wild rumors of setting Sacramento up to be the new capital of the United States. Russians. Chinese. Nuclear war. Alien Invasion. (Secretly, Ray thought that would be pretty cool.) Civil war. The works. One thing came through again and again though: the West Coast was screwed. TV was off or in standby mode, there were no radio stations broadcasting, and the government wasn't talking. It had been a little over two weeks since the bomb. Definitely a lot bigger than anyone really knew. People were getting edgy, and with all the stress—financial, racial, political—that the state had been under prior to The Day, Ray had the distinct impression that California was a powder keg. The fuse was lit, and they were sitting on the lid. They needed to get *out* of here before everything blew up. They had to move faster, he thought, grinding his teeth.

* * *

From the Journal of H. Rayton Townsend
December 2, 2016 (Continuation)

I almost forgot! No wonder I felt a little weird writing the date earlier! Today is my sister's birthday. I will have to find a carrier pigeon to send her a card. I have been doing a lot of thinking since my tour of the local watering holes earlier. If it's the whole West Coast that's screwed, my window is closing radically to get out of here. I had hoped that once I left the greater Bay Area, maybe I could find some kind of transportation hub where I could use a credit card, make a phone call, maybe get a Greyhound bus ticket home. I had hoped that this was a localized event. But it has now been two weeks with no further information being given. No one seems to have a plan, and it doesn't look like help is on the way beyond the local FEMA camps. And we all know that's not an option! Where is everybody? After a devastating hurricane or an earthquake, supplies get flown in, disaster-relief agencies are on the ground with doctors, health care, medicine, food, and bottled water, right? Generators are set up, power is restored. It may take a while, but it gets done, right? Everyone is making do with what they have, and to be honest, it's starting to run out. If the whole coast is gone, that explains a lot, the delays or outright absence of anything resembling a prompt response to the disaster.

What happened? Why doesn't anyone have anything to go on besides rumors? How big is it? Are we at war with a major nuclear power? If so, then who? I would think that in the event of a real nuclear war, things would be much worse than they are. ICBMs would have leveled everything by now. There would be nothing left. So that rules out Russia, China, and our allies. Maybe it was a limited exchange, or an accident? A computer gone crazy like in that eighties movie WarGames? Maybe there was truce or a ceasefire after the first exchange of missiles? Maybe we will learn more in Sacramento. We have to go by there anyway. I need sleep, and then we are going to have to talk this out as a group.

* * *

Ray stumbled back to the gymnasium and wrote for a while, sitting on his cot. Ben Webb had opened his eyes as Ray walked past and then closed them again. He had been writing sporadically and thinking when Ben sat up and looked at him.

"One of these days, I'm going to have to see what you are saying about all this," he said.

"Maybe I can get a movie script out of it someday," he replied bleakly. "I'm going to get some sleep now, Ben. I'm wiped out." Ray yawned. "Have Kyle and Carly been back yet?" he asked.

"Kyle came in for a bit and told us what was going on, then he went back to the clinic to spend the night with Carly and the baby."

"That makes sense," Ray muttered, leaning back. "We all need to talk in the morning about some important stuff." Ray pulled the blankets up. "You gonna be awake for a while, Ben?" he asked. "You got this?"

"Yeah. We slept all afternoon," he replied, nodding at Becky and Brian, who were still out.

"Keep an eye on things and wake me up if anything gets weird, okay?" Ray asked.

"Will do," Ben replied. "I'm gonna go see if I can find some coffee in this place."

Ray was already asleep.

* * *

From the Journal of H. Rayton Townsend
December 3, 2016
Winters, California

Having slept on things last night, I have come to a few conclusions regarding the rest of the West Coast. It's bigger than we thought, but until we have solid facts, it will all remain a rumor as well. There is nothing that we can do about that, so we should carry on, try to make it to Carly and Kyle's cabin, and hole up until springtime. I will discuss things with the Webbs today and the Meyers when they return from the clinic.

* * *

He sat down with the Webbs after breakfast to discuss everything that he had seen and heard the day before. He started with the deteriorating situation at the clinic and what Carly was doing to make sure the little kid had the best fighting chance to defeat whatever was wrong with her. He then moved on to what he had discussed in the bars around town and what the rumor mill was churning out. How the situation seemed to be bigger than previously thought. He

174

shared his thoughts on the situation and his fears and concerns about getting over the mountains before the situation deteriorated further. He told them about the new camps near Sacramento and the visiting president elect, Bowman. He also laid out a few concepts that he felt they should consider as a group before going further.

"At some point, guys, you were going to have to turn north anyways to try to make it back to Washington, right? If the rumors are true, though, then Seattle and Portland are gone. Tacoma is just south of Seattle, right? So it's kind of up in the air right now, and it's impossible to tell if there is anything worth going back to or not."

"Those *are* just rumors, Ray," Becky replied. "Besides, everything we have is wrapped up in the business. We have to get back so that we can make sure our people get paid, protect what we have, and maybe get a few bids in on rebuilding in the affected areas. Right, Ben?"

Ray blinked at that then shook his head. Ben shook his head as well and looked worried.

"Beck," he began, "what if it *is* all gone? What if it's more than just rumors?"

"Please!" she said dismissively. "The government would have told us, right? Do you really think they would just sit back and not say anything at all about the entire West Coast being destroyed? For God's sake! It's just rumors!"

"All I am getting at is this, guys," Ray continued. "It sounds like we got hit harder than anyone realized, and Kyle and Carly's cabin is *way* closer than Tacoma. It will be safer in the Sierras this winter than down on the flats. People down here are going to be doing anything and everything they can do to survive. God knows, California is dangerous enough when times are normal. If we split up now, it makes us easier targets than we will be if we stay together. Why don't you guys come to the mountains? Ride out the winter and see what the lay of the land is come springtime?"

Becky had an even more stubborn look on her face. Ben looked even more worried, and Brian was just sitting and staring off into the distance, thinking. Becky had just opened her mouth to make another, no doubt, searing point when Kyle came back into the gym.

"We lost the baby," he said and then turned to stumble back out again.

Ray hurried after him to join him on the walk back to the clinic. Catching up, he started to raise his hand to put on Kyle's shoulder and then let his arm drop. He instead matched his pace to Kyle's, and the two men continued in silence for a while. They walked that way for about ten minutes before Ray could gather the nerve to speak.

"What happened, Kyle? It was just a bad cough, right?" he asked quietly.

Kyle didn't respond; he just kept walking with his head down and his hands in his pockets. Ray was just about to give up when Kyle answered him.

"Carly hasn't put her down since she died this morning. The doctor said it was a respiratory infection that they just didn't have the right medication to treat. Her breathing got worse last night. She was fighting so hard, Ray! Then she just stopped breathing."

Again, Ray didn't know what to say. He just walked along with his friend.

"If you don't mind, Ray, I'd like to spend some time with them alone."

"Of course," he replied.

As Ray watched Kyle walk away, he was saddened for his friends. He also realized that he didn't have anything worthwhile to say to help them. They were devastated. What can one say to a parent who has just lost a one-year-old child, "I'm sorry"? It is such a lame response. It doesn't make anything better; if anything, sometimes, "I'm sorry" just makes things worse. He walked back to the gym, thinking, and ultimately, he realized there was nothing he could do to help. Kyle and Carly were Catholic, though, and they were staying in a Catholic gymnasium, next to a Catholic school. So maybe, if he couldn't come up with something, there had to be a priest around there somewhere. That was, like, their job. He thought, nodding. A priest would know what to say and do. He would find a priest, tell him where his friends were and what had happened, and maybe he could go to the clinic and help them. That guy would know what to say.

When he ultimately returned to the gym after finding the priest, Ben, Becky, and Brian had made up their minds. Now that the situation with Lena was resolved and they were rested, they would be moving on soon. They felt badly for the Meyers, but they had places to go as well. Ray argued again, futilely, for everyone to stay together, but their minds were made up. Becky definitely wasn't having it. His arguments to wait a few more days fell on deaf ears. Deep down inside, he was troubled. In fact, he found himself tempted to go with the Webbs. Nature and time were conspiring against him; he needed to move, and soon, if he was going to get out of this state. Leaving now, however, would be just another example of people turning their backs on one another, leaving those that really needed his help. He didn't know what to do, so he sat back on his cot, back against the wall in the corner, and began to write in his journal, hashing out all the pros and cons of staying or going. Honestly, the thought of spending just one more minute in Becky's company disgusted him. She just wouldn't see! She didn't get it, and her hardheadedness could get other people killed.

If he was going to leave without the Meyers, he was going to be leaving alone, he decided. His path lay to the east, and cabin or no cabin, that was the way the path led, and that was the way he was going.

* * *

From the Journal of H. Rayton Townsend
December 4, 2016
Winters, California

Kyle and Carly came back to the gym late last night and fell into an exhausted sleep. No one really wanted to talk about anything. Needless to say, they aren't aware of the Webbs' decision to move on yet, nor do I think they will really even care at this point. The Webbs will probably allow me to go with them, but I still feel that leaving Carly and Kyle behind will be the worst kind of selfish-

ness. They need someone to stand with them right now. Besides, I trust the Meyers way more than the Webbs. If I fell by the roadside and broke my leg, I feel that Kyle and Carly would do everything in their power to get me up and going again. Becky, on the other hand, would most likely leave me to die, stripping me of everything that I would need to survive. I can see it in them now. Ben wouldn't stand up to her, and Brian would continue to be a shadow, trailing behind. I'm going to wait for the Meyers. Gotta follow those gut instincts.

* * *

It was a cold, drizzly gray dawn. Like all of them for the last few weeks. Six people stood by a small grave in a cemetery in Winters, California. No one had an umbrella. Father Mike, the local priest, was giving a quiet eulogy for a little girl who would never grow up. Her parents stood silently nearby, rain mixing with tears, as the two of them pondered the ashes of a future where dreams would not come true and potential would not be realized.

What must it be like to lose a child? Ray wondered yet again. It was incomprehensible to him. Even having a child in the first place must be close to terrifying. But to have one and then lose them this way, under these conditions, must go far beyond terror. He had wanted a family when he was younger. Being married to a thankless job, though, had left little enough time for himself, much less finding the right lady who would be gracious enough to bear his children. His string of tragic, failed romances was evidence enough that he probably wasn't exactly father material. Maybe that would change someday, now that the world was different. If he survived this, he owed it to himself to find that girl, whoever she was. One thing at a time.

Laughing at himself for being a complete and utter moron, at a funeral no less, he tuned back in to what was going on around him.

Father Mike was wrapping things up. Kyle and Carly knelt to place two roses on top of the casket, and then they turned and walked away. The Webbs weren't too far behind them. All of a sudden, it was just him and Father Mike standing there. Ray studied the priest across the small grave. Ray didn't think the man was even aware that he still stood there. He was a sparrow of a man, very thin, but he moved with surprising speed and grace. Sure, assertive motions that showed an inner strength and self-confidence. He was normally a font of positive energy. At that moment, he was raising a shaking hand to his brow to wipe away raindrops. He wore a pair of round glasses over a rounded nose, and at that moment, it seemed like he was far, far away.

"Do you think it will be okay, Father?" Ray asked politely.

He gave a start as he realized Ray was still standing there, then he uttered a short, bitter bark of laughter.

"For them? Or for all of us? Who knows, Ray?" Shaking his head, he corrected himself. "Well, God knows, I suppose. I have been struggling with my faith these past few weeks. I am not sure of how many more of these I have in me."

Father Mike nodded in the direction of over a dozen mounds that dotted the cemetery in all shapes and sizes.

Ray studied him again, briefly, before replying. "As many as you have to, I guess," he said. "People need someone to turn to at moments like these. But who helps the helpers, right? If you don't have it in you, at least fake it. I don't think God would mind too much if it helped someone like them feel better."

Ray stepped back under the still-leafy branches of a tree nearby. It cut the drizzle somewhat. He reached into his jacket and withdrew a small silver flask; he had won it gambling the night before along with a fifth of good brandy to put in it.

"A little nip of something, Father?" he asked, raising an eyebrow.

"Don't mind if I do," Father Mike replied with a small grin. "It seems like an appropriate day for a drink."

"Assuming that God is real," Ray began, "why would he allow something like this to happen, Father? Punishment? Did we fail him in some way beyond our understanding? The Meyers are good people, and they simply didn't deserve this. She was a sweet little kid." He nodded at the grave.

Father Mike was silent for some time, thinking of how to respond. Finally, he looked over at Ray. "I have been thinking the same thing for quite some time," he finally said. "I'm not going to give you that 'God works in mysterious ways' crap. It's part of why I have been struggling lately."

Ray took another swig of brandy and handed the flask back to the priest. He nodded his thanks.

"Maybe he did it just for you, Ray," he finally said.

Ray blinked. *Not* the answer he had been expecting.

"Come again, Father?"

"Maybe he did it for all of us and the reason fits the individual. We have free will, but sometimes it seems that God needs all of us to use that free will to make a choice, to choose whether we will be good people or bad people. Maybe all of us before this—those of us that are left anyway—maybe we were all too close to the middle of the road, you know? Those that were truly guilty or truly innocent are gone, maybe on The Day. All that's left are us, and maybe we have a choice to make. Look deep inside yourself, and you may hear his reasons for doing this just for you. So you can make a decision, Ray, or many of them, for that matter. Will you be a good person or a bad one? Or will you just *be*? Maybe he put you in a world where you will be forced to choose. I hope you make the right decisions. That's all I can tell you. Hope it helps."

"That's a real comfort, Father," Ray said dryly. "You know I'm Presbyterian, right?"

"God won't hold that against you," he replied with a straight face. "Thanks for the drink, Ray."

"Take care of yourself, Father," Ray replied, walking away.

Choices—how about that? Maybe there was something to that.

When he got back to the gym, the Webbs were packed and ready to leave. Ray hadn't given them a definitive answer yet whether he would keep traveling with them. Carly was lying on her cot off to the side, staring into space, and Kyle sat on the ground next to her, holding her hand. Ray walked over to them slowly.

"Well, I guess this is where we part ways," he said.

Kyle's eyes were bleak as he looked up at him. "I know," he replied.

Carly dropped Kyle's hand and turned away from Ray, facing the wall.

Ray glanced over at the Webbs. They were waiting impatiently by the door. He walked over to them, making his way through the maze of cots that covered half the gymnasium floor.

"Good-bye and good luck, guys," he said, extending his hand.

Brian and Ben shook his hand. Becky just turned and walked out the door.

Good riddance! he thought.

"I hope you make it where you're going, Ben," Ray said. "I can't leave just yet."

"We understand," he replied. "Good luck."

Just like that, they were down to three people. Idly, Ray wondered how long Ben and Becky's marriage was going to last, then he shrugged. He gave a snort of laughter as he walked back across the gym to Kyle. His mood had lightened now that the decision to stay was made. Choices.

"I decided to stay here in Winters for a few more days, guys. My feet are kind of sore from all the walking we have been doing lately. I could use a break."

"Thanks. Thanks, Ray," Kyle replied. "I know."

Leave-Takings

24

From the Journal of H. Rayton Townsend
December 8, 2016
Winters, California

Today dawned bright and cheery. It feels like the first time I have seen the sun in ages. It has been four days since the funeral, and this is our sixth day in Winters. The pregnant storm clouds of the last few weeks have moved off to the east and are way ahead of me in their trip over the Sierras. Kyle and Carly have had a rough couple of days since we buried Lena. I have heard them crying at night, not sleeping, and they spend their days looking like zombies, barely moving from their cots, staring off into space. They haven't really been eating either. I am honestly worried about them both. I am not sure how much longer I can stay here. We need to move on, and soon.

Last night was a little different. I think all the stress and grief and depression finally caught up to them, and they slept like the dead. Maybe today will be different. I certainly hope so, at least. When we do leave, we should be in good shape for supplies for probably a week or so minimum. The food here has been free so far,

and we haven't had to dip into the traveling food at all.
I have been playing poker with a few folks the last few
nights to pass the time, and I'm having pretty good luck.

* * *

Ray was sitting outside the gym, on the flat part of one of the brick banisters lining the stairs that led to the gymnasium doors. The sun was an orange fireball coming up in the east and looked somehow larger than normal as it crested the treetops. Ray gloried in the sunshine, closing his eyes and letting his head rest for a moment against the brick wall behind him. He had woken up early today and was writing again. He was feeling rested and a little edgy. It was time to be moving forward. He was ready to take that next step on the long way home.

Yawning, he stretched, arching his back and flexing the muscles there. He tucked the journal away and pulled out the Rand McNally road atlas. Flipping to the large map of Sacramento, he looked at the areas he had circled and frowned. Camps. For people. People like him.

His lips twisted with distaste. Looking at the other red markings, he had placed red Xs that noted roadblocks on highways in and around the city that others had told him about. Looking up, he frowned as another convoy rolled through Winters. A long line of military vehicles that passed, carrying supplies, food, people, and presumably, weapons. They were all headed for Sacramento. Two helicopter gunships provided close air support for the convoy. The rumors had hundreds of thousands of people in the camps around Sac at the moment. He wondered when they would get around to emptying out Winters and the people and resources that were left there as well.

Spitting over the side of the railing, he jammed the atlas back into his pack and stood up. He glared at the last truck driving through town.

"Nothing to be done for it now," he muttered. "Coffee is what I need."

He shouldered the pack as he went back inside. On one side of the gymnasium, the Catholic Ladies' Auxiliary was setting up breakfast. Chafing dishes full of powdered eggs, sausage patties, biscuits, and gravy awaited along with coffee. He walked through rows of cots, people that arrived after them, and went to the corner where he and Kyle and Carly had been sleeping. He stuffed his pack under his cot. Both Kyle and Carly were still out cold.

He walked to the buffet and smiled at one of the ladies when he got there.

"Mornin', Ray!" a large grandmotherly lady greeted him.

"Good morning, Leah," he replied.

"Let me guess, three breakfasts and three coffees?"

"Yep. And maybe a tray?" Ray laughed.

"Coming right up, hon. If you want to pour your coffee, I'll get the rest dished up for you guys."

Juggling the tray and weaving through cots, he made his way back to their sleeping section and put it down on his empty cot. He grabbed one of the mugs and waved it under Kyle's nose. One bloodshot eye opened, and he yawned.

"My hero," he muttered, taking a sip.

Carly was beginning to stir, so he gave her a mug as well. She nodded her thanks to Ray before taking a sip.

Ray busied himself for a minute while they ran to the bathroom. He gathered utensils and napkins and placed their breakfasts carefully on their empty cots. When they came back, he was sitting cross-legged on his own cot, wolfing it all down. Ray watched them carefully, hoping that at least today, they would eat. They did. Hesitantly. That was promising. He finished his own breakfast and sat calmly, savoring his own coffee. He had neatly stacked his plate and utensils back on the tray, which now sat on the floor.

When Kyle and Carly finished, he did the same with theirs. He took the tray into the kitchen and washed their dishes, putting everything away so that no one else would have to do it. He went back out, got a second cup of coffee, and rejoined Kyle and Carly in the corner. They were murmuring quietly to each other when he got back.

"So," he said as brightly as he could manage, "the sun came out today!"

They both grunted something unintelligible.

"It's the first time I have seen it out since . . . well, since everything."

Nothing.

"Well," he sighed. "I was happy to see it, at least. It was nice to sit outside this morning and watch it come up."

"How long have you been up, Ray?" Kyle asked neutrally.

"Oh, I woke up early, feeling pretty well rested, and decided to do a little writing. Maybe an hour before dawn or so."

The silence stretched out uncomfortably.

Father Mike saved him. "Good morning, Meyers! Good morning, Ray! Nice to see you all up and about," he said. "How was breakfast?"

"It was pretty good, Father," Ray replied. "It filled us up, and that's a good thing."

"I'm glad to hear it," he replied with a smile and a twinkle in his eye. "Being 'filled up' is a good thing. How was it, really?"

"Awful." Carly shuddered, making a face.

"Biscuits and gravy *rule*!" Ray muttered.

Father Mike laughed.

"I've never been a fan of powdered eggs either," he agreed. "So! This is what I was thinking. I wanted to invite the three of you before you move on to come to dinner tonight. It's not much, but I am making spaghetti and meatballs and homemade bread with fresh butter and garlic. I thought you could all use a home-cooked meal before hitting the road again. Say, around seven tonight? It gets lonely sometimes, just cooking for myself."

Ray's mouth started watering immediately. They hadn't had fresh bread in weeks.

Kyle and Carly looked at each other for a long moment and then finally nodded.

"It's settled, then!" he said briskly, giving Ray a wink. "I will see you all tonight. Can you believe the sun came out today? It's beautiful outside!"

185

Father Mike walked on, greeting a few people here and there and making sure they had everything they needed. Ray could have hugged him. He had done with a dinner invitation what Ray had been trying to figure out how to do for days, bringing up leaving.

Carly looked thoughtful. Kyle shook his head slightly as if waking up from a bad dream, and his eyes seemed a little brighter. Ray began to hope.

"If you'd like, Kyle, Carly," he began tentatively, "I have been working on something that I'd like to show you this afternoon. It's kind of important, and it will help us in our preparations for when we decide to move on."

"Yeah," Kyle said softly, "we should probably start thinking about that, shouldn't we?"

That afternoon, the three of them sat down with Ray's road atlas and began to go over the map of the Sacramento area. Camps, both military and refugee, dotted the area, circled in red. Checkpoints were marked out by red Xs. It looked like their best bet and safest way to continue would be to follow County Road 31 to Davis. From Davis, they could get back on I-80 and head toward Sacramento. By traveling at night and keeping a low profile, they figured they might be able to circumvent the checkpoints and avoid being readmitted to the refugee camp system.

Once the ball was rolling, he saw Kyle and Carly moving with more purpose than they had in days, and he was mildly surprised when Kyle brought up leaving that very night. After their meal with Father Mike, of course.

They spent the next hour and a half redistributing gear, food, and supplies among the three packs and planning out the next few days. Then everyone tried to sleep as much as possible until 7:00 p.m. and dinner.

* * *

"Father, I don't think I could eat another bite even if someone threatened me," Kyle said.

Ray groaned in agreement. Carly rolled her eyes but nodded as well.

Nothing remained of the loaf of bread except a few crumbs. The good Father Mike had also made artichoke-cheese dip, and it was better than most that Ray had tried. The little bowl was licked clean as well.

"I'm glad that you all enjoyed it. I know there won't be too many more meals like this for you for a while. It is nice to be able to send you away with full bellies. I am actually kind of glad that we will have the cots for three more people as well. Folks have been flooding into our little town here for the last two days, and Winters is packed to the gills with people that need shelter."

Ray was nodding; he had noticed the same thing.

"I suppose we may have to send some others on to the FEMA camps soon," he said sadly. "Maybe all of us will have to go soon. I feel that we are being stripped to the bone here. We will hold on as long as we can, I suppose, but there just isn't enough to go around for too much longer. That's why I wanted to have this last meal."

Everyone was feeling a little mellow. The good father had produced an *excellent* bottle of wine from somewhere, and they were sitting around the table, savoring the last of it. There was a comfortable quiet in the room, and everyone was relaxed. Father Mike cleared his throat.

"I had told Ray, on the day of little Lena's funeral, that I was suffering from a crisis of faith. The last few weeks have been hard on all of us, and I was giving in to self-pity. Ray answered me. His answer made me take a good long, hard look at what I was doing here. It made me look around and open my eyes. He told me that if I had to 'fake it,' God wouldn't mind. That I could still help others whether I believed anymore or not." He laughed.

Ray started to raise his hand to explain what he had meant. Father Mike quieted him with a hand on his arm.

"There are many ways to serve God, I think," he said. "But 'faking it' has never been one of them, at least for myself. You made me take a good look at myself, Ray, and for that, I thank you. Being able to help as many others as I can has helped me. He may put us through any number of trials in this life, and this is simply another one. Every test has made us stronger, coming out the other side of them. We learn some lesson, or we discover a new way of looking at things or how we deal with them. It is that moment of realization, that perfect twinkling of self-awareness, that we realize that we are loved. We learned a lesson because *we didn't give up*! He is proud of us at that moment, like a parent, because we learn something. There are many kinds of love, I think. They all descend from him."

Father Mike took a sip of his wine.

"When I was a very young priest, there was a very old man in my first parish. I don't know how old he was, but he was very devout, and he never came to Mass. He had a way to get there, people that loved him that would have driven him there. He only lived about five houses down from the church. The other, older priest in the parish, had tried for years to get him to come but had been politely refused over and over again."

He shook his head.

"I had puzzled over it, tried to figure it out. So finally, one day I went to see him at home. It was a short walk. I was young and direct, so in not so many words, I asked him what the problem was. Why we never saw him there. Apparently, no one had ever asked him why. They had always just tried to talk him into going without ever getting to the root of his refusal to go. He thought about it for a moment, and finally said to me 'No one laughs at Mass.' I stared at him. 'What do you mean, no one laughs at Mass?' I asked. He thought about it for a minute and then tried to explain. 'They say that God is love, right?' I agreed. 'Well, I have never been in love with someone that I couldn't laugh with. My wife, before she passed, we laughed all the time. When my children were born and got old enough to get around on their own, we laughed with them too. The girls I went steady with before my wife, the ones that lasted awhile, we laughed together as well. All our married friends, in long-lasting marriages, through the Depression, through the war years, through heartache and sadness, joy, and victory and loss, we were able to laugh together. Laughter and love are linked, Father. When I laugh at something, I feel love as well. Laughter *is* love. If God is love, then he must be laughter as well, and yet no one laughs in church. It is always so solemn and, sometimes, depressing, and when I go to Mass, I don't feel better about myself. I feel worse. If God loves us, then he should be able to laugh with us in his house, even if we are being reprimanded for being a little less than perfect.'"

"Needless to say, I left his home feeling a little chastened," he continued. "After that conversation, I tried to work a little more humor into my sermons and lessons, and I was able to get him to Mass on Sundays."

Father Mike looked at Kyle and Carly for a long moment.

"You two love each other very much. You have been tested. You cry together, support each other in all that you have lost, and that is as it should be. I want you to promise me that in the future, you will laugh together again as well. Laughter *is* love. As long as you remember that and have faith in that love, you will eventually come out of that other side of the tunnel and find that glimmer of hope."

"What happened to him?" Carly asked. "The old man."

Father Mike blinked. "A tree fell on him," he replied.

"That's terrible!" she exclaimed.

"A windstorm came up on a Sunday after Mass. He was walking home, and a tree fell on him. I ran out to see what I could do to help. He looked up at me and said, 'See? I *told* you he had a sense of humor!' Then he passed away."

"That's actually kind of funny," Ray said, finishing his wine.

Carly punched him.

"There's a lesson in there for Presbyterians too, Ray," Father Mike said.

"Oh, don't worry, Father. I laugh all the time," he said with a wink.

They spent another hour chatting and laughing around the table and helped Father Mike do the dishes and clean up. Finally, it was time to go. They all had their packs on and were standing in the doorway. Hugs and handshakes went around, and they started walking and left Winters behind.

Missing Something

CHAPTER 25

Offutt AFB, Omaha, Nebraska

Colonel Johns had the priceless luxury of having an hour to himself. He was looking out his office window, sipping a cup of coffee, and watching transport plane after transport plane touching down. Every one of them had tons of needed cargo, food, medicine, blankets, communications gear, staff, doctors, and vehicle components. Omaha was secure. The Bridgeport nuclear facility was guarded and online, the water and sewage treatment facilities were working, additional National Guard units had been reporting in, the FEMA people were pleased, and at the moment, all his hard work was paying off. And he, strangely enough, had nothing to do. There were a few reports of his people tangling with some Road Warrior types, but those incidents had been shut down rather quickly. The men's morale (and that of the ladies, he mentally added) was high, and everything was working just like it should.

He was surprised when a hesitant knock sounded at the office door.

"Come in," he responded, turning away from the window.

One of his communication officers came to attention with a number of dispatches clutched in his hands.

"At ease," Johns said. "What do you have for me, Al?"

"Well, sir, it's pretty exciting news," he said, handing the dispatches over. "We're going to be hosting a summit meeting between the two presidents. They want to meet here and hammer everything out."

Johns raised one eyebrow and began to read.

"That will be all for now, Captain," he said. "And, Al, keep this meeting under your hat for the moment, okay?"

"Yes, sir," he said, saluting, and then he left the office.

A summit. Here, on a base that had just rejected the directives of a dictator. With violence and death and acrimony on both sides. Now that same dictator wanted to come here for a meeting with his very hostile counterpart. For some reason, this had Johns really, really worried, and his gut was telling him that not everything was as it seemed.

They were to provide security to both presidents, and they were to accommodate both advance security details. They were to provide a neutral meeting space where both presidents and their cabinets could sit down and discuss the details of resolving hostilities inside the continental United States. Johns was to take personal responsibility to make it so, and his stomach did a slow flip-flop.

"Goddamnit!" he whispered. "What am I not seeing?"

The presidents and their staff would be arriving in five days, on December 11.

"Lots to do and not a lot of time to get it done," he muttered. "Well, security we can *do*!"

Johns pressed the intercom on his desk. "I would like to see the commander of our Navy SEAL contingent, with my compliments, ASAP!" he snapped.

Johns was reading yet another condition of this meeting when there was a knock on the door.

"Enter!" he said.

Tony Bride entered and raised an eyebrow at Johns sitting behind his desk reading a report with thin-lipped concentration.

"You wanted to see me, Colonel?" he asked.

"Yes," Johns replied absently. "Have a seat, Tony."

In the unusual events the week before Thanksgiving, the officers of the different services that had been passing through Offutt had come to a somewhat-informal agreement. They deferred to Johns and acknowledged that he was in charge of the situation now, but mostly they attended to their own men and their own missions. So for example, while Johns's own staff officers adhered to their service regulations and SOPs, the SEALs were a little more informal, the Marines *very* formal. The Eighty-Second guys went back and forth between informal and formal, and the National Guard guys didn't know what to do half the time, so they saluted everybody and pursued their own agendas when not brought into a specific arrangement. To an outsider, it would have been very confusing, but for right now, everything suited Johns's purposes. After all, if it weren't broken, why fix it? Everything was working, *had* been working, until now.

Johns turned his rather-disquieting, direct gaze on Tony for a moment, now seated across the desk from him, then seemed to come to a decision about something.

"Tony, I want you to read these and think about them for a minute. Then tell me what you think."

Tony took the proffered papers and began to skim them quickly, then did a double take, and began to read in-depth. Johns let him get into it for a bit, satisfied to see his eyebrows raising as well, his brow furrowed. He took a contemplative sip of his coffee for a minute and digested all the information that he had just read.

"Tony, you want a cup of coffee or anything?"

"That would be great, Colonel," he replied absently, completely absorbed.

Johns rose and walked over to his side bar to pour another cup. "Cream, sugar?" he asked.

"Just black, Colonel, thank you," Bride replied, turning a page.

Johns waited until Tony had finished reading, and then with a sigh, he sat back in his chair.

"Interesting," he said, looking at Johns.

"What are your thoughts, Tony?"

"Well, Colonel, the way I see it, Hotchkiss is kinda putting himself right into the proverbial lion's den. We could renege once he got here, arrest him, put him to work resurfacing highways or something, or just flat out shoot him. He knows this is hostile territory, and yet he asked to meet here. So what gives? What are we missing?"

"I had the same thoughts myself," Johns admitted. "I think he's going to make a play to take Bowman out of the game somehow. With his rival eliminated, he's the last man standing, and I suppose he thinks that everyone will have to fall in line with his way of thinking. It ain't going to be obvious, though, so we're going to need to think outside the box. That's where I need a Navy SEAL to think sneaky. How would you do it? How would you kill the president?"

"Well, we have to assume that this guy has his own Special Forces teams in play somehow as well, right? My guys and I, we're here, the Eighty-Second is here, so who's to say he doesn't have another SEAL team en route right now somewhere on our perimeter with a clean shot and a great line of sight to the meeting place? They'd have their orders to take out the rebel and restore the political authority to their guy. Take the shot and fade away, just a terrible misunderstanding and an accident. Or this summit could be legitimate. Or there could be stealth helos inserting a team as we speak, or a mad bomber loose, or just about anything." Bride sighed.

"So what do we do?" Johns asked.

"I'll have an action plan for you in a few hours, Colonel."

"That's why I'm glad you're here, Tony, and on our side."

"Does it seem like politics in this country has just gotten plain ugly the last few years, Colonel?"

"Nope. It's always been a mean, nasty business, Tony. People have just removed the veneer of manners from it so that we see it for what it is now."

"I'll get back to you soon, Colonel."

"Please do, Tony, and keep thinking about the angles on this. We need to keep our guy alive."

Tony saluted casually and walked out.

Johns spun around in his desk chair to look out the window again, at the transport planes landing and taking off.

The next few days flew by, and Johns was busy making arrangements for the summit. Both advance Secret Service teams had arrived, secured quarters for the two presidents, and were going over the plans for getting their respective presidents there with a smooth efficiency that Johns approved of. Bride and his SEAL teams were dug in around the base for sniper-countersniper precautions, and he had Lieutenant Brady and Lieutenant Evans sweeping the country-side with the Eighty-Second Airborne farther out. Looking Glass was monitoring all air traffic. They had BigEye drones aloft as well as a contingent of stealth helos with quick response teams. His air patrols were burning copious amounts of jet fuel monitoring the situation under the guise of escorting the transport planes in and out of their airspace, and everything seemed on the level.

Comms was monitoring all surface chatter in the Lower 48, and nothing seemed out of the ordinary. He had even set up a few stealth satellites to keep an eye on Mount Weather and Sacramento. He could count the buttons on a woman's blouse from eighteen miles up. Everything was going smoothly, everything was happening according to plan, yet Johns could not shake the feeling that he was missing something, something obvious.

Dismissing the impending summit for the moment, he signed off on some local reports. Most of the major metro areas in his AO were clear of civil unrest and had lights and power restored. People were having their ration cards issued, health care administered, and some were being allowed to return home. Essential services and resources were being moved out to camps for the dislocated and those displaced by The Day. His numbers were starting to come in for technicians and essential job fields. One of his people had rec-ommended that they take a census and find out who knew how to do what, and that was satisfying, putting people to work. They had managed to send troops out to cordon off contaminated zones, do triage on the wounded, and arrange more serious cases to be flown out of country to specialists in unaffected zones.

There had been no more ugliness on military reservations or impacts on civilian leadership since the initial few days of the crisis, and Johns was grateful for that. Common sense seemed to be taking precedence for a change. Oh, there were bureaucratic squabbles, cries for more resources, but he felt that they were getting what they could to where it was most seriously needed, and things hadn't boiled over into violence again.

Finally, the day of the summit arrived. Johns was still nervous, but it all seemed to be going according to plan. He visited SATCOM again, watching footage come in live of the two jumbo jets being prepped on their respective runways. He reviewed footage of the Western White House in Sacramento (even though it was painted a coral pink and done in a Mediterranean style). He viewed Mount Weather the same way. Everyone seemed to be behaving themselves. Around 1400 hours, flash traffic detected a tragedy unfolding in Europe. In a wave of violence that made his heart sink, he watched in horror as the Second Day attacks unfolded and the European democracies burned. They needed this summit more than ever now. The United States was on her own.

Well, there goes our foreign aid, he thought.

Johns watched personally as the presidential motorcades arrived at their respective airfields. Their escort fighters took off and maintained a holding pattern above. He watched Bowman board *Airforce 2.0* and Hotchkiss do the same. He watched their cabinets board, zooming in to see if his sister, Kath, was with Bowman, and it didn't look like she was. Both aircraft took off, and the acknowledgment came into the tower that they were on their way. Everything was ready. Everything was prepped. Now all Johns had to do was wait and see what was going to happen. He blinked and realized he was chewing a nail.

Calm down, he thought to himself. *Everything is going according to plan, and in a few hours, the civil war will be resolved. We will have one way forward, and we can get on with fixing the country. It's all going to work out just fine.*

Double Cross

CHAPTER 26

Hotchkiss, Mount Weather, Maryland,
December 5, 2016

Ted hung up the call with a sense of growing satisfaction. He had never really been a good actor, but he hoped that little display of gentile frustration and bizarre behavior had snowed them into thinking he was frazzled. He wasn't frazzled, but he *was* frustrated. Just the fact that Bowman had 70 percent of the domestic assets under his belt had given him pause. The program should have been working.

"No plan survives first contact with the enemy," he quoted to himself. If the country was resurrected, he planned on writing in his memoirs that they would definitely need to factor in an election-year scenario.

Hotchkiss informed his cabinet to begin preparations for the summit, which he had no intention of attending, but they didn't need to know that yet. He had concerns that Bowman had infiltrated his command structure, so he made absolutely sure to stick to the plan, just in case anyone was watching. The week went by quickly, and he made sure to play the part of a diplomat, sending his advance team to secure quarters and establish security. He didn't allow anyone to put any additional dirty tricks and safeguards in place.

That Colonel Johns was a crafty one. A crusader for democracy. A true believer. And men like that couldn't be bought or coopted or compromised as far as their values were concerned. Ms. Johns, his sister, was the same way, a superstar second-term senator from the state of California. Both were as clean as the driven snow; there simply wasn't any blackmail material available for either of them. Usually, Ted could find some kind of wedge to drive into a crack, but there was nothing, so it had to look like he was willing to compromise. Neither the colonel nor Bowman would be allowed to suspect that anything was out of the ordinary. He needed Bowman to go to Omaha.

A week and a half ago, his people had hacked into the information systems available to the opposition, in a passive way. They were monitoring, recording, and listening to everything said and not reacting in any way. Passive hacking let Hotchkiss see what his opponents were seeing, listen to what his opponents were listening to, and tap into the way they thought and acquire tactical information.

He had been right about Johns. He had no less than six SEAL teams in position, the Eighty-Second Airborne, drones, and covert aircraft available. They were mounting round-the-clock SATCOM intel, drone coverage, and chatter monitoring. That was frustrating in and of itself, but it would work right into his plans. He was counting on them watching him. He had taken great pains for them to see what he looked like so they would know whom to look for on the day of the summit.

Hotchkiss had acquired a nonconventional suitcase nuke from his special ops people. It was a low-yield weapon, about six kilotons, enough to level Offutt and everyone in it. He had also acquired a suitcase monitor with satellite-uplink capabilities that would allow him to be "present" to talk to Bowman. He planned on sending his entire cabinet along with a lookalike on his Air Force One Boeing 757. Getting his people to Offutt, delivering his message, and coercing the rival president and his cabinet onto *his* plane was how things were going to work. If not, then there would be another "unfortunate" nuclear attack on American soil, easily linked to terrorists, and unfortunately, the president and all his people would be dead. Who better to pick up the pieces than Ted Hotchkiss? So either Bowman agreed to be placed under arrest and brought back to Mount Weather or *boom*! He couldn't wait to see the look on the guy's face when presented with the option. Surrender or die. He was planning on sending Sue from DHS to be his unwitting messenger. She wouldn't even know until they were airborne that there was a nuclear weapon on the flight. It would be interesting.

While they were flying there, he would be flying to a different hardened facility in Kentucky. The week went by quickly, and he maintained his facade of nervous energy, talking to his people about how he hoped the summit would go well, that there was a way planned forward for reconciliation. He wasn't sure whom Bowman had subverted on his staff yet, but he could figure that out later.

Finally, the day arrived. The plane was fueled, and his escort was in the air, a refueling tanker on position in case it was needed. Hotchkiss nodded to his chauffer as he entered the limousine, a briefcase in each hand. No one had ever noticed how alike the two men looked. Hotchkiss glanced up as he stepped into the car. *Are you watching, James? How about you, Colonel Johns? Keep your eye on the marble.* Once he was in his limo with Sue, the chauffer got into the driver's seat and then slid over to the passenger side. The other man in front took the wheel and began driving them to the airstrip. His chauffer wormed through the divider, and the two men began changing clothes.

"What the hell is going on, Mr. President?" Sue asked, scandalized.

"Simple, Sue. I'm not going to the summit," he replied through his shirt. They had ten minutes to drive to the airstrip.

"Excuse me, you're what?"

"I'm not going, Sue. You are. And the rest of the cabinet is. But I'm not. I'm gonna do this one remotely. See?" He pointed at the attaché case with the satellite monitor inside.

"With all due respect, sir, are you out of your mind?"

"Never been better, Sue," he said with a wink. "Alan here is going to take my place boarding the plane so that they think I am onboard, and the rest of the cabinet are going to board afterward from their own cars. No one needs to know until you get airborne that I'm not there, okay?"

"Yes, sir, but I'm a little confused. You called for this summit, made all the arrangements, planned everything out, including the menu, so what's the point? We could have done another conference call from the situation room."

"The point, Sue, is that we need to get Bowman to Omaha somehow, and from there, you guys will be bringing him back on my plane."

Sue opened her mouth to ask just how in the world she was going to accomplish that.

"Trust me, Sue," Hotchkiss said, "once he listens to what I have to say from the SatLink, he will run to get on that plane. I'm going to talk him into it."

The two men were finishing their changes.

"When you get on Air Force One, Alan, give Sue the two briefcases. The first one is my SatLink, and when you meet Bowman, make sure to open it up, and I'll take everything from there. The second briefcase is a surprise. Just keep it by your chair, all right? Bowman may ask for it, and feel free to give it to him, but you must wait until he asks."

Hotchkiss grinned and then squeezed through the partition to the front seat.

The car pulled up to the base of the jet, and Ted got out, adjusting his cap. He walked to the passenger door, and opened it. Alan got out, and Ted winked at him. "Mr. President," he said.

Alan and Sue walked up the gangway, and Ted got back in, driving the armored limousine to a nearby hangar. He got out inside and watched as the rest of the president's cabinet boarded the jet and flew off into the sunset.

"Mr. President, your jet is ready, sir."

"Well, do you think they bought it?"

"I guess we'll find out, sir."

Hotchkiss nodded.

"I guess we will."

Hail to the Chiefs

CHAPTER 27

Sacramento, California
December 11, 2016

James Bowman was going over a few points that he'd like to make at the summit that evening when there was a polite knock on the office door.

"Come in!" he called.

His Secret Service agent opened the door and ushered in Senator Kathie Johns.

"Hi, Kathie! Come on in and have a seat. I'll be right with you."

"Mr. President," she said warmly.

James wrote a few notes in the margins of the document he was working on quickly so that he'd remember his train of thought later and closed the file folder.

"Thanks for meeting with me and taking a little time out of your undoubtedly busy day."

"Well, here I am," she said with a wry grin.

"How are things out there?"

"Well, like you said, busy. I'm happy that I already have an office here in Sacramento, and it helps to be the local girl on the ground, coordinating between local governments, law enforcement, the Army, FEMA, and your office, sir. But it's getting done and, so far, with a minimum of griping by all the respective agencies involved."

"Good, good," Bowman said, nodding in agreement. "I bet you're wondering why I asked you here today. Right?"

She nodded.

"You probably think it has something to do with the summit, right?"

She nodded again.

"Well, it does, and it doesn't," he replied. "Sam Clark has been after me to appoint a vice president, and based on everything I have seen so far and with the limited pool of qualified individuals we have, I would like to offer you the job."

Her mouth dropped open for a moment, in a very satisfying way, and Bowman hid a grin.

"With all due respect, Mr. President, you must be joking. I am not even a member of your party. I voted for the other guy, remember? It was just plain luck that I was on Catalina, meeting with you on The Day, and not in the Bay Area or Washington, DC. After that, I sort of just got caught up in things. Now that we're back in Sac, I was kind of getting my feet back under me and doing what I can to represent my state and my constituents."

"I see," Bowman said, pausing for a moment. "Aside from party politics and disagreeing with me on a number of issues, I thought we were finding quite a bit of common ground."

"We are, sir, and I remember you reaching out across the aisle quite a bit when you were a senator. That still doesn't change the fact that we come from very different political backgrounds."

Bowman thought for a minute and then walked over to a mission-style buffet at the side of the office. He poured himself a drink.

"Want one?" he asked.

"Good stuff?"

"Of course. I'm the president now. Rank has its privileges, you know."

"Then, yes, sir, I will join you in a drink."

"Want it straight up or over ice?"

"Straight up, if you don't mind, sir."

Bowman poured two fingers' worth of scotch into a tumbler and brought both drinks back to the desk.

"When our country was founded," he began, "before the two-party system that we now own to our dubious credit, the runner-up in the general election became the vice president of the United States. Did you know that? Two men would hit the campaign trail with very different political views, campaign against each other, and the second-place guy took the number 2 spot in office. I have always felt that maybe that approach supplied a balance to the executive branch in the early years of our republic."

"Again, Mr. President, I am a member of the Democratic Party, and you, sir, are very much a Republican. Maybe that's the way that it was then, but we *do* have two parties now. And besides, I didn't run against you. So what's your point? If I had, I would have won," she said with a twinkle in her eye.

Bowman sighed then laughed.

"Look, Kathie," he began, "Democrat, Republican, we have the same goals now, rebuilding the country. The people need strong leadership and a balanced approach to things. Maybe all that bullshit mattered before The Day, or maybe it never did, and we fooled ourselves into thinking that way, but for whatever reasons, that world is gone now. It's just us. You're a moderate, sharp. You have good leadership skills. I was thinking on Catalina, on The Day, that it was a shame to let the Obama staffers from the transition team go, that there were a lot of bright folks in that group, but that party politics wouldn't let me keep them, and now I can! I have a scary, competent team of people working for me because they have to compromise on their proposals and, don't get me wrong, they fight like cats and dogs! I get the very best results presented to me, and it's working! For the first time in thirty years, government is actually working for the people and not the other way around. We have had four major power plants come back online already in three weeks, communications are back up more or less, people are starting to return home, folks are getting the health care and medical attention that they need, and we are putting people to work in droves. All because of a horrible accident that occurred, I will have the most bipartisan administration in history. With the exception of the country east of the Appalachians, the part that is directly under Hotchkiss's thumb, America is lining up nicely with the goals that we have set. We're going to do it! Wouldn't you like to be part of that? You'd be a heartbeat away from this office. Won't you think about that?"

She sighed, staring into her drink for a moment.

"To your credit, Mr. President, I will think about it. Can I have a few days before I get back to you?"

"Of course," he replied, "but think about this. I'm headed off to this summit tonight in Omaha, and based on what we know about this Hotchkiss fella, he's got a trick up his sleeve. There's a very real possibility that you could be the president as of midnight. I hope not, but there it is. Sam Clark has been after me for this very reason. There was one direct attempt on my life and two more that we got to before the plotters could act. I like your brother, by the way. That was well done out there in Omaha. I might try to bribe him onto my staff at some point as well."

"Good luck with that, Mr. President. David has always—and I mean always—gone his own way. It was positively infuriating when we were kids!" she said with a laugh, and Bowman joined her.

"I'm stealing two moderate judges from this state and one from Nevada for the Supreme Court as well. I have a whole stack of records to go through at some point to appoint them. I wish we had been able to save a third senator on The Day. That way, we could have Senate confirmation hearings with a majority vote."

She laughed. "Let me guess, two senators with an R behind their name and me so that it would be two to one on every appointment?"

"Actually, on a more serious note, we should have a few more before too much longer," Bowman said with a grin. "Hawaii and Alaska are each appointing two. The governor here is going to be appointing one, seeing as how one seat is already filled. Two if you take my offer. The governor of Nebraska is appointing a pair, Maine, and Texas. So at some point real soon, we will have the beginnings of a real representative government again. Executive, legislative, and judicial. Then we can all go back to playing golf and living the good life, making speeches, and getting fancy perks from lobbyists."

"So that was it, sir? This was a recruiting effort?"

"Yes, ma'am."

"I'll think about it, Mr. President."

"You do that," he replied as she rose to leave. "And, Kathie?"

She turned at the door.

"You're doing a great job out there. I mean it!"

Bowman shook his head and put Kathie Johns on the back burner. He had a feeling she would come around, and based on what he'd seen since The Day, she was just the right person for the job. He had a few other choices, but he had wanted to talk to her first.

He spent the rest of the afternoon going over what he was going to say to Hotchkiss. He also had to be very careful about how he said it. He had no intention of backing down, and Hotchkiss seemed like the type that would go for the kill as soon as there was blood in the water. He also had a weakness. People had been underestimating James Bowman his entire life, people just like Mr. Ted fucking Hotchkiss. They always ended up being incredulous when they lost. Bowman planned on giving that chump enough rope to hang himself with, and then he was going to, James had no doubt.

Hotchkiss. Bowman had been looking over Hotchkiss's staff at the same time he had been inspecting Bowman's people on the video conference call a week before. A familiar face had been in the background from the days when he had been new to the hill. Craig Kilbourne was involved in the program. That had come as a bit of a surprise. He was a Washington insider and had served as a senior aide to Senator Trujillo on the Senate Armed Services Committee. Bowman remembered him and Carl palling around together, playing basketball, and attending social events, dating in the same circles. It hadn't taken much to get the number from Carl's cell phone. Right after the meeting last week, he had texted Kilbourne and been pleasantly surprised when he received an immediate response. Kilbourne was unhappy with the situation out east and had been feeding Bowman updates as the week progressed. It seemed that everything was on the level for the summit this evening.

At 2:00 p.m., things took another lurch to the surreal, and he joined the rest of his staff, watching events unfold in Europe. Another sixty or so nuclear detonations, mostly in Western Europe, but a few in the former Soviet satellites as well. The Second Day attacks. It looked like what was left of the United States was on its own for the moment. The Middle East was toast as well. Netanyahu had been true to his word. Backed into a corner, Israel had unleashed hell.

Suddenly, the president felt very old and very vulnerable. He left the briefing room feeling ten years older than he had going in. The country and the world needed this summit to go off without a hitch, and it was with some relief that his aides informed him that their jet was prepared for anytime he was ready to leave. It wasn't Air Force One, of course; that old girl had died on the ground in DC on The Day. It was a nice, newer 757, though, and it would do in a pinch.

Bowman spent a little time with his wife and kids, like he traditionally did before any diplomatic trip, and made sure to tell them that he loved them. He dressed presidential in a suit that cost more than he had made in a year back in the old days, petted the dog, grabbed his attaché case, and stepped into the limousine. Senator Paulson would be joining him and his staff for this trip to Nebraska. Kathie Johns and Carl would be staying in California.

He was about to climb the stairs on the Jetway when his phone pinged. Looking down, he read "Ghost en route" and grinned. Hotchkiss was on his way.

He was settling into his first-class seat when his cell rang again.

"Mr. President? I'm glad I caught you before takeoff. It's Kathie Johns."

"Yes, Kathie? I only have a minute here."

"I've thought about it all afternoon, and I'd like to take you up on your offer, sir."

"I'm glad to hear that, Kathie. That's great news! Tell you what, talk to Sam Clark, and I think he can take care of the details! You can even have the pick of my Obama staffers, if you want them," he said with a smile in his voice.

"Thank you for this opportunity, sir. I won't let you down."

"All right. We have to roll here, Kathie. I'll talk to you when I get back."

"Good luck, Mr. President!"

Smiling, Bowman powered down his phone. Well, that was one less thing to worry about.

* * *

Sue Stevens looked out the window of the 757 at their fighter escort and nodded. She had always liked looking at fighter jets—she loved air shows. Something about the sheer deadliness and speed both fascinated and enthralled her. They had finally reached cruising altitude, and she opened the attaché case containing the SatLink and powered up the screen. It pinged a few times, searching for its counterpart, and in a few moments, Ted Hotchkiss's face appeared onscreen.

"Hi, Sue, I was sorry to dump this little errand on you last minute, but I think everything is going to work out just fine."

Sue plugged an earbud into her ear and attached her jaw mike, effectively making the conversation private. Most of the staff hadn't realized the president wasn't on board yet.

"Do you think you can explain to me, sir, just exactly what we are supposed to accomplish on the ground in Omaha?"

"Well, Sue, that's simple," Hotchkiss replied. "I gave you *two* briefcases, right?"

"Yes, Mr. President," she replied.

"The SatLink will allow me to speak with Bowman, essentially ordering him onto your plane after the meeting. The second attaché case has a small-yield nuclear weapon inside it that will vaporize Offutt AFB and all involved if he doesn't comply. Cool, huh?"

Sue paled visibly and swallowed while Hotchkiss laughed.

"He's going to *run* to get on that plane when I am done with him, Sue. Don't worry, I don't think you or any of the other guys are in any danger. We'll take Mr. Bowman and company into custody for safekeeping for the duration of the crisis, and I can get on with fixing things."

"Sir, how do you know that he hasn't left orders to do the same to Mount Weather?"

"He wants to believe that everything is a go with this summit, Sue. He's an optimist, but just in case he's a little sneakier than I thought, I am no longer at Mount Weather. I'm headed for the fall-back position. Remember where that is?"

"Yes, Mr. President," she whispered.

"Good. Let me know when you land. It should be another two and a half hours or so, right?"

"Yes, Mr. President."

* * *

Hotchkiss had boarded his executive-class Gulfstream Sabre for the flight to Kentucky. They had departed a few minutes after the 757 took off. He lounged in his extracomfortable seat. He had spared no expense for this beauty of a plane and had had it brought up to Mount Weather at the first opportunity. There was even a bedroom in the back, with silk sheets for long international flights. Gold fittings, expensive creamy leather, even the cockpit was luxurious for his well-pampered staff. Sometimes he'd go up and hang out with the crew. But not today. The flight to Kentucky had to weave its way through restricted airspace, so he'd be arriving at the cave about the same time that the others would be arriving in Omaha. No worries. He might even take a nap. All was well with the world, except for Europe and the Middle East, of course, but he was extremely confident that this little civil dispute in the country would be resolved by early evening.

His phone pinged, and he looked down to see the message, "Eagle aboard." Grinning, he powered down his phone, flipped off his SatLink, put his arm around the waist of his *very special* Argentinian stewardess, and walked back to the bedroom.

* * *

Craig Kilbourne was texting Bowman furiously. He had caught a glimpse of Hotchkiss in videoconference with Sue Stevens and, after walking casually through the flight, realized that the president was not aboard. "Ghost not coming. Summit is a sham. Have no details. Something is up." He had gone to the washroom to send the messages. He hoped Bowman had his phone on. He tried Carl next. He had been pleased to find out that he was Bowman's chief of staff.

Since he was *still* Bowman's chief of staff, that meant that he had turned as well; otherwise, he would have been swept up in the purge after the coup attempt.

* * *

Carl looked at his phone and read the message from Craig Kilbourne and sighed. Too bad. He had rather liked Craig, but he was going to have to go. Carl hoped Bowman left his phone off for the duration of the flight. They were too close now to having this situation resolved rather bloodlessly. It could have been way worse. Bowman was competent enough, but he didn't have the experience and the credibility with the program members to win over their confidence. That he had been the sitting president was one thing, but that sham of a swearing in ceremony had left a bad taste in Carl's mouth. Now he was appointing Supreme Court justices, and for all Carl knew, he was looking at a replacement VP. That would cause all kinds of problems and deepen the rift between the two governments. He had been working tirelessly with Hotchkiss to bring this summit off in addition to doing the necessary duties of a chief of staff. Hotchkiss had endorsed every project that Carl had worked on, as it was for the greater good, restoring infrastructure and solving problems. Doing his job while doing his job was exhausting, though, and he was looking forward to putting all this double-dealing behind him.

He still wasn't sure how he had avoided the purge of program assets in Sacramento, but he had been taking full advantage. He had texted Hotchkiss immediately upon receiving Kilbourne's text, forwarding the contents. He hoped Ted had his phone on. Carl moved forward to first class to keep Bowman occupied and distracted until they touched down in Omaha.

* * *

Bowman suppressed a grimace as Carl came forward to sit next to him. He had been trying to keep him busy with projects that both Hotchkiss and himself could agree on, restoring infrastructure and managing the day-to-day stuff that Bowman didn't have time for himself. He hadn't assigned him anything too sensitive, though. He didn't want any unfortunate mistakes to sabotage his hard work so far. Carl was an excellent manager, and that was why he had hired him in the first place. This betrayal with the program had cut him to the quick. Bowman didn't accept or approve of any of it. He had understood the necessity of it when he had read the briefing, but as far as he was concerned, the United States *had* a civilian leadership, and this Hotchkiss fellow was an unnecessary redundancy. The program should have stayed inactive once it was ascertained that the country had a president. Carl should have known better. Bowman had been feeding him bullshit ever since he had read the name on the list. He had been having him quietly watched ever since he found out. He was really looking forward to firing him after the summit. Bowman smiled and greeted Carl and asked him if he needed anything. Inside he was seething.

* * *

Colonel Johns had been watching the flights from Mount Weather and Sacramento respectively ever since they had taken off. The drone coverage and SatCom data was actually kind of interesting in a way. He almost wished he had gone into that branch of the service. The satellite watching Mount Weather had picked up another jet taking off after Hotchkiss. A really sleek executive Gulfstream. That wasn't too unusual. There was a lot of smaller, fast private transport moving around. What was unusual was the fighter escort accompanying it.

"I wonder where you're going," he murmured. Knowing Hotchkiss, he knew somehow it was another scheme of some kind.

"Control, place a tracker on that Gulfstream for me, would you?" he asked.

"Yes, sir."

Security was at its highest level. So far, his perimeter was clear. There were no bad guys out there, but the feeling he was missing something hadn't left him for the last five days. He had doubled down on everything. A mouse wouldn't be able to fart within five miles of Offutt without him knowing about it in seconds. He was paranoid as hell and couldn't wait for this summit to be over.

"Sir, we have flash traffic from NORAD."

"Put it through, please." The two 757s were fifteen minutes out, and local air traffic control was lining them and their fighter escorts up for final approach. He was planning on landing Bowman first. He hoped the pettiness of it would get Hotchkiss's panties in a bunch. He might even leave him circling for a few minutes just for spite.

"Launch! We have launch! Multiple ICBMs launching from Atlantic and Pacific sites!"

"Say again, NORAD?"

"We have multiple incoming warheads, ocean-launched over the eastern and western seaboards!"

"Get Space Command up on the screen," Johns ordered tightly. Coincidence or planned? "How close are we to landing presidential aircraft?"

"ETA ten minutes, sir."

"Tell them to punch it. We have a situation here!"

Johns watched helplessly as the missiles went hypersonic, streaking through the upper atmosphere.

"Detonation! We have detonation! Multiple detonations! Go dark for pulse!"

Johns closed his eyes. Prayed.

"Rebooting systems."

"Sir, we have lost contact with Air Force One."

"Which one?" Johns asked tonelessly.

"Both of them, sir."

* * *

They were seven minutes out from Offutt, and Carl grinned inside. He had done it! The president hadn't turned his phone on. The captain had just announced final approach, everyone was strapped in, and suddenly, the lights went out, the engines just stopped, and the 757 started to fall straight down and to the left. Everyone was screaming, and the jet was dropping like a rock from twelve thousand feet up. Everyone except the president. Bowman looked at Carl with a ghastly grin.

"Did your boss plan this, Carl? Is this Hotchkiss's doing? Was it worth it, you little shit? You just killed the country with your fucking *program!*"

From the cockpit, he could hear the pilots trying to call in the mayday. *He knew!* That was the last thought Carl had as they crashed into the Nebraska countryside.

Sue Stevens pinged the president that they were on final approach. She had calmed down substantially since the initial call a few hours earlier. She was a professional, and this wouldn't be the first tight situation she had been in. Somehow, they would all get out of this and finally start addressing the details that the program had been designed to deal with. They were about ten minutes out when she heard alarms from the cockpit, and suddenly, the plane's engines just shut off, and they were in free-fall from sixteen thousand feet. She wondered wildly if somehow Bowman had found out about the summit. This wasn't supposed to happen. Who would run the program now? She looked out the window at the ground rushing up to meet them and giggled as a fighter jet's pilot ejected from his cockpit, then she screamed as the F-18 slammed into the fuselage of the 757. An enormous fireball erupted, and the remains of the two planes were scattered over six square miles of Nebraska farmland.

Ted Hotchkiss smiled smugly and enjoyed the view as his stewardess poured herself another glass of champagne. He was reknotting his tie, and she was wearing nothing but the silk sheet and one stocking. He had just turned his cell phone back on when it pinged. He read the text message with a little irritation. Kilbourne hadn't been on his short list for leaks, but Carl's forwarded message made sense now. He wished he had seen that earlier. He would have had him taken into custody. With a mental shrug, he finished tying his tie. His phone pinged again, and he saw the message from Sue that they were on final approach. Good. The captain had informed him a short while ago that they were about seventeen minutes out from the private airstrip at the cave.

"Better get dressed, mi amor. We're almost there," Hotchkiss said to her reflection in the mirror.

"Okay," she said, stepping out of bed and looking for her clothing.

Hotchkiss stepped through the bedroom doorway to the small lavatory and closed the door. He had just unzipped his fly and was taking a leak when the plane did a barrel roll and the chemical-blue fluid, combined with urine in the toilet, doused him. It went in his mouth! *His mouth!* He was soaked. His Armani suit was ruined, and he was filthy. Gagging and choking, Hotchkiss screamed in rage and frustration. He was going to *kill* those worthless fucking pilots. He was going to *kill* them. He was the president of the United States! He was . . .

He was dead.

The gulfstream slammed into the mountainside and erupted in a devastating explosion.

All over North and Central America, aircraft dropped from the sky, and the lights went out. The United States entered a new phase of darkness. They were really on their own.

Davis and Beyond

CHAPTER 28

From the Journal of H. Rayton Townsend
December 12, 2016
Clay, California

This is my first opportunity to write anything in the last few days. Something huge has happened. We stopped in Davis just two mornings ago, yet what has transpired since then feels almost as if months have passed. The whole world has really changed now. We are free for the moment to continue, but we almost got stuck again. I think a lot of people are going to die now.

* * *

Davis, California,
December 10, 2016

Ray, Carly, and Kyle were approaching the outskirts of Davis, California. They had been seeing air traffic all morning—jets, transport planes, helicopters, that kind of thing. It almost felt . . . well, normal. They were regular enough in their appearances for everything to seem normal. It was a good sign that something was being done. The university in Davis drew them in like a magnet, and they seemed to be doing all right there. The power was on, things were organized on campus, and the three of them were able to do some laundry and take a glorious, hot shower for the first time in what felt like forever. It had been a few days since they had left Winters, mostly traveling at night.

The university still had that atmosphere of compressed energy that places of higher learning all seemed to have. Young people with ideas and the young at heart always seemed to have that effect. Apparently, they still had sporadic Internet service, and news was trickling in a little at a time. News from overseas, Canada, Mexico, the Lower 48 in isolated areas, and so forth. Sometimes it was a five-minute clip of a nuclear detonation; other times it was demonstrations of thousands waving small flags or burning flags. Ray couldn't make sense of a lot of it. The students, though, were gathering information like squirrels stored away nuts for winter. Every sound byte, every news clip was posted and reposted to advance one theory after another. There was so much raw data available, but Ray didn't have a context to fit it into for his worldview to make sense. It had been twenty four days since The Day, and a lot, it seemed, had been happening.

They were so busy gathering information and speculating excitedly about what was going on that Ray thought wryly they hadn't yet fully considered the implications of what they were talking about. A few seemed to get it; they were the quiet ones, laying plans. The rest were almost giddy with speculation, gloating over the dark paradise that they fantasized about but really, really wouldn't want to live in that was evolving while they hunted nuts. The reality, the *realness* of the life he and his friends had been living hadn't set in yet for most of them. It would in time, probably very soon, and he wondered how many of these kids would be alive by this time next year. Until it did, though, he planned to milk as much information out of them as he possibly could. They were happy to show him.

There were a million theories about the bombs. That was bombs—*plural*, it seemed. SF, LA, Seattle, Portland, and Phoenix were confirmed. There had been another detonation somewhere in Nevada, Las Vegas probably, a few others farther east, but nothing was coming out of those areas yet. Some speculated that that crazy guy in North Korea, the one with a bad haircut, had pulled the trigger. Others claimed it was everything from Mexican Narcotraffickers to Russian mobsters, Islamic extremists, or Central American rebel groups. Whatever had happened was pretty scary, though, and it was much bigger than they had thought.

When they had first arrived on campus in the morning, the big news was the Middle East. Netanyahu and the Israeli Knesset had nuked the entire Muslim world into radioactive dust, from the west coast of Africa all the way to Indonesia. There were two presidents as well, it seemed. Bowman, the president elect, and some guy out east named Hotchkiss; they had been exchanging a constant stream of threats and statements that had largely gone unnoticed in the aftermath of The Day. He was in some kid's dorm room, looking over his shoulder at a news feed from the BBC somewhere in Europe, when a Breaking News icon flashed across the screen. The student clicked the link, and Ray was appalled to see a map of Europe with icons flashing around just about every major European city. The West had just taken a terminal blow.

"There goes our foreign aid. *Fuck!*" he whispered.

"What was that, man?" the kid asked, looking over his shoulder.

"Nothing," Ray replied. "Hey, thanks for letting me watch that. Take care of yourself."

He practically ran to find Carly and Kyle. Ray had had high hopes that San Francisco had been a one-off. A really horrible *localized* event. As if a nuclear detonation was a localized thing. It wasn't. Five confirmed strikes and a possible sixth in the United States made his blood run cold. With what he had just seen about the Middle East and Europe, it was a full-blown international crisis now. They were *so* screwed. With the western half of the country on life support and in chaos and Europe having just been removed from the equation, this was bad. Very, *very* bad. It might even mean that he wasn't going to find that Greyhound bus ticket home. He talked to as many kids as he could, marking his atlas with what was known to be true, what people were speculating on, rumors, and half-baked ideas. He made notes along the way.

He finally found Kyle and Carly sitting by the fountain on campus and eating oranges. *Oranges!*

"There he is," Kyle said. "Here, have an orange."

"Thanks," Ray said absently, looking around. "We need to get moving, guys. It's bad."

He noted that Kyle had acquired a nice new winter coat from somewhere.

"What is bad, Ray?" Carly asked. "You look like your pony died."

"I think it did."

They glanced at each other then looked at him.

He told them.

They agreed with him that things were about to get a lot worse. That they shouldn't be too forthcoming about their destination from here on out. Just in case. The three of them got what sleep they could before pressing on at nightfall. I-80 was still their best bet and the fastest, straightest route to the cabin.

Ray had been leading the way, hiking quietly along the side of the interstate for about three hours. He guessed it was getting close to 11:00 p.m. when he heard a stick snap off to the side of the road. It was *so* dark out there. The three of them froze in place, straining to hear something. They watched the sides of the road for danger. They waited that way for almost five minutes.

"Probably a deer or a coyote," he whispered, shrugging.

Taking a deep breath, he started walking again. Someone ahead stepped into the road.

"Stop right where you are!"

"*Shit!*" Ray muttered as perhaps eight more soldiers appeared from either side of the interstate. They had walked right into a checkpoint.

The original soldier approached until he was right in front of them. He had three stripes on his sleeves.

"Well, three more." He shook his head.

"Sergeant," Ray began, "we are just trying to—"

"Shut. Up. Listen to me," he rasped out. "I am *tired* of being up all night *every* night because stupid fucking civilians like you are too fucking stupid or inconsiderate to follow *directions*! Got it? There is a *curfew* in effect. Iit starts at *sundown*, and that means that wherever you are when it gets dark, you *stay there* until it gets light outside again. You don't go wandering around! We have had to *shoot* people, and I am getting pretty fucking tired of that too. Johnson, Edwards, Get up here!"

"Sergeant!"

"Check 'em for weapons and ammo and dump 'em in with the rest."

"Yes, Sergeant!"

After being frisked, they were made to dump their packs out on the road and then hustled through repacking everything. They were herded up the roadway to a truck with one guard, where perhaps a dozen other people had already been loaded in the back.

"No talking. No noise," the guard said curtly before turning and jogging back the direction that they had come from.

Ray thought that sounded like excellent advice after being yelled at. His ears were still ringing from the dressing-down they had just received. The next few hours were tense as a few more were herded in and rounded up. It was about 4:00 am when the truck began to roll toward Sacramento. Ray had dozed on and off until the engine started, and then he got a spot by the tailgate so he could look out the back. Progress was swift until they hit the suburbs, then things slowed to a crawl. The roads were packed. Sacramento was being seriously fortified. There was vehicle traffic everywhere, the power was on, helicopters buzzed by overhead, and everywhere, there were people digging, building, doing roadwork, soldiers manning check-points, floodlights being inspected and installed. And barbed wire was being laid down. It looked like they were preparing for a siege.

For the first few hours, it had been too dark to write, so Ray had left his journal in his pack. He pulled out the atlas and began making notes in red ink very, very unobtrusively. The truck stopped around midday, and they were given rations and water and a chance to stretch and use the bathroom. Then they got back on the truck and continued. Eventually, around 6:00 p.m., they pulled into what appeared to be a very large refugee camp. Ray glanced at his map and saw that it was very close to an area that he had previously circled. The driver was about to park alongside many other trucks full of people when an MP on duty began waving his arms in a circular fashion, directing them back onto the road. Apparently, that camp had been full. He had already put his atlas away when another soldier jumped into the back of the truck with them before pulling out. They drove for two more hours. It was drizzling off and on again, and it was fairly dark outside. Ray was drowsy. They had spent all day just driving through Sacramento. Apparently, they were headed for a new camp just north of Galt, California, and they were almost there.

The sky suddenly went from pitch-black to daylight blue with scattered clouds for about four seconds. Then everything died. The truck engine just quit, and the long line of trucks following them had apparently done the same. The glow of lights over Sacramento blinked out. Ray even thought he heard a plane going down somewhere nearby, and it was confirmed a few seconds later by a loud *crump* and a fireball maybe six miles away in the hills. Ray could see other aircraft dropping from the sky like meteors.

"What the fuck?" the soldier breathed out just as another flash appeared in the sky farther east.

Ray lit a match for light just in time to see one of his truck mates looming over the soldier. It burned out just as he was punched in the face with a meaty sound. Then things were happening very, very quickly. Ray jumped out the back of the truck and was followed immediately by Kyle and Carly. They took off for the side of the road, slipped over the barbed wire fence, and then just ran pell-mell into the darkness.

Behind them, shots rang out, people were screaming, and farther back, one of the trucks that had been in their convoy was burning. They just simply ran and ran until they couldn't run anymore. The three of them found a small ravine and huddled together for warmth. They slept straight through until dawn the next morning. When they awoke, they were three miles from the town of Clay, California.

* * *

Kyle woke Ray with a hand over his mouth. Carly was rigid next to them, staring wide-eyed at the large bull eying them curiously from about ten feet away. The bull snorted, blowing steam from his nostrils. He pawed the ground a few times, and Carly squeaked. Then he seemed to be distracted by something, and he trotted away, little tail held straight up in the air like a flag. Everyone exhaled the breath they had been holding.

"We're getting too old for shit like that," Kyle muttered, standing up and looking around.

A roadway ran by about four hundred feet from where they had been holed up, sleeping. The three of them made their way quickly over to it and through the fence nearby, stepping onto the paved surface.

Ray scanned the horizon, and in the distance, tiny columns of smoke rose into the air, scattered over a broad area.

"You guys have *any* idea where we are?" he asked.

"No clue," Kyle replied.

Carly shook her head.

"That was some crazy shit last night, huh?"

"Yeah. We got lucky, I think," Ray replied.

The sun was just peeking over the foothills to the east and the mountains beyond them. The grass was white with frost. Their breathing made plumes in the air, and it was quiet. Nothing was moving anywhere except the bull in the distance. They all had to pee, and once the call of nature was satisfied, they began walking along the roadway, heading northeast. It was a two-lane country road, the kind with goblet-trained vineyards and small ranches that were so prevalent to Northern California. It never ceased to amaze Ray just how *big* this state really was and how little you actually had to travel to get away from the large population centers that crowded the transportation corridors. You could be surrounded by urban and suburban sprawl and find a completely uninhabited valley, or a mountain, or a beach just twenty minutes away by car. Of course, those estimates would need to be reevaluated now that cars wouldn't be running anymore.

"Either of you guys have a clue just what the fuck that was all about last night?" Carly asked in a low voice.

"EMP, I imagine," Kyle replied.

Carly gave him an exasperated look.

"Electromagnetic pulse," Ray said quietly. "It's a side effect of a nuclear explosion."

"So we have been reexposed to radiation? Is that it? We're all going to die now?" Carly was sounding a bit frantic. "That was right over our heads, Kyle! There were *two* of them!"

"I don't think it works that way," Kyle replied. "It looked like they were in outer space, too far away for the blasts to hit us. I watched a DVD about it once, called *The Rainbow Bombs* or something. Back in the sixties, they were testing nuclear weapons in space. It looked just like what we saw last night. Pitch-black and then daylight blue for a few seconds. Anyway, one of the big ones they tested apparently blacked out the entire Pacific Rim. That's when they figured out what it does and that nukes in space is probably a bad idea. That was the sixties. Can you imagine what EMP does today? Smartphones, tablets, all the electrical power that everyone relies on daily? Just to live? Man . . ." he trailed off.

"Well, the timing was perfect anyway. Whatever the point of it was, we'll never know, but we got away because of it."

"So nothing is going to work anymore?" Carly asked.

"Nope," Ray replied. "That's pretty much it for electric mixers, toasters, microwaves, DVD players, and the thousands and thousands of miles of electrical lines we have in the country. That's also it for my Greyhound ticket home. We're fucked. Welcome back to the eighteenth century, guys. *Two hundred years* of history just got erased."

They both looked at him.

"It's a lot different when it's happening, right?" he finally said.

"What?"

"I said it's a lot different when it is happening, the end of *everything*," Ray explained. "In a movie or a book about the end of the world, it always takes place *after* it is happening, decades, years. The hero always has the answers and the skills to survive. There is this mythology that has grown up around what happened, and everyone seems to know and accept the world the way that it is. There are hidden treasure troves of stuff just waiting to be discovered, and you just know that the guy it's written about is going to make it out of there against impossible odds. The villains he encounters are illiterate savages or cannibals, or they have forgotten how to make fire or something, or I don't know . . ." he trailed off, frustrated. "It's just that no one wrote about it while it was happening. The pain, the fear, the hunger, the cold, the leg cramps, the *violence and death!* The sudden sense that there is no safety anywhere! The hero is always some glib talking, svelte, know-it-all—*God*—kind of guy, a badass hero with crazy weapons and martial arts skills, and yet *here we are.* I am still overweight, out of shape, balding, and not sure of where our next meal comes from when we run out of food, walking along a two-lane road to God knows where, and I sure as shit don't know if we're gonna make it someplace safe or not! Do you?"

They just looked at him.

"Well, I am for sure *not* a fucking hero! We could get stuck in a camp, robbed, and killed for our boots or something terrible. We may *never* know what happened or *why* it happened or how big it is, and in the meantime, there are a lot of dangerous fucking people around while the world where we are tears itself to pieces. I wish someone would have written about that so I knew what to do!"

They all trudged along for a few more minutes, not saying anything. Carly and Kyle were kind of shocked, actually. This was the first time that Ray had complained about anything.

"This is the first holiday season I have had off in fifteen years," Ray muttered. "And it *sucks!*"

"The holidays can be a real drag, Ray," Kyle finally said. "A lot of people commit suicide this time of year."

"I can see why," Ray replied.

"Well, at least we have our health," Carly said brightly and so innocently that you couldn't even detect the sarcasm.

For some reason, they all came down with a case of the giggles.

They arrived in Clay fifteen minutes later.

* * *

Clay was a whole different mind-set than Winters or Davis had been. People weren't overtly hostile. Yet. Things were definitely different, especially with three strangers strolling into town like nothing was happening. They had decided to pass themselves off as through hikers on the Pacific Crest Trail. It ran near here and was the western equivalent of the Appalachian Trail that ran back east. They could explain their presence, lack of information, etc., that way without going into details of why they were there or where they were coming from. Clay was a little harder. A little more suspicious. You could tell that people here were going to hang on a little tighter, be a little slower to smile. It seemed amazing that it hadn't even been a month yet since The Day, but it was starting to sink in everywhere that people were soon going to be dying off in a big way. With winter coming, many more would be going soon.

Ray wouldn't be surprised if the aftermath of the bombs killed more people than the bombs themselves. He had the distinct impression that Clay would be happy to see their backs when they left town. The whole place was abuzz with the EMPs witnessed the night before. Everything had stopped working.

Once they knew where they were, they were able to sit down with the road atlas and figure out how to get where they were going. The cabin was at Lake Alpine, just a little under a hundred miles away. There was not a lot in the way of food and water to be had in Clay, so what they had now was going to have to last them until they got there. They needed to move faster somehow without depleting their supplies until they really needed them.

Ray had noticed a high-end bike shop as they had walked into town. Three mountain bikes would probably cost the earth, but they had to try.

Ray had sewn three ten-dollar gold pieces into the waistband of his pants before leaving Petaluma. Maybe the bike store would take them as payment for three bikes. He fingered the outlines of them lovingly. They were the last of the coin collection that he and his grandfather had worked on together from the time that Ray had been a small boy. They had been a gift to him the Christmas before his grandfather had passed away. All the other coins had been locked up in a bank deposit box on The Day, but Ray had always kept the gold ones with him. He liked looking at them occasionally. They came with good memories, and 1908S, 1910, and 1898, were the dates. He remembered that Christmas now. "Keep 'em, trade 'em, or pawn 'em, it's up to you. I just wanted you to have them. If you *do* decide to sell them, make sure that you get what they are worth. That's a fair amount of gold there." Then he had winked. He knew Ray would never sell the coins. Except now he had to *spend* them.

Sighing, he walked into the bike store.

The bike shop owner, after a little talking, had been open to the sale. Ray had seen the greed in his eyes when he flashed the first coin. He had hesitated, as if thinking hard, and pulled out a second coin as well. *That* had pretty much guaranteed that they were going to get three top-of-the-line bikes. Gold had been selling for $1,800 an ounce prior to The Day, and it hadn't yet sunk in what the EMPs meant to transportation. He had held back the one with the *S* mintmark. For some reason, it seemed like a talisman of good luck to carry a coin that had been minted in San Francisco. They were able to get three carbon nanofiber bikes with all the accessories and saddlebags in exchange for the two coins. A hundred miles to go on bikes. That seemed a little more reasonable.

Four hours later, as they were huffing and puffing their way into the foothills of the Sierras, Ray looked at Carly and Kyle and grinned.

"Best twenty bucks I ever spent!" he whooped. Clay lay twenty miles behind them.

"Eighty miles to go!" Kyle replied.

Then they were all too busy trying to breathe to try talking more. So they focused on pedaling instead. Ray hoped his grandfather would have understood.

Late-Night Television

Harley Earl spent the week following The Day mostly awake and watching television. He hadn't blinked or slept for three days. He was glued to the patchy, static-plagued satellite feeds coming in from around the world. Incomplete footage of nuclear detonations, governments and stock markets in disarray, communications gone, rioting, and the chaos that was going on in the United States. He watched celebrations in the Middle East, where American flags burned, and prayer vigils at the Vatican, where St. Peter's Square was filled with thousands of candles and silence. Governments were falling overnight and, sometimes, being replaced within twenty-four hours of that as more extreme groups took control. *Every* terrorist organization in the world wanted to claim responsibility for the November 17 attacks, it seemed. That only added to the confusion.

At the moment, he was drinking coffee and watching the Iranian president rally his people. Iran would "throw the remaining crusader armies into the sea," and the president was reaching out to Shia and Sunni alike to rise up and attack the invaders, from the youngest child to the oldest grandmother. "Now! *Now* is our chance to destroy them, to bring down that painted whore, that immoral prostitute Israel . . . that unnatural plague upon the land." People, it seemed, were believing his message. Renewed violence across North Africa, the Middle East, across Afghanistan, Pakistan, and into Southeast Asia was the result. It testified to the convictions of the true believer.

He changed channels to a BBC newsfeed, where the British prime minister was promising aid to the United States. On another channel, the Chinese were offering the same, along with most European countries and Australia. Worldwide, the reactions were mixed. Some nations mourned for America, others rejoiced in her suffering, but most were stunned and feared for the future. Others everywhere plotted how to take advantage of it. *Change* was coming no matter what. Putin was quietly building up and preparing for something. What exactly that was had yet to be decided.

Sometimes he slept, sometimes he was awake. His systems recorded everything, burning backups to disc for future review and retrieval. Someday, if anyone survived, people might want to know what happened. Harley went on air twice a day to relay the information he was seeing. Hopefully, people were listening.

San Francisco, Los Angeles, San Diego, Portland, Seattle, Las Vegas, Denver, Albuquerque, Dallas, Houston, St. Louis, Chicago, Indianapolis, Minneapolis, New York, Philadelphia, Boston, Atlanta, Miami, New Orleans, Baltimore, Columbus, Charlotte, Nashville, Tampa, Fort Meyers, Little Rock, Green Bay, Phoenix, and Washington, DC, went up in flames, burning from existence in the first seventy-two hours. Millions were incinerated, and millions more were made homeless. The cities that weren't vaporized were abandoned by people, afraid that they might be next. The roads were choked with refugees. Several hundred thousand more were slowly freezing to death in the upper Midwest, with no power, water, supplies, or social services.

Chaos enveloped the country as people stockpiled and hoarded what they could gather. Social and legal precedents went right out the window in some cases. Road gangs coalesced almost overnight as the strong took from the weak, the helpless died, and those in between did whatever they had to to stay alive.

The thermal plumes from the detonations blasted superheated air and debris into the atmosphere in a toxic cloud that circled the earth seven times before its lethality dropped to normal. It disrupted weather and reflected light back into space. The Northern Hemisphere, already dealing with a strange early winter, froze even harder as the jet stream dipped down past Florida. It rained for a week in the Sahara Desert, seeds that had laid dormant for a thousand years bloomed suddenly, and nomadic herders stopped in awe of fields of flowers and plants that covered sand dunes as far as they could see. Drought racked the Southern Hemisphere, and crops failed. It snowed on the equator, and the climate went haywire trying to correct itself.

Globally, the political situation worsened. Governments in unstable areas rose and fell with more frequency, the Saudi Royal family fled to Britain, tensions escalated beyond belief between India and Pakistan, and it started as a conventional war that went nuclear in a heartbeat. Cities burned after missiles were launched, and one-fifth of humanity died on November 23. In poorer countries, dirty bombs were used, and biological and chemical weapons came out of hiding, including a nasty version of an airborne Ebola virus. The Israelis were under siege, and so far, they were holding their own.

Sleep and wake and watch television, rebroadcast, repeat. Harley fell into a new routine. On December 10, he watched the fall of Jerusalem. Later that day, he watched as the Islamic world burned. That afternoon, he watched the Second Day attacks in Europe. Putin was rolling through Eastern Europe with tanks before all footage cut off. Taiwan rejoined China without a shot being fired. Harley watched as station after station overseas went off the air permanently due to rioting or fallout or radiation screwing up the signal. He watched as two presidents threatened each other domestically. He slept for two days almost after that.

While Harley slept, something happened that he never saw coming—in fact, no one did. On the evening of December 11, two Iranian oil tankers arrived just about a hundred miles off the United States coastline. Two in the Atlantic Ocean and two in the Pacific. They were Iranian oil tankers, but they were flagged out of Yemen. The Iranians had been training for years to do what they were about to do. Since 2002, crews had trained to set up missile gantries on cargo ships and oil tankers and had actively been pursuing a "space program." That was what they were doing right now. These rockets would be shot into space; only they didn't carry a human payload.

These rockets were nuclear-tipped. The Ayatollah, along with the fundamentalist government, had wanted for years to initiate an EMP attack against the Americans, and that silly treaty from a few years before gave them the means to acquire the technology to do so. They would never have been able to engage the Americans in a stand-up nuclear engagement, but blacking out the North American continent seemed like the perfect way to remove them from the world scene permanently.

A total of eight missiles were fired into low earth orbit over the continental United States, Canada, Mexico, and Central America. Two splashed harmlessly into the ocean, but six hit their escape velocity and detonated right on target. The pulses of the detonations fried out every remaining circuit in North America, unless it was shielded, hardened, underground, or in a faraday cage. Power plants that had gone back online in the previous weeks since The Day stopped producing power, vehicles stopped running, aircraft dropped from the sky, and thousands of miles of high-voltage lines sizzled and warped from the energy surge.

When he got up to have his coffee on December 12, everything everywhere was off the air. Harley was truly alone now. That was definitely something to worry about.

CHAPTER 30

Stockville

The Friedmans took two vehicles into Stockville two days after the blackout. Everything was good. They were all together, and they were on a quest for information and supplies. Josh was hoping that some of his fellow ranchers were in town to swap materials and stories. The kids looked at it as a semipermanent vacation from school and were happy to just be doing something different.

Brian was getting a little worried about Trish. She was afraid of how much trouble they were going to be in when Mom and Dad found out that they were in Nebraska with the Friedmans. He knew now deep down inside that that was the least of their worries, but he reassured her anyways.

"They know, Trish," he said. "Remember? I left them a note."

"Okay," she replied. "I miss Mommy, though. Are we going home soon?"

"Maybe not for a few weeks, Trish," he replied, squeezing her hand.

"Are you sure, Brian? I mean really, really sure?"

"Yep, Trish, they know, and they are happy that we are here and that we are safe with the Friedmans."

"Okay," she replied, sounding mollified for the moment.

Abby had charge of the younger Friedmans for the moment, and she was having fun with them.

"Hey! You guys want to get some hot chocolate?" she asked.

The answer was a resounding yes, and they went into the ice cream shop across the street from the VFW, where the elder Friedmans were going to a meeting with other concerned citizens.

The next few minutes were some of the last unconcerned moments they were to have for some time. Everything happened very, very fast, and had Brian known what was about to happen, he would have savored them even more. Josh was licking the whipped cream from his hot chocolate, and so was Trish. Brian had just gotten his, and the two boys were planning on giving Abby a hard time for flirting with the kid working the counter when a single motorcycle went past on the street outside. Brian looked up through the plate glass window and saw him go by real slow, holding an assault rifle of some kind. Josh saw him too, and so did Abby.

"Cool," Josh said, pressing his face up against the glass.

"Guys, I think you should get away from the window," Abby said in a tight voice.

"Come on, Abs, that is *way* cool. You know it is. I bet that dude is a total bada—"

Brian was backing away when an explosion rocked the store next to them. The plate glass window shattered, and the ceiling tiles dropped from above in a shower of dust and debris. Brian took it all in, his hot chocolate forgotten, dripping over his hand. One snapshot at a time. Abby running for her brother curled up on the floor in front of the window, his hands wrapped around his bleeding scalp. Trish curled into a ball under one of the tables, screaming. The kid behind the counter running out of the back door of the store behind the freezers.

More explosions rocked Main Street, Stockville. The bikers, there were a lot of them now, were throwing lit sticks of dynamite into shop windows, hurling Molotov cocktails into vehicles. Brian watched in horror as Mr. Friedman ran out of the doorway of the VFW across the street, desperately searching for his children. Abby screamed a warning as a biker rumbled past, his arm back and then, moving forward with a samurai sword, decapitating him as he turned. The man on the bike turned circles in the street, gesturing with the bloody blade, his face a mask of rage and purpose. He was wearing a spiked helmet, the beard hanging down his chest braided and flapping in the wind as he roared off down the street. Mrs. Friedman was outside the VFW now, and Abby was helping Josh to his feet. She looked down at her husband, in total incomprehension, just as another biker flew past, hurling a Molotov cocktail into the open doorway behind her. Flames gouted out the doorway, her hair on fire, her clothes burning, as she ran up the street, unable to think as another biker cut her down. Her body lay in the street, burning. Trish was still screaming under the table. Brian took it all in, his chest hitching as he struggled for breath, looking both ways, sobbing. He ran across to Mr. Friedman's body and got the .45, crouching as bikers flew past to either side, then he ran back to the ice cream store. All over Stockville, shots, explosions, and screams rang out. Buildings were ablaze, and people ran and hid and were rooted out and killed.

Brian got Trish out from under the table and screamed out Abby's name. She looked up, stunned. Brian would forever remember the look in her eyes that day.

"This way!" he shouted, pulling Trish by the wrist toward the back door, where the counter jockey had fled. They emerged into an alleyway. There was a single biker sitting at the end of it, and he whooped as he saw the children exit the building. Gunning his engine, he began to ride toward them, presumably with the intention of riding them down. Brian shoved Trish back inside the doorway. Smoke was billowing out now. He flicked the safety off on the .45, pointed it at the biker, closed his eyes, prayed, and squeezed the trigger. The recoil ripped the gun out of his ten-year-old hands, and he dove back inside just as the biker flew past and crashed into a dumpster with a final-sounding heavy thud. The four of them ran outside and made their way down the alley.

At some point, Brian and Trish got separated from Abby and Josh. Brian still wasn't sure when it had happened. One moment they were there, and the next moment they were gone. They stumbled through choking smoke and debris to the edge of town, where they collapsed into some bushes, crying. Behind them, the sack of Stockville went on through the rest of the afternoon.

The Dog ran from the noise behind him. He wanted his ball, and he wanted to leave. Now. He made for the bushes, where he had stashed it earlier, and when he got there, he found two little people huddled and whimpering. In his bushes, with his ball! He paused, unsure of what to do, one paw raised, his head tilted quizzically. His ball was in there, and he wanted it, but there were little people there. What to do? Maybe they would leave soon. Sighing, he crouched down until he was lying with his nose on his paws. Maybe in a while they would leave and he would get his ball. If they didn't go soon, he would get his ball anyway. He settled in to watch as the children fell asleep.

Brian and Trish had eventually cried themselves out and fallen asleep in the bushes. Brian awoke around sunset to an odd feeling. There was a very *big* dog licking the cuts on his face. He put both hands on the dog's chest and pushed him away. For a moment, he felt really bad about leaving Dagwood behind and almost started crying again. The dog sat down and stared at him and Trish for a moment and then whined deep within his chest.

"Hi there, dog," Brian whispered.

Smoke rolled over the prairie around them, and there was a flickering reddish light everywhere. The dog approached again and began licking Trish's face.

"Eeeewwwwww!" she said. "Stop it!"

The dog sat down again patiently and stared at them. As the two children stood up, the dog rose and went to where they had been lying and dug under the grass for a moment. He came up with a tennis ball. He tossed it into the air and then caught it, almost seeming to grin at them. He seemed happy.

They emerged from the bushes and stared wide-eyed at what was left of Stockville. Clutching each other's hands, they began to walk toward the town, the dog keeping pace with them. He angled his body in front of them to redirect the way they were walking. They began to walk around him, and again, he cut them off, whining. They tried a third time, and this time, he dropped the tennis ball and snapped at them, barking once.

"Okay," Brian said, "we won't go back into Stockville. Geez."

The dog gave them a push, and they began to walk south, away from the burning town.

Restless

Harley slept extralate on the morning of December 12. He took his time waking up. The previous weeks almost seemed like a bad dream. He used the bathroom and took a long, hot shower. Wandering into the kitchen, yawning, he put some coffee on and absently clicked on the television as he went by. There was static. He wondered what today's news programs would bring. When the coffee was ready, he poured a huge mug and went into the living room, flopping on the couch. He clicked from the static-filled channel to the next one. That one was off the air as well. Shrugging, he went through all 121 satellite channels. *Nothing!* That was odd. Someone somewhere should have been broadcasting. He brought up the Menu option and hit Autoprogram while he went to get dressed. Maybe the television had reset itself the night before for some reason.

When he went back out, the television had finished cycling through things, and he only had three channels left with a signal. He was receiving a very faint feed from the BBC, but it was so broken he found himself grinding his teeth in frustration, and he couldn't see or hear anything being broadcast. Every three seconds, "Signal Strength Is Low" would flash across the screen. Flipping to the next channel, he had a feed from Australia, and it was the same thing that he was getting from England. Broken, unintelligible, and very, very frustrating. The third and final channel was from China, and they were really only covering their local news, nothing international.

He briefly considered driving into town to see if anyone knew anything and then quickly dismissed it. He had tried that right after The Day, but after noncommittal comments by the locals and some envious, poisonous looks at his Land Rover, Harley had decided not to do that again unless he was in extreme need. Just because he was a hermit was no need for people to be impolite. He paid his taxes and tried to be a good neighbor. He didn't bother anyone, and they shouldn't bother him. Crazy locals.

Harley fixed breakfast and decided he was going to barbecue later as well. He laid out a steak to thaw and then made up his bacon and eggs and toast. He wandered into the radio room, breakfast in hand, and sat down to start fiddling with the dials. He inflated his antennas, and outside, at ground level, the doors were opening up, the large rubber bladders inflating, his antenna going up. He looked at some of his dials and gauges as well. That was odd. He'd lost all surface solar power and was running on the battery backups. Maybe there was too much snow accumulating or something. He'd go out later and take a look.

Harley couldn't raise anyone on any frequency. He did hear a series of faint beeps and clicks on one channel, but that faded as he listened. *Everything* was off the air, it seemed. No television, no radio, zero, zilch, zip, *nada*! He tried the Internet, both wirelessly, dial up, and the fiber-optic connection, and got *nothing*. Was anyone still alive out there? Harley checked his consoles and rewound to the night before. He had recorded hours of static.

"That was a waste of storage," he grunted. All of a sudden, there were images. He watched all the backup newsfeeds, and everything pretty much cut out right around 9:00 p.m. Some people were mid-broadcast, and they were just cut off.

"Very, very weird," he said.

Leaving the radio to scan channels and the television and the Internet to do the same, Harley went to wash up his breakfast dishes. Then he spent the rest of the morning reading. He would occasionally wander into the radio room just to see if anything new was happening, but nothing.

Harley spent the afternoon watching movies, made himself a salad for lunch, and walked into the control room. Nothing still. Harley was getting irritable and restless, so he decided to go topside for a walk. He really needed that interaction with people. People were okay, at a distance, where you could just turn them off when you didn't want to talk anymore. He had never thought that all of them would just stop being there, though. Now he was what? Lonely? When he got upstairs, Harley zipped up his parka and crunched out into the snow. It was *so* cold out and snowing more. The air had a fractured-glass feel to it as wind-whipped snow stung his cheeks. It was a short walk. He was still going to barbecue, though. Later.

Suddenly, the snow stopped, and the air became very still. The sun peeked out for a moment, and Harley peered across the distance at large smoke plumes on the horizon. Stockville was about six miles away, and it was burning.

"Uh-oh. I wonder what happened there."

It kind of looked like there were no more crazy locals, or maybe they had finally all gone and killed one another. At any rate, Stockville was close, and Harley wondered if it was something to worry about. He had an idea suddenly on how he could find out, and he hurried back inside.

Harley checked on his steak; it was thawing out nicely. He mixed up a bowl of marinade to let it soak for a while. He was going to light the grill in an hour or so, but he had thought of something while he was topside a few hours before. After prepping his dinner, Harley wandered into the hobby room, and after a little searching, he found the drone he had purchased months before and never used. He spent a little while locating all the accessories, charging up extra battery packs, attaching the camera, and making sure everything was in good operating order.

He had decided to get up early the next day and make a stealthy aerial observation of the town. Harley figured, with the drone, he'd be close enough to see what had happened in the town but not close enough to get into trouble should things go awry. The camera worked, the drone worked, the battery packs were charging and doing their thing, so that was one less thing to worry about.

Harley went to the radio room next to do his daily programming and systems checks. He recorded his greetings and playlists, reported the little bit of news he had about the world in general, and then depressed, went to choose a movie to watch for the evening. Harley finally settled with an old black-and-white Jimmy Stewart flick. *It's a Wonderful Life* seemed like just the ticket, considering the mood he had been in lately. He would watch that while eating dinner.

Grilling was a quick affair. It was too cold outside to linger. He simply fired up the gas grill after brushing snow off it and let it warm up for a few minutes. While he was waiting for it to heat up, he started up his Land Rover and got the snow chains on the tires. He would need that in the morning. Harley laid some night vision goggles on the passenger seat. He would also need those, as he planned on leaving while it was still dark out. No point running over a deer, and he planned on driving with the headlights off so as not to attract attention.

While the steak and potato were on the grill, he ran a few aboveground status checks as well. The gas tanks were still almost full, and his solar power systems were toast. He would need to monkey with that soon, but it wasn't a priority at the moment; his underground turbines provided all the power he needed. It was concerning, though. He'd need to figure out how to rewire some of the minor systems that had depended on them for power.

The steaks finally done, Harley turned off the gas grill and covered it. He trudged through the snow back to the garage, locked up for the evening, powered up the security system, and prepared to take the elevator back down. The wind was really kicking up now, and with a final glance over his shoulder at the clouds of blowing snow, he shivered a little. What a sucky winter.

Harley was wolfing down his steak, baked potato, and Caesar salad when his perimeter alarms tripped. He quickly got up and walked into the control room. Pulling up the various cameras—a few were still working at any rate—he panned the complex but kept the exterior lights off, and he didn't activate the intercom either; he just watched. What he saw made him shiver again. It was snowing like crazy outside, and the wind was howling.

"I'm not going back out there," he mumbled. "Looks cold."

The shortwave system next to him crackled to life, and he almost wet his pants at the suddenness of it all.

"[Static] I . . . [static] . . . repeat, is there any . . . [static] . . . there?"

Harley snatched his microphone and headphones off the desk.

"Hello?" he replied. "Hello, unidentified transmitter! This is Harley Earl, receiving, KPAR, Nebraska! I can barely hear you. I'm going to try to amplify signal. Please repeat. Over!"

"[Static] [static] [static] . . . es! Repeat, we're dying here! Please send *any* assistance, military, police, or government authority! We simply cannot hold out much longer!"

Harley took a deep breath. "Where are you calling from? Over," he asked.

"We're forty miles south and west of Pittsburgh, and we are under attack. Food is running out, and we have been under continuous assault for three weeks! Please! We have women, children, elderly, and disabled that we are trying to care for . . . [static] [static] [static] . . . don . . . ow . . . ha . . . e'll . . . ease! [Static] [static] . . ."

"Last transmission garbled. Please repeat. Over," Harley said.

Harley sat there in the dark, repeating himself for thirty minutes, but no one responded. Finally, with a snarl, he ripped off his headphones and hurled them across the room, unaware that he was crying.

* * *

Brian and Trish wandered with The Dog for two days as the weather got colder and colder. Snow fell softly at first and then gathered in intensity, the wind howling and blowing across the open countryside. The children slept when they were tired, curled into the warmth of The Dog's fur. He kept trying to bring them rabbits to eat, but Brian had no way of starting a fire to cook them, and he wasn't sure how to fix a rabbit if he could.

The dog seemed to have a direction he was going, and he gently herded them the way he wanted them to go. The snow made going difficult. They went through and over fences on a few occasions, and

236

Brian wondered whose land they were on. The second day out, they had crossed a fence in near-whiteout conditions and crested a hill to see the strangest thing Brian had ever seen. The Dog hunkered down at the top of the rise, and Brian wondered if he was hallucinating.

Under a tree, there was an older kinda hippie-looking guy grilling out a steak and singing at the top of his lungs. Brian and Trish gaped at each other in amazement. Eventually, the man pulled the meat off the grill, went through a doorway at the base of another snowdrift, and didn't come back out again.

"Brian, what was that man? Where did he go?" Trish asked, coughing.

"I don't know, Trish," he replied. "We'll sleep close by here tonight, though, by that big tree. We can keep warm from the gas grill."

"Okay. Brian? I don't feel good."

"I know, Trish. We'll be warm tonight, though."

"I'm hungry too."

Brian was still drooling from smelling the meat.

"Me too, Trish."

The Dog had brought the little people to the Lonely Man that lived inside the ground. It had seemed like the right thing to do. Maybe when the Lonely Man went back outside again, he would take the little people inside and help make the little one better. The Dog knew she was sick, and the Lonely Man seemed like maybe he would be able to help her. He whined, pressing the length of his body against "Trish." Maybe that would help keep her warm. He had been bringing them rabbits, but they would not eat. So he had eaten them himself. Maybe little people didn't eat rabbits. "Brine" hadn't really known what to do when he had made the offerings. The Dog eyed the slope down from the hill and pushed the little people toward the tree with his nose. Soon he would hunt again then sleep. It had been a long day.

They spent the night outside, on the lee of the tree, the snow drifting to either side of them. The little people huddled in with The Dog, getting up occasionally to warm themselves by the fire thing.

Very early in the morning, the garage door opened, and the Lonely Man left in his four wheels. The Dog ran to the opening and barked, and the children ran inside with him. Suddenly, the door began to close, and they scampered out again. *Foolish little people!* He ran out to get them back in, but the door was closed now. Now they needed to wait in the cold again. The Dog chuffed in exasperation.

A short time went by, then a longer time, and The Dog could hear the four wheels returning. Behind them, the door began to raise again, and The Dog barked at the little people again to join him, pushing "Brine" and "Trish" into the opening. The four wheels skidded for a moment, and then the Lonely Man got out, yelling. The Dog danced in place. He knew he was *good*, that the little people would be okay now. He wondered if the Lonely Man had more meat—maybe he would share.

The Lonely Man adjusted the way he was talking and seemed to make up his mind. Another door opened, and The Dog ran inside and barked. All the people joined him, the door closed, and then they were moving without moving. The Dog sniffed at the door and then licked "Trish." She pushed him away, and he sat down. Then they were somewhere else. The Dog could not *wait* to see what was behind the next door. He got up with his tail wagging and his tongue hanging out, panting.

* * *

Harley had gone straight to bed after being unable to raise the stranger from Pittsburgh again. He had decided not to watch the movie—he was just too depressed—and opted for any early bedtime instead. He was planning on getting up at 4:00 a.m. to drive as close to town as he dared, and then he would deploy the drone, make recordings, and then get the heck out of there. The alarm went off way earlier than he thought it should, but after slapping the Sleep button a few times, he got up anyway, grumbling. Yawning and cursing because he had stubbed his toe, Harley hopped into the kitchen to put some coffee on and decided he needed a really hot shower to get going. Once that was taken care of, he dressed hurriedly, grabbed his AR15 from the armory, and rushed upstairs. Raising the garage door, he looked around and noticed that the snow had stopped and things seemed a little warmer. He glanced at the thermometer.

"Well, it's warmed up to freezing anyway," he said.

Harley started the Land Rover and let it warm up while he stomped around outside in the snow. The stars glittered overhead, and he shook his head in amazement at how many were visible. In the limitless white expanse, he felt almost as if he were drifting in the universe for a moment, so much so that he had a mild case of vertigo.

The snow chains on the tires made it relatively easy to get where he was going, but at times he drifted off the road because he couldn't see the pavement. Eventually, though, he pulled off about a mile outside town and got the drone ready to fly. There was nothing moving anywhere. Harley took his rifle anyway just to be safe and trudged to the top of a small hill. He activated the camera, turned on the drone, and began flying it toward town.

He flew it high on the first pass then descended and flew it back toward himself. Harley made about ten passes the length and breadth of the place and then flew it back to himself. He swapped out the battery pack and did it again, this time completely circling the perimeter and surrounding areas. Finally, satisfied that he would be able to see all that he needed to see, he landed it, set it back in the passenger seat, and got out of there.

Harley wanted to get home so he could see the footage. This was his first attempt at drone photography, and . . .

"Should have done a test run back home first. Well, live and learn," he muttered. "I can always come back out if I need to."

Harley noticed the wind kicking back up again, and it was strong. Some of the gusts rocked the Land Rover on its suspension, and he slowed down. Glancing in the rearview mirror, he saw snow billowing across the road in his wake. He almost missed the turnoff to his lane, but grumbling, he backed up fifty feet and turned in, sliding a little.

The final mile to the garage was driven in almost complete-white-out conditions, but he made it. He had activated his remote garage door opener when he got close and was planning on driving straight in when he almost ran over two small figures and a very large dog.

"Son of a bitch! What the fuck?" he yelled, slamming on the brakes and almost sliding into them anyway.

Harley looked out the windshield at two little kids and a . . . wolf?

There are strange things afoot at the Circle K, Harley.

He opened his door and stepped out. *Kids*! What was he going to do with kids? Harley didn't know very much about kids, and he looked around, hoping, maybe dreading more of them, and where were their parents? Who lets their kids run around in the middle of nowhere with a big-ass dog in the middle of a snowstorm?

"Ummmm," he began and then cleared his throat. "Hi."

The older of the two, a boy, replied, "Hi."

"Can I help you?" Harley asked. "Where did you come from? I mean, what are you doing here? I mean, ummm, where are your parents? What are you doing here?"

The smaller one, a girl, began to cry.

Now Harley was really confused and wary and a little . . . guilty, maybe?

"Please don't cry," he said.

The little girl sobbed harder, and the boy squeezed her hand. The dog-wolf moved in on her other side and tried licking her face.

Harley took a deep breath, about to say something else, but the boy spoke first.

"Please, mister, can we come inside with you just to warm up? Tricia is sick, and the people who were taking care of us are gone, and I don't know what to do. I'm trying, but I don't—"

And then *he* began to cry too.

Who leaves kids all alone outside? Harley thought, shaking his head. *Especially a sick kid?* This was definitely something to worry about.

"Yeah," he replied. "Let me get the car parked, and please stop crying, okay?"

Feeling completely out of sorts, Harley pulled the Land Rover into the garage and shut it off. He grabbed his night vision goggles off the seat along with his AR and turned just as the two kids entered the garage along with the big-ass wolf pretending to be a dog.

Seeing the rifle, the two children shied back a little, and glancing from them to the gun, he realized he must look a little intimidating.

"Sorry," he muttered. "This is just to keep the bad people away."

"Are you a good guy, then?" the boy asked.

Harley thought about it for a minute then laughed.

"Today I am," he replied. "What are your names, anyway? Me, I am Harley Earl."

"My name is Brian, and this is Tricia, and this . . . we just call him Dog."

"Well, nice to meet you, Brian and Tricia and . . . Dog. Is he your dog?"

"I'm not sure," Brian replied, "if he's our dog, but I think we might be his kids. He saved us."

"Well, we can sort that all out later," Harley said. "Is Dog housebroken?"

"I don't know," Brian replied. "I guess we'll find out."

"I guess we will," Harley agreed, smiling. "Well, come on in. Let's get you warmed up."

Harley armed the security system and closed the garage door.

"You sure live in a small house out here in the middle of nowhere," Tricia declared. "But it's lots warmer than out there."

"You mean my garage?" Harley asked, puzzled.

"Yeah," she said very seriously. "But I guess you don't need much 'cause you're all alone. How come your 'lectricity is still on? Ours went out and didn't come back on a long time ago."

"Well, I'll show you that secret when you feel better, okay?" Harley replied. "Why don't you guys come in? And we'll take care of stuff."

"But we *are* inside!" Tricia scowled.

"Trust me," Harley said, grinning, "this is just the beginning of inside."

Harley pushed the button for the elevator, and the doors swished open. The dog rushed inside and barked. Harley stepped inside, and the children followed, holding hands. Tricia was coughing. He waited for the doors to close, frowning. That cough didn't sound good. What was he going to do?

Harley pushed the Down button.

"How come you have an elevator in your garage?" Brian asked as they began to descend. "Do you have an underground house?"

"Something like that," Harley replied absently, thinking. He was going to have to dig out those medicine books. Harley had gone through a holistic phase, and that had led to other studying, but he had forgotten most of what he had read.

The elevator finally reached the bottom, and Harley's ears popped. The doors swished open again, and the three of them stood looking at a large circular door with a spoked wheel in the middle of it. The motion-sensor lights went from low to normal illumination, and the burnished steel glowed softly.

"Wow!" Brian exclaimed softly. "Are you a spy or something, mister?"

"Nope. Just Harley Earl," Harley replied. "This is where I live."

Stepping out of the elevator, Harley punched in his security code and then spun the wheel to open the door. The children and the dog followed him inside.

Now that they were inside, Harley wrinkled his nose a little. These kids needed to be warmed up, and they needed a bath. Brian's nose was running a little, and he kept wiping it away with his sleeve. And Tricia was still coughing. Harley decided that he needed to appear confident and in charge and like he knew what he had to do. He could tell they needed that. The dog needed a bath too, and he was limping, favoring a front foreleg. Harley had briefly considered getting some animals during his "hobby" phase but had never gotten around to it, but he had some veterinary/animal husbandry books around somewhere too. Maybe that would let him help the dog as well. Three sets of eyes were locked on him, waiting for . . . what? Oh yeah, he was supposed to be in charge. Kids, of all things. Good grief!

"Um . . . follow me," Harley said, going farther inside. "Are you guys hungry?"

They nodded.

"How about some hot chocolate?" he asked.

They nodded again.

"How about a nice, hot shower or a bath?"

"Oh yes, please!"

"We need to wash your clothes and find some dry and warm stuff for you to wear," Harley said, leading the way toward one of the guest rooms. Harley was flipping lights on as he walked, and since the kids were following behind, he didn't see their eyes getting bigger and bigger as they took more and more of it in.

"You really live here all alone?" Tricia asked. "This is bigger than our whole *school* was!"

Harley turned suddenly, and the kids stopped suddenly, almost running into him.

"Yes," he said softly, "it probably is. If you are up for it later, I'll give you the tour, but until I do, there are a few ground rules, okay?"

They nodded.

"First, don't go anywhere in here without me, at least in the beginning. I don't want you to get lost or get hurt. This is a big place, and I don't want to have to try finding you or worry about you falling or drowning."

"Drowning?" Brian mouthed incredulously.

"Second rule, we're going to get you guys clean and warm, but stay in this room until I can come back to get you, okay? There's some stuff I need to find really quick, and hopefully, it will make you feel better, Trish. Okay?"

"Okay?" Harley repeated.

"Okay," they answered.

"This is one of the guest rooms. It has its own bathroom with a shower and a Jacuzzi tub. I don't care which ones you use. You guys can settle that yourself. But I want you out of those clothes and getting clean and warm as soon as you can."

Harley vaguely remembered his mother saying something like that to him when he was ten or so, and cold and wet from sledding all day, he hoped that sounded adult enough. He grinned as the kids began taking care of business.

Stepping into the bath, he began to fill the tub, and he turned on the shower as well, letting the water heat up so that steam began to fill the air.

"There are warm, fluffy towels here to dry off with when you're done, soap and shampoo and stuff in this cupboard, and while you guys are getting cleaned up, I'm going to see what I can do about some clothes, okay? I'm going to take your stuff and wash it, and when it's dry, we'll get it back to you so that'll be one less thing to worry about."

Harley closed the bathroom door and scooped the kids' clothes off the floor. These were going in the washer, like, right now. The dog accompanied him down the hallway to one of the laundry rooms, sniffing occasionally at Brian and Trish's clothing.

Harley eyed the dog trotting along beside him.

"You could use a bath as well, you know."

The dog just looked at him coolly.

"Well, we'll figure that out later," Harley said.

Harley loaded everything into the washer and set it to Heavy Soiled and maxed out the rest of the settings. There! It would run extralong, but everything would come out clean. After that was done, he trotted to the library and grabbed a few books. He stopped by his own bedroom and grabbed a few soft wool sweaters, an some medication. He was just returning to the guest room when the door flew open and Brian came sprinting into the hallway.

"I thought we had an understanding that you were going to stay put—"

Harley began sternly but was cut off by Brian.

"Mister, please! Tricia just fell down, and I can't wake her up! Please hurry!" he said, running back into the room.

Harley sighed then followed.

One more thing to worry about.

Climbing

CHAPTER 32

From the Journal of H. Rayton Townsend
December 17, 2016
Sierra Nevada Mountain Range

We have maybe fifteen miles to go to the cabin. Had to
stash the bikes about ten miles ago. Maybe Carly and
Kyle can come back for them in the springtime, but I
doubt it. Snow. There is snow everywhere and piling up.
It is so cold that I can barely write. We have to climb to
the pass. No one has plowed the roads this winter, and
no one probably will for a long time. Got to keep going.

* * *

Ray, Carly, and Kyle were hiking quietly, saving their breath. Every single footstep took effort and conscious thought. They had been making good time on the bikes, but as they had climbed into the Sierras, the light drizzle had become heavy fog, then a light rain, then a heavy downpour, the wind howling around them as they pumped legs on pedals, trying to go faster. The rain had started freezing after a while, and then heavy clumps of snow began to collect on the roadway. The third time one of them had wrecked because of the icy conditions, they had decided to leave the bikes and continue on foot. They had stashed them in a cleft in the mountainside about ten miles back, with heavy vegetation all around to hide them so they would be out of sight to the casual observer.

Now they were walking, and it took everything. Wet, cold, miserable, noses running from the wind, eyes tearing up, and every bit of exposed skin being sandblasted with ice particles that slapped like miniature razors. Ray was exhausted, every third step slipping out from beneath him, where the snow covered the ice.

"This sucks," Kyle began.

"Kyle! Knock it off!" Carly snapped. "It sucks for all of us, not just you, and complaining about it just makes everyone else miserable."

They continued in silence once more.

"Yeah, well, Mad Max never had to put up with snow and shit," Kyle finally said.

They all stopped for a minute, and Ray felt his lips cracking from grinning. They were all smiling, actually. The first smiles in what felt like forever.

"Mad Max, huh?" Ray said. "That was a great series of movies."

"Which one was your favorite?" Kyle asked.

"Why, the *Road Warrior*, of course," Ray replied as they began walking again.

"Yeah, that was the best one," Kyle agreed. "*Thunderdome* sucked, though. Tina Turner kinda ruined it for me."

"I liked that one," Carly said quietly.

They kept walking, and slipping, and talking about end-of-the-world movies and books. *The Postman, Waterworld, Mad Max, The Walking Dead*, zombie movies, anything and everything to shake off the cold and keep putting one foot in front of the other. Eventually, they fell silent again and continued trudging along.

"*Threads*," Kyle said at one point.

"Threads?"

"Yeah," Kyle said, focusing on his walking for a while. "That was a movie about a nuclear war."

"Never saw it," Ray replied.

"It scared the shit out of me when I was a kid," Kyle said. "Remember how a few days ago, you were talking about how no one ever focuses on all the pain and death and destruction when the world is tearing itself to pieces? The millions of people losing everything and everyone they love? That movie was almost too much. My folks didn't let me watch it at first, and when they did, I had nightmares for weeks afterward. Anyway, that one did, and now I know why it scared me. We're living it right now, and so is everyone else."

They were quiet after that, making their way through the storm, alone with their thoughts. They stopped at one point to heat some water for hot drinks and tie a rope to one another so that no one would get lost in the near-zero visibility that was becoming the norm, and no one wanted to go over the edge of the high mountain roads they were walking either. The snow was knee-deep now.

They passed through a few more small towns, not stopping, flinching as drapes were twitched aside to eye the strangers passing through. Ray knew they would get nothing now from any of those people other than hurt or getting robbed or killed, so they kept pushing forward. They were totally committed now, and it was too late to turn back. The cold was a constant danger now, a constant physical presence, a pressure on the inside and outside, an enemy that constantly assaulted the unwary. It lulled them, affected concentration, slowed the thoughts, made them aware of every bruise, every scrape, every hurt that they had felt. And then they went numb. The opposite started to happen; they would get warm flashes and bursts of euphoria and feel very calm and sedated so that they had to stop, jump in place, yell, scream, and rage to shake it off. They burned through the rest of their food at a frightening pace. The energy needed to fuel three bodies pushing upward through thigh-deep snow was amazing. They had to sleep outside at night—if possible, finding a wayward pine with low boughs that they could crawl under to keep the snow off. They slept together, huddling for warmth under every scrap of cover they could spare, but they didn't really sleep; the cold or nightmares kept them awake most nights when they closed their eyes.

In the morning, they would shake the snow from the blankets and themselves, making a quick dash to pee. They would stretch and work the cramps out of muscles stiffened and sore from lying on the frozen ground. And then they would continue on. Helping one another, coaching one another, encouraging one another, bitching and laughing at one another, they made it ever higher into the mountains, running out of food and patience and energy. They didn't give up, though, and six days after abandoning the bikes, in the middle of the day, they were traversing another featureless stretch of snow-covered road when Kyle suddenly stopped walking. They were in a broad stretch of the mountain pass, and trees stretched away to either side going farther up the mountains. Ray, just focused on moving, walked right into his back. Carly, in turn, ran into Ray's back. All of them took turns breaking a trail through the deep snow, and at that moment, Kyle had been leading.

Ray mumbled something, and Kyle didn't reply.

For some reason, that really irritated Ray, and he had to *think* about what he had just said before repeating himself.

"I *said*, why are we stopping in the middle of the fucking road, Kyle? We gotta keep moving."

"We're here," he said wonderingly.

Carly took a second look around and slowly smiled, then she nodded.

"We almost walked right past it."

"What do you mean *we're here*?" Ray muttered. "There's . . . there's nothing, *nothing* here except more snow!"

Ray looked at them suspiciously, squinting his eyes, wondering if they were starting to crack up on him. Snow fever or some shit.

"With all the snow, you can't see it, but we are right at the base of an access road that leads up to the neighborhood with our house, Ray! We have three miles to go! We're almost there!"

The three of them turned left and worked their way over to the access road. The snow was a little lighter under the trees and drifted in places, but for the most part, it was only calf-deep. Two hours later, they were there. Ray stood in the lane, crying, on the very edge of final exhaustion, staring at the most beautiful home he had ever seen. He would have probably frozen to death within feet of salvation if Kyle hadn't smacked him on the shoulder. Kyle hugged him.

"Come on, dude. Let's go get warm."

* * *

From the Journal of H. Rayton Townsend
December
Lake Alpine, California

Well, we finally made it here, and honestly, the place is amazing. The view is incredible. Kyle has been going on about this place, this cabin for the last month, and it was starting to take on mythic proportions in my head. I wasn't even sure if I believed him anymore or not. Cabin is a bit of an understatement, though. It's a three-bedroom home. There is running water—they tapped a natural spring when they were building it—food, clothing, a fireplace. There is electricity because they have a generator, and more importantly, Kyle has two hunting rifles and a decent stockpile of ammunition for them. Warm beds with down comforters, hot showers, and best of all, safety!

It is a large three-bedroom home built from weathered logs and stone. The inside is ultramodern. There are two large full propane tanks out back to provide gas for heat and cooking, and Kyle's folks had always stocked enough food on hand to feed a dozen people three squares a day for a month. With just the two of them, they should be okay here after I move on. There are fish in the lake down in the valley, good hunting in these parts, and wild berries in season. It's far enough off the beaten path that no one other than a few year-round locals even know that it is here. I am a little envious— all kinds of other things, too. Just haven't had a chance to explore yet. More later.

* * *

The three of them stood in the snow-covered driveway for a moment longer, just staring at that glorious house, and then Kyle got them moving. There was a good six feet of snow drifted over half of it, but it was snugly built and solid. The only tracks they had seen so far were deer, raccoon, and squirrels. Around the bend farther uphill, Ray could make out the shapes of three more large homes, and Kyle had told him that there were about a dozen more beyond that. No one was around; it was just the three of them. Kyle was hunting under a snowdrift for the spare key, swearing as snow went down his collar and cuffs, but eventually, he found it and stood up with a triumphant shout. Steam was rising off him from the effort as he unlocked the door and staggered inside.

Overhead, the pines were creaking and swaying in the rising wind. Dusk was falling, and the storm was ramping up again. Ray was mesmerized by the sound before joining the other two in the mudroom. When they entered the home, there was a silence so profound it made Ray's ears ring. The house smelled as if it had been shut up for a few months, but it was clean and much warmer than being outside. It was growing dim too, and Kyle began to issue instructions.

"Ray, why don't you get a fire going in the fireplace? I'm going to light the pilot lights on the furnace and water heater and stove. Carly, can you turn on the propane when I give the word?"

Everyone nodded and started moving.

Ray went to the fireplace and knelt down on the hearth. He reached inside to pull the lever that would open the damper, and as the metal turned to open, small twigs and dead bugs pattered down inside. Next to the fireplace was a small keg that held fatwood, another old wood box that held newspapers, and a recessed niche holding kindling and logs. He crumpled up a few of the old newspapers and laid a few sticks of fatwood across them then added a few twigs and smaller pieces of kindling. Looking around, he saw a tall glass on the mantle that held long matches, and he grabbed one. Before lighting it, though, he paused for a moment, listening to the keen of the wind outside the walls. He could feel minute movements against his skin as the cold pulsed along them. It seemed as if the house held its breath. Striking the match, he held it under the damper for a moment, watching as the flame was drawn up and into the chimney. Happy that there was a good draw of air up the flue and he wouldn't smoke them all out, he set fire to the wadded-up newspapers.

Tiny flames curled up as they approached the fatwood and the tinder. There was a sizzle as the oily wood caught flames growing larger, the light illuminating his face from below as he knelt there. Gradually adding more wood until he had a real fire going, Ray contemplated *fire*. Tonight, they would have fire, such a simple, useful thing and sorely lacking in his life for the last few weeks. Fire had the power to heal, build, create, and destroy. Fire was the tool that had lifted man above his fellow animals, giving him additional tools and dominion over the world. Fire was what had destroyed the world. It was a symbol of councils and remembrance, storytelling, and myth. Fire was where history was recorded, both orally and on cave walls. It pushed back the darkness where man had feared to tread before the Written Word. Fire had baked pottery vessels for storing food, it cooked meat, and it had wrought tin and copper and bronze, iron, and steel for the making of tools and weapons. Fire was life. Fire was death. Fire was *all*.

Ray added logs now, and the hearth blazed with light. He huddled before it, oblivious to his surroundings, like some primitive god worshipping the fire. Finally satisfied, he rested on his heels before the hearth and watched the dancing of the flames, his hands stretched out to it, alone in the dark, the fire his companion.

Kyle had entered quietly behind him with a prickle down his neck and back. He had not wanted to disturb the primal way in which Ray had been sitting before the fireplace. He had seemed too intense there for a moment, unconsciously leaning forward as the flames grew and beckoned.

"Nice fire, Ray," he finally said.

Ray jumped, startled from his reverie.

"Yeah. Wanted to make sure we got warm *fast!*" He gave the fireplace a critical glance. "Might have overdone it a bit, though."

The fire was roaring on the other side of the chain-link curtains in front of it. It was throwing heat five feet into the room.

Kyle flipped on the lights.

"Got the genny running too. Can't run it long because we don't have a lot of gas for it, but enough for a little while tonight. Electricity. Pretty neat, huh?"

Ray agreed that electricity was indeed pretty neat, but deep down inside, he added the addendum, that *fire* was better.

"We should have hot water in a bit too. I kicked on the furnace as well. It'll take an hour or so for everything to heat up all the way. Tonight, Ray, we will have hot showers, hot food, warm beds, and we will be safe."

Dinner consisted of hot soup and biscuits, but the real highlight of the evening was a hot shower and a warm bed. After turning off the generator, they turned in early. It had been a great day, the first great day in a month, and Ray dropped off into an exhausted slumber, listening to the wind outside. He took a great deal of contentment in being warm, clean, safe, and fed well. Tomorrow was for tomorrow to worry about.

Lake Alpine

CHAPTER 33

From the Journal of H. Rayton Townsend
December

I don't know why I am still bothering with this, except to put my thoughts down on paper. I think I said in the beginning, though, that it is cheaper than therapy. I have lost track of the days. It may be Christmas for all I know. It feels that way. Maybe I just feel the urge to record something, to have the hope that someday, some-one else may want to read this and know what we, who are alive today, went through to get there. I woke up this morning not knowing who I was. I didn't know my name. I didn't know what I was doing here. I only knew that I was clean and dry and warm and more rested than I have been in weeks. I knew that I existed, that I was me, but I didn't know anything beyond that. I guess that kind of makes sense in a weird way. The time since The Day seems to have redefined all of us, made us more than we were. It is very hard to explain on paper what I am feeling right now. First, I was confused, and now I am not. Not exhausted anymore, just tired, like I could sleep for a week and take a break from that with frequent naps. I savored all of it, stretching and yawning, and then I finally remembered who I was and where I was and that I was safe and thankful for having good friends who helped me to get here. We are very, very lucky today. I don't know that we would have survived another night in the open. I honestly don't. Things were getting blurry there at the end. Privacy. Wow. First time I have woken up without being in arm's reach of someone for a month. It makes such a huge difference to wake up on your own, without having to follow a schedule.

* * *

Ray yawned and blinked awake. He had woken up briefly, much earlier, as watery gray light had seeped into the window of the bedroom. He had rolled over and pulled the goose-down comforter up over his head. *Too early!* he had thought, falling back into a deep, dreamless sleep. Thankfully dreamless. He hadn't known anything beyond the fact that he was warm and was too exhausted to care beyond that. Now, hazy sunshine was coming in through the window, and grumbling to himself, he realized he needed to pee with a vengeance.

Like an old man, groaning, he pushed the bedding off to the side and sat on the edge of the bed for a moment. Wearing only boxers and yawning again, he scrubbed his hands across his face and through his hair. He marveled at the plush carpeting under his bare feet. Getting up, he padded to the door, pulling a T-shirt over his head. As he stuck his head into the hallway, Kyle was approaching his door with a pile of neatly folded clothing in his hands. The two men grinned at each other.

"Morning!" Ray whispered.

"How'd you sleep?" Kyle whispered back.

"It was . . . *delicious!*" Ray replied.

"I know. Carly's still asleep."

Kyle pushed the folded clothes at Ray and smiled.

"Here, these are some clothes my dad used to keep here, and he was about your size, so they should fit."

"Thanks, Kyle," Ray said. "That's awesome!"

"I'm gonna go make coffee."

Kyle headed for the kitchen, and Ray quickly set his clothes on the side of the bed then went to take a leak. When he returned to the bedroom, he saw that he had new jeans, a couple of T-shirts, socks, boxers, a nice flannel shirt, and a couple of sweaters. He dressed and shivered at the feel of clean clothing against his skin. Luxury!

Ray joined Kyle in the kitchen, and he saw that Carly had woken up and already had a cup of coffee in her hand. She waved sleepily and yawned, which was contagious. Ray got his own cup and sat down at the table. Kyle was making breakfast, pancakes, and sausage, and his stomach rumbled embarrassingly loudly. The three of them ate quietly and looked out at the view beyond the windows. The storm had dwindled to flurries again, and wide-open patches and columns of sunshine streamed down through breaks in the clouds. That sunlight alternated with dark shadows as it moved across the valley below, across the lake, and up the slope of the far side of the valley. The light illuminated snow-encrusted trees in all directions. It looked cold, deadly, and beautiful.

"I prefer being inside and looking outside at a view like that rather than vice versa, I think," Ray said quietly at one point. The others nodded in agreement and understanding.

Lingering over their coffee, they talked about what they would need to do. Short-term plans and long-term plans and Ray's plans for moving forward. They assured him that he was welcome to stay for as long as he needed, and they would do what they had to in order to ensure that he was prepared for the next leg of the journey. Ray told them how much that meant to him and how much he appreciated that. They replied that his staying with them in Winters had meant even more after being abandoned by the Webbs. They all laughed, shaking their heads over and speculating what would ultimately happen to the Webbs and people like them.

It was a lazy day full of naps and books, admiring the view, making lists, and taking stock of things. None of them even considered going outside, and they rested, watching the fire, watching the clouds play across the landscape, watching one another, and finding themselves grinning silly grins, just happy to be happy, safe, and warm and on their own schedules. They needed the rest and gloried in the resting after a month of filth and pain and terror. Tomorrow they would work. Today, they planned and threw out ideas and talked over potential lists of things that would be needed. The reality was that Carly and Kyle were home now; they at least would be going no further. Ray could see it in their body language, a relaxing of stress and a sense of starting over. It would be a long winter, but they were home, and they were starting over. Today, they would rest and dream and plan, but tomorrow, they would start securing their future. It was another great day.

The next morning, they got an early start. There was a lot to do. Laundry, for one. Their clothes hadn't been washed since Davis. They were caked with sweat and mud and were just unpleasant all the way around. So they sorted what was wearable from what was not, washed everything, washed it again, and relegated what was unusable to the ragbag. Even if it weren't wearable, it would be usable in some form going forward, until it disintegrated. None of them wasted anything anymore. Everything that they owned mattered going forward. So it would be saved, repaired, sewn up, and recycled.

Carly had decided to spend the day inventorying everything in the house. Food, clothing, medical supplies, cleaning supplies, equipment, fuel, literally everything was going to get organized and go on a checklist. Kyle and Ray decided that they were going to meet the neighbors, if there were any, and just generally see what was out there. They cooked a decent breakfast, and they loaded the two rifles, leaving one with Carly. Kyle took the other one as they went out the door.

None of them had gone outside the previous day, and they noted as they did step outside how the storm and the wind had essentially obliterated their tracks leading to the cabin. The two men agreed that that was a good thing as they didn't exactly want to announce their presence to the world yet. They were, however, surprised to note that while their tracks had been obliterated, fresh tracks had been laid around the perimeter of the house during the night. A bear, a big one, maybe even a grizzly, had been checking them out. Probably an old guy, out doing a little final forage before that long winter's nap.

The two men headed up the lane and stopped in turn at the two other homes that Ray had noted upon their arrival. No woodsmoke, no tracks, and both stood solid, dark, and completely uninhabited. Kyle explained that these people had also been from the Bay Area, and they probably hadn't made it out. He knew where the spare keys were located, and they entered each to take a quick look around. Ray felt a little crawling up and down his spine at entering the unoccupied homes, which he quickly shrugged off. Then he laughed. Kyle raised an eyebrow at him, and it took a minute to explain.

"Do you remember how shocked all of you were when I broke out that first car window north of Santa Rosa?" Ray asked.

Kyle thought about it for a minute and then slowly nodded.

"Yeah," he replied. "We've kind of evolved a little bit from there, huh? I never thought that we could become so casual over it. We have, though. Things *have* changed, and like you said that first night, if it's not *us* taking that stuff, it's gonna be whoever comes after us. At this point, I think, I would like us to get everything we can rather than leave anything useful behind for a stranger. Better us than them, right?"

The mild sense of trespassing and violation passed, and instead of getting freaked out over it, the two men shared a growing sense of excitement and a sense of purpose. First things were first—essentials. Food would be a priority, and they checked both kitchens, locating pantries and canned goods, utensils, gadgets, and tools. They checked the bathrooms and closets for medications, cleaning supplies, clothing, and blankets. Both garages held tools and fuel. Some held camping gear and bicycles and sporting goods. Locking the doors behind them, they proceeded up the lane, leaving two sets of footprints behind them.

Every house held treasure and was abandoned, locked up for the winter, waiting for people that would probably never arrive. They were completely alone so far. Kyle had known that most of the homes here were weekend homes or seasonal escapes for people looking to get out of the city for a little while. Most of these homes were merely for entertaining, and they were stocked to do just that.

Finally, they reached the top of the lane and arrived at a home that was different from the rest. An elderly couple lived there, and they were the only year-round residents of the cul-de-sac. They were both retired, but it looked like they hadn't been around for weeks. A Jeep Patriot stood in the driveway, completely covered with snow and ice, and no tracks or woodsmoke even hinted at an occupant. Kyle wondered what had happened to them. Ray shrugged.

They walked up to the front door and began pounding on it.

"Mr. and Mrs. Simmons?" he yelled out, thumping away on the door. There was no answer. Puzzled, the two men circled the house a few times, peering in through dark windows, but nothing moved inside. Finally, they gave up.

"Maybe they went somewhere on vacation or for Thanksgiving before The Day, ya know? Probably didn't make it back would be my guess," Kyle said, sounding a little frustrated. "They have *always*—and I mean *always*—been here, Ray. Since I was a little kid. I used to mow Mr. Simmons's grass when I was kid. I wonder where they went."

Ray shrugged again as they began walking back to the lane. The two men stopped there and looked down the roadway to where it curved around the side of the mountain.

"Well," Ray said with a sudden grin.

"Well what?"

"We have seventeen homes to scavenge," Ray replied. "All with detached garages. All have at least three bedrooms, kitchens, closets, etc."

Kyle waited patiently while Ray was thinking.

"How long do you think it will take to get *everything* useful down to your place?" he finally asked.

"Well, let's head back and talk it over with Carly," Kyle finally said. "Let her know what we found out here. Get her take on it as well."

"I guess we should probably break it down into categories, right?"

"Yeah, that sounds good. That way, we can prioritize. Food first, definitely, followed by health and hygiene, luxury goods, and irreplaceable things, then raw materials and tools?"

"Sounds good to me," Ray replied. "I'd say we get the food first, start at the top, and work our way down. That way, as the time goes by, we will have a shorter and shorter distance to travel. Think we could get all the food by tonight? If we bring things back one category at a time, Carly can inventory it all and stay organized."

"Lunch sounds good."

"Hmmmmmm. Lunch sounds like a great idea," Ray agreed. "I think it's going to be a busy afternoon and a busy next few days."

"Kinda fun, huh?"

"Yeah," Ray agreed, "it kinda is."

They headed back down the lane, looking at tracks in the snow. They saw deer sign, elk sign, squirrels and raccoon, and the bear again. Others were a little smudged. The hunting would be good, at least. They talked about fishing in the lake for Kyle next summer, and he mused that there had always been fishermen out there. With what they could scavenge and what they could hunt, they figured that Kyle and Carly were going to be just fine for the long-term. That was good.

An hour later, the three of them were sitting down over grilled-cheese sandwiches and tomato soup. Ray cracked open a beer with an appreciative glance at Kyle and Carly and took a long pull on it. Carly had spent the entire morning inventorying foodstuff and working with a planner. Just based on what was already in the house and not taking into account anything they might find outside, she cheerfully informed them that with a small breakfast and one large meal a day, they could eat for the next four months. She was practically dancing at the thought of it and had a twinkle in her eye. Just based on what they already had, that wasn't counting hunting or fishing or foraging in the neighbors' houses yet, so they would have the minimum covered no matter what. Both guys agreed it was nice to see her that way later on in the afternoon; she hadn't really been like that since Winters, and it was awesome to see her bouncing back.

Kyle and Ray filled her in on what they had found as well, and she agreed that the food should probably be priority 1 since that was the first project she had done a complete inventory on anyway. Ray, feeling pretty mellow, said what was on his mind.

"You know, Kyle, there's a lot of meat on a bear. Fat too."

Kyle grinned back at him.

Carly looked between the two of them and threw up her hands. "Oh. My. God," Carly said, looking from Ray to Kyle. "You guys saw a freakin' *bear?*"

Kyle rolled his eyes.

"No, babe, we just saw the tracks. It's okay." He laughed. "*But* there's definitely one in the neighborhood."

Carly was *not* happy about that at all.

"Bears scare me half to death," she muttered.

After lunch, Kyle pulled out a Smith and Wesson .44 and loaded it with magnum rounds. Carly had insisted on it. If they were going to be out and about with a bear in the neighborhood, she wanted something a lot closer to hand than the rifle. The two men each took a rifle and headed back out with the wheelbarrow and all the plastic totes they could scrounge up. They walked all the way back to the top of the lane, where the retired old couple had lived. They figured they would start there and work their way back down again. Plus, since they normally lived there year-round, Kyle figured it would be the best-stocked house with food.

When they got there, Kyle banged on the door again for a while, just to be polite, and they waited a few minutes more just to observe the correct forms. Kyle didn't have keys for the place. Eventually, they walked around back, broke a porch window, reached through, and unlocked the door.

They hit the kitchen first. The cabinets were absolutely *packed* with food along with a full-sized pantry. They spent twenty minutes loading all the totes and the wheelbarrow, and glancing out the window, Ray noted the Jeep again. The road was steep. Why not?

"Hey, Kyle," Ray said.

"Yeah? What's up?"

"We could probably carry a lot more in that Jeep, don't you think?"

"Yeah, but it probably won't turn over with the EMP, right?"

"Yeah, but it's a steep road, right? Couldn't we, like, coast it down? Just drop it into neutral and ride the brakes? The snow's only two or three feet deep. I bet we could do it," Ray said.

Kyle looked out at the Jeep critically.

"We should try to find the keys so we don't have to break the steering column open."

Ray picked up a set from the countertop. One even said "Jeep" right on the padded top of it. He dangled them in front of Kyle.

"Shall we?"

The two men walked out and began clearing the snow and ice from the vehicle. Kyle was right; it wouldn't turn over, but they were able to pack the entire contents of the kitchen cabinets and pantry into the whole vehicle with just enough room left for a driver. It would have taken them four trips at least with the wheelbarrow, maybe more, to get it all down to the cabin. They had really scored, though. Canned goods—it felt like they won the lottery there. Beans, peas, vegetables, fruit, condensed soups, ravioli, SpaghettiOs, mac and cheese, and other canned pastas. Dry goods like dried pasta, sauces, dried fruits, nuts, processed-cheese spread, salsa, chips, snacks, flour, salt, condiments, beer and soda—there was really too much to list— they took it all, including an entire spice cabinet that was hanging on the wall. They checked the fridge too; everything in there had gone bad, but they pulled more drinks out of there in bottles and cans.

Finally, they were ready to go. They left all the totes there along with the wheelbarrow for the next trip.

"All right, man, give me a push," Kyle said, climbing behind the wheel and dropping it into neutral.

Ray walked around to the backside of the Jeep and dug in. *Man, this sucker is loaded!* Kyle had rolled his window down.

"Are you pushing?"

"Yeah!" Ray replied. "How come you get to drive anyways?"

"I have experience," Kyle replied with a straight face.

Ray strained and pushed as hard as he could, the Jeep rocking back and forth. Suddenly, the front tires went over the ridge of ice in front of them, and the thing was moving. He jumped up on the back bumper as it started to roll. With a whoop, Kyle started steering them downhill, the Jeep going faster and faster. Ray hung onto the top tie-down rails and whooped as well, the wind beginning to lash his face. Kyle braked once, and the Jeep began to slew to the side. Uh-oh! Kyle corrected, and they began to slide the other way. They were almost down to the cabin and started to go into a spin.

"Oh, fuck *me*!" Ray groaned, the car spinning now, whipping him around and around, Kyle still whooping it up in the front seat. On its final revolution, the rear wheels slammed into something below the snow, and the sudden stop sent Ray flying about fifteen feet into a snowdrift. He lay there stunned. Amazed beyond all rational belief that he wasn't injured. Nothing seemed to be broken, but he had the wind seriously knocked out of him.

"Asshole!" he wheezed.

Carly had come running from the cabin as soon as she heard the whooping and the impact, and she and Kyle came running over just as Ray was getting his breath back.

"Oh my god, you guys! Ray, are you okay? Kyle, what were you thinking?"

He glared at both of them. They looked worried.

Finally, he sat up, still half-buried in the snowbank. He pointed his finger straight at Kyle. "I'm driving next time!" was all he said.

They collapsed in gales of laughter while Ray was still spluttering with outrage.

* * *

Eventually, Ray got out of the snowdrift and dusted himself off, still a little grumpy about it, and walked around for a bit, but everything seemed okay. They left Carly unpacking the Jeep and made a second trip up the hill. Having gotten the food, this time they were after pharmaceuticals and hygiene products.

"Toilet paper!" Carly called after them.

"Yes, dear," Kyle sighed.

Ray laughed at him.

Eventually, they got to the top again, and Kyle apologized for dumping him in a snowbank. They went right back to work. Ray was having great luck in the medicine cabinet of the downstairs bathroom when he heard Kyle call him.

He ran upstairs to find Kyle in the doorway of the master bedroom with a cloth over his mouth. He pulled the door shut just as Ray reached him.

"What's up?"

"Well, I know now why they haven't been around for a few weeks," he said grimly.

Ray nodded at the door, and Kyle responded with a grimace.

"Yeah. They're in there." He took a deep breath. "Murder-suicide. The old man left a note."

"Shit. Really?"

"Yeah." Kyle nodded. "Seems his wife was moving into mid-stage Alzheimer's. Kids lived in San Francisco with their kids. He just didn't want to go on by himself. Killed her then committed suicide."

"Well, their loss is our gain, then. Fuck it! I'm going to stop feeling guilty about them maybe coming back and finding the place stripped. I guess we should probably bury them, right?"

"Yeah." Kyle nodded.

"Shake it off, Kyle. They're the ones that checked out, not us. It sucks, but like I said, their going gives us more of a chance to live and live well. That's the endgame here."

"Yeah."

There was a second vehicle in the garage, and they packed it to the rafters with stuff too. They were also up two more weapons—a twelve-gauge shotgun with two boxes of shells and a nice .40 Beretta semiautomatic with two boxes of shells as well. It took them three days to strip the Simmons place to the floorboards. Tools, food, both vehicles (which had had full tanks of gasoline), medicine, books, board games and playing cards, linens, blankets, booze, and clothing. They buried the old couple out back. Carly recommended that they start looking for shelving as well, a lot of it. Much of what they scavenged would need to be stored in the garage until it was organized and packed away. Carly had been reorganizing the basement while they worked, clearing space to store the food. The plan was for it to become a canned-goods pantry.

On one trip through the garage, Ray nodded at the late-fifties pink-and-white International pickup truck sitting in there.

"Does that thing work, Kyle?"

Kyle shook his head. "Not yet at least, *but* Dad and I were working on it. It was a project that we were sharing until his heart attack last spring. I have high hopes that we'll be able to get it running once we get everything else done."

Ray looked around their spacious garage and noted the neatly organized shop area. The tools were neatly racked and organized. There were boxes that were labeled and stacked nicely. There were also an oxyacetylene torch and welding gear, drill presses, and all the other bric-a-brac that such places seemed to collect. He nodded in approval.

"I wish I knew why Carly has us grabbing clothing and shoes and other stuff that don't fit any of us," Kyle grumbled.

Ray glanced at Kyle out of the corner of his eye. He was being serious, and he was puzzled.

"Your wife is thinking ahead, Kyle," he replied slowly. "She's looking to the future. It won't fit her or you or me, but there's no telling what other people might need at some point. Down the road, you guys might be able to trade this stuff for what you *do* need. Look around. Before all this happened"—Ray waved his arms for effect, gesturing in a circle—"no one thought about where it all came from, the synthetics and the fabric, the leather, electronics, tools, whatever. Anyone could just go to a store and buy what they needed, right?"

Kyle nodded uncertainly.

"There are no stores left, Kyle. What exists right now is what there is, and there may not be anymore for a long, long time. That's why we have forty sets of silverware, clothing that doesn't fit, shoes, dishes, tools, kitchen gadgets, and bottle openers. All this is *wealth* now, my friend. At some point, you will be able to spare some to get more of what you can't. You have a potable water source right in the house. It's naturally filtered. At some point, people may want to move in up here by you, and you will have a very big say in who that's going to be. Maybe right into the very houses that we're cleaning out. I think Carly is *counting* on it at some point."

The scavenging continued, one home at a time. Their place filled up while the others emptied out. All the homes had had fireplaces too, and toward the end, they were moving all the precut firewood they could find as well. Ray looked at the stack at one point and estimated they had about twenty cords of wood laid in. He had insisted that they keep it sorted too, hardwood with hardwood, pine with pine, kindling with kindling; there would be a reason for that later, but he needed to do the research and then discuss it with Kyle. Some of the trees nearby would probably need to come down as well. The tops were brown and dead. One thing at a time, though.

They stuck to the plan: food, medicine, and weapons first. The basement filled up quickly, and sometimes, they had to take a break from acquiring stuff and go hunting for more shelving just so Carly would have a place to put everything away. They came across more ammunition from time to time but did not find the rifles or handguns that it was chambered for, but that didn't stop them from taking it, though. Once the idea of trade goods got into Kyle's head, he was looking at things in a whole new light. Their alcohol stock soared. There was *so much* booze up here. They had hard alcohol, beer, wine, foofy cider drinks and coolers, plus a ton of stuff to mix it with. And there were sodas in the fridge and garage of most places.

Gradually, the two men worked their way downhill. The second-to-last house closest to them had a major jackpot.

They were scavenging the garage when Ray idly lifted the lid on a chest freezer. It had been running right up to the EMP and had a thick layer of ice on the inside walls. When the power had cut out, it had already been early winter in the Sierras, and so everything in the garage had remained frozen. There were steaks, chops, hamburger, bacon, sausage—*meat*.

"Oh wow!" Ray exclaimed. "Hey, Kyle, sheck this shit out!"

Kyle came over quickly.

"Wanna barbecue tonight?" Ray asked.

Kyle was actually salivating and wiped a little drool away from the corner of his mouth.

"Oh yes, I think so! Canned goods are great when you're hungry, but *man*, let's burn some steaks!"

The two men did a little improvised square dance right there.

Meat.

Ray went inside the home, and above the fireplace in the den was a .58 Hawken black-powder rifle. Custom job, beautiful curl in the wood stock. He whistled as he pulled it down. Someone had spent a *lot* of money on this rifle. The maker had even signed the barrel. Ray could barely make out *Jud Brennan*. He didn't know who that was, but he admired the craftsmanship. There was a nice poured-pewter fore-end cap, a few tasteful inlays, engraved wedge key escutcheons. It caught the light from the windows and *glowed*. Kyle walked in and saw Ray admiring the gun.

"Nice! I didn't know that Tom had been into black powder!"

A little bit of looking let them find percussion caps, black gunpowder to shoot it with, a beautiful leather shot pouch holding all the necessary tools for maintaining the rifle, a powder horn, lead ball, and other accoutrements. There was a whole closet full of gear, actually. There were knives and tomahawks, and on the desk sat a matching percussion pistol, also in .58.

Ray looked at Kyle with a glow on his face.

"I simply *cannot* wait to shoot his rifle, Kyle," he said.

Three more days passed, and they were done. The third bedroom and the basement were packed with foodstuff as well as most of the rest of the living space. The garage, except for where the truck was parked, and the workshop area were stacked to the ceiling with totes and boxes and wall to wall with stuff. The living room was full of board games and books and other sundries. The house looked like an episode of *Hoarders*. It had taken them a month to pillage seventeen homes. They had taken everything except the nails, furniture, and curtains. Now they needed to organize it all. Kyle and Ray were exhausted, and Carly was right there with them. They all agreed it was time for a break. Their foraging had yielded food, drink, seeds, toilet paper, cleaning supplies, blankets, clothing, hardware, tools, books, recreational materials, containers, storage tubs, terra cotta pots stacked in the backyard, waiting for spring, along with almost a pallet's worth of bagged topsoil. Firewood, lumber, concrete, and thousands of other items.

There were enough books on hand in enough different subjects and disciplines to read a book a week for the rest of their lives. Ray couldn't wait to dive into the "primitive living and survival skills" books they had found in the Hawken house. There were sets of buckskinner books, back issues of muzzle-loading magazines, trapping, skinning, hunting, and off-grid living. The entire Foxfire series had been there as well. Everything from how to craft snowshoes to brain-tanning a deer hide. Kyle had found a wind-up record player somewhere, a real antique, but it worked. They had also found a ton of old vinyl records, so they actually had music as they ate dinner that night. They listened to music, read books, played board games, and relaxed. As always, a hot shower was to be relished. Things were going to be good for a good long while. They were, in a word, *set*.

As Ray dropped off to sleep that final day of foraging, he did so with a smile on his face. They were going to be well-fed, the supply situation was good, and they would be entertained and warm. There would be many projects over the next few weeks, and he dreamily fantasized about designing and building things that would help Kyle and Carly construct a new life up here in the mountains.

Trying Hard

34

Harley followed Brian back into the bedroom, where they found Tricia lying on the floor, unconscious and unresponsive. He wasn't sure what to do, but he found himself doing stuff anyway. He checked her pulse, and she was breathing shallowly; she was also burning up. Harley lifted the child from the floor, wrapping her in blankets, and laid her gently on the bed.

"Brian, we need to lower her fever, I think, before we can do anything else," Harley said.

Harley looked over at Brian, who was still wrapped in a towel.

"Oh," Harley said. "Here, put a couple of these on."

Harley gestured at the oversize sweaters, and Brian grabbed a few, slipping them over his head.

"When was the last time you guys had something to eat?"

"Three days ago," Brian replied.

"Okay," Harley said. "Come with me for a minute."

"But—"

"I know. We need to get some more stuff if we're going to help her, though, and some of that stuff is in the kitchen, and I need your help, all right?"

"Okay."

"Come on. Let's go. We'll come right back, I promise."

Harley guided the boy to the door and then led the way to the kitchen.

He quickly started heating water for drinks and soups. He grabbed washcloths from the linen closet, occasionally flipping through the holistic herb book, looking for anything to lower a fever. Harley also figured that if the kids hadn't eaten in three days, they were probably dehydrated as well as being hungry, so he needed to get them rehydrated as well as fed, but something that they would be able to keep down. He figured chicken soup would probably help with the latter. Maybe the former too.

He quickly mixed a cup of hot water with a teaspoon of salt and a teaspoon of sugar (he had read somewhere that that would help, at some point) and handed it to Brian.

"Drink this slowly, Brian. Sip it. Make sure you drink a lot of water, juice, Gatorade, stuff like that, over the next few days, okay?"

"Okay."

"When the soup is done, turn the burner off and eat some of that as well. Okay? Can you do that for me?"

"Okay."

"I'm going back to check on Tricia. Come and join us when you are done eating. But I need you to be strong, so you need to eat and drink right now. Don't have too much, because if you do, it may make you sick, but have some now, and in an hour, we'll get you some more. And then you probably need some sleep as well, right?"

"Okay."

Harley grabbed some ice from the freezer, filling Ziploc baggies with it and wrapping them in the washcloths.

"You remember how to get from the kitchen here back to the bedroom?"

Brian nodded.

"Come join us when you've eaten. I'm going to need your help. Okay?"

"Okay."

Nodding, Harley left the boy sitting at the kitchen table. When he returned to the bedroom, he found the dog curled up on the floor near the bed. He groaned softly as Harley entered and kept his head down, but his ears were pricked, and his eyes followed Harley alertly as he moved around the room.

"You're probably hungry too, right?"

The dog's tail swished across the carpet a couple of times and then was still.

"I'm trying, Dog," Harley whispered. "I'm trying really hard. We'll find you something in a bit, okay?"

Harley put his hand on Tricia's forehead, and she was still burning up. She moaned softly when he took his hand away.

Harley ran into the bathroom, wetting the washcloths, then he wrapped the ice bags inside them. He put one under each of her armpits and laid one gently across her forehead. He added a few more blankets and propped her up a little more with an extra pillow. He had some flu powder medication to mix with hot water, but he wanted her a little more conscious before he tried to give it to her— he didn't want her to choke. He rubbed some mentholated gel on her chest. He hoped that would help with the breathing and wheezing. Then he just sat in the room, holding her hand.

Brian came back in a little later, and Harley tucked him in on the other side of his sister, and in a short time, he was completely out. Harley stood a short time after Brian fell asleep. He looked at the two children for a moment. He checked Tricia's forehead again. She seemed a little cooler than before, but still very hot, and Harley decided to get more ice bags. He dimmed the lights to a soft glow as he walked out of the room, the dog still watching him.

"Come on, boy, let's get you something to eat. Hungry?"

The dog licked his lips.

"Let's go," Harley said, thumping his thigh.

The dog rose to join him.

Leading the way back to the kitchen, the massive dog walking beside him, Harley tried to figure out what to feed this beast. He got a mixing bowl down from the cupboard and filled it with water. The dog immediately began lapping up water as soon as Harley set it on the floor.

"Guess you were thirsty too, huh?" Harley said.

Harley looked through his canned goods until he found a huge can of beef stew. "This looks like just the type of thing a big guy like you would like to eat," he said.

He opened the can, and as soon as the can opener pierced the lid, the dog's head came up and he licked his muzzle again.

"Yep. This is for you."

Harley dumped the whole can into another mixing bowl and set it on the floor by the water.

The dog set to eating immediately.

Harley ran his hand down the dog's back one time, and the dog tensed but then relaxed and kept eating. Harley petted him again, and the tail swished this time. With his refilled ice bags, Harley headed back to the bedroom.

He replaced the now-melted bags and rewet the cool washcloth on Tricia's forehead then collapsed into the oversized armchair off to the side. Harley pulled out another blanket and snuggled in under it, reading from the medical text for a while. Both kids were still out. He glanced at his watch. It was only 2:00 p.m., but it had been an eventful day so far. The dog went back in and curled up on the floor at the base of the bed. Harley grabbed another blanket and draped it over the dog. His tail thumped the floor twice, and he put his head down, mismatched eyes watching Harley thoughtfully.

"You're a smart fella, aren't you?" Harley said softly.

The dog closed his eyes.

Harley had some of the herbs that the book mentioned growing in his garden, and he also had a pretty good supply of medicine to supplement them, so he began to make a list of what he would need. Other than the raging fever, he had no idea what other things might be wrong with Tricia. It might be the flu, or it might just be exposure and exhaustion and hunger combining to make her sick. A common cold could kill if you were outside long enough. Harley thought about the weather for the last three days, and he shivered at the thought of two little kids out in it constantly. They probably wouldn't have lasted another night out there. Well, they were inside and warm now, and Harley was going to do his best to keep them alive. The dog too.

He must have dozed off, because he woke with a start at around 5:00 p.m. Muttering to himself, Harley got up to check on Tricia. She was a lot cooler now and breathing easier. She was still warm, but Harley didn't need to replace the ice anymore. He did rewet the washcloth on her forehead, though. Glancing around, Harley heard gnawing sounds and realized with a wince that the dog had gotten ahold of a signed Babe Ruth baseball from his collection.

"Hey!" Harley said, and the dog looked up at him. "Gimme that!"

The dog growled, and grabbing the baseball, he turned and ran into the hallway.

"Not cool, man," Harley said, pursuing. "I want that baseball!" he hissed, and the dog kept running down the hallway toward the villa.

Glancing back at the kids, who were still out, Harley shrugged and began jogging after the dog.

The pool deck in the villa was wide, and the dog was on one side of the pool while Harley was on the other.

This was only going to end one way; Harley wanted that baseball back. He chased the dog around for a while, getting nowhere. Finally, exasperated, Harley went and found a can of tennis balls.

"Here you go, you beast! I'll trade you!" Harley began bouncing the tennis balls off the deck.

That got the dog's attention, and his ears came up. Watching Harley bouncing the balls and ignoring him, the dog trotted to Harley's side of the pool. He approached cautiously, finally laying the baseball down and dancing around Harley, trying to grab one of the tennis balls as it bounced from the deck up into Harley's hands.

"You want this?" Harley asked him.

The dog crouched down, rump in the air and forelegs extended in front of him, his tail wagging.

"Go get it!" Harley yelled, throwing the ball into the far end of the pool.

The dog launched into the air, chasing the ball, and entered the water with a huge splash! While he was swimming to get the tennis ball, Harley grinned and walked over to retrieve his now-partially chewed autographed baseball.

"Not too bad," he muttered, rinsing it off in the pool. He dried it carefully on his shirt, careful not to smudge the autograph any more than it already was. Harley sighed. The dog was paddling back toward the shallow end, tennis ball in his mouth as he climbed the stairs and jumped out of the pool. Laying the ball down, he shook the water off in a tremendous spray, getting Harley all wet.

"Ugh!" Harley exclaimed. "Well, at least you got a bath, sort of. Me too, I guess. Want me to throw it again?"

So Harley threw the tennis ball again, and the dog launched back into the pool to get it.

They played ball for an hour or so, until the dog was clean and Harley was thoroughly drenched as well. Finally, laughing, Harley grabbed a few towels and dried them both off. He noticed while handling the dog the wound on his foreleg. Harley gently rubbed the worst of the grit and grime away from it, and the dog tensed, growling softly, but he let Harley work. Harley decided he would try again later, if the dog would let him, maybe get a bandage and some antibiotic ointment on it, but that was something to worry about for later.

"I told you I was going to get that ball back," he whispered to the dog. "And I did. I also said you needed a bath, and you got one. How about that?"

The dog cocked his head at Harley.

"Come on, let's go check on the kids again."

Harley walked out of the pool area, the dog accompanying him with a soggy tennis ball in his mouth.

Harley moved the children's clothes from the washer to the dryer and then went back into the bedroom, the dog flopping on the floor with a sigh. Harley covered him with the blanket again. Tricia's color was a lot better, and she was breathing easier. Brian was still asleep as well. As Harley went to wet the cool washcloth on her forehead again, Tricia opened her eyes and looked right at him.

"I don't feel good," she said.

"I know, but it's going to be all right," Harley whispered back.

Harley had been waiting for her to wake up so he could get some fluids into her, so he made her drink some of the flu stuff, and she took most of the glass that he had mixed it in and drank it. Then with a sigh, she closed her eyes and was out again.

Harley nodded in satisfaction. He was experiencing feelings that he had never felt before, responsibility, caring, and of all things, protectiveness. Go figure. He tucked the covers up under her chin and slipped out of the bedroom. The dog came along too. The dog went to the big steel door and began pawing at it.

"Do you need to go outside?" Harley asked him.

The dog pricked his ears and pawed at the door again.

"I think you do, all right. Let's make it quick. It's cold out there," Harley said, grabbing his jacket.

They jumped in the elevator, and the dog didn't waste any time, he took care of business and came right back. When they got downstairs again, Harley found Brian wandering around and yawning.

"Hello, sleepyhead," Harley said. "How are you feeling?"

"Better."

"Your clothes are on the dryer over there. They're clean and folded. Is your sister still asleep?"

Brian nodded.

"Good. We don't want to wake her up for a while yet. She was a very sick little girl for a few hours there. I think she's getting better, though. Her fever broke about twenty minutes ago. Are you hungry?"

Brian nodded again.

"Good. How does some more soup sound? I'll join you. We can talk some, and then I'll give you the tour. Sounds okay?"

"Yes, please."

"Clam chowder sound okay to you?" Harley asked, pouring the leftover chicken soup into the dog's dish.

"Yeah, I like clam chowder," Brian said.

"How about a grilled-cheese sandwich to go with it?"

"Yeah, I'm kinda hungry."

"Me too," Harley replied. "Were you and Tricia from that town that burned down a few days ago?"

Brian didn't say anything, and Harley looked at him expectantly. Finally, he sighed and began to tell his story.

"We were there, but we weren't *from* there. We were with the Friedmans, and then the motorcycle men came and started killing everyone, and Trish and I . . . well, we just ran."

"That sounds like a smart thing to do, Brian," Harley agreed. "Running away sounds like the absolute best thing that you could have done to me. You saved your and your sister's lives by running away."

Brian nodded thoughtfully.

Harley served up two bowls of soup and two grilled-cheese sandwiches and took a mouthful of chowder. He slid a glass of milk across the table to Brian and cracked open a beer for himself.

"Why don't we start at the beginning, Brian?" Harley asked casually. "Where were you and Tricia on The Day?"

So taking a deep breath, Brian began to talk, and Harley listened, fascinated.

You Win Some . . .

CHAPTER 35

Cain had almost 450 bikers riding with him now. They had roamed the western plains states, hitting where they could and taking what they could carry. Supplies were good. Morale was *great*. The plundering was fun, and the spoils of war made it even better. He grinned into the wind. By last count, they had sacked close to forty small towns, and people whispered his name in dark places like that of the boogeyman. Stockville had been hit a week before, and they had ridden in there and owned it. He was considering a change in course, maybe heading for warmer climates. Take his army and go while no one was around to oppose him. He was considering it.

At night, they camped under the stars. The weather was cold, but a big-enough bonfire and some good liquor put paid to that. Every guy that wanted a chick had one now, spoils of war, and they had even acquired a few trailers to haul food and loot, tents and supplies, ammunition and weapons, and slaves. Cain had a command tent and people to set it up for him, and he truly felt like a warrior king. A nomad of the plains.

Maybe hit a few more towns and go. They could swing back through here when the weather warmed up, and he was considering a push into Oklahoma before swinging into the south. The boys were leery of trying a run through Texas. There was just too much firepower there to deal with, day or no day. Tonight when they stopped, he planned on talking to everyone and planning out another direction to travel. There was one thing to deal with soon, and that was the granny in the minivan. That old lady had to pay. She had gotten away from them a few miles outside of some pissant town a few days before. Fred Kneller and about a dozen of their outriders had tried taking her out. Her minivan had been packed with supplies, and they had seen it as a total target of opportunity.

They had tried running her off the road, and suddenly, the van's side door had slid back, and there had been granny, firing from the hip. She'd dropped four of the bikes in six seconds and caused a few of the others to wipe out when they'd run into the wreckage. Fred had a serious road rash because of it. So they had to get even for that. Tonight they were going to party and plan, and tomorrow, they were going to hit the town. Cain grinned at the thought of it.

Far ahead, he saw his advance party. About thirty bikers. It was a sunny day. Suddenly, there were flashes from ahead, booms, and it looked like everything piled up fast. People were down. Cain held up his hand for a stop, and the main column came to a halt.

"Mack, take a few of the boys ahead and see what just happened up there," Cain ordered.

"Sure will, Johnny," he replied, whistling up about a dozen other guys.

"Lock and load people. We may have a situation!" Cain roared.

* * *

It had been a rough eight days for Abby. In the last week, she had seen her parents murdered along with her younger brother. The other two children she had been responsible for were lost. She hoped they had gotten away at least. She had been passed around like a party favor after the fall of Stockville, during the looting, and at the partying of the bikers afterward. She had been forced into slavery basically, she and another dozen young women from Stockville. When she wasn't being violated, she was cooking, cleaning, and carrying things. At night, she was tossed into a guarded pen with all the other captives. The first few days, she had been numb, almost catatonic, going through the motions. Then she had attached herself to one of the younger bikers and his stash. In all the possible futures that she had seen for herself, becoming some loser biker's stoner bitch hadn't been one of them. She stayed high all the time now just so she didn't have to care.

At the moment, she was riding behind Lucky Stevens way out in front of the rest of the gang. She was wasted. The air felt good, and looking around, she realized they were right in the middle of a group of thirty other bikes. There were some other girls on the backs of other bikes. Some were even there willingly. The thought that one mistake by one biker on these slippery roads could bring down everyone kind of made her shiver a little bit. It would be a huge mess. She hugged Lucky a little tighter, and her hand brushed across something hard in an elastic loop on the front of his jacket. Were those . . . ? Yes, they were grenades. He had six hanging on the front of his jacket.

Abby closed her eyes for a moment, drifting. She thought about dying, an end to pain, an end to this daily routine of rape, forced labor, and perpetual drug use, an end to the guilt and sense of worthlessness and shame that this life engendered. If it was fast, she wouldn't even know she was dead. She could be gone. She could be *free*. She could get even for her family and all the other families that these animals had done this to. Abby took a deep breath and let it out, then another. She hugged Lucky even tighter and ran her hands across his chest. She whispered in his ear.

"Can we go faster? It kind of turns me on a little."

So Lucky put the hammer down, showing off a little and moving his hog to the very front of the pack.

Abby squeezed her thighs closed around him, then she began to pull the pins on the grenades.

Lucky didn't notice for a second, and then the spoons flew away, and he was wearing six little bombs.

"What the fuck?" he screamed.

"Oops! My bad," Abby cooed in his ear.

"You crazy bitch! Jesus!"

He managed to get two of them off his jacket before the other four detonated, blowing him and Abby into hamburger meat.

The other two grenades hit the pavement, bounced twice, and detonated about chest level in the rest of the pack. Had she lived to see it, Abby would have been proud. She killed most of the advance party and severely injured the rest.

* * *

"Well?" Cain asked. "What happened?"

Mack brought his bike to a stop near Cain's and leaned in close to talk.

"Bad shit, Johnny. One of those girls we picked up a week ago in Stockville wigged out on the back of Lucky's bike, pulled the pins on his grenades, and decided to opt out of living. She took out most of our outriders."

"How many?" Cain asked flatly.

"Twenty-six dead, four severely wounded, and two are okay."

Cain winced. He took a deep breath and then motioned for his lieutenants to come in for a brief parlay.

"All right, people. Here's the deal. We're going to camp here tonight, bury our dead, and plan out tomorrow's course of action. And, gentlemen? We need to have a few new rules regarding captives. Get your people organized and then come see me at the command tent."

Mack gave him a look.

"See about getting our guys settled, Mack. I'll be up in a few. That little woods looks nice."

Everyone scattered and started setting up camp. Cain sat there, surveying the road, and thought about it. Finally, he reached inside his jacket and pulled out a flask. He took a deep pull of double-distilled brandy and shivered in the wind. A big fire would be nice tonight.

Setting camp took about an hour. Tents were put up, fires started, meals were cooked. Guards were posted, and those with no guard duty made fun of those whose names were pulled from hats. The partying started up soon after everyone had eaten. Drinking, smoking, laughing, and fucking soon took over as the men did as they wanted. Cain walked through the bedlam, exchanging a word here and a drink there. Finally, he entered the command tent and spread his maps out on a small collapsible table. Mack entered, handing him a hot bowl of beef stew and some biscuits, warm from the small Coleman oven. Cain ate slowly, studying the maps in front of him. He heard a small *crack*, *hiss*, and Mack put a beer down on the table in front of him. Cain nodded his thanks.

He had a few minutes yet before the other guys arrived, so he was able to put the warrior chieftain hat down for the moment. Chewing steadily, he looked at Mack across the table. Then he raised an eyebrow. Cain took a long swallow of beer to clear his throat and mouth.

"Well, Mack, what do you think? Is it time to move to warmer climates? Me, personally, I think we may have worn out our welcome in this part of the country. It's cold as shit, the pickings have been getting slimmer, and people are getting more desperate to hang on to what they have. Honestly, it's just us here right now."

Mack thought about it for a minute and then took a long pull on his own beer.

"Well, Johnny, we've been following your lead from the get-go. Me and the original group of guys, you've done all right by us. We've been having a good time, but you're right, it's getting harder. This little coalition of gangs we've put together has been working out all right. There's enough to go around at the moment, but what happens when there's not? A lot is gonna depend on what the rest of them want to do. Every one of those guys that are coming in here tonight sees himself as a mini warlord. They have ten guys behind them, or twenty, or fifty. You're the alpha dog, but they'd go for your throat in a second if they thought you were easing up. You can count on us, me and the rest of the *angels*, but I think most of these fellas are just along for the ride. If you want to move south, we'll move south, but there are no guarantees the rest will come with us."

Cain sighed and stretched, standing up.

"That's my take on it too. Tell you what, Mack? Let's just hit this town tomorrow and then go to Mexico or something. Deal?"

Mack nodded.

"All right, round 'em up and get them in here. Let's go over this again."

About twenty guys showed up fifteen minutes later. Some were drunk, some were high, but most were clear-eyed and hungry-looking. Cain smiled ruthlessly. He started immediately as soon as the last one entered.

"By now, all of you have heard what happened out front today, right?"

There were mutters and nods around the tent.

"So from here on out, we need to discuss better ways of dealing with and transporting captives, or we may even need to discuss getting rid of captives altogether. How many do we have anyway? Do any of you know?"

"A hundred or so?" one of the guys ventured.

"Anyone else?" Cain looked sternly around the room. No one else ventured a guess.

"Mack?"

"We have one hundred seventy-three captives, Johnny, mostly young women."

"One hundred seventy-three?" Cain asked.

Mack nodded.

"As of this morning, how many guys did we have riding with us?"

"Before or after the incident with the outriders?" Mack asked.

"Before," Cain replied.

"We had 457 guys."

"And after?"

"It was 431 in good shape, four wounded, three of them are gonna die."

"What's your point, Cain?" asked one of the other bikers present.

"My point? My point is that *one fucking captive* just killed almost thirty guys, you stupid fuck!" Cain roared back. "*My point,* is that you people are getting lazy, sloppy, and stupid out there, and that. Gets. People. Killed!"

Cain glared around the tent, and no one met his eyes for a moment. He took a deep breath.

"Now, we are gonna discuss how to prevent that in the future. Whether we kill the rest of them or we guard the rest of them. Basically, one quarter of our population is slaves, and any of them at any time, may take the opportunity to cut your throats or, how did you put it earlier, Mack? Opt out of living? And how many of us are they willing to take with them?"

"The guys aren't gonna like not getting laid regularly, Cain."

"Yeah, Sam, they're not. But we gotta look at it this way: I'd rather have 431 guys alive and horny than thirty guys dead and satisfied. Going forward, I don't want any of those people riding with us when we're out on the road. Anything can happen. In the morning, we load them into trailers and we lock them up for the duration of each day's trip. Got it?"

There were reluctant nods all around. Cain nodded himself, satisfied. Point made.

"If there is just one more incident like today, we're getting rid of the captives, all right?"

There was a little more muttering, but they all agreed.

"Now, about tomorrow's action. Mack, why don't you tell us what you were able to find out about Jenner, Nebraska?"

The planning went on into the night, and at dawn, they'd be hitting the town of Jenner.

Kids and a Dog and Stuff

"Evenin', folks! Harley Earl here. Just checking in to let all my listeners know that we are still on air. We will continue to play music for you here on KPAR Postapocalyptic Radio! Tonight is a slight diversion from my regularly scheduled broadcast. We have no news for you, the weather sucks, but look at it this way: since the bombs, those commuter times have dropped to next to nothing. You might even say it's dead out there, so if you have a working vehicle, put the pedal to the metal and drive! Be careful out there too. There are some rather-rude fellows on motorcycles looting and plundering the countryside. If you meet them, be sure to exercise your Second Amendment rights and do us all a favor. Blow away as many as you can! Here is Twenty One Pilots with 'Ride'."

Harley and Brian had had quite an interesting conversation the day after they met. They had come all the way from California, it seemed, lost their parents in the process, and lost the people that had taken care of them. He had heard firsthand all about the gang that had taken out Stockville, but what had captivated his imagination the last few days was the two hundred head of Black Angus cattle on the Friedman's ranch. The kids had described it as being up in the hills quite a ways back from the main road, hidden in a fold of the land. Harley wondered if anyone had been through there yet and if it was worth the risk to try to acquire some livestock. There was apparently more on the ranch than just cows; there were chickens and a few goats as well. The idea of eggs over easy for breakfast kind of appealed to Harley.

The other thing that appealed to Harley was the supply out at the ranch house, not to mention clothes for the kids and other things. He wanted to wait a few more days so that Trish was fully recovered from her illness before trying it. That didn't mean he couldn't do a little research beforehand. Harley had a map around here somewhere of all the local landholdings, and he wondered just how far away the ranch was. The chickens alone would be worth their weight in gold, but goats meant milk and cheese and fresh meat too, and they ate just about everything to stay alive, or at least that was what Harley thought. With the weather and the abrupt power failures everywhere, though, if he was going to make a move, he'd probably have to do it soon. He assumed the chickens would probably have some kind of autofeeder thing and probably hadn't been fed for a few days, much less water or heat.

Responsibility was a difficult thing for Harley. He had pretty much done what he wanted to do his entire life, and it was so terribly difficult to have to think of someone else before he ran off in pursuit of his latest idea. If Brian and Trish hadn't been here, not to mention the dog, why, Harley could have just gone out and gotten all that awesome stuff to bring back already. Of course, if he hadn't met Brian and Trish, and the dog, he wouldn't even know that that awesome stuff existed. The other thing was, having kids and a dog around and stuff was exhausting. The dog wanted to play all the time, and it was impossible to keep track of Brian now that Harley had given him the tour. He grinned. That had been satisfying. It was the first time he had ever really shown anyone around his place other than contractors. His grin faded as he realized that most of those guys that had helped build this place were probably dead now.

Harley had told Brian all the rules about everything. He had never really realized that he *had* so many rules when it was just him at home. Explaining about safe-climbing in a harness was necessary, though; he didn't want to find Brian with a busted neck after a six-story fall from a cliff. The trout pond was for catch and release only, until they became monsters, at least. Harley recommended not swimming in the pool until Trish was better: always go swimming with a buddy. Harley had shown him where the video-game room was, and the library, and the fitness center, and gotten him on a schedule where he checked in with Harley once an hour or so just so that Harley knew he was still alive. The dog was usually running around with Brian, and when he wasn't, he was curled up in the bedroom with Trish. Trish, Harley thought he'd better go check on her. Make sure she had everything she needed.

He had located Friedmans' on the plot map of the county and was pleasantly surprised to see the ranch closer to him than the town had been. Why, they were practically neighbors. He wondered why they'd never met. Only one other large acreage separated his property from theirs, as a matter of fact. Well, he'd worry about that later. He was going to see how Trish was doing.

Harley walked to the bedroom where Trish was ensconced and knocked on the door before going inside.

"Come in!" a little voice called, and Harley went in the rest of the way.

The lights were dimmed a little bit, and at that moment, Trish had a TV remote in her hand and was watching *The Powerpuff Girls*.

"Hi, Harley!"

He heard a tail thumping the carpeting and looked over to see the dog curled up in his blanket and peeking out at him.

"Hi, Trish. Hi, Dog!" he said quietly. "How are you feeling, kiddo?"

"Okay, I guess. I'm a little bored, though," she replied.

"Well, you were very, very sick just two days ago," Harley replied. "It takes time to feel better, and I think you should probably rest up for at least a few more days. Are you hungry? Thirsty?"

She shook her head.

"Want me to get you a few more cartoons or movies to watch?"

"Yeah."

"What would you like to watch?" Harley asked. He had an *extensive* collection of cartoons and movies, at least.

"Do you have any movies with unicorns in them?"

"As a matter of fact, I do." Harley mused, thinking.

He took her temperature again, made her drink some more of the flu stuff, refilled the plastic cup on the nightstand with cold juice, and went to find movies about unicorns.

Brian wanted to go swimming that afternoon and talked Harley into going in with him. They had a squirt-gun fight and contests to see who could hold their breath the longest underwater and were eventually joined by the dog. They took turns throwing the tennis ball across the pool for him. Then they relaxed in the hot tub, and Brian told him all about what he had been doing all day. Finally, they dried off, and Harley went to fix dinner.

They ate in Trish's room and watched *The Last Unicorn* together, and Trish, at least, really enjoyed it. Harley did up the dishes and tucked her in for the evening. He played video games with Brian for a bit and got him into bed finally as well. Then he and Dog went for a walk outside. It was a little cold, though, and the whole western horizon was piling up clouds again with what was looking to be another epic snowstorm. Sighing, Harley, and the dog, turned around to walk back up the lane and went back inside.

The dog settled in with a *whuff* sound and began licking his foreleg slowly. He had kind of claimed an overstuffed beanbag in front of the television for a bed. Harley went over to him and crouched down and took a look. It looked like the leg was healing just fine now, and Harley ruffled the fur between the dog's ears.

"You're going to be just fine too, it looks like," he whispered.

The dog relaxed onto his side with a sigh, and Harley threw a blanket over him.

He walked to the media room with heavy steps. With all the activity and excitement of the last few days, he hadn't really had a chance to review the video footage he had shot with the drone camera. Talking to Brian had cleared up what had happened there, but Harley kind of deep down inside needed to see what the world had come to. With the kids and the dog all settled in for the night, he decided to take the opportunity. He was horrified, of course. Zooming in with the camera, he inspected smoldering buildings and bodies in the streets with pools of blood around them. The bikers had vandalized every remaining unburned surface with swastikas and mottos. One really grabbed his attention, though. It said one thing, but the way it was written made Harley's blood run cold. It was one word: CAIN. The letters were about four feet long. For some reason, seeing that name made Harley start to think. To really think about how lucky he was to be where he was. There were other people out there, he knew. That was their new reality. To be hunted by Cain, to have everything taken from them, life, love, family. Harley's reality hadn't changed one bit, at least until Brian and Trish, and the dog, came into his life. He had been incredibly selfish, he suddenly realized.

Oh, he didn't feel bad about where he lived or how he lived, what he had that others didn't. It was the way he had looked at the world that was selfish, and he realized, all at once, that he had been a fool as well. All the things that made life important, Harley had missed out on them, it seemed. Anything worth having was worth feeling discomfort over, apparently. *Life* was supposed to be uncomfortable. It shouldn't just happen to you; you had to earn it. All the things that Harley had dismissed as one less thing to worry about should have been things that he was worrying about all along. Because they were worth having. In spite of the discomfort they caused or the embarrassment or the inconvenience, they were worth having.

So the question now was, what was he going to do about it?

Brian and Trish had grown on him in the last two days—them at least he could help out and take care of. But what could he do for other people? Should he take more in? And *if* he did so, how could Harley be sure that they were the right kind of people? What if he let in someone like Cain? Harley shivered. This was new territory for him, and he should just let it go. Then it would be—*No!*

"No more," he whispered. He could offer people hope on the broadcasts, give pep talks and that sort of thing, but what else? Should he go looking for others? Maybe.

"Kids and a dog and stuff," he muttered. "One more thing to worry about."

Tomorrow, if Trish felt better, he and Brian would take a field trip to this ranch and see if there was anything worth having from there.

CHAPTER 37

Settling In

From the Journal of H. Rayton Townsend
Late January 2017
Lake Alpine, California

Kyle and I have been taking down the dead trees on the property, along with the dead ones close by, at the neighbors', etc. We decided that while I was here, and we knew that we could depend on each other, that it would probably be for the best to get the area as prepped as possible for their (the Meyers') long-term use. We are constructing a smokehouse for any meat that we can hunt up later, as well as a storehouse for items that aren't going to be needed immediately. Stuff like the extra clothing, shoes, and household goods that we plundered from the other houses. All the things that may be traded off at some later time. We can salvage locking doors for them from the other houses to keep them secure from potential thieves, or bears and raccoons for that matter. I have to be honest with myself, I am stuck here for now, at least until springtime, if spring ever comes again anyway. The pass is, well, impassable, and even if I cleared the Sierra Nevadas alive and sane, I would still need to cross Nevada and the Rocky Mountains after them. The

Rockies are even higher and scarier and more treach-
erous than the mountains that we are in right now. In
the summertime, it will be a daunting task. My goal
is to still get home eventually. Maybe things won't be
so bad farther east, but I still feel guilt and shame for
not being able to go any farther. It gnaws at me. By the
way, Happy New Year! We celebrated it about two weeks
back, kind of around the time we thought it should be.
We're still not sure what day it is, but I am pretty sure it
is January now.

* * *

The sound of axes rang through air, so pure and clean that Ray felt like he should be exhaling diamonds with every stroke. It was a good sound. Kyle was alternating swings with Ray on the far side of the tree that they were currently in the process of taking down. It was the seventh one.

"Break!" he shouted out after taking a final savage swing at the tree.

Leaning on their axes, the two men stepped away from the forty-five-foot pine. They were breathing hard and wiping away sweat in spite of the thirty-degree temperature outside.

"Whooooooo!" Kyle exhaled.

"Kinda gives you an appreciation for the guys that used to log the old growth forests, huh? All those redwoods and sequoias, right?" Ray asked.

"Yeah," Kyle agreed. "This one is only five feet across. Carly and I drove *through* some and under others on our honeymoon up the coast. They had carved tunnels through the trees. Some were so big."

Ray stretched and felt his back pop. He twisted and felt everything kind of settle into place. He was developing great muscle tone now and felt fitter than at any time in his life. He had finally achieved those washboard abs he had always wanted. Something he *never* thought he would be able to obtain. Even in high school, when he had been in the best shape of his life, cranking out two or three hundred sit-ups a day, he had never had the chiseled look that he now sported. He grinned in pleasure at the simplicity of the jobs that they were doing now.

"Ready to finish taking this bitch down?" he asked.

"Let's do it!" Kyle replied.

The two men went back to work, and Ray thought about the coming months, the things that he might see and do and experience. He grinned at how far he had come from where he had been. He was laughing outright as the tree began to break, and both men dodged back out of the way. The first tree had been a near disaster, with neither man knowing what to expect. The trunk had jumped off that stump, twisting through the other trees and shattering, as it tore away limbs and rained debris on both of them. Now they at least knew which way to jump. They had been sawing the trunks into usable lengths and constructing a smokehouse for anything they could hunt later on. It was going to be a good one, and it was almost complete. It had a floor of interlocking pavers that they had stolen from up the hill, bringing them down one wheelbarrow at a time and laying out the original dimensions. It had a nice fire pit in the middle of it, and the outside walls now stood about six feet off the ground. Ray figured this tree might do it and they'd be done with that building project soon.

They fell to the job of pruning the branches from the log, measuring what would be needed, and began to saw it into the appropriate lengths to get the job done. During the sawing, stacking, splitting, and chopping, Ray found his mind wandering again. There would be roads to follow, of course, a luxury that the early pioneers had had to do without. In many ways, though, Ray was betting that it would probably be just as dangerous. Instead of Indians, there would probably be biker gangs or rogue military units, maybe additional camps to avoid. Who knew what awaited him? He had the feeling that he might finally see the *real America*, like some sixties drifter that he had read about hiking the back roads through small towns and farms and vast open spaces. He would see a country stripped of all pretensions, false pride, and possibly humbled by tragedy.

It could very well be vicious and unruly and governed by mob justice as well. He imagined that maybe he might end up doing things, to stay alive, that he had never considered doing before, that never in a million years would have occurred to him. People would be at their very best, or their very worst, or maybe he would be surprised. Maybe, he would make it over the mountains and it would all still be there. That Greyhound bus ticket home. He *would* get home. His mom would give him a hug, and his dad would be sitting, watching TV, and flipping the channels, a dog curled up in his lap. They would have long talks about everything and nothing, and he would help them by doing chores around the place until he could get back on his feet again economically. It was nice to think about a happy ending, but for some reason, Ray just didn't think it was going to work out that way. So instead of moving onward, he stayed, learned, and got stronger. He focused on what he *could* do. Right now, that was the repetitive rhythm of splitting, chopping, and stacking kindling and firewood.

"Ready to knock off?' Kyle asked.

The question startled Ray out of his reverie. He had been in the zone, that rhythmic, repetitive place where all thought had faded to be replaced by almost a Zen blankness. He had heard runners and joggers refer to it as runner's high, only he hadn't been running; he had been chopping. *Chopper's high* sounded so ridiculous in his head when he thought of the term that he started laughing. When he explained the thought process to Kyle, he grinned too.

The two men arrived back at home at dusk. They paused on the stairs as Kyle gripped Ray's shoulder and pointed quietly. Far away across the valley, down the other side of the lake, a pinprick of light was moving. It was very visible as that side of the valley had been in deep shadow for a while now. It had the look of a lantern the way it flickered. Then it moved a few more feet and disappeared.

"Looks like we have neighbors," he said with a grin.

Ray followed him up the steps and into the house and wondered if that was a good thing or a bad thing. Time would tell.

Dinner was the last of the steaks from the Hawken house. Canned peas, homemade sourdough bread, and cherry cobbler finished it off. They had coffee with dessert and played cards, mostly 500 rummy, throughout the rest of the evening. Ray had noticed, with the electricity turned off most of the time, they all had a tendency to go to bed a little earlier and had started keeping farmers hours. Up with the dawn and to bed when it got dark outside. Tonight was a little different, and they stayed up later, reading, playing cards, and listening to music on the windup record player.

"You know, Kyle, I think we should probably build something like this too," Ray said, showing him the sketched picture of a primitive forge. "Some simple blacksmithing skills may help you out a little later on as well."

"Yep. Might as well learn what we can while we can. Never know when it'll come in useful."

"Seeing as how that was the last of the steaks tonight, we might want to go hunting soon as well. Maybe bag one of those deer we have been seeing tracks from."

Carly rolled her eyes.

"You, sir, just want to go play with the fancy rifle that you guys found," she said. "Boys and their toys, I swear . . ."

Ray and Kyle grinned at each other.

"You better believe it! I cannot *wait* to shoot that rifle. Besides, some more steaks would be good, and the smokehouse is almost finished. So is a day off for hunting totally out of line?"

"Go kill Bambi," she said with a sniff. "You guys better do the butchering too, though! Do *not* expect me to clean what you kill!"

"Nice!" Kyle exclaimed.

* * *

From the Journal of H. Rayton Townsend

We have been hunting for the last week or so. We finished the smokehouse too! So far, I have gotten two cow elk, and Kyle has nailed three deer. I have no idea why they are still up here at this time of the year, but they seem to be finding food, and so they have become food for us. We have the bodies hung up in the garage across the street, draining, after we field-dressed them, and we

have a ton of butchering ahead of us. What I really want
to talk to you about is the bear! It's quite a story.

* * *

"Dude!" Ray hissed in disgust, pulling the scarf up and over his nose. He edged away from Kyle on the tree stand they had built. "*That* is fucking rank and uncalled for!"

Kyle was laughing quietly and waving the fart in Ray's direction. "Ugh! No more beans for you, ever!"

The air was still in that just-past-dawn kind of way, and it was quiet in the part of the forest they were hunting today. They had constructed a few tree stands, and this one was about three miles downhill from the cabin, almost to the main road. They hadn't gone quite to the edge of the forest, but they were close. They had also removed the Private Driveway sign from the side of the highway. The road was windswept and covered in snowdrifts, looking like a vast white meadow. No one had been through since their arrival the previous month, and that was the way they liked it for the moment. Ray was just about to comment on Kyle's rank, dead, zombie gas again when both men grew silent and alert as a single shot echoed through the trees.

"Did you hear that?" they both started to whisper at the same time.

A piercing scream followed the shot, accompanied by the enraged roars of what sounded like . . .

"That fucking bear," Kyle said.

There were more shots and screams.

"Someone's in trouble," Kyle said in a normal voice.

"Wanna go check it out?" Ray asked.

Kyle hesitated for a moment and then sighed.

"Yeah. Let's go!" he replied, shimmying down the trunk.

Ray followed as fast as he could, and the two of them began to plow through thigh-deep snow. They pushed as hard as they could for the final half-mile to the roadway. There were more shots and more screaming, and they tried to go quicker. The roaring had continued as well, and when they got to the roadway, they found a complete and utter mess.

A *very* large bear was floundering through the snow, swatting at, chasing, and biting someone dressed in multiple layers of winter clothing. Sometimes the bear connected, and sometimes he missed, but when he hit, the results were devastating. The person they were watching was being mauled. Without even exchanging a word, both men raised their rifles to their shoulders and commenced firing. There was no time to consider the victim getting clear of the target. Ray hit him at least three times, and so did Kyle. At any rate, the bullets striking distracted the hell out of him. The bear dropped its now-motionless victim in the snow. It was actually kind of funny for a moment, the bear in his winter coat swatting at the rounds hitting him. He was standing on his hind legs and looking around, puffs of snow and dust blowing off the heavy fur. Then it stopped being funny really fast, because the bear had seen them and was charging. Kyle pushed Ray one way and went the other himself.

"Split up! And for God's sakes, keep firing!"

Ray ran behind another tree and continued to fire at the bear running straight at him. It had seen his dash away from Kyle and changed course to get him. Distantly, a part of his mind was aware that Kyle was yelling about his rifle jamming just as he dry-fired his own. He was out of ammunition, and all he had was the Hawken strapped to his back. Ray hadn't even test-fired it yet, but it was loaded, and the 30.06 wasn't. The bear was fifteen feet away from Ray, coming on like a snowplow, when Kyle yelled at it from behind his tree.

As the bear was distracted by Kyle, Ray swung the rifle around, pulled the butt into his shoulder, and thumbed back the hammer to full cock. As he came abreast of him, Ray pulled the trigger, and 120 grains of black powder exploded, throwing the .58 ball across the short distance to the bear. Ray knew he had a kill shot just as soon as the rifle barked. The grizzly's entire side erupted with blood and fur. The shot had pierced heart and lungs before exiting, pretty much killing him instantly. He did take three more strides before slamming headfirst into the tree that Kyle was hiding behind. The bear looked at Kyle, gave a strangely human-sounding sigh, and died. Kyle sat down suddenly in the snow, eyeing the dead bear with his rifle across his lap.

"I wet my pants. I can't believe it!" he said in disbelief. "Jesus!"

Ray snorted and grinned a tight grin. He didn't feel too dry himself at that moment.

"Well," he said, looking at the Jud Brennan Hawken in his hands, "that's a pretty sweet rifle."

"Fucker has to be seven feet tall, easily . . ."

Ray ignored Kyle and looked across the roadway toward a shredded brightly colored winter parka.

"I mean, he almost got me . . ."

Ray gave the bear a leery look and edged around the carcass, heading for the road.

"He almost got you too . . ."

Kyle was still sitting in the snow as Ray followed the bear's path back to where the mauled person was lying. She was lying in red snow. Ray would always remember that part of it. A disjointed heap, arms and legs akimbo and looking slightly out of place. Very carefully, he rolled her over, stripped off a glove, and felt for a pulse. There was a lot of blood.

"A guy could just *die* out here—"

"She's alive!" Ray yelled to Kyle.

Kyle was *still* in the snow, staring at the bear and breathing hard.

"Dude! Kyle! She's alive! What do we do?"

Ray knew that you should never ever move someone that has been in a serious car accident. This was much, much worse than that. There were no paramedics to call to the scene. The closest medical help was four miles away. There was no 911 to call, no handy field guides for surviving a bear attack on a lonely snow-swept road in the middle of the mountains during a postnuclear winter. All that went through Ray's mind bitterly. Finally, in his cheeriest tone of voice, Ray called over to Kyle again.

"Hey, Kyle! You done looking at that bear yet?"

"Yeah," he said, blinking.

"I said she's alive! I'm not sure for how much longer! We're going to have to move her, man! Can you carry my rifles?"

Kyle went over to grab the Hawken after picking up Ray's 30.06 where he had dropped it in the snow. Ray picked up the girl in a fireman's carry, and they began to head back up the mountainside. As they passed the bear, Ray nodded at it.

"See? I *told* you there was a lot of meat on a bear!" Ray laughed.

The next two hours were an agony of climbing. The three and a half miles to the cabin were marked by bruises, scrapes, slips, falls, and pain. He didn't drop her, though. Ray's lungs were working overtime by the time they made it to the cabin, and he was graying out a little. Carly strolled out of the front door, ready with a comment about "the great white hunters, returning with their prize" when she realized it wasn't a deer slung over Ray's shoulders. She went as pale as a sheet.

"Jesus! What did you guys do now?" she exclaimed.

"Help her," Ray gritted out through chattering teeth.

"We need her inside right now!" Carly snapped, taking charge. "I'll do what I can."

Ray laid her gently down on the couch in the middle of the room and then staggered into the kitchen to gulp down some water. Behind, he could hear Kyle explaining quickly what had happened. As he reentered the living room, Carly was competently and quickly examining the injured woman that they had brought in. She thumbed up an eyelid, checked her pulse, and gave her a cursory examination. She was inspecting lacerations, bite marks, puncture wounds, and the large spectacular bruise on the side of her face. A flap of skin had torn loose on her scalp and was hanging down over one eye. Ray felt a little ill.

At that point, Carly looked at the two men and started issuing instructions.

"Okay, she's out cold. We need to get her cleaned up and warmed up," she said, pointing at the torn scalp. "And *that* is definitely going to need some stitches. I think her shoulder is dislocated as well."

Ray looked at Kyle, and he shrugged.

Carly clapped her hands sharply, and they looked at her.

"*Gentlemen!* I need the first aid kit supplies, washcloths, a turkey baster, boiling water, rubbing alcohol . . ."

The list ended with *sewing needles* and *boiled thread*.

"We gotta move if we're gonna save her! *Now!*"

Carly began cutting the woman's clothes away with Kyle's buck knife, deft fingers moving surely and quickly, while Ray boiled large pots of water on the stove, boiling washcloths, thread, needles, and utensils. He spent the entire afternoon doing that and feeling useless as Carly set about trying to save a life. She washed the wounds with the cloths, irrigated the area where the skin had torn away, and stitched up her scalp. She flushed out the puncture wounds with the turkey baster and stitched up a few other places as well. She wrapped her head with gauze after smearing antibiotic ointment along the stitches, wrapped other parts of her as well in bandages and gauze, all the time muttering about blood loss and how she wished they had an IV with plasma or saline. With a final critical glance, she put her foot into the woman's armpit, and with a wrench that made Ray and Kyle wince, she popped the dislocated shoulder back into place. After three hours, she had her cleaned up, sewn up, wrapped up, and into Ray's bed with as many of the old-fashioned rubber hot-water bottles that they could find. They had scored enough antibiotics in their plundering to hopefully stave off infection.

"That should do it," she said finally. "If she has ruptured her spleen or has internal bleeding, though, she's done for. We'll know in a few days for sure."

Then Carly broke down completely, sobbing into Kyle's shoulder. Embarrassed, Ray took that moment to go to his room and strip off his filthy, bloodstained clothing and get in the shower.

He had been covered in her blood by the time they made it back to the house. He looked at his shaking hands, staying in the hot water longer than normal until he felt clean again. Carly got cleaned up after he got out, and the three of them sat down for a subdued but welcome dinner.

They ate quietly, until Carly rallied at the end. She looked at Kyle with a twinkle in her eye.

"What?" Kyle asked.

"You know what this place needs?" she asked quietly.

"What's that, babe?" Kyle replied around a mouthful of green beans.

"A bearskin rug!" she said, laughing.

Kyle choked, and Ray patted him on the back. He thought that was pretty funny, until he realized she was serious. She was insisting that they go back down for the bear after dinner.

* * *

From the Journal of H. Rayton Townsend
January
Lake Alpine, California

The date doesn't seem as important as it once did. Carly wasn't kidding. After dinner, she made us go back down for the bear. We moaned and groaned and said it could wait until tomorrow, but she wasn't having it. So we pulled on warm clothes again, reloaded the rifles, and went back down for the bear. When we got there, Kyle and I followed the woman's back trail a little ways, and we retrieved her pack and rifle from where she had first encountered the bear.

* * *

They set out after dinner with a large tarp and a couple of poles to build a travois. They figured they could skin out the bear while down there, load the hide and the meat, and drag it up to the cabin. The wind moaned through the trees above them, and a few more flurries drifted down through the branches. The pines creaked and swayed in the wind, and both men were tired from the adrenaline crash from the events earlier in the day. Full stomachs made them a little drowsy as well, but after a mile in the snow, they found their rhythm, their muscles loosened up, breath came easier, and they started talking again.

Ray was about to recap his flask of brandy but instead held it out to Kyle.

"Want a little motivator?" he asked.

Kyle grunted and took a long, healthy swig before handing it back.

"Good," he wheezed out after a second. "Where did that come from?"

"Winters. I played a lot of poker there," Ray replied.

"Nice score."

The two men continued crunching through the snow downhill.

"We *could* have done this tomorrow, you know," Kyle grumbled.

"Yeah," Ray agreed, "but Carly has a point, dude. There *is* a lot of meat, fat, and fur on this guy, so why let it go to waste? I'm sure there are wolves and other scavengers around up here as well. Why let them reap the benefit of what we did earlier? Besides, this sucker could freeze solid tonight, and we would have a hell of a time doing this in the morning. We might as well just get it over with."

"Yeah."

They continued on for a few more moments, and then Kyle brightened up a little.

"Hey!"

"What?"

"That girl had a rifle of some kind too, remember? And where's her shit? Remember? We heard the shots first?"

"That's right."

Both of them agreed that another rifle around was a good thing, and they stepped up the pace a little. When they reached the bottom of the lane, they turned onto the main road and followed her back trail for a while. Eventually, they found her rifle and a small pack.

"This must be where she first ran into him," Ray said, gesturing to the snowplow trail leading away to the far tree line and then her own tracks stretching back down the pass.

"Here's her pack!" Kyle said, digging it out of the powder. "And her rifle . . ." Kyle whistled slowly through his teeth. "Look at this, Ray."

Ray took the rifle and saw it was a .22. He shook his head slowly, wondering what kind of a woman entered the mountains in winter armed with only a .22 and was willing to take on a grizzly with it, no less.

"Girl has some balls to take on a bear with a small-caliber rifle, ya know? She's real brave, or she just didn't know what else to do, or both," he said, smiling.

"Like throwing rocks at a freight train," Kyle agreed.

"Ready to skin that sucker out?" Ray asked.

"Let's do it, to it!"

The two men approached the bear and again marveled at its size before beginning.

They stretched the bear out on the ground, and Ray had brought a tape measure along, checking the length of the bear. They both whistled. He was eight feet long.

"Big motherfucker. Glad we didn't meet him first, ya know? *Look* at the size of those paws!"

They both agreed that would have probably been a bad thing.

They built their travois out of the tarp and poles, knelt down, and began to skin out the bear. It was slow-going at first, but eventually, they got the hang of it, got the pelt off him, and laid it on the travois. It was going to be an awesome rug! They removed as much meat and fat as they could and stacked it on the skin. Ray pulled out his hatchet and hacked through the bear's skull to get the brains. Those went into a Tupperware container. As an afterthought, he got out his Leatherman and used the pliers to remove the bear's canines as well. He slipped them into his pocket. Kyle gave him a quizzical look, and Ray just shrugged and smiled. They had taken about six hundred pounds of meat from this animal, and it was about all they could manage in one trip. They would need to preserve it as soon as they could. Ray guessed the smoker was the best bet. Finally, they were ready to go.

Looping straps over their shoulders, the two men began to pull the travois up the hill and through the woods. It was a long three and a half miles and well after dark when they arrived back home. They staggered to a halt in front of the garage. The snow was coming down in earnest again, and Kyle lifted the door up. Ray absently noted that the thermometer outside the door read twenty-seven degrees.

"It ought to be cold enough out here tonight to keep the meat fresh, right, Kyle?" he asked.

"Oh yeah. We're done with this for tonight. Tomorrow, we'll need to cut it up, wrap it up, and get it put away somehow."

"Feel like having a bear-b-que tomorrow?" he asked.

Kyle just punched him in the shoulder. Hard. Which made Ray laugh even more.

After everything was put away and situated, they closed the garage door and went inside to find Carly reading a medical text by lantern light. She had put some coffee on for the guys for when they returned, and they sipped it gratefully, standing in front of the fireplace.

"How's our guest?" Kyle asked quietly.

"She's sleeping now. Really sleeping, I mean, not just unconscious. She came to for a bit, flailing and screaming at one point, and I got some water and painkillers into her, but she went right back out again," Carly replied. "It's a step in the right direction, at least. We won't know for a bit whether she has internal injuries, but if she lives through the night, her odds go up quite a bit. As it is, I am fairly concerned."

"Bear is in the garage, Carly." Ray sighed. "Rock, paper, scissors for who showers first, Kyle?"

"Go ahead, man. I'm gonna get more coffee in me, but make it *fast*, Ray. I'm feeling a bit yuck as well, ya know?"

Ray jumped in the shower and groaned as knots loosened and punished muscles relaxed. He adjusted the showerhead to the heavy-massage setting and purred as the water pulsed over abused muscles and between his shoulder blades. When he dried off after getting out, he glanced at the soiled clothing on the floor of the bathroom and winced. Those would probably never be the same again. He padded into his former bedroom to get some fresh clothes, a T-shirt, some fleece pajama pants, and warm wool socks. He studied the woman in the bed as he dressed, who was completely motionless except for the rise and fall of her chest as she breathed. Her face was a spectacular collection of bruises, cuts, scratches, and scrapes. It was amazing that she had even survived. Carly had put thirty-two stitches into her scalp and another sixteen into her midriff area. The puncture wounds made him wince and shake his head. He was glad she had been unconscious while those were being irrigated. He grimaced again thinking about it. She was breathing steadily, though, and he wished her a silent "Good luck" before leaving the room.

When he returned to the living room, he felt like a new man. Well, *newer*, at any rate. Clean and wearing warm and fuzzy clothes. Carly had stacked some blankets on the couch for him to curl up in, and he nodded his thanks as he did just that gratefully.

"Tired?" she asked him.

"Yeah," Ray replied, having to think hard just to get the word out. "I thought I would read a few pages on the tanning process"— he yawned—"before I fall asleep."

"For my bearskin rug?" Carly smiled.

"Yeah," he replied.

Carly nodded.

Ray laid back on the couch, snuggled into his blankets, and read about four words before his eyes drifted shut, the book open on his chest. Carly walked across the room, closed the book gently, and set it on the end table before lowering the lantern to a dim, soft glow. She put the rest of the lanterns out then went to put Kyle to bed as well. She still had a long night ahead of her and was planning on spending the night in the room with the injured girl just in case she needed anything.

38

The Ranch

Harley spent two days building a fenced-in area in his garage. It was a big garage, designed to hold three vehicles, but Harley only had his Range Rover. What would he have done with more cars, anyway? It had only been him, Harley Earl. One guy, one car. It made sense. So the rest of the garage was a big, open area, and he hoped that soon, there would be goats and chickens in there.

Trish was on her feet again, but taking it easy. Harley had told her not to push it too much and explained that he and Brian would probably be going to the Friedman ranch today to check stuff out. He would be leaving the dog with her for company, and he explained that it might take them a few hours to get what they were after and come back. She seemed to be okay with that, and he made sure that she had stuff to do, more movies and cartoons, snacks, and juice and stuff. She had been absolutely enchanted by the game room when he had given her the tour, and she and Brian had been competing fiercely since last night in a video game marathon.

The animal pen complete, Harley checked over his vehicle. He loved this car. It had a seven-inch lift kit on it, big knobby tires that retained their snow chains at the moment, a winch on the front, and a spacious interior. He ran back inside to the armory, checked and reloaded his AR-15, and grabbed a few extra magazines full of ammunition. And his binoculars, of course. He did a final check on

Trish to make sure she had everything she needed and told her that he and Brian would be leaving in a few minutes. Trish gave him a big hug, and he felt something melt inside him as he hugged her back. Then he knelt down and looked her in the eye.

"We'll only be gone for a few hours, Trish, okay? We'll be right back, I promise."

"I want to go with you."

"I know, sweetie, but seriously, you'll be fine here. There's lots to do, and Dog will keep you company."

She followed him and Brian to the big steel door and waved as they left, Dog standing beside her.

When they got upstairs, Harley pulled out his map of the area, and with Brian riding shotgun, they headed off into the storm. It took about an hour to get to the Friedman ranch, crunching through and over the snow-packed roads, but Harley was pleased to see that there were no tracks in the long drive that ran to the ranch complex. They passed a few cows along the way, grouped together for warmth. Finally, they pulled into the dooryard of the ranch house. It was silent as Harley cut the engine.

They got out and cautiously approached the door to the house. Harley knocked loudly, but no one answered. He looked at Brian and shrugged.

"Let's go in. Doesn't seem like anyone is at home."

They opened the door and went inside.

"Hello?" Harley called out. "Anyone? Anyone? Bueller?"

"*Hello!*" Brian called out.

There was no answer.

"All right, Brian, let's grab your and Trish's stuff, and then we'll go see about the chickens and goats and things, all right?"

Brian nodded decisively. It felt weird to be in someone else's house when they weren't there.

They were about to start doing stuff, Brian heading for the bedroom that he and Trish had shared before going into Stockville, when someone spoke from behind them.

"Very slowly put your rifle down and turn."

Harley felt a prickle between his shoulder blades and did as he was told. He carefully laid the AR on the kitchen table. Then he turned around.

A woman stood there with a shotgun leveled, pointing at him.

"Who are you, and what are you doing here?"

Harley tried to grin, but he couldn't pull it off.

"I'm Harley Earl," he said. "We're neighbors, sort of, and we just came to get some stuff."

She flicked the safety off.

"You mean you came here to rob us?"

"Mrs. Friedman?" Brian said from the doorway.

She blinked, lowering the shotgun a little.

Harley was confused. He thought they had all died, from what Brian had said.

"Brian?" she said slowly, recognition seeping in through the paranoia, and lowered the shotgun altogether.

"What are you doing here? Who is this?" she asked, pointing at Harley.

"This is Harley Earl," Brian said with a grin. "He saved me and Trish, Mrs. Friedman. We didn't know how to get back here, and so we found this dog, and . . ." Brian was explaining. It was a long story.

After introductions were made all around, it turned out that *this* Mrs. Friedman was his friend's aunt, the lady who actually lived here. She had made it out of Stockville during the attack the week before and had returned home on foot.

"Come on out, guys, it's okay!" she yelled over her shoulder.

Brian's eyes grew wider and wider as his friend Josh came into the kitchen along with two of his cousins, Sandy and Olivia.

"I thought that all of you were dead!" he said with a grin.

"Nope. Aunt Angie got us out of there. I lost Abby somewhere in all the fighting," Josh replied. "I don't know what happened to her. So we came back here to wait and haven't really been outside since. No one else has come home, though."

Off to the side, Harley was quietly talking with Angela Friedman while the children were getting reacquainted.

"Honestly, we didn't mean any offense," Harley was saying. "I have my own place not too far from here, found the kids wandering around last week with a big-ass dog, and they told me about this place, chickens and baby goats specifically, so I thought it would be worthwhile to come and get them some real clothes other than what they were wearing when I found them and anything else that may be useful that was lying around. Brian thought you were all killed in Stockville, so rather than have looters or more bikers get what was here, since it wasn't too far away, I thought we'd make the trip and get what we could, you know? Seriously, I apologize. We didn't mean to scare you half to death."

"Tell me about your place," Angela said seriously and suspiciously, glancing at the kids. "I don't remember seeing you around before, and believe it or not, we *do* know all our neighbors. So I am finding it very hard to believe that you live where you say you do, unless . . ." Her eyes widened a little. "You're *him!* The crazy guy that bought the old missile base about eight years ago! Right? There were rumors that someone had bought it, and there were outside contractors and big trucks coming and going for a while there, and then nothing." She shook her head. "We thought *whoever* had just given up on the project, seeing as how the whole place was falling apart. It would have taken a ton of money to get it livable—I mean, I *know* it would have! Josh and I used to party there with the other kids when we were in high school. It was just a big damp hole in the ground."

Harley laughed quietly. Then he nodded.

"Yep, I am the crazy guy. If you want to come with us, I am sure that your opinion of the place will be vastly improved. I think it's only a matter of time before your place here gets hit by bad people. It seems to be happening everywhere. In all honesty, though, I could use help with the kids. I've been doing my best, but . . ." Harley spread his hands and shrugged.

So Angela made a decision. Harley's place sounded safer than the ranch, so she got the kids packing bags of clothes in a hurry. They emptied their closets into duffel bags, stuffing in underwear and socks, shirts, and pants, and Harley noted with approval that the clothing situation at least would be under control. They loaded totes with food and ammunition, and Angela cleaned out the gun safe. Josh Friedman had had a surprisingly good-sized collection of firearms on the premises. Angela packed her own bag full of practical clothing and some valuables, documents, and that kind of thing. All that stuff went into the back of the Range Rover until they couldn't fit any more.

The next thing was the livestock. Angela led Harley to where a large plywood-sided trailer was sitting under a three-walled steel barn, and he backed his vehicle up to it so that they could get it hooked up to the trailer hitch. They spent the next two hours loading feed and hay into the back of it. Finally, they loaded two-dozen chickens, a rooster, and sixteen goats as well, four nanny goats and twelve little ones. The chickens had their own cages, so that was relatively easy. The goats had to be chased down in some cases, but the work progressed. Finally, everyone crowded into the vehicle, and boy, was it loaded! They just couldn't fit anything else.

Harley drove slowly back to his place, with the blizzard howling around them. It was near-whiteout conditions. So he took his time. Safety first. His garage at the end of the lane looked like a solid hill of snow now, so he had to spend forty-five minutes clearing it away from the doors with a shovel. Finally, he was able to get the Range Rover into the garage. They detached the trailer, got the goats and chickens into their pen after laying down hay for them and after stacking the rest of the baled hay and feedsacks off to the side, and Harley closed the doors, leaving the trailer outside.

There were a few murmurs when he hit the call button on the elevator after keying in his security code. And a few moments later, it arrived. Everyone packed inside, and Brian began excitedly telling the other kids what to expect. Trish had been alone for almost seven hours with the dog, and Harley was feeling a bit anxious about it for some reason. He saw Angela looking at him from the corner of her eye and grinned. The elevator reached bottom, the doors swished open, and the illumination went from low to normal. The brushed steel door gleamed softly as Harley went to key in his security code.

"What are you, Harley? A spy or something?"

"Nope. Just Harley Earl," he replied soberly.

Spinning the large spoked wheel in the center of the door, he pulled it open.

"Welcome to my home," he said.

He gave them all the tour, of course, and Trish was overjoyed to have more kids around, but Harley was interested in Angela's reactions to things. She was the first adult that he had ever had in here. It almost seemed as if he was being judged. It was an uncomfortable feeling. He assigned bedrooms and asked if anyone was hungry and took the dog out. Everyone got cleaned up and warmed up and fed, and eventually, the kids went to bed.

Finally, it was just him and Angela awake. They chatted for a while, exchanging stories of what they had been doing since The Day, and Harley heard all about Stockville and the ranch. Mostly it was all small talk.

Finally, Angela asked him point-blank what he had done before The Day.

Harley tried to figure out how to answer that, and finally, he replied.

"Nothing," he said softly. "I did nothing."

"Well," Angela replied, standing up and getting ready to head off to bed, "you did something today. That's all that matters. Thank you, Harley. Good night."

"Good night, Angela," Harley replied.

A New Understanding

39

From the Journal of H. Rayton Townsend

It has been a few days since I have logged anything of interest or resembling an actual journal entry. Mostly I have been copying useful information or random thoughts that I have been gleaning from the books I have been reading. So here goes. Kyle and I completed the construction of the storehouse for all the additional items that we don't use. We finished it completely yesterday morning. It has a good, sturdy door with multiple locks on it. We ended up building shelves to go inside and clothing racks, where clothing will eventually hang by size and gender. All in all, it's going to work out fine. We are pretty proud of ourselves at the moment. With the smokehouse and the storage house complete, we will begin construction on a greenhouse soon. Kyle thinks we can salvage windows and frames from the houses farther up the street to aid in its construction. We will incorporate it into the deck that already exists on the outside of the home here, and by salvaging the lumber from the decks of the other homes, we are confident that not only will it be a great addition to the house, it will be built

*solidly as well. The next few days, we will rest and plan
and inventory stuff needed for the construction.*

* * *

Ray's nose twitched. He was dreaming about playing poker with
a bear and a dog at a big round table. Nothing about the dream
seemed all that extraordinary, and everything made sense at that time
in the manner of dreams. A talking bear dealing cards, for one thing,
and a dog making a cup of coffee while the bear dealt. They had
been playing poker for some time, and Ray glanced at the winnings
stacked before him. He had been doing well, it seemed. Stacks of
gold coins gleamed against the green felt surface of the table, and
the bear was telling some far-fetched story about a time he had gone
to Santa Fe. The dog was silent, simply going about the motions
of preparing his hot coffee, grinding the beans, and brewing it. It
smelled delicious. Finally, matter-of-factly the dog offered him a cup
of that delicious-smelling coffee, and Ray's nose twitched again. He
was delighted to accept. That coffee seemed like the most important
thing in the world at that moment.

"Thank you, Dog. I will have a cup of coffee if you don't mind!"

Laughter made him open his eyes. He hurt everywhere, it
seemed, and he groaned. Carly was waving a cup of coffee under his
nose.

"Did you just call me a bitch?" she asked. "I can keep the coffee
if you don't want it."

Ray snatched the mug and sat up, yawning.

"Man"—he yawned again—"I was really out. Was I talking in
my sleep?"

"Yeah, you called me a dog, I think.," she replied with a twinkle
in her eye.

"It wasn't you. I was playing poker with a bear and a dog or
something." He blinked. "Never mind. It's gone now."

He sipped at the coffee. *Necter!*

"It's okay, Ray," she replied, grinning. "I am a bitch sometimes!"

They laughed easily together while Ray drank his coffee. Then
Carly grew serious.

"You guys did a good thing yesterday, Ray."

He shrugged, suddenly embarrassed. "Did we? I would think that just about anybody would have done the same if it were one of us . . ." he trailed off.

"Would they?" she asked. "I used to think so, but I'm not so sure anymore. Things are different now. You could have just left her there to die. You guys didn't, though. You risked your own lives to save someone else's. I think that's an old-fashioned sentiment at the moment."

"Well," Ray snarled, disentangling himself from the blankets, "I am an old-fashioned guy!"

As he struggled to get up, his thighs above the knees knotted up in savage cramps, doubling him over almost immediately. He hit the floor with a whimper, grinding his teeth to keep from screaming. He almost blacked out. The pain was so intense. When he could see straight again, he realized that Carly was kneading the pain away from his left thigh, and he groaned and just lay back, letting her work. The cramps were so intense that the muscles were writhing and dancing just below the skin, almost like he had small animals living in there.

Minutes that felt like hours went by as the pain faded. When he could speak again, he just shook his head and took a deep breath.

"I don't know what you just did, but that was awesome! Would you marry me?"

Carly waved her ring in his face.

"Oh yeah, right," he replied. "Man, it was like someone was beating the muscles in my thighs with red-hot hammers. I have never had a cramp like that in my life! How did you learn to do that?"

"I'll probably have to do the same thing for Kyle when he wakes up in a little bit. You guys really overdid it yesterday, but it was needed. Thank you, Ray, for everything. That girl," she paused. "I mean, if you weren't with us, I don't honestly know that I would have been able to save her, you know? If Kyle had been down there alone, he might be dead now along with that girl. I don't know if *he* could have saved her, or . . . I don't know. But you *were* there, and

Kyle and the girl are alive, and I think it's going to be okay now." She wiped away a tear.

Ray changed the subject.

"Is Kyle still asleep?" he asked.

"Yeah. But not for long. His coffee radar works perfectly. He'll be up in a bit."

"I ache all over," Ray replied. "I can't even imagine how *she* must feel." He nodded toward the bedroom. "How is she this morning? Any better?"

"She's hurting, a lot. She came around a little earlier, and I got some water and Keflex into her before she dropped back off. We'll have to wait and see."

Ray nodded.

Kyle came shuffling into the living room in his pajama pants and yawning.

"I smell coffee," he announced as Carly and Ray grinned at each other.

The three of them had breakfast shortly after that and began to plan out their day. The meat had to be a priority, and Kyle and Ray were going to be busy with that. Carly would need to be inside and close by should their guest need anything. Finally, with a plan in mind and the breakfast dishes done and put away, it was time to go and do. Grimacing as he pulled the dirty clothes back on from the day before, Ray joined Kyle in the garage. First, they went out to the smokehouse and fired it up. They didn't want too hot of a fire; they wanted the smoke, though. That was where all the hardwood firewood would come into play, which Ray had insisted they keep separate from the pine. With the initial fire going in there and waiting for it to die down into coals, they returned to the garage. They set up a table to work on and began the process of slicing and butchering. They set three large steaks aside for later. The rest went into thin strips for jerky, additional steaks, roasts, chops, and burger. Hanging on a kitchen wall for decoration had been an old-fashioned meat grinder, hand-operated, that was going to be worth its weight in gold. They had taken it apart and cleaned it, oiled it, and sharpened the blades before putting it back together again. It was clamped to the side of the table now, and they took what was left, scraps, and fatty portions of meat and made bear burger. They mixed up a briny solution of salt and spices to baste the meat with as it smoked. With it as cold out as it had been, they would be able to freeze some of the meat after wrapping it, but Kyle wanted to get the whole smoking process down pat too for the months when it wouldn't be below freezing, and the bear was the perfect opportunity to practice.

Once they had finished with the bear, they started bringing the deer and elk over, one at a time, to be processed as well. It took them pretty much all day. They frequently ended up resharpening blades, but by dusk, the two men had enough meat put away, frozen, or being smoked to feed an Army. They smoked meat for the next few days. After everything was cut up, they made sausages and jerky, and the pleasant smell of woodsmoke hung heavily in the neighborhood. They had a couple of bear-b-ques, and seasoned right, it wasn't half-bad.

Finally, Ray was able to grab his *Big, Big Book of Buckskinning Secrets* and read up on how to tan a bear hide.

After lunch one day, the two men built a large wooden frame from scrap lumber. It was trial and error until they got it right. Then they stretched the hide out, and it was massive. The rug would probably end up being about twelve by nine, and it would look great if they did it right. Carly was going to get her rug in front of the fireplace. Leaving Ray to happily experiment with the pelt, Kyle went to start on another of his own projects, the planning and layout of a storehouse.

The next day, Kyle and Ray cleared the ground for the construction of a storehouse. They dug a pit that would be the floor of the building and leveled it all out, lining it with landscaping pavers and gravel. They wanted it to be about twenty by twenty, and they were disassembling two of their former neighbors' garages to do it. This project would probably take them a week, working all day every day, but they weren't going anywhere for a while, so what the heck? It was slow-going with the frozen ground, until Kyle got the idea to build a fire and thaw things out. Pickax and shovel and repeated fire-buildings let them breach the frozen earth. They cut more logs and began to lay them out around the stone-lined pit in the center, log-cabin-style. Once they had the dimensions in mind, they began to frame out the structure. By noon, they had the outside walls about waist high and the framework complete.

"Good thing I am a fan of that log-cabin look," Kyle said at one point.

"Yeah, this place is starting to look like an old west fort," Ray replied.

"Yeah, about that." Kyle explained that at some point, he wanted to build a palisade around the perimeter.

"Sure that's not overdoing things, man?"

Kyle just smiled.

During lunch, Carly informed them that their guest was awake now and officially on the mend. She was aware of her surroundings but still in a lot of pain and very weak. Her name was Margaret. She could speak and seemed to be all right mentally. It would be a few days before she could even get out of bed on her own. Carly asked both men to take a break at some point in the day and introduce themselves. Encourage Margaret to get better.

Ray found himself feeling a little shy. He couldn't explain it, really. He was so vocal and outgoing around people that he knew. He spoke his mind, felt comfortable, and always had a million things to talk about and say. Add a new person to the mix, though, and he always became quiet and reserved and shy. It took him a while to get to know people now and to make up his mind about them. As a younger man, he had made friends at the drop of a hat, but a lot of those friends hadn't worked out so great, so as he had aged, he had become a little more conservative in the friendship department. Nowadays, prior to the events that had driven them here, it was about quality and the content of a person's character, not how many contacts he had had in his smartphone.

Another reason that he was hesitant to introduce himself was that old legend about saving someone's life. That once you did that, you were responsible for them. He was pretty sure that that was just superstition talking, but as Carly had pointed out, the world had changed, and so had he, and maybe old things were becoming new again. Traditions, superstitions. He shivered, wondering how long it would be before old gods walked the earth once more and people offered up sacrifice to appease them. For all he knew, the Maya had returned to their ancient cities down on the Yucatan and were cutting out the hearts of their enemies. Time would tell, he figured. He hoped that the Written Word would not fall by the wayside, though. People someday would need to know what had happened here after they who had lived through it were gone. Words would need to suffice somehow to convey the terror and the anarchy and the pain that had come with The Day. He threw all his energy into the building of the storehouse that afternoon, thinking dark, cold thoughts. Kyle, realizing Ray had gone away into some heavy thinking, remained quiet for the rest of the afternoon while they worked.

Carly had a pot of stew simmering on the stove when they went inside for dinner, and it was delicious. She had made fresh corn bread to go with it, and they ate with pleasure. Ray was attacking his second bowl with gusto when Carly broke into his blissful gluttony.

"Have you introduced yourself to Margaret yet, Ray?" she asked.

Ray shrugged. "Not yet. Soon, I guess, probably after dinner."

"Would you take her some broth and some stuff to eat when you do?"

"Sure," he said.

"That way, you guys can chat a little. We're all going to be stuck here for a while together, so it would be nice if everyone has a chance to get to know one another."

After dinner, while Kyle and Carly were doing the dishes, Ray carried a tray into his former bedroom. There was a bowl of rich, thick broth with bits of meat and vegetables floating in it for Margaret. The lamps were turned down low in the room, and he turned them up some. She blinked awake with a start at seeing him and then relaxed some.

"I brought you something, if you're hungry," he said quietly.

He helped her sit up in the bed a little more by placing a few pillows behind her back, and she winced a little as she straightened.

"How are you feeling?" he asked.

"Pretty goddamn sore," she replied. "I met a bear a few days ago."

"I met him too," Ray said. "Are you hungry, Margaret? I brought in some soup for you."

"I could eat, I guess. I'm a little thirsty too."

Ray took the hint and poured her a glass of water from the pitcher on the nightstand. They talked while she ate. She was from the Portland area in Oregon, and she had left the day after the bombs had gone off, hiking out. She was on her way home to Missouri, where she had grown up, where her family was.

"Lot of that going around," he muttered.

Ray told her that he had lived up that way once himself. A little town called Longview just about an hour north of Portland on the Washington side. How beautiful it had been. Vancouver with its nightlife and things to do. Backpacking and camping in the forests. They talked for a while, and gradually, her eyes began to close, the pain medication taking its toll, and she fell asleep. Ray took the empty soup bowl back to the kitchen and turned the lamps back down again as he was leaving. Margaret seemed nice. That was a good thing, he thought as he closed the door behind him.

"So you met her finally," Carly said. "What did you think?"

"She seems nice," Ray replied.

"Good."

"Hey, guys, when we're done with the dishes, you wanna play some cribbage?" Kyle asked.

"Of course," Ray replied, "but if I catch you cheating again, I'm going to make you play against Carly for the rest of the night."

They had worked out a routine after dinner, where two people would play cribbage while the third would read or entertained themselves, the loser sitting out of the next game. Ray was really into reading the buck-skinning series at this point. There was simply *so much* useful information there. Low-tech survival skills that were so appropriate to what he would be facing in the springtime that he had started making a habit of noting particularly noteworthy things into the margins of his journal while he read. Carly thumped him on the head at one point, where he had become superabsorbed in what he was reading.

"You're up!" she said, gesturing at the board.

Ray waved her off and kept reading, so the pair of them settled in for another game. He winced as Kyle pulled twenty-three points on the first hand.

"See?" he said, gesturing idly. "That could have been me that that happened to!"

Carly stuck her tongue out at Ray and proceeded to crush Kyle for the rest of the game. They *both* cheated! Kyle was shameless about it, though.

You Lose Some . . .

CHAPTER 40

Captain Pilson and his company had been deployed to help restore order and help the people right after The Day. His National Guard outfit had been participating in a joint training mission outside Omaha when the news had come in concerning the rest of the country. Orders that had made sense at that time. Someone somewhere was in charge, so they had established garrisons in some of the smaller towns. Providing security and distributing supplies had seemed to be the way to go. Then the Second Day attacks had occurred, the night the EMPs had gone down and basically fried out his communications and vehicular transport. At that point, he was on his own. At least until someone further up the food chain made contact and gave him new orders, he'd keep doing the job. At least they had winter gear, so the men were warm.

He had set up his company command post in a little town called Jenner. Three days ago, an old lady and her family had come tear-assing into town, screeching about renegade motorcycle gangs terrorizing the countryside, and had demanded that he and his men do something about it. Pilson assured her that she and hers would be safe here. A few other families had wandered in since then, and he had been working with the mayor and city council to make sure that everyone was quartered and fed. He had spent the last few days making the town look defenseless. The two immobile Bradley Fighting Vehicles were under tarps in the town center, and he had doubled the watch on the rooftops. The men were dug in and behind sand-bagged positions throughout town. All things considered, he felt he had done everything he could to lure the bikers in, but the waiting was hard.

Yesterday at sunset, one of the sentries had reported activity about a thousand yards out, and he had glassed the area, seeing a few bikers reconnoitering the town. He had ordered the men into their positions and asked a few of the locals to wander around looking unaware, just business as usual. It looked like they had taken the bait, just another easy, soft target waiting to be hit. After about an hour of watching the bikers circle the town, they had vanished, and the men had relaxed somewhat. Pilson had a feeling though that it was coming soon.

Shortly before 4:00 a.m., one of his men had awakened him, and he had returned to his fourth-floor, rooftop position in the business district to scan the surrounding countryside.

"Come on, you turkeys," he whispered, looking around. "Come take the bait."

"Patrol's back, Captain."

"What's up, Ed?'"

"Well, sir, we saw them, but they didn't see us. I'd guess about 320 up to 350 hostiles, getting ready to hit the town, sir."

"Show me."

Lieutenant Ed Parsons pulled a map out of the breast pocket of his BDUs.

"They've split the force into thirds, sir, here, here, and here. A slightly larger group is going to be coming in on the railroad tracks here."

"All right, guys, just like we planned, we let them in, drop the bar, and try to make sure not too many of them get back out. I assume the larger group is probably their boss. I'm going to want mortars and RPGs and some serious automatic fire on them as soon as they are well and truly inside the boundaries of town. Everyone know what to do?"

There were nods all around.

"These people are counting on us. Go. Lieutenant, you're with me."

Boots thumped as men ran back to their individual units. Other than that, the town was silent. Pilson looked across the street to the rooftop of the old-fashioned limestone bank building. The mayor waved back at him enthusiastically, and he snorted.

"The townsfolk all prepared, Ed?"

"Yes, sir. We have around five hundred armed and enthusiastic volunteers on rooftops all over town. We have a few of our guys mixed in with them to help direct fire and keep things under control."

Pilson grinned in the darkness. "How about the rest?"

"Well, sir, that bank might as well be a fortress. We have all the kids gathered in there and the old folks, the handicapped, and so on. If anything, I'd feel sorry for anyone that actually made it in that far. Some of those old folks are veterans, and they are packing some serious heat."

Pilson's eyes turned a little steely at that. "I don't feel sorry for any of these people coming in here, Ed. They are going to reap what they have sown."

* * *

Cain looked at the sleepy little town of Jenner. He counted three lights lit in the darkness. The rest of the place seemed pretty quiet. Everyone slept later in these winter months, especially with no electricity. It didn't even get to be light out until around seven this time of year. Why bother getting up when you couldn't see anything? Well, this would work to their benefit—get in, hit them hard, take what they wanted, and burn the rest. He had split the gang into thirds. They would hit them from all directions, overwhelm them before they were well and truly awake, spend the daylight hours looting, and be long gone before darkness fell again. All the captives were locked up in three trailers back at the rendezvous point and under guard. He glanced at his windup wristwatch. They'd be going in in fifteen minutes. The men had pushed their bikes up to within striking distance so as to not to alert the good townsfolk before they were ready to attack. At five fifteen, they'd fire up the engines and go tear-assing into town. The men were well armed. That National Guard shipment they had confiscated three days after The Day had been solid gold. Three trucks loaded to the canvas with assault rifles, ammunition, grenades, rations, and other goodies had basically fueled his ambitions to become a new Genghis Khan. It was almost time, and he felt the same excitement he always did right before the action began. This was going to be *great*!

* * *

"Man, you never really realize . . ." Ed whispered softly and trailed off.

"You never realize what, Lieutenant?" Pilson asked softly.

"Just how much bigger four-hundred-plus people look all gathered in a group. I mean, it's a number, right? But when you actually see them, it can look like a lot more."

"Yep."

In the darkness around the town, engines snarled to life, headlights stabbed the darkness, and whoops and yells of startling animosity rang out into the crystal clear morning air.

"Here we go!" Pilson said. "Let them come in."

Pilson stood up, looking at the three avenues of approach in turn. There they were, coming in on the railroad tracks. There they were to the east and the south, racing along the main streets, throwing grenades and dynamite. The explosions rang out, and the rest of the bikes entered the killing zone. He watched in satisfaction as men ran across the roads, stringing wire at head and chest height and dropping antitire spike strips

"Now," he whispered, and the streets erupted into gunfire, muzzle strobe flashes, the streets lit up.

* * *

The beginning went just like it always did, Cain noted with satisfaction. Engines snarling, explosions ringing out. The angels tore into Jenner with their straight pipes roaring. The beginning went just like it should. Then things got a little hairy. Cain drew his sword as he saw figures rushing out of a building ahead.

"This is so *fucking* great!" he screamed out. He and his group were approaching the center of town. There were two blocky shapes there. He squinted his eyes and realized that white canvas was being ripped away from—*Oh no.*

"OUT! OUT! It's a trap! Get the hell out of here!" he screamed, spinning a U-turn in the middle of the street. Laying down smoking rubber, he followed his own advice.

Not too many men heard him over the explosions and the rush of the assault. At that moment, the "Sinful Archangels" got the shock of their lives. As the canvas hit the ground, the two Bradley IFVs were revealed. The turrets' 30mm chain guns began firing at the oncoming bikers. The high-explosive rounds took out the first thirty bikers in Cain's group in a spray of red hash and flying cycle parts. Then rifle fire came down from the rooftops of the square, emptying many a seat. As Cain accelerated away from the carnage behind him, red tracer fire lanced down side streets at knee level, spanging off the corners of buildings and ricocheting away, sometimes finding flesh and a wrecked bike.

Glancing around, he dropped the sword and drew his Python instead. They were getting close to the tracks now. He had about a dozen other guys riding with him. They needed to get *out!* That was when the mortar rounds began to fall, walking back up the tracks right at them. Cain gunned it, gesturing forward. *Go through! Go through!* They were almost out.

The bikers fanned out, loosening their formation as bombs rained down around them. He saw the first one, then another bike, go cart-wheeling away as it took a direct hit. Cain varied his speed and direction, fishtailing around craters in and near the tracks. He had six guys left. Up ahead, he saw a guy attempting to string some fencing across the tracks, trying to cut them off. He took careful aim with the .44 and pulled the trigger three times, the massive weapon recoiling in his hand. The figure dropped, and they flashed past.

Mack was riding right next to him when they hit open pavement and Cain looked over. From the other two directions, he saw maybe twenty other bikes emerge from the chaos.

"What now, Johnny?" Mack yelled.

"Back to the rendezvous point!"

Behind them, more explosions and shots rang out, the chain guns echoing eerily in the predawn darkness, then nothing. Cain led his people out at high speed. Thoughts raced through his mind. Who were those people? Where did they come from? How did they know that the angels were coming?

On the other side of town, Fred Kneller lay bleeding slowly to death from numerous wounds he had received. The ambush had left his fellow bikers' bodies shredded and lying in pools of blood. Three 40mm grenades had gone off near them, and automatic weapons fired from across the street had ripped the bike out from under him. Everything was a little foggy, and he blinked as he realized that someone was leaning over him. He tried to focus and saw a Kevlar helmet and BDUs. The figure wavered a little and then snapped into focus. He was holding a trench shotgun.

"Who are you guys?" he asked, choking back unbelievable pain. He was damned if they were going to see that he was hurting.

"C Troop, 1st of the 167th Cavalry, Nebraska, National Guard," the figure replied. "Who are you?"

"Nebraska National Guard," Kneller sneered. "You dumb fucks, there *is* no Nebraska anymore! You can go straight to—"

Kneller was cut off rather abruptly as the shotgun swung toward him, and the trigger was pulled.

Throughout town, the firing had dulled down to a single shot here and a single shot there as the enemy combatants were dispatched and otherwise put out of their misery. Squads of soldiers were at street level, actively patrolling and pacifying the area, and the whole thing came to a conclusion just after dawn.

Cain counted bikes coming in. Factoring in the guards he had left back at camp, he had sixty-one remaining archangels.

"Hey, Johnny, are we going to take all this with us? I don't think we have enough people anymore."

"We're taking one truck, one trailer full of food, and ammunition, and I want everyone who is left armed with a rifle, a sidearm, and all the ammunition they can carry. We're going to put as much distance between us and Jenner as we can before nightfall. Get moving."

"What about the captives?"

Cain mulled it over for a moment. Then he sighed.

"Right before we leave, unlock the trailers they are in, and we're going to leave the rest of this shit for them."

"Seriously?"

"Yeah, Mack, seriously. They've earned it. Maybe they can meet up with the people in that town back there. We can't afford to take them with us, and I have had enough of killing today. What about you?"

"Yeah."

They waited for another hour after the last bike came in, and then they left.

Pilson looked around the carnage, fighting the urge to retch. It always crept up on him after combat. The nausea. The smells of cordite, burned flesh, shit, and blood, along with the visual aftermath of what happened, always combined first to make him want to vomit up everything he had ever eaten. But not only that—it gave him the shakes and nightmares for weeks. He simply could not let the men see that side of him, though, for their sakes. So he always, somehow, kept it together, kept it professional and calm, so that they could do their jobs. This was going to be a bad one, though.

He saw Ed jogging toward him from down the street. That young man was a leader, he thought, nodding approval.

"What's the butcher's bill, Ed?"

"Well, we have about 370 enemy KIA, sir."

"Any prisoners?"

Ed shook his head.

"Good," Pilson replied. "Our casualties?"

"Um, three dead and fourteen wounded, sir."

"Not bad. It would have been better to have lost none, but not bad, all things considered, about 120 to 1."

"What are our orders, sir? Should we pursue them?"

Pilson thought about it for a moment.

"Nah," he eventually replied. "Let's get the town policed up and pick up all the pieces, and then we will continue on with the orders we already have, help the people and restore order. I think we just made a great start on the latter. Tell the men they did a great job, Lieutenant. Let's get back to work."

The Bitch

41

From the Journal of H. Rayton Townsend
January 2017
Lake Alpine, California

Starting to feel really proud of everything we are accomplishing here. Margaret "my friends call me Maggie" is healing up well. Kyle and I have fallen into a routine where we go hunting in the morning and work on projects all afternoon and into the evening. With Ol' Griz out of the way, the hunting is better than it has been. We finally figured out why the deer and elk are up here. There is a natural salt lick not too far away, and that has been working in our favor. Our next big project is the pickup truck in the garage, and if we can get it running, that is going to be a major score. Planning on learning and using that Hawken rifle a lot over the next few weeks. We have plenty of cap and ball and powder.

* * *

Kaboom! The report echoed among the hills and mountains near Lake Alpine, and a large cloud of smoke wafted away on the morning breeze. The sun was just clearing the far mountains on the other side of the valley. The day looked to be snow-free and sunny, but it was going to be cold again.

"Nice shot, dude!" Kyle called from a few trees over.

Ray reloaded automatically now and watched his downed prey for a moment. He slung the rifle over his shoulders and climbed down from his treetop perch. Once down, he paused for a moment, massaging his shoulder. This beast of a rifle kicked like a mule.

He walked downhill to check out the cow elk he had taken with his Jud Brennan Hawken. He knew who that was now, and it turned out, after reading several of the black-powder hunting books and *Living History* magazines, that he had scored a rifle by one of the best in the business. He was apparently a premiere rifle builder, and his guns fetched, *had fetched*, thousands of dollars for an accurate reproduction. Ray shook his head, just good luck again. So far, he felt like he'd been really lucky. He wondered what things were like in January in the rest of the country and carefully pushed that thought process away. He didn't want to know. Yet. The cow elk kicked twice as he approached, sighed, and passed. Kyle joined him a few minutes later. He had been tracking the same elk with his 30.06, just in case Ray had missed, but it had been a clean kill.

The two men butchered the elk where it lay and packed another couple hundred pounds of meat back to the cabin. They were old hands at the smokehouse now, and this should probably hold them for a while now. Kyle and Ray estimated roughly a thousand pounds of smoked and frozen meat over the last three weeks. They would probably get sick of it after a while, but when the lake thawed in the spring, at that point there would be fishing as well.

Carly was seriously hinting that she would like them to start on a greenhouse soon, and Ray and Kyle had been puzzling out how to do just that. It would go a lot faster if they had a vehicle to haul the parts though. So their next project was going to be that ugly pink-and-white International in the garage. Both men were in seriously good shape now, and Ray had high hopes of maintaining his newly found abs. There was so much to do.

The next morning, they smoked meat and worked on the truck. Ray felt like a mad scientist with manuals and parts spread out all around them. He lubricated gaskets and built and rebuilt parts, tightened screws, and basically did what Kyle told him to do in the order that he told him to do it. They had an engine hoist, and after getting that sucker completely rebuilt with new parts for the most part, they were finally able to lower the engine into the frame, where Kyle bolted it securely down. They had had to improvise there a little bit. The frame on one side was a little broken up, so some work with the torch and welding had to be done. Then new holes drilled to accept the bolts that would hold the engine in place. Ray got really into it, the mysteries of a chemical combustion engine.

It was a learning process, and once again, trial and error and patience and, sometimes, starting over completely was the key. They scraped skin from their knuckles and swore, laughed and told stories, fought and argued, and generally had a great time. They tightened bolts and belts until everything was as taut and ready as it could be. Mostly, they enjoyed the challenge of it all, the higher purpose involved with this task. A working vehicle meant unimaginable luxuries that could be hauled back and utilized. They drank beer while they worked, and an easy friendship that had been enjoyed for weeks became something a little closer. Ray was seriously starting to feel like these people were family; in fact, they felt more like family than his family sometimes. He had been out on the West Coast for fifteen years now, and before that, he had spent six years in Montana. Most of his adult life had been spent away from the people he was related to back in Illinois. He loved them and missed them sometimes, but he had always had to go to them; they never came to see him. Quick short visits where they would spend a week pretending to be a family. Or a quick trip home for a funeral.

Carly would come out and watch them working sometimes, making a comment here and a suggestion there. Now that Maggie didn't need constant attention, Carly was organizing all her loot and moving the extra stuff into the storehouse. Neatly labeled totes were beginning to line the walls of it, and she had started hanging up clothing on the racks that they had constructed for her. She had cleared most of the stuff out of the house the last few days. Except for their food, the basement would remain the ultimate food pantry for the foreseeable future. Now she was starting on all the stuff that they had stashed in the garage. So she would come out and chat with them while they worked, and she moved stuff, often hinting that if they felt like taking a break from the truck, some fresh salad or greens would be nice, that maybe, they could start on a greenhouse soon. They bundled wires with zip ties and ran them to the lights and instruments. They charged up car batteries with the generator and found that a few of them held a decent charge. They spent the next three days from dawn to dusk working on the truck, breaking only long enough to eat and refuel, and then they would go back to it. They had done enough hunting for a while.

On the afternoon of the third day, they were ready to test-fire the engine. Carly, Kyle, and Ray gathered inside the garage for the big event. All three were really excited. They had fueled it up, oiled it up, lubed all the necessary parts. The hoses were on, the coolant was full, the battery was charged, all the wires and fuses were where they should be, and the belts were taut. Kyle had the honors of turning the ignition key. He took a deep breath and turned it. The starter clicked and whined, and nothing happened. Kyle gave them both a frustrated look.

"COME ON, YOU BITCH!" Carly shouted at the truck.

Kyle tried it again. The starter clicked and whined, the engine turned over for a few revolutions, and then the truck died. They waited a few anxious minutes until Ray and Carly started chanting together, "Bitch! Bitch! Bitch! Bitch! Bitch! BITCH! BITCH! BITCH!"

Kyle tried it a third time, the exhaust backfiring, scaring them half to death, and with a belch of oily black smoke, the engine turned over completely and settled into a steady purr as they ran choking and wheezing and still chanting out of the open garage door and into cleaner air. The three of them hugged one another, dancing in a circle and yelling, until the air cleared enough for them to go back inside and admire their handiwork. Kyle grabbed Ray by the front of his shirt, eyes wide in mad-scientist fashion.

"She's alive! Alive! Alive, Ray! Muahahahahaahhaaha!"

It worked. The truck was working and running smoothly. Carly ran back into the house to grab three Guinnesses, three pint glasses, and three shot glasses, as well as a bottle of Jameson.

"Irish car bomb, anyone?" she asked innocently.

The two men roared their approval, and after carefully turning off the truck, they downed their car bombs right there in the garage. They had transportation again, and all was right with the world. The entire rest of the day was a celebration of sorts. Lots of booze, dancing, music, and silliness. Margaret even joined them for an hour or two before returning to bed. She was starting to be able to move around on her own, and everyone was happy to see that. Her color was much better, and Carly was positive that the worst was behind her. She still had a long road to recovery ahead of her, though, and it would probably be a month before she was approaching anything like a normal state of health.

Kyle had dug out some party hats and noisemakers and fire-crackers for their impromptu celebration.

"I found these when we were scavenging and put them away for something exactly like this!" he said.

The drinking went late into the night, with them setting off the firecrackers at one point, cheering as Kyle lit them and tossed them into the yard from the back deck. Ray was well and truly sauced at one point and just stood and stared out at the fog-shrouded valley below. He could see the light moving again far off in the distance, and he raised his glass in a toast to it. He walked back inside, where another round of shots awaited.

Outside, the snow was beginning to fall again. At some point, he just passed out.

* * *

From the Journal of H. Rayton Townsend

I was really, and I mean really, hungover this morning. I haven't drunk that much in a decade. It was like all the holidays that we missed getting here kind of rolled into one. We just celebrated Thanksgiving, Christmas, and New Years all at once! We needed the break. Seriously. All we have done is work, and that blowout last night was the break that we needed from it all. There has just been so much to do! It is beyond satisfying to provide for yourself, though. To create things that are going to help people to live a better life. Maggie came out and joined us for a little while last night. Didn't talk much, though. There are still walls there that need to be broken down, I think, perhaps a little tragedy as well beyond bear attacks. I know she feels a bit like an outsider, given how close the rest of us have become. It will just take time, I guess. All we can do is try to make her feel welcome. So in this new year, I have a list of things to be thankful for. I am thankful to be well-fed and safe in this place, I am thankful to be alive and healthy, and I am thankful for good friends to stand by me. It is more than most have at the end of January, I am sure.

My plans were originally to have been moving on as soon as it was possible to do so. Rest up, gear up, and continue my journey, but I have to be honest with you right now. Brutally honest. I am reconsidering that decision. I still feel guilty a little, but let's look at the facts. The sole reason for my wanting to go home was to surround myself with people that I knew I could depend on, right? Family, old friends, etc. To create a strong point, to survive this new world with good grace. I have that right here, in this place, right now. Right? Is it simply wasted effort to keep going? Would my family want me to be safe and alive and healthy? To know that I was living a good life somewhere far away? Or are they, right now as I speak, struggling to stay alive? Do they need my help? Would they hate me for not coming back and spend the rest of their lives worrying about whether I was alive or dead? What if everything I know is gone? The trip back will take months. Why make it if I am only to arrive too late to do anything to help? These questions keep me up at night. Is it selfish to stay, or is it selfish of them to expect me to go? At what point do the needs of the

*individual and his obligations to other people and places
outweigh those bonds of familial obligation?*

So many questions.

*Maggie is heading for Missouri at some point, and
for a time, at least, maybe we can travel together. A few
months remain yet for decision-making.*

* * *

A blizzard had locked them inside for the last four days. They busied themselves with board games, music, books, and long decadent naps. Kyle and Ray sometimes sat down together and sketched out what a greenhouse should look like, with a lot of input from Carly, of course. She definitely wanted a say in the design of it all. With the truck running, they could haul lumber and windows and siding back by the bed full. They finally settled on a plan and a design, and Carly was pleased, which was important as well. Kyle had turned out to be a remarkably good sketch artist, and the concept sketches that he had come up with were beautiful to behold. If only it would stop snowing. They had probably received two feet of snow in the last three days.

On the third day, after relaxing for a while, Ray was feeling restless and needed to do something with his hands. He wandered out to the garage and rounded up the tools he would need to start a small project. Kyle, curious, wandered out about an hour later to see what he was doing.

"It's a surprise!" Ray replied.

Kyle shrugged and went back into the house.

Ray had remembered the bear's teeth that he had taken on the day they found Maggie. There were four of them, and there were four of them living in the cabin now. It seemed symbolic somehow that they each have a memento of the occasion that had brought them together. Ray had just finished the chapter on scrimshaw in the *Big, Big, Big Book of Buckskinner's Lore* that he had been reading, and he wanted to try it out. He cleaned and polished the teeth using the buffer in the shop, and they were much larger than he remembered.

They were bigger around than his thumb, and each about six inches long. Ray thought that they would make excellent pendants.

He set up the vise very carefully, padding the metal edges, and secured the first tooth. He moved a few kerosene lamps very close to his work area and very carefully began to etch a design into the first tooth. He had found a template for the kind of lettering he wanted to use, and scrimshaw looked like an awesome way to kill some time on a cold winter's day. There were colonial and modern designs in the book, and he set about incorporating some of them along with his own ideas into decorating each tooth. He wanted to make each pendant very personal for the person who would be wearing it. He had started with Maggie's first, blushing a little bit. Maggie had a tattoo next to her belly button that coincidentally was a stylized tribal paw print of a bear. Ray had decided that that was what he would use as a border for the top and bottom of this first tooth. He grinned to himself as he worked. He was willing to bet that she didn't even know that he knew that.

When they had been fixing her up, though, and cutting off her clothes that day, there had been very few details about her that had remained private. Ray blushed a little again and focused on the design. He incorporated other designs as well, dots and starbursts, some stylized trees, and a bear, and in the very center, surrounded by scrollwork, he etched the name Maggie.

He threw his coat on and waded through the snowdrifts out to the smokehouse, where he grabbed some charcoal, and then went back inside of the garage. With a mortar and pestle, he ground it very finely then added a little water to the mixture. He began to rub it into the fine scratches he had made, filling in each little line. Every once in a while, he would take a rag and wipe the excess away. He gave the tooth another buffing all the way around and sat back to admire his work. The white of the tooth gleamed around the inscribed black images and lettering. Very nice. Very satisfying. He had nailed it. Just like the pictures in the book. He drilled a small hole through the tooth and laced it on a finely braided leather thong. It would be a beautiful thing to wear.

Glancing at the windup alarm clock ticking on the workbench, he was astounded to see that he had spent eight hours on this one project, and his stomach growled.

"What a perfectly awesome, restful, productive way to waste a day inside," he said to himself.

One down, three to go. Ray walked from the garage back into the house, and he paused for a moment. He took in the snow falling all across the valley and breathed in the clean, cold air. What a beautiful place. Smiling, he went back inside.

Everyone greeted him as he entered, and they sat down to dinner and a hotly contested game of Monopoly. It had been another good day. Kyle and Ray went over some sketches of the greenhouse. They were very detailed and incorporated the growing needs of four people and the assortment of seeds that Carly had inventoried. Most of the seeds were heirloom varieties, which meant if they were harvested correctly each season, each plant type could be replanted the following year. Their food would produce more food essentially. Carly had high hopes for that and had been reading up on saving seeds to reuse, not just for something that could be eaten, but also as something that could be traded later on. The two men looked out the windows at the yard in the gathering darkness, discussed a few more trees that might need to be taken down, and went over their lists of lumber, nails, windows that needed to be scavenged, and a couple of heating options for it so they could grow food in the winter months.

It had been another great day. Restful, but productive. Full of good things and good people to share them with.

Significant Changes

42

From the Journal of H. Rayton Townsend
February 12, 2017
Lake Alpine, California

If you will note, dear reader, it is with some satisfaction that I would like to point out that there is a solid date on the above journal entry. We were bored last night, so we consulted my journal and a calendar, counted days, and argued about time and generally worked our way back to The Day. As near as we can determine, today is the correct date, February 12, 2017. A little stab at normalcy to know what day it is, right? Such a small insignificant thing, but civilized as well, to have the luxury of knowing where you are in the history of the world. Winter up here will probably last a few more months. Some days have been a flurry of effort and seemed like weeks have passed. Other weeks have seemed like just a few days and have gone quickly, so it has been a challenge to know just where we are and what we have been doing.

Having stripped all the essentials out of the neighboring homes, we are now going for bonus points. The smokehouse functional and working, loaded with sau-

sages and jerky and hams from the deer and elk; the storehouse complete and loaded with dishes, silverware, clothing, and luxuries; and the house restored to its neat and well-maintained order and cleanliness, the carpets vacuumed, etc., it is time to address the other projects and the extras that will make life worth living here. We have had a break in the weather, and before the next snowstorm comes through or other people arrive, Kyle and I have decided it is time to start working on the greenhouse.

With "the bitch" running and our scavenged gasoline supply, we have decided to plow the lane from the cabin all of the way to the top, where the old retired couple used to live. That way, we can start taking back windows and lumber and pavers by the truckload in order to start work on Carly's plan to get some fresh produce. I have to admit that we are all getting sick of canned goods, and the thought of a fresh salad makes my mouth water uncontrollably.

If I never end up going any further than this, it will be okay. I have calmed down considerably in the last few weeks, and the working rhythm of life here in the mountains is keeping me focused and physically fitter than I have been in some time. The company is good, and we have enough and more to make a good life here. Maggie is bouncing back quickly now, and the side effect of plowing the lane is that we all now have a place to take a walk in. Maggie and I take a walk every morning now to the end of the lane and back. It is slow-going, and I have to measure my pace to hers. The important thing is that she is healing now. I have gotten to know her much better over the last few days, and if I am any judge of character, there is a lot going on behind those brown eyes. The bruising is fading, and Carly says her stitches can probably come out soon. She was very lucky to have avoided infection from the attack and is lucky to be alive.

I gave Maggie her pendant today.

* * *

"Here," Ray said, holding out something for Maggie. "I made this for you. Happy belated Chrismahannukahwanza or whatever. It's kind of a souvenir."

The two of them were standing at the top of the lane, looking out through the trees across the valley to the lake below. Maggie accepted the small package wrapped in an old brown paper bag and tied with twine. She opened it and saw the scrimshawed bear's tooth with her name on it. Subdued emotion swirled behind her eyes as she turned it in her hands. Then without a word, she quietly slipped the leather thong over her head and tucked it into the top of her jacket.

"It's from the bear that almost got you," he said.

"I gathered that," she said a little dryly.

They were both quiet for a few moments.

"Well, I just thought that maybe you'd like to have a souvenir from the whole experience and bragging rights farther down the road, when you are telling someone about what happened to you. You can pull it out and say, 'Here's its tooth, see?' I mean, it's better than having a T-shirt that says, 'I was mauled by a bear, and all I got were these stupid stitches,' right?" Ray laughed. "Now you can say, 'All I got is this stupid pendant.'"

"No, Ray," she replied, "it's not that at all. I like it. It's beautiful. It's very cool that you took the time to do it for me. That's what I was thinking. Where did you learn how to do something like this?"

"I read a lot," he replied, shrugging. "So you really like it?"

"Yeah, I do."

"Good. I have one too. So do Carly and Kyle. We're like the bear-tooth club now."

Laughing quietly, they continued their walk. Turning at the very top of the lane, they began their way back down to the cabin. Chatting quietly and occasionally laughing. For a while they would walk in silence, alone with their thoughts. They were both thoughtful people and were troubled by what the future might hold. Ray was happy to see her bouncing back as fast as she was. Maggie was tall, about five feet ten inches, and had brown hair and warm eyes. She had an easy laugh and was easy to talk to once he had gotten past his initial shyness. She was way out of his league as well, but come to think of it, most of the women he had ended up with had been out of his league. He laughed when he thought about it.

"No one ever asks the pretty girls to dance," a friend had once lamented in high school, and it was true. It wouldn't be fair to either one of them to get involved, though, or for Ray to even make the attempt. Maggie had given no signs that she was interested in anything more than a casual friendship and survival. For one thing, she was at least ten years younger than him, and for another, Ray sighed, she was way out of his league. She had an edginess that he liked, though, and a wicked sense of humor, and he enjoyed spending time with her.

Is this a crush? he wondered. *Not now, damn it!*

It wasn't fair. He would have to watch himself. More like a lack of dating options than anything else. He resolved to try to distance himself from her a little bit. If it was a crush and he made a pass and was rebuffed, it could impact the entire social order that they had constructed here. It could hurt more than just his feelings if he wasn't careful.

When they weren't walking, they worked on projects together, and it was pretty cool what a team player she was. Maggie wasn't afraid to work, that was for sure. She and Carly had developed a pretty close friendship rather quickly. When they were together, they always had their heads together, plotting and scheming and planning. Sometimes they would fall silent when Ray walked into a room, and he went about his business like he didn't notice. It set his teeth on edge, though.

The walks continued, and it had finally reached the point where Carly and Kyle exchanged knowing looks as they went out the door. Ray hated that. He was going to have to set them straight soon. *Both* of them. Neither one ever said anything, but it was infuriating. When Ray wanted something, he preferred to get it on his own. He had always hated being *set up* with a friend of a friend. There was simply too much pressure. Public pressure, even when unspoken, to do what he wanted to do anyway didn't help. Sometimes, public pressure and expectations ruined things as well, things that might have happened anyway without speculation. Neither ever said or implied anything, but their expectations were clear when they looked at him, and he just *knew* that there was talking going on when he wasn't around.

Two weeks later, Ray was wound pretty tight. The giggling from the other room, the looks—all of it—had him feeling as jumpy as a cat. He still acted like he didn't notice, but he did, and he wasn't sure what *he* wanted anymore. Ray threw himself into one project after another, the greenhouse, reading and studying, chopping firewood, anything to keep busy. One day found him working on the bearskin rug, and he lost himself in the tanning process. It was going to be great when it was finished. Kyle went out to join him at one point, sipping a cup of coffee. He started to say something, but Ray cut him off.

"Hey, Ray, Maggie was wondering—"

"Don't" was all he said.

"Don't what?" Kyle said, blinking, all bland innocence.

Ray went back to scraping the rug, sighing.

"I'm going to be moving on soon," he finally said.

"Well, we figured that," Kyle replied. "Maggie was wondering if you would help in sketching out the specs for a smaller cart to pull behind you when you guys leave in the springtime. You're still planning on going together, right?"

"Yeah," Ray replied quietly. "I mean maybe. Probably. I don't know. She may have her own plans. You know?"

"Having a cart would save you guys some pain. You could take more. Maybe we could do that later?"

"Sure," Ray replied, grunting, scraping at a rough patch of skin.

"You won't be able to hold out forever, man," Kyle said, winking.

"What's that supposed to mean?" Ray asked.

Laughing, Kyle went back inside. Ray scraped the hide harder. He was really going to have to say something soon.

"Maybe it's all just in your head, you idiot!" he muttered at one point. "Just be cool. Relax."

That didn't seem to help much.

The next day's walk with Maggie was a little different. The two of them walked mostly in silence, quieter than they normally were. There was more light snow hissing down between the trees, just flurries mostly. Ray would glance at Maggie from the corner of his eye occasionally, but she seemed lost in her own thoughts today, so he didn't say much to break the mood.

Finally, she broke her silence.

"So," she finally said, "I knew that you guys saved my life and all, but I finally got the whole story out of Kyle and Carly yesterday. If I have the facts right. *You* killed the bear that was trying to kill me, saving Kyle in the process, correct?"

Ray nodded hesitantly.

"*Then* while Kyle was freaking out and staring at the bear, you found out that I was still alive. *You* carried me almost four miles, uphill through a raging snowstorm, without dropping me once and effectively saved my life. Am I right?"

Maggie had stopped walking.

Ray sighed. "That's about it," he said quietly, turning to face her. "Yep."

Her cheeks were flushed from the cold and the effort of walking, but her eyes were hot. She was wearing a stocking cap that Carly had knitted for her. The neck of her sweater was sticking through the top of her winter coat, where it was zipped up, and she looked beautiful. Downy flakes of snow were falling on and sticking to her shoulders and her long brown hair, where it emerged from the cap. Ray stood there and looked at her, memorizing the image. Maggie sighed, took three deliberate steps forward, and put her arms around Ray's neck. Then she gave him a light kiss on the lips. The whole time she had been looking directly into his eyes.

"You're welcome," he said, laughing quietly.

She didn't step back, though; if anything, her arms tightened around his neck, and she pressed herself against him. She continued to stare into his eyes, as if memorizing the lines of his face. She smelled fantastic.

Ray cleared his throat, his voice hoarse.

"Would it be too terribly out of line to kiss you again?" he finally said.

"That would be great!"

Ray kissed her again, firmly this time, way more than a mere brush of lips, and when they broke from that one, they were both a little surprised, it seemed, that she had her back to a tree, and they were breathing hard. It might have lasted moments, or it might have been an hour, but that kiss had lasted a long time.

Breathing hard, Maggie shoved him back a little bit.

"Well," she gasped out, "we finally got *that* out of the way!"

"Do you have, like, a checklist or something?"

"I think I popped a few stitches!" she said, laughing.

They held hands walking back to the cabin, stopping occasionally to kiss again. That was how it started. When they returned home, both went back to their projects, glancing at each other occasionally and smiling. Neither one noticed Kyle and Carly watching them watch each other.

* * *

Ray lay awake on the couch in the living room that night and mulled over the day's events. He couldn't sleep, staring at the ceiling and thinking about Maggie. He hadn't seen this coming in the beginning, when he had pulled her from the snow, covered in blood.

"The whole fucking world ends," he muttered, rolling onto his side, "and *now* I find the girl of my dreams. It figures."

He stared into the darkness, listening to the wind howl outside, sleep out of reach. He thought about that first light kiss, her lips brushing his for the first time. The solid warmth of her body pressed against his own. The way she had stood in the snow. Her eyes. The way her nose turned up a little at the tip. The snowflakes that had dusted her parka and her hair. He thought of the short, intense kisses on the walk back to the cabin, and then getting here and acting like nothing had happened. Maybe he was delirious and lost in his imagination. Maybe nothing had happened at all.

It was well past midnight when he heard the door to his former bedroom creak open quietly. He lay there on the couch, in the darkness, and watched as Maggie padded into the living room with a blanket wrapped about her. She stood in the darkness for a moment, hesitating, trying to decide if he was awake or not.

"Hi," he whispered quietly, letting her off the hook.

"Hi," she whispered back. "I understand that I took your bed too."

"Yeah," he replied with a smile, "you sure did."

"Well, if you don't mind a little company, you are welcome to have it back."

Maggie turned around and walked back into the bedroom, leaving the door open.

Ray gaped in disbelief for a moment, marveling at how wonderful women really are. Then he was off the couch like a shot. As he padded into the bedroom behind her, he closed the door quietly. Maggie turned to face him and let the blanket drop. She was wearing nothing beneath, and it took his breath away for a moment.

He studied her in the moonlight coming through the windows, trying to memorize every curve, hip, belly, breast. He touched her skin lightly and shivered as goose bumps rose on her shoulders and midriff. He kissed her lightly and then once again, more firmly, as they wrapped their arms around each other. Her hands trembled as she removed his shirt, his pajama pants. They stood in the moonlight holding each other, kissing, skin to skin, flesh to flesh. Breathing each other in, kissing, smelling each other's scent in the darkness.

Ray realized that he was so erect it almost hurt.

Maggie knelt down, and he moaned as she took him in her mouth, her lips enveloping him. He was growing impossibly harder, her tongue teasing the tip of his cock. He let her do that for moments before bringing her back upright to kiss her again. He tasted her and himself on her lips as he slowly lowered her to the bed. Everything, everything was *right* about this, more right than he had ever experienced.

She gasped as he took each nipple in his mouth, lightly tracing each with his tongue, grazing them slightly with his teeth until they stood erect as well in the darkness, like impossibly firm berries. He gently traced the scar where she had had stitches and inhaled her scent. He trailed his tongue down her belly, lightly blowing the saliva dry, kissing her navel, going past the bear paw, until he reached the soft, damp area between her legs.

She panted harder as he probed her with his tongue, tracing the outlines of her in the darkness. Savoring every fold of soft skin, tasting her, teasing her. She moaned, and her hips twitched into his face. He rose back up and kissed her again, their scents and flavors combined on their lips as he put his tongue in her mouth. She kissed him back fiercely as he entered her, moaning into his mouth. He went slowly at first, conscious still of her recent injuries, deep, slow, thrusts, almost pulling out completely on the upstroke and burying himself inside her, grinding slightly on the downstrokes. Grinding together, feeling her pushing back into him. It lasted for an eternity. It didn't last long enough. They were lost in each other, kissing, tasting, panting, moaning. She began to scream lightly, and she bit his shoulder as she came. Ray felt his own orgasm coming fast, and he began to pull out of her.

"Don't you even dare!" she hissed at him savagely, wrapping her legs about him tightly and locking her ankles in the small of his back,

"Babies!" he managed to gasp out.

"I want you to come in me, Ray," she moaned out. *"Come in me!"*

So he did. He buried himself inside her, impossibly wet now. As deeply as he could. She rose to meet every thrust, and he grasped the headboard above them, trying to push deeper. She came again as he jetted into her, the orgasm going on and on. He almost blacked out from the intensity of it. They cried out together, and he held her tightly, panting hard, shaking, and remaining inside her glorious wetness.

When he could think again, he opened his eyes to find Maggie staring into his own and was astonished to realize that he remained hard. They remained that way for a while, moving lazily against each other, feeling the play of skin on skin. Ray remained enveloped in what seemed like the entire universe. They touched with hands, fingertips, stroking and caressing, all while remaining connected in that elemental way, exploring. Eventually, they began to move faster again.

They made love three more times that night, waking up each time to do so. Ray was awakened at one point as she straddled him, still half-asleep, sinking onto him with a sigh. Her hair fell forward across her face as she rode him, grinding into him. When they came together at the end, she leaned forward and kissed him and then stayed there. They fell asleep like that, Ray inside her, feeling whole. One mind, one body, one soul.

Dawn arrived, and Ray quietly slipped Maggie's arm off his chest. He needed to use the bathroom. A sense of wonder filled him, along with awe and lust, at seeing her sharing his bed. The amazing thing was that she was still there. Ray had had a brief disappointing fear prior to awakening fully that it was all a dream, some random crazy thing that he had invented in his mind. But she was still there, and it was all real. There is nothing better in life than waking up next to a warm, willing wanton woman.

After he had taken care of business, he padded into the kitchen to make coffee and was surprised to see Carly and Kyle already up. They exchanged glances and smiled.

"Glad to see the two of you getting along so well," Carly drawled out.

"I was just tired of sleeping on the couch, that's all," Ray replied.

Kyle raised an eyebrow at him and shook his head.

"Nothing happened," Ray assured them.

They looked at him in frank disbelief, Carly laughing outright.

"Seriously," Ray said, all wide-eyed innocence, "I just came to get some coffee."

"So what exactly was all that commotion last night?" Carly asked with a straight face.

"I don't know," Ray replied. "Squirrels?"

Kyle choked on his coffee. Feeling utterly routed, he grabbed two cups of coffee and retreated to the bedroom.

"Hi," he said softly, waking her with a kiss.

"Hi, yourself," she replied.

"I brought you some coffee."

"My hero."

The coffee grew cold on the nightstand as they made love again.

Getting It All

Harley dodged out of the way as a running, yelling knot of children flashed past him, going down the hallway, chased by a barking dog. Who would have thought that his hidden lair could have been so enriched by the rough-and-tumble antics of little people? Harley certainly hadn't thought of it. He stood staring after them and shaking his head. The addition of four more people, though, certainly brought a liveliness to the place that it had never had. The kids had adjusted well enough, he supposed. Kids were flexible.

Angela, on the other hand, troubled him a little bit.

They had made a few more trips to the ranch, mostly for hay and feed for the chickens and goats and some other odds and ends that they had thought might be useful, and then they had stopped going as winter settled in even more firmly than it had been. Angela, in the beginning, had seemed competent and in charge of herself, but as the days dragged on, she seemed to be falling into a deep depression. It couldn't be easy losing a family, Harley figured. That was what had happened to her, though. She ate, she responded to things that were said to her, but it seemed to Harley like she was going through the motions. The lights were on, but no one was home.

Harley had his hobbies to keep him busy. The kids treated the place like it was Disneyland, playing and having a constant great time. Harley played with them too. Angela hadn't really settled in yet, though, and it was something Harley had decided to address. He had always felt like a big kid, and being able to pursue any impulse, any dream at any time had reinforced that about Harley. He was such a total innocent about so many things. Angela was disturbingly an adult and seemed to be having a hard time coming to terms with her new situation and relating to the rest of them.

He found her in the library. She went there a lot, it seemed. The whole top floor of the control dome—well, the former control dome, anyway—had been converted in the early days by Harley into a large library space. It held literally thousands of volumes on every subject that had interested him, plus he had a ton of fiction in there too. Fantasy, sci-fi, action, adventure, alternate history, and the classics as well as real history and all the subject matter as it related to all his different hobby phases. There were a few even he hadn't read yet, but that had looked good.

"Hi," Harley said brightly.

"Hi, Harley," Angela replied.

"What's up? Find anything to read yet?" he asked, gesturing awkwardly at the bookshelves.

Angela was silent for a moment.

"Have you read all these?" she asked.

"Most of them," he replied seriously.

"Wow." Angela once more scanned the room, taking it all in. "So you know a lot of stuff about a lot of stuff, huh?"

"Well, I know a lot about a little bit and a little bit about a lot," Harley replied, laughing. "I never studied one thing exclusively, so I figured, the more I studied, the more useful I would one day be. It's important, learning stuff, I think. I was always interested in every-thing interesting, but I never got a college degree. I just couldn't stay on one thing long enough to become an expert in it."

"Well, at least you're honest about it," she murmured.

That right there, he thought, was what puzzled him about Angela. She would say stuff like that all the time. He wasn't sure if she was impressed or praising him in some way or being dismissive and condescending. Or just making small talk to say something. Was she shallow or stupid? Or did she just not care?

"Did you ever go to school?" Harley asked politely.

"Yes, I did," she replied, not elaborating.

"Well? What did you study?" Harley asked, curious.

"I studied natural sciences, ecosystems mainly, and I figured that when I married a rancher, it would come in handy."

"Did it?"

Angela laughed. "No, it did not."

"I like ecosystems," Harley said innocently.

"I can see that," Angela replied.

There it was again! "No. I do!" Harley protested. "The fish tanks and the garden silo were fun to design. I had to factor in everything, how one species depends on another, to attain that balance so that the whole system could grow and mature into something special . . ." he trailed off, frustrated. "Every aspect of this place depends on every other aspect for balance. Ecosystems within systems. Understand?"

"I do," she replied, nodding. "And yet?"

"Now it's out of balance a little," Harley mumbled.

Angela laughed again. "And you are trying to figure out how everything fits together, right?"

Harley nodded.

"Do you want me to explain it to you?" she asked.

"Yes, please. I have been a little out of my depth lately, trying to figure things out."

Angela took a deep breath. She had actually been waiting for a conversation like this for the last week or so. She would need to do this delicately so as not to offend Harley too much, but she needed to make a point as well in a way that he could understand. Harley was either dysfunctionally brilliant or brilliantly dysfunctional. He had grasped instinctively what so many students had to struggle with regarding systems integration. She was so impressed with what he had accomplished here it was maddening. She had seen this place as a teenager, and where she was standing bore no resemblance to that memory at all.

In fact, had she seen the potential of this piece of property like Harley had instinctively done, she would have pressured Josh to buy it when it was listed on the market. She had had no idea, none, of what he had accomplished here.

"Harley, before The Day, you existed in an open system, right?"

He nodded hesitantly.

"What that means is, you were able to interact with the outside world as much or as little as you wished, right?"

Now he nodded firmly.

"Your system here, with all its subsystems, was merely a part of something greater, a product of an outside system. Follow me so far?"

"Yep."

"That outside system consisted of roads, towns, people, parks, dogs and cats, power lines, music, and universities and countries. You were a part of that. Just a subsystem operating independently of the greater system, right?"

Harley nodded again.

"Now, on The Day, your interaction with that system collapsed, right? Maybe not right away, but you were so specialized here that you almost didn't realize that it was gone, because within your own system, you had balance. It was you and all the subsystems that you created, and in itself, the missile base became a closed system and no longer part of the whole. When you brought Brian and Trish and the dog in, your system had to adapt to outside pressures, and you either had to change a little, or the outcome would have been negative. Right?"

"Yeah."

"Then you brought us here from the ranch, and more pressure was exerted on the closed system, right?"

"Yeah."

"Harley, the out-of-balance feeling that you are experiencing is *you*."

"What do you mean?" he asked.

"You have had to change, Harley, and now you need to change a little more. Don't you see? By letting people in, you simply cannot continue to exist in a little Harley bubble. You have to take responsibility for what you have done, or you need to eliminate the variables that caused your system to get out of balance, that thing that is instinctively making you uncomfortable. You yourself have been a closed system, perfectly in balance with and adapted to your environment. Your environment is changing, though, and you need to change with it. You need to grow up. It's time to be an adult. I'm sorry if that offends you, but it's true," she said, standing.

Harley stared off into space, dumbstruck. She patted him on the shoulder as she walked past, exiting the library.

What a complete bitch! he thought.

He *was* an adult. He even had a driver's license to prove it. He could drink, he could smoke, he could fight, he could build, he could take *responsibility* for things. What in the world was she talking about? Yeah, he was a bachelor with no experience with kids. Yes, he had a lot of stuff and a lot of hobbies and interests that really didn't include interacting with a lot of people, but so what? Hadn't he opened his home to them? Hadn't he taken responsibility for their future? Hadn't he provided them with a safe haven from what was happening out there? *This* was why he didn't like people; they were always trying to force their ways on him, their beliefs, their opinions. Why should he be the one that had to change? Why couldn't they?

He spent the entire rest of the day sulking and trying to figure out what Angela had been talking about.

Except for meals, he avoided her for the next few days, keeping busy with the chickens and goats and reading up on the keeping of them. He continued to play with the kids and take the dog for walks outside. The whole time he did so, he was thinking about their conversation in the library. What did she mean he had to grow up? All he knew was that his system was out of balance, both personally and atmospherically inside his home.

Testing the Waters

From the Journal of H. Rayton Townsend
February 26, 2017
Lake Alpine, California

It's been a busy couple of weeks! A lot has happened. For one thing, I am no longer sleeping on the couch, and the rest I won't go into, but Maggie and I are getting along just fine. Kyle and I put the snow chains on "the bitch" this morning, and we're going to try to drive down to the marina store on the lake to see if anyone is around or if there is going to be more salvage to haul back.

* * *

Kyle and Ray kissed their women good-bye and hopped into the truck.

"Ready for this, Kyle?" Ray asked.

"Yeah, man, but I'm a little nervous."

"I'm sure it will be fine," Ray said, "but I have to admit, I'm a little amped up myself. Think they'll be hostile?"

"Well, as long as we keep our composure, it should be good. Vic has owned the marina since I was a teenager. There's no telling if it's him down there or someone else now, though," Kyle replied. "If it's Vic, we should be good. If it's someone else, we'll have to negotiate.

Remember, we're armed too, and if it *looks* like no one should fuck with us, then more than likely, no one will fuck with us."

"Let's hope," Ray muttered, looking out the rear window of the truck as they crawled away down the lane.

Maggie and Carly waved as they drove toward the main road, and Maggie blew Ray a kiss when she saw him look back. The two women went inside.

It was a slow drive down to the marina. No one had come over the pass from the west or had driven the main road at all since their arrival. They left a solitary track of churned snow in their wake. They had to use the winch and the plow a few times as well to get through some of the drifts, but eventually, they made it to the valley floor.

"We should have looked for snowmobiles somewhere," Ray muttered as they worked their way through the third drift.

When they pulled up outside the marina, they noticed a single plume of woodsmoke rise from the sheet metal chimney on the building. Other than that and some footprints in the snow outside, there was no sign of life. A sign over the door proudly proclaimed, VIC'S MARINA. BAIT. TACKLE. COLD BEER. GENERAL STORE.

As they entered, they saw an old man in a rocking chair parked in front of the wood-burning stove. He had a blanket wrapped about himself, and he was smoking a pipe. The fragrant smoke filled the interior. A little bell over the door rang, and they courteously stamped the snow from their feet before going any farther. An old yellow Lab looked up from his bone and wagged his tail. The plank floor creaked, and the three men looked at one another for a moment.

"Vic? Vic Mazetti?" Kyle asked.

"Who wants to know?" the old man replied, voice like gravel.

"It's me, Kyle. Kyle Meyer," he said, unwinding the scarf from his face.

"Well! I'll be a sunofabitch!" the old man replied. "How the hell are you, son? You guys up at yer dad's place?"

"Yeah," Kyle replied. "We've been up there for about three months now."

"That's real good! Real good to hear!" the old man replied. "I thought someone was up there! I been hearing gunshots every now and again, and it looks like someone's been cuttin' down trees! Glad it's you! How are the Simmons doing?"

"Well, Vic, they didn't make it," Kyle said, explaining what they had found upon arrival.

"That's a goddamn shame," Vic said sadly. "They've been here a long time. Makes me sad. Who's yer friend?"

"Oh!" Ray said, stripping off a glove and extending his hand for a shake. "Ray Townsend."

The old man stood up to take it, and as the blanket fell away, it revealed he had been holding an HK submachine gun the entire time.

"Vic Mazetti," he said, shaking Ray's hand firmly.

Kyle whistled appreciatively, eyeing the weapon.

"That's some serious shit there, Vic. Trouble with shoplifters?"

Vic looked down at the gun and set it on the countertop.

"Can't be too careful these days," he replied, patting the weapon. "We had some troublemakers through here right after the night bombs went off. No one else through since, though."

Vic looked at Kyle.

"You've lost a little weight, huh? Looks good on you, though. Been kinda lonely 'round these parts with just Bob and me," he said, nodding at the yellow Lab. "So you been poachin', huh? No one around to say otherwise, though. Any luck?"

"Yeah, the hunting has been good so far," Ray replied with a grin.

"See you finally got that piece-a-shit truck running. Well, if you need gas for it, I can spare some, if you wanna trade for some fresh meat. Carly and the baby fine?"

"Lena didn't make it," Kyle replied tightly.

"Sorry as hell to hear that, kid," he replied. "Well,"—Vic paused for a moment—"there's a few dependable folks around. Regulars like you. The Campbells are at their place across the lake, haven't been in since it froze up good, probably snowed in like everyone else. Don Bromsey and his clan are up t'road apiece. A few good folks. We were kinda helping one another out before the weather turned. Come springtime, I am sure the roads'll open up too. How're things on the flats?"

Ray and Kyle filled Vic in on what they knew about the whole situation. San Francisco, LA, Seattle, and Portland, the other suspected cities that had been hit. They told him about Bowman being in Sacramento, the camps, and the other rumors that they had heard—pretty much, they gave him everything they knew. Vic listened without interrupting. They told Vic exactly where they were, what they had been doing. Ray filled him in on his own plans to keep heading east.

"We got lucky," Kyle finally finished. "We got out ahead of it, but I think once the passes open, there will be more people coming through. A *lot* more people, Vic. We'd just as soon keep a low profile if we can. Come springtime, I want to camouflage that access road and make it look like no one has ever been through there."

Vic was silent, chewing the inside of his cheek as he thought things over. Finally he spoke.

"I'm not crazy about hordes of people coming through here, Kyle. They will strip my place bare in just a few days, assuming it doesn't just get confiscated by the government. Bastards!" he spat.

Ray and Kyle glanced at each other.

"I have always liked that place up the lane from you guys. Tell you what, Kyle, maybe it's time to circle the wagons a bit, get Bromsey and the Campbells up there by you too. How many you got up there now?"

"Just the four of us right now, Vic, and Ray and Maggie are probably gonna be moving on in a few weeks as soon as they can, weather permitting."

"Tell you what. You think about this good, okay? I'll supply all the gas you need if you help me move my inventory up there just in case we get flooded with people. I'm thinking we could help one another out, more hands to do work and security, and if we're lucky, no one will even know we're there. I like all of you folks, and I bet we could make a go of it if we move fast. You come see me again soon, Kyle."

They nodded, talked a little more, and then Ray and Kyle left.

"He's quite a character, huh?" Ray asked as they drove back up the mountain.

"Yeah. Truth be told, I am glad that Vic made it. He's an old Wall Street–trader, business-pirate, corporate-raider kinda guy. He moved out here after 9/11 and never looked back."

"I imagine he's pretty pleased with that decision at the moment," Ray replied.

Kyle was quiet for a while, concentrating on his driving.

"By the way, Ray, Carly's pregnant."

"Really?"

"Yeah, we've been trying for a little while now, and it finally took. Kind of scary and exciting at the same time, you know?"

"Congratulations!" Ray said, grinning.

"Thanks," Kyle replied. "The thing is, our daughter can never be replaced, but we have always wanted kids. Lena would have been the eldest one, but she wasn't going to be the last. Know what I mean? It will be hard with no hospitals or anything, but we'll figure it out, I'm sure. More hands will be a big help too."

"I'm sure you guys will be just fine," Ray replied. "Seriously, Kyle, that's great news! I think maybe Maggie and I will be leaving you guys in a month or so. But it sounds like old Vic there is fired up along with some of the other neighbors to get up there by you guys, so that should offset us moving on."

"Yeah, I figured that was coming soon. We should be able to outfit you both, start planning your route, and figure out how much you can carry and will need to carry. It's gonna be hard just me and Carly again. We've gotten used to having you around."

"I know what you mean, man. I am a little scared about what's actually out there myself. I have to find out, though. I have to go and see it."

"I know," Kyle said, nodding.

Being an Adult

Harley Earl was a little beyond pissed; in fact, he was white-hot as he stalked down a corridor in the complex. He had approached his conversation in the library with Angela from a few days before from every direction that he could and could find nothing wrong with himself or the way he lived. He had tested hypothesis, done his own behavioral analysis, and reexamined his systems theories. If anything, he had discovered he needed to be a little firmer with the kids, establish some boundaries and rules, and maybe start up a schooling process so that they didn't grow up to be completely ignorant of the world around them. He had, far and away, enough books to make that happen, not to mention all the recent 24/7 data that he had recorded from The Day up until the Second Day attacks on December 11. Nope, Harley could be a great schoolteacher if he wanted to, and he *had* accepted the new world as it existed. Now he could really do whatever he wanted. There were no laws to say otherwise. If he wanted to teach the kids, he would, and he didn't need a useless piece of paper to do it. That was a whole separate issue, though. Right now, he was going to find Angela and give her a piece of his mind.

Just because he didn't necessarily like to interact with people on a one-on-one basis didn't mean that he couldn't be articulate when he wanted to. Most of the time, he was just shy, or bored, or disconnected, and simply put, he didn't want to invest the effort to get a point across. It seemed, though, that Angela had her mind made up about him, and Harley had spent the last few days making up his mind about her. She was rude, pure and simple, and he was going to let her know that. If she had merely been withdrawn, or a hermit, like himself, he could have lived with and understood where she was coming from, but the smug, superior, know-it-all attitude and the little *judgy* comments had to go. Plus the condescending, parent-to-child approach, whatever the fuck that had been, during the other day's conversation, it was just, well, it was rude. If he were any judge of character, there was self-pity there as well, and she was envious of what he had and was willing to share out of the goodness of his heart. Harley *was* a good person. He had been a little selfish in his life prior to The Day, but the only person that that selfishness had hurt had been him. He realized that now that there were kids around. Had he known they were so much fun, he would have adopted a few, or maybe tried to get into a relationship when he was younger, and had a few of his own. That was water under the bridge. He was almost fifty, and there was no going back.

He found her in the library, of course. As Harley entered, she looked up and then went back to what she was reading. The next five or so minutes needed to be private, so Harley quietly closed the door behind him and locked it. Then he walked over to where Angela was sitting and sat down directly across her. He leaned back in the over-stuffed leather club chair and stared at her, not saying a word.

Angela continued to flip through her book for a few more moments and then sighed and set it aside. She looked up finally and met his eyes. Harley let the silence drag out for a few more minutes before beginning.

"I think we got off on the wrong foot the other day. So I wanted to have a serious conversation with you and start over without the kids around. If anything, they need a little stability right now, and what I have to say might distress them."

Angela opened her mouth to say something, and Harley held up his hand.

"This won't take long, what I have to say, and when I am finished, you will have a chance to talk. That's how *adults* do things, is it not?"

Angela nodded tightly.

"So. Let us begin again. My name is Harley Earl. This is my home. You are all welcome here. I have food, security, recreation, water, and resources that will allow all of us to live comfortably for some time. That being said, I wanted to tell you about myself. How I got to be where I am and how I became the person that I am today. I was not a popular child—in fact, I was bullied from an early age—so I became comfortable doing things by myself, and it became a life-style. I was a functional hermit. I had jobs, I interacted with people on a surface level, and I did what I had to do to survive in the world the way it was before The Day. It was not a privileged life, I can assure you! I came from a single-parent home. My father left when I was three, and my mother did the best that she could, but she passed away when I was a teenager, sixteen, I think, and I had to become a ward of the State. No one wanted to adopt a sixteen-year-old. For the next two years, I was moved from foster home to foster home. I grad-uated from high school, couldn't afford to go to college, worked odd jobs in a shitty economy, and hoped and dreamed for a better life.

"I played the lottery religiously, the same numbers every week, buying only one ticket each time. That let me dream that there was something better out there for me, but the reality was, I was scared and alone in the world, and I had no one to help me become more than I was. I read a lot," he said, gesturing around the library, "and I dreamed of places that I could never afford to visit. Then one day, I won the lottery. I *won*. For the first time in my life, I had won something! Now I could afford to follow those dreams. I was thir-ty-three when that happened. Most people would have just blown all that money and had nothing tangible to show for it, but I invested wisely and grew it bigger. I was able to look at the stock market as a system, and it made sense to me. I didn't really have people skills, but I could understand numbers and how they worked. I was able to identify trends and capitalize on them before other people, so I had a pretty good income. That was when I realized I could afford to do whatever I wanted, not in a capricious or cruel and uncaring way, but I could follow my dreams and become the kind of person I always wanted to be. I went to college for fun, taking classes that interested me, and probably learned more than the drunks and potheads I was surrounded by. I made a choice to not engage in that kind of culture. Although, every once in a while, I like to get a little stoned. I liked music and bands and a good microbrew. I traveled to all the places I couldn't afford to visit before, and I built this place. See, money lets you disregard the things in life that you would rather have nothing to do with, and it lets you engage in the things that you do.

"I don't particularly like being around other people. It's not selfish, it's not childish, it's simply who I am, and I have accepted that about myself. It may not be ideal for others, but that is *their problem*, not mine. I have my happiness by being apart from the rest of the world. I had the means to make it so, and so I did. I like to learn things and know how they work, how to do stuff, and so I do that constantly as well. I got lucky winning the money, but everything since then has been a calculated effort. Understand? I earned all this, the lottery winnings merely the launch pad to get me where I am. Now, I know people with fancy degrees, and even with a bit of financial help, they never would have been able to figure out how to get here. I think self-awareness is the only step that one needs to take to reach the status of adulthood, and believe me, lady, I have been self-aware for quite some time. I am comfortable with who I am.

"Now, on The Day, things changed out there in the world, and to a certain extent, you were right when you said that not a lot changed for me then. I built this place to be self-sustaining and off grid. I wasn't dependent before, and I am not dependent now. What changed for me was the realization that I could probably afford to help people that might be in a tight spot, but which people? The Cains of the world, who would slaughter an entire town? Like I said initially, I don't particularly like being around other people, so who am I to judge who gets in and who doesn't? I found two of those kids wandering around my property in a blizzard, and I took them in. One of them was so sick she almost died, but I was able to nurse her back to health, and I took responsibility for them. Me. Harley Earl. Then I took the responsibility of trying to find additional resources for them, clothing, the chickens, and the goats that they told me about, and at great personal risk, Brian and I set out to secure those resources. He thought you were all dead, by the way, and from what I saw of that town, it is a stone-cold miracle that you people made it out. We were gonna grab the kids' stuff and a few animals and get the hell out of there. Instead, we got lucky. We found you and three more kids. Now, in addition to the first two kids, again, I took the responsibility of bringing the rest of you in here. Me. Harley Earl. Again.

"So far since The Day, I have now officially helped five children and one adult that needed it, and I am considering bringing in more, but they have to be the *right* more, understand? I broadcast messages of hope and what news there is on a daily basis, did you know that? I *know* more about what happened than just about everyone on this continent at the moment. Dig?

"I am self-aware, I take responsibility, I plan and execute, and I adapt to situations. Maybe before all this went down, you could have called me childish, and by the pre-Day definition, you might have been right. I would have blown you and your opinion off as one less thing to worry about and had nothing more to do with you. And you would have gone on about your business of being an *adult* in the pre-Day world, and my childishness would have had no impact on you and yours. That being an *adult*, that mentality, is what killed the world, Angela. Where are all those 'adults' right now? Starving, dying, being raped and tortured and killed—all those horrors are being perpetrated on them by other *adults*. Maybe they were lucky and got incinerated on The Day, with their 'adult' ashes floating around the stratosphere somewhere." Harley laughed bitterly.

"What really pisses me off at the moment is your whole attitude. The little condescending, smirky, judgy comments. The self-pity. The separation from everyone else. The *hermit*, the *child*, has been taking care of the kids and the dog. I have been feeding them, cleaning up after them, and getting them to bed on time and keeping them entertained. The guy who should have no responsibility at all is buried in it, and here you sit, thumbing through a paperback in my library, with the fucking *nerve* to call me a child and telling me to *grow up*! If what I have been doing offends you in some way, then spill it! I've had my say now! What the fuck exactly is your *definition* of an *adult*?"

Harley nodded once firmly, sat back and crossed his legs, and waited.

Angela stared at him, her eyes wide. She opened her mouth as if to speak a couple of times and closed it again. She looked almost like one of his fish downstairs. She was very pale as well, and Harley wondered if anyone anywhere had ever talked to her like that. He was patient. He waited, staring at her levelly and holding her eyes. Angela blinked a couple of times, and then she burst into tears. Sobbing uncontrollably. Harley watched her cry for a while, uncomfortably. He didn't know what to do. Finally, he stood up, got her a few Kleenex from a box on an end table, and took them to her.

"Thanks," she whispered, wiping her eyes and blowing her nose.

Angela finally looked at him again. Her eyes were bleak.

"You're right," she said, shaking her head. "You are absolutely right. I have been selfish since I got here. I apologize for offending you, Harley. I just didn't *know* . . . all of that."

"Why would you?" he replied.

"I don't know," she replied. "When we came in here and I saw you and where you lived, I just assumed that you were some kind of shallow, rich guy, that life had just blessed you with everything, and that you didn't *know* what the world was doing out there. I was wrong. I guess I just needed a little time to process everything."

"That's understandable," he replied, "but I meant what I said the other day at the ranch too. I need your help. I haven't been around other people for a long time. Emotionally, or physically, or any of it. The kids are easy. They're kids, and they're fun and exasperating, but everything they do is done with integrity. The world hasn't ruined them yet. I am still out of my depth with them and people in general. I need another adult here that knows what kids need beyond feeding them and taking care of them and keeping them healthy. I suppose in time I will learn that too, but it is hard work to go from being a committed bachelor to having a house full of kids. I suppose it would have made a great sitcom before The Day." Harley laughed.

"Oh god, it's all gone, isn't it?' she said. "Everyone and everything that I worked for my whole life."

"No," Harley replied. "That's where you are wrong. You still have your kids and your nephew. You have lost *some things*, but not everything. Your ranch will still be there. We need to figure out how to save some of the cattle at some point, but no one can just take the land away. Raiders may burn your house down, but you can rebuild it. We have chickens and goats upstairs too. You are here now. You are safe, and at some point, things will stabilize. That's the nature of systems. They get a little out of whack every once in a while, but eventually, things stabilize and become ordered again. They don't always go on the same way, though," he said with a grin.

"Thanks, Harley. Thank you for being patient with me. I will try harder."

"That's all we can do, right? Just try harder."

Harley glanced at his watch. It was almost time to feed the kids lunch.

Into the Great Wide Open

CHAPTER 46

From the Journal of H. Rayton Townsend
March 18, 2017
Lake Alpine California

This will be my last journal entry from this place. I can't believe it, really. The next time I write, I will be somewhere else. It's a little scary. After putting as much effort into everything here as we have, it seems like home. I have been around Kyle and Carly since The Day pretty much, and moving forward without them will feel strange as well. I have Maggie, though, and I think I love her. I can't imagine life without her now either.
Kyle and I finished the greenhouse, and it turned out awesome! Carly has a lot of space to grow things now. Two wood-burning stoves salvaged from other homes provide heat at either end of it, and we have been using them to boil water into the air so that it's downright tropical in there. Everything she has planted so far has sprouted, too much to list here actually, and I envy them, the salads they will be having with meals soon. Maggie and I won't be able to partake of that particular pleasure. I leave here knowing that we have done everything we can to make Kyle and Carly self-sufficient, that they

have good neighbors who will be able to help them. We met some of them the other day, the Campbells moving in with Vic Mazetti and the other locals on the way as well. Kyle has been very busy hauling stuff in his truck, and we didn't quite destroy the other homes completely. The passes, while still snow covered, have melted some. The days are growing longer, and they should be naviga-ble with the winch and the snow chains that we have on "the bitch." The four of us have worked out a plan to get Maggie and me back on the road again. Kyle will drive us the rest of the way over the Sierras and into Nevada. He will take us as far as he can or until the gas tank stands at the halfway point. We have constructed a cart that Maggie and I can pull together.

* * *

The cart was about six feet long and four feet wide, and it rolled well along the graveled roadway the few times they had tried it out. Maggie and Ray had rigged a few harnesses with which to pull it, and so far, it worked great. They had had several strategy sessions over the previous weeks, packing and unpacking it and getting a feel for their equipment. They had come up with a plan. The cart was constructed from parts cannibalized from the neighbors' vehicles, tires, axles, and a bed made from two-by-fours. The torch and the welding equip-ment had made things easier. Along the edges were several tie-down points made from metal D rings and riveted to the wood.

They would load the trailer along with the cargo that it would carry in the back of "the bitch." Food, water, ammunition, tools, clothing, and shelter. Plus a tarp and bungee cords to secure it all. They had spent days rinsing out and sanitizing empty two-liter soda bottles. They filled them finally with springwater and a few drops of bleach to keep them potable for the long haul. Jerky and sausages from the smokehouse, canned goods, instant soups, and dried vege-tables went in as well. Drink mixes and a few bottles of booze, along with necessary trade goods, kind of topped things off. They still had their backpacks as well, filled with excellent outdoor gear and the lightest materials; in case they'd have to suddenly ditch the cart, they could continue on their way and still have everything they needed.

Kyle would drive them the rest of the way out of the Sierras and down into Nevada. He would take them as far as a half-tank of gas would get them, and then he would need to turn back. They had gone over the list again, and again and again. Loading and unloading the cart, testing its capabilities up and down the lane. Sometimes they cut down on the weight, and other times they added things to it that would be indispensable. With four brains working on the project, Ray felt confident after the second week that they weren't forgetting anything, but every once in a while, someone would have an "oh yeah" moment, and an additional thing would go into the cargo.

Maggie had her .22 rifle, and when they had been foraging, they had uncovered absolutely ridiculous amounts of ammunition for it. It seemed that almost all their former neighbors had owned one at some point. So they had almost five hundred rounds of that now. Maybe they could pick off small game and varmints with it to fill the cooking pot along the way. Ray had his .58 Hawken as well, plenty of lead, powder, and caps to fire it with, but it was a single shot. He could knock down a bull or a bear with it, but it took time to reload and would probably not be of too much use in a stand-up firefight. It was what they had for weaponry, though. Kyle was trying to get them to take more in that department, but Maggie and Ray insisted that they were going to need what they had at the cabin come springtime, with the passes open and more people coming through. So they refused, and somehow they would find what they needed along the way. They had a good attitude, excellent gear, and the will to make this trip. They were going to make it. Once they left, there would be no going back. They had to think of everything; the alternatives didn't even bear thinking about.

The final day before they had to leave was a celebration. Full of good things and memories being made. Carly built a snowman in the yard with a pipe and a fedora, button eyes, and nose. They went over their lists a final time, and everyone agreed that it looked good. They couldn't think of anything else to take. The cart and their supplies were loaded into the back of "the bitch."

That night, they had a huge meal that Carly prepared. Dancing, drinks, and board games followed. Carly got a little teary-eyed about halfway through it and ran out the room. She bounced back quickly, though. The four of them stayed up late, sprawled out on the bear-skin rug in front of a roaring fire and talking. There were a few final small presents exchanged.

"Ray, I put together a first-class med kit for you guys, and I wrote out a pamphlet for how to deal with some things you may run into along the way," Carly said. "Hopefully, there will be no more bears, but you never know, right?"

"Thanks, Carly," he replied. "What kind of topics?"

"Oh, frostbite, infection, loose teeth, lacerations, things that are bound to occur at some point or another. Either to you guys or people that you may encounter on the way, people you don't even know yet but might end up caring about. Things you may need to deal with. You still need to make it over the Rockies in springtime, and that may be a mean bitch. Getting here almost killed the three of us, remember?"

Ray nodded.

"It's important to stay warm, so I knitted you guys extra hats and mittens and scarves too, I want you to take this book with you as well. I found it when we were looting and plundering."

Ray looked at the title and grimaced.

Where There Are No Doctors: A Field Guide to First Aid in the Third World.

"That's where we are now, huh?" he said quietly/ "Fuck."

Carly smiled.

Maggie had been looking over Ray's shoulder at the book.

"Oh wow," she said. "Thank you, sweets!"

She gave Carly a big hug.

They talked a little more, and then it was time for bed.

Ray and Maggie made love slowly that night, tenderly, and then they held each other, shaking in the darkness.

"It's going to be okay, Ray," she said against his chest. He just squeezed her tighter.

The next day dawned bright and clear, and they loaded the rest into the truck early, well before the sun came up. When they came back in, Kyle and Carly were preparing a big breakfast to send them off with. They had some great last-minute conversation, and then it was time to go, time to say good-bye.

Carly hugged Ray and kissed his cheek.

"I am going to *miss* you," she said, glancing at Maggie. "I am going to miss *both* of you so much!"

"I'm going to miss you too," he said. "Someday, when this is all over, I am coming back here, or at least—"

Carly put her hand over his mouth.

"I know."

Ray stepped aside, and Maggie gave Carly a hug that lasted a while too.

"Thank you," she whispered, "for so much, for everything. For my life . . . my future—all of it. Thank you."

Both women had tears in their eyes.

"Are you both *sure* about this?" she asked. "It's not too late to stay. We can unpack everything, wait a while, see—"

"It's time, babe," Kyle said. "They have places to go, things to see, other people that they care about. They have to know what happened."

"We do," Ray replied thoughtfully, "but this is a lot harder than I thought it was going to be."

There was another round of hugs, and Carly waved until they went around the bend in the lane, and that was that.

They saved their good-byes for Kyle about five hours later. He was eyeing the gas gauge, trying to squeeze every mile out that he could, but finally it was time. Kyle pulled over to the shoulder of the Nevada highway and killed the engine. They got the cart down and loaded, tied the tarp down over it to secure their precious cargo, and made sure they hadn't forgotten anything. It was all there. Finally, it was time for Kyle to get going.

"Well, this is it, man. For now. I can hardly believe it," he said, giving Ray a big hug. The wind gusted past them for a moment, stirring up dust.

"I have a few more things for you guys," he said. "These are from Carly."

Kyle handed Maggie a kerchief folded around about a dozen fresh biscuits, and they all laughed.

"And this is from me," he said, handing Ray a heavy package wrapped in deerskin.

Ray unwrapped it and saw Kyle's .44 along with a box of shells for it and a holster.

"Kyle, we've been over this—" Ray started to say.

"You *need* to take this," he replied just as firmly, "where you are going. You're going to need protection and the firepower. Carly and I have the rifles, the shotguns, and that semiauto we picked up at the Simmons' place. Vic is moving into the neighborhood, and if I know him, he has more guns than he knows what to do with. He'll be packing some serious heat. So you need to take this."

"All right, then," Ray said, smiling, "I will."

Kyle thumped him on the shoulder, gave Maggie a quick hug, and then jumped into the truck.

He started it up and got turned around while they stood there watching.

Kyle pulled up even with them and rolled down the window.

"Normally, I'd say, 'Call us when you get there,' but . . ." He waved his arm futilely.

"Good luck, Kyle!"

"You too!" he waved. "Be good!"

Ray and Maggie stood on the shoulder and watched him drive away. They were on a lonely stretch of Nevada highway, and they stood there until the truck was an ugly pink dot climbing into the foothills. They had their arms around each other, and the wind gusted again. Ray pulled Maggie close and gave her a long kiss.

"Alone at last," he said with a grin.

"Let's go," she replied, hugging him back.

He took a long look around at the emptiness surrounding them and sighed. The world seemed so much bigger now. They hooked the harnesses over their shoulders and began to walk, pulling their meager valuable possessions behind them.

"I think Kyle took us a little farther than he should have," Ray said at one point.

"I know he did," Maggie replied with a wink.

"Maybe we should send them a Christmas card. Next year." Ray laughed.

"Pony Express carries Christmas cards?"

"Smart-ass."

Tough Times

March 20. 2017, Nevada

They walked, pulling the cart, for about eight hours the first day, taking frequent breaks and drinking lots of water. Ray was happy that they were crossing the desert in early spring. No rattlesnakes or other venomous critters had woken up yet, for starters, and the sun was bearable. But it was still dry, and the water, when they drank it, tasted like nectar. They made a little fire when they stopped that first evening and ended up outside the town of Yerington, Nevada. After a small dinner and the fire had died down to coals, the two of them were lying on the tarp, with their backs to a stone outcropping. They were watching shooting stars, and they were tired, but not excessively so. It felt good to be snuggled in next to someone after a long day on the road. The cart worked great, and they had high expectations of making some good miles the following day as well.

"Ray?" Maggie asked.

"Yeah, babe," he whispered back.

"I'm crazy about you."

He smiled before replying, "Well, I kinda like you too, lover."

"Good." She elbowed him in the ribs. "'Cause you're stuck with me at least as far as Missouri."

Ray laughed and then dropped off to sleep.

The next day, they walked all day again, taking frequent breaks, and eventually, in late afternoon, they reached the town of Schurz, Nevada. There was a hostile vibe in Schurz. As they entered the town, they noticed a few of the locals eyeing them and their cart. Mostly looking at their cart, it seemed. A large man with a potbelly and a cowboy hat lurched off the sidewalk toward them. He seemed drunk, and he was sneering at Ray's Hawken rifle.

"Does that old thing really shoot?" he snarled.

The man took another step toward them, and Ray, on impulse, almost instinctively brought the muzzle to bear on him. The huge .58 bore gaping, he replied, "Do you want to find out?"

The man backed away quickly, half-raising his hands. He tripped over the curb and went down hard on his ass. Maggie and Ray glanced at each other warningly. Ray unzipped his jacket so that the butt of the .44 would be exposed as well. Unspoken, they decided to keep their weapons handy for the hopefuly short time they would be passing through Schurz.

Schurz wasn't exactly what you call a going concern. They looked at the lean, dirty, unshaven faces around them, at the tattered clothing, and just kept walking. The town seemed half-empty, and those that were left seemed to be hanging on by their fingernails. Maggie and Ray would find no help there, it seemed. They were a little shocked. The winter in the mountains had insulated them to reality, it seemed. They had known on an intellectual level what they might find out here, but actually seeing it hammered home how bad things could get and how quickly. This town would be just another Nevada ghost town soon. It was dying.

They were starting to get very concerned about the way people kept looking at them. Ray could see the speculation in the piggy little eyes as they walked past. The unspoken question seemed to hang in the air. "What's on the cart?"

He and Maggie didn't have much, but what they did have would be needed in the coming weeks and months. He wondered when someone was going to make a move.

"Babe, we gotta get out of here, or we're not going to survive the night."

"I know," she whispered back. "Let's just keep going. Maybe we should walk all night and put as much distance as we can between these people and us."

"Might not be a bad idea," he replied.

As they continued through town, eventually they reached a residential neighborhood that had been solidly middle-class at one point. They saw a man and his family packing a pickup truck to leave town.

"Afternoon," Ray said politely.

The man started as he noticed the guns. Ray and Maggie were alone at that moment with the stranger and his family, the other locals having melted into the woodwork.

"Afternoon," the man replied cautiously. "I see ya'll are traveling too."

"Coming from California, headed east," Ray replied.

"On foot?" the man asked.

"If we have to."

The man thought for a moment and then called his wife over. Their names were the Carters, and they had two little kids, a boy and a girl, aged six and eight. A long conversation ensued, and they got down to business.

"All right, my name is Toby Carter," the man said, "and this is my wife, Tracy. We're heading east to a little town called Ely, and we're going to be leaving early tomorrow morning. Headed up to my folks' place. They have a ranch there. Seems like a good time for families to be together, and this town just went belly-up in the last few days. So we talked it over, and if you'd like, for a price, we can take you that far. It's about 250 miles to get there and might save a little wear and tear on your feet."

"What kind of price?" Ray asked.

"Well, the grocery store finally ran out of food, and there's nothing left in the whole town. That's why we're leaving. We have a working vehicle, and a lot of folks don't. Everyone worth a damn left already, and those that are left are gonna start preying on one another soon. We'd rather it not be us, if you know what I mean. Got any food on that cart of yours?"

"Some," Maggie replied.

"Well, we can start with that, then. How about half of your food?"

"Let us talk it over for a minute," Ray replied.

He and Maggie stepped off to the side with the road atlas. They did some math and determined that it might take them a month to walk that far. A month's worth of food for two people versus a five-hour ride in the back of a truck.

"Give 'em two weeks' worth?" Ray asked Maggie finally. "We'd still come out ahead on the deal. What do you think?"

"Yeah, that sounds fair. Throw in a couple packs of smokes, and I'm sure we'd have a deal," Maggie replied. "We would have used twice that to get that far, and this way, we save time, energy, and resources. Offer them two weeks and see what they say."

"Okay," Ray said, turning back to the Carters. "We can spare two weeks' worth of food for two people. Two people meaning two adults, like *us*." He gestured to himself and Maggie. "How does that sound?"

"Well, gas was expensive before The Day, and now it's almost impossible to get for any price. We barely have enough to get where we're going. Do you have anything else? Maybe some more food or something?"

They went back and forth in that vein for a while before settling on two weeks' worth of food and two packs of smokes.

"After all, man," Ray said to Toby, "you can't beat tobacco as a trade item. In fact, I bet there is even less of this than gasoline remaining at this point."

"Done!" Toby said.

They camped out nervously in the Carters' backyard that night, one of them awake at all times until they left Schurz. Toby and his wife didn't want strangers in the house, and Maggie and Ray didn't blame them a bit. They wanted to leave *early* as well. The sooner they left Schurz behind, the better.

From the Journal of H. Rayton Townsend
March 22, 2017
Back of the Carters' Pickup Truck, on the Way to Ely,
Nevada

We left Schurz in the dust early this a.m., and not a minute too soon. People were throwing rocks and bottles at us as we left, and a few actually chased behind on foot as we left town, before turning away and slumping back into that shithole. No one shot at anyone, but we thought they might for a minute or two there, and we were ready to retaliate. We camped in the Carters' backyard last night, and we were happy to get moving this morning. We gave them one week's worth of food before we left and a single pack of smokes as a down payment, promising the rest when we arrive in Ely. Hopefully, Ely will be in better shape than Schurz. At the moment, we are riding in the back of Toby's pickup with our stuff, and it's a little chilly and windy back here. Maggie has been snuggled into me since we left and is sleeping at the moment as I write this. It's midmorning, and we are making great time. Another few hours, and we'll be there.

* * *

Ray closed his journal with a good feeling. The miles were bleeding away beneath the tires, and he rested his head back against the glass of the cab of the pickup. He felt good about the deal they had made and the progress they were making in getting there. An abandoned car sat on the side of the road, facing the opposite direction, and Ray had just enough time to read the bumper sticker as they passed it:

The problems that we face *now* will not be
solved by the minds that created them.

"Amen, brother," he murmured.

The rhythmic susurration of rubber on pavement lulled him, and drowsy, he dropped off to sleep as well. It was warm under the blankets with Maggie.

The next time he awoke, the truck was stopped, and as he blinked awake, he became aware of a hard, cold pressure on the side of his face. Flicking his eyes to the right, he realized that the barrel of a 9mm was shoved into his cheek. *Shit!* he thought. Toby was on the other end of the pistol and shaking like a leaf.

"Be cool, man," he said, a lot calmer than he felt.

"Get out! Both of you! And leave your stuff! We are not taking either one of you any farther!" he yelled.

Ray felt Maggie stirring beside him, feigning sleep, as her hand closed around the butt of the .44 in Ray's waistband. Ray raised his hands slowly, stalling for time, moving to shield her from Toby's sight.

"But we're not there yet," Ray replied lamely. He stood up slowly, hands still raised, and prepared to jump down from the truck. Toby retreated another four steps as he did so.

"Both of you! Out! Now! Hey, bitch, wake up!" His voice had taken on a hysterical edge. "We're leaving you right here!"

"What's going on?" Maggie asked sleepily. As Ray jumped down, she used his movements to mask what she was doing.

"I'll tell you what's going on, lady, we're—" Toby started to say as his head suddenly vaporized like a watermelon hit with a sledge-hammer. The report of the .44 right next to his head left Ray completely deaf out of one ear for a moment. He watched, ears ringing, as the now-headless corpse took two staggering steps backward, blood jetting five feet straight up into the air, before collapsing spread-eagled in the dirt.

"Jesus," he breathed out.

From the other side of the truck, Tracy Carter began to scream. The kids began to cry out hysterically as well. Ray still stood there for a moment, stunned, ears ringing and feeling like a fly trapped between two windowpanes.

"Don't you understand? We need that stuff more than you do! We have kids, and we *need* it! We *need* it! You don't need it as much as we do!" Tracy was repeating herself over and over as his hearing came back. Ray walked over to the body and retrieved the 9mm.

Tracy had walked around the truck, and as she did so, she saw what was left of Toby lying on the ground. She went berserk then, began screaming obscenities and denying that anything was wrong. Maggie jumped down from the bed of the truck at that point.

"SHUT UP, BITCH!" Maggie snarled.

Tracy lunged at her, fingers like claws, and as she did so, Maggie backhanded her with the barrel of the .44. She followed that with a vicious punch to the nose and kicked her a few times when she hit the dirt to make sure she didn't get back up again.

Total time elapsed was about thirty seconds. Ray stood there, his ears filled with cotton, hearing the kids screaming from far away and looking at the headless body in the dirt. Maggie stalked away from the now-cowering Tracy Carter, the look on her face positively terrifying. She opened the passenger side of the pickup and ripped the kids out of there. With one under each arm, she walked back and dumped them by Tracy in the dirt. Turning, she walked back to the driver's side door and looked at Ray still standing there, the 9mm down by his side hanging loosely by the huddled little family.

"Get in, Ray!"

Ray just looked at her.

Maggie sighed. "Ray . . . it's okay. Get in the truck," she repeated in a softer tone.

Ray started walking for the passenger side door, and it must have penetrated Tracy Carter's mind what was about to happen. She grabbed his pants leg as he walked past, pleading. She would not let go. She was keening out the same words over and over.

"No! No, no, no, please! *Please*! I told him not to. I told him— no! Please, no! I told him . . . please, please, *please*!"

"Let go, please," Ray said like a robot. He reached down and removed her hands from his pants leg.

She promptly grabbed it again, and he looked across the bed at Maggie. She shook her head sadly. He bent down once again firmly, and as he detached her hands from his leg, he felt her nails scrape him through the Gore-Tex. He slammed the door in her face, and she ran alongside as Maggie dropped the truck into drive and they pulled away. Ray watched her in the side-view mirror for a bit and saw her crawling toward her husband's corpse, the two children still screaming in the dirt. He had to look away.

They made it two miles up the road.

"Stop the truck!" he choked out.

Maggie slammed on the brakes and stopped just in time, and he threw open the door, vomiting onto the shoulder. Her expression didn't change the entire time he was getting sick, and she didn't say anything. When he got back in the cab, she wordlessly handed him a bottle of water. He rinsed his mouth out and spat, trying to get the taste of bile out of the back of his throat. Maggie rubbed his back between his shoulders.

"Feel better? You all right?"

Ray nodded. "I've never killed anyone before," he said, shuddering.

Maggie looked at Ray a long time before replying.

"If it makes you feel better, Ray, you didn't kill him. I did. And I have never killed anyone before either." She shivered a little. "It doesn't feel very good, though, does it?"

Ray shook his head as she put the truck back into gear and kept driving.

* * *

Ray was standing in a muddy ditch, looking at Maggie. The rain was pouring down, and he was cold, so cold. Maggie was lying there, arms and legs at impossible angles, and half of her head was missing. Pinkish matter and blood was washing away with the water running away down the center of the ditch.

"Don't you understand?" someone was saying mockingly, slyly. "Don't you understand yet? We *need* this stuff more than you! We *need* it! We have kids. We need it more than you! We need it, need it, need it! Why don't you understand?"

He was cold, very, very cold. Why was it raining so hard? And why did they have to do this? He took a long, shuddering breath then another one, plumes of steam coming off him with the cold. The blood was so red. He took another deep breath, about to scream out all the rage and grief and loss, the indignation . . . he . . .

He sat up suddenly in the darkness, panting. Shaking, shuddering. He hugged his arms around himself, rocking back and forth. His teeth were clenched, and he was sweating. He felt Maggie rubbing his back.

"Bad one?" she asked.

Ray merely nodded. He couldn't reply yet.

"Do you want to talk about it?"

He shook his head.

"In that case, would you mind if I got some sleep myself?"

"Not just yet," he replied.

He lay back, holding her in the darkness until the shuddering stopped.

"It was us or them today, right, babe?" he finally asked.

He felt her nodding in the darkness.

"If we had just given up and let them take everything, just let them leave us by the side of the road, we would eventually have been just as dead as if they had shot us, right?"

He felt her nod again.

"Baby, you saved our lives out there today. Do you know that?"

That was when the dam burst, and hanging on to Ray tightly, her fists knotted in his shirt, she began to cry. Not just for the Carters and the afternoon, but for everything. It finally caught up with Maggie. Deep, gut-wrenching sobs wracked her. She screamed, she scratched, she sobbed and bit, and finally, she just slumped, exhausted, into merely crying again. Ray held her throughout and reflected on just what kind of woman he had ended up being with. In a lot of ways, Maggie was a lot tougher than he was. Probably tougher than he would ever be. She had an instinctive way of seeing right to the heart of things, acting and reacting before he had a chance to really realize what was going on. She was faster to judge, to make a decision, and if she weren't that way, they would both be facing a long, slow death at the moment if they hadn't just been gunned down by Toby Carter on the side of the road.

He stroked her hair softly as she began to calm down. Not for the first time, he was examining his own reaction to things, almost like an outside observer, noting that he would need to become stronger for her. That he would need to become harder emotionally, spiritually, ethically in just about every way possible if he was going to be able to protect her the way that she had protected them both today. She had chosen them, their lives, over everyone else this afternoon, and Ray was glad that she had it in her to do that.

"Don't you understand . . . ?" seemed to echo in the wind.

Ray did. He did understand. There were formerly good people, scared people out there, making really bad decisions right now. Really, really bad, shitty decisions. Their shitty decisions would get him and Maggie killed if he wasn't always careful from now on and watching. There was no law, no society, nothing anywhere other than themselves to protect them and keep them alive and safe on this journey. He knew that now. It was everywhere. The feelings that he had for this woman, the fondness, changed into something more as he held her in the darkness as she cried. Finally, Maggie sat up and pushed him away a little bit. She rubbed her palms over her face and eyes and spat into the darkness.

"I'm a fucking mess," she said.

"I love you," he said wonderingly.

"What?"

"I love you. You're amazing," he repeated.

Maggie was very still for a moment. Then she laughed.

"What brought that on?"

"I just realized, it is all," Ray replied quietly.

"Well, I love you too, Ray. How about that?"

"Still feeling sleepy?" he asked.

"No."

"Good," he replied, kissing her.

They made love right there on the shoulder of the road, savage, quick, desperate love, tearing at each other's clothing, because they were alive, and they were in love, and they intended to remain that way.

* * *

They jerked awake slightly before dawn the next morning. Building up the fire, they cooked breakfast. They took a little extra time to brew some coffee on their little camp stove. It was glorious. They got back on the road right after that.

A short time later, they arrived in Salina, Utah. Salina was in a little better shape than the other towns they had passed through or driven around on their way so far. For one thing, there was gas to be had in Salina. It was beyond expensive, but they traded all the Carters' things and some food for a full tank. While Ray was gassing up the truck, he was approached by a clean, well-dressed young lady with an AR-15 on a strap over her shoulder. She handed him a pamphlet and chatted for a little bit as he filled the tank. There were Mormons in Salina. Apparently, Salt Lake City had come through The Day just fine.

Making small talk, Ray inquired about the road ahead. Denver had been hit along with Las Vegas. People were running in all directions, it seemed. The Deseret Industries people had been on it, though, and relief supplies were going out locally along with polite, smiling people carrying pamphlets and assault weapons. Ray thanked her politely for the pamphlet, and afterward, he shook his head. What a weird world this was turning out to be.

Pulling out of Salina, they discussed it a little.

"Did anything about that stop seem a little . . . weird, babe?" he asked.

"Yeah. Mormons give me the creeps, love, but they are fascinating too," she replied.

"They don't even drink coffee!" he exclaimed in disgust. "*How* do you trust people who don't? They're just so freakin' healthy!"

"And *blond*!" she added.

They both laughed.

"Well, we were able to gas up there, and that's more than we've found anywhere else, ya know? They can't be all bad," Maggie said.

"They gave me a pamphlet," Ray grumbled.

"Did they really?" Maggie laughed. "They gave me one too!"

Smiling, they drove on in silence for a while.

Maggie had been studying the map for a bit.

"With a full tank of gas, we should be able to make it to Colorado," she said. She sighed, and Ray glanced over at her.

He raised an eyebrow.

"I miss my Garmin!" she said, laughing.

Ray extended his right hand without taking his eyes from the road, and she took it in both of hers while he drove.

"So . . . Colorado, huh? Not bad."

"Yep. But I don't think we'll find another fill-up after this, Ray, so it's probably going to be walking rather than riding for a while. Maybe we can try siphoning from abandoned cars or something, or maybe trade the truck for some more stuff. A working vehicle has to be worth *something*, you know."

"Well, we'll just have to keep our eyes open."

The Rockies awaited them, a thin blue line on the horizon now, and Ray knew they were going to be far more challenging than the Sierras. Snow was falling again as they made their way across Utah, draping everything in a shroud of white. They drove on into it and, a few hours later, saw the sign: WELCOME TO COLORADO.

"Want to stop for a bit?" Ray asked. "I could use a stretch."

"Sure," Maggie replied.

"We've burned half the tank already," he said, glancing at the fuel gauge.

They pulled into the welcome center, stretched out all the kinks, and made lunch. They explored for a little while, looking for anything useful, but the vending machines lay smashed, their contents taken by enterprising travelers before them. Maggie grabbed a few tourism pamphlets, and then they got back on the road.

* * *

They had been following I-70 along the Colorado River since Grand Junction a few hours before. The going was slow as the snow piled up. They had to stop and backtrack occasioanlly around wrecks, the remains of rioting, and what was left of some of the larger towns. The interstate was occasionally blocked by a jackknifed big rig or some crashes, but they were managing so far. Maggie was driving slowly to conserve fuel and to keep from slipping off the road, but they were running on fumes, and it wouldn't be long before they were on foot again.

Ray looked up and saw a sign that said DE BEQUE: 3 MILES as the engine coughed once, twice, and died. They were on a long downgrade, so they were able to coast for almost another mile before Maggie pulled to the shoulder and they stopped.

"Well, that's it, babe! We're out of gas!" She smiled.

"You mean we ran out of gas in the middle of nowhere?" he asked.

"Yep."

"I think I have heard of this move. Are you sure you're not trying to take advantage of me?"

Maggie winked at him.

"Nope. I saved that one for the second date."

They opened the doors and shivered as the wind knifed inside the cab. They unloaded the trailer from the back, strapping their possessions and gear down to it. They did a quick once-over of the vehicle for anything else useful. Maggie came up with two full magazines for the 9mm they had gotten from Toby Carter.

"These'll be handy," she murmured.

They found a few other things, tied the tarp down, and started pulling the cart toward De Beque. Ray patted the truck fondly as they walked past it.

"I can't believe we covered this much ground in three days," he said.

"I know. With how things are now, it almost seems like a miracle, huh?" she replied.

"We used to live in an age of miracles," Ray said grumpily. "Transportation, warm clothes, hot showers, plenty of food, health care—there was enough for everybody."

Maggie threw a snowball at him, and he spluttered.

"What do you miss the most right now? Think quick!"

"Hot pizza," he replied with no hesitation.

Laughing, they advanced through the snow toward De Beque, the ground ahead rugged, the air cold. There was no going back.

Ever Onward

CHAPTER 48

From the Journal of H. Rayton Townsend
March 28, 2017
Rocky Mountains, State of Colorado

We are very, very tired. We have been pulling that damn cart through snow for the last five days. Two days ago, we broke into a ski shop to spend the night, Big Al's Ski and Snowboarding, and to use one of Kyle's expressions, we "borrowed" some snowboards to lash to the wheels when going through some of the larger drifts. When we reach open pavement on the other side, we have to stop and remove the snowboards so that the wheels can roll again. We have snowshoes to wear too. We are burning through food and supplies at a startling rate. All the effort to keep moving onward is making us ravenous. Saving as much food as we did while driving the truck is proving to be a godsend. We would probably be completely out of food at this point had we walked the entire way. We're looking for a place to hole up in for a few days. We need the rest.

* * *

"Where *is* everyone?" Maggie asked again.

"I don't know, but it's a little creepy, huh?"

"You would have thought these little mountain towns would have done better than this," Maggie said, outraged. "They were used to winter. People knew each other. You would have thought that they would have been able to count on each other to get through it, right?"

"Yep," Ray replied.

"I am *so* disappointed in Colorado, babe."

They were on the outskirts of Eagle, Colorado, and the town seemed from a distance to be completely deserted. An hour earlier, they had pulled the cart past a roadblock, two yellow sawhorses, with large yellow-and-black radiation signs on them. There was no one manning it. A larger printed sign advised that the interstate ahead was not safe for traveling. Poor Denver. Ray had rather liked the Mile-High City. They would have to give it a wide berth to stay on the safe side, and that would prolong their stay in the mountains.

"Sometimes it feels like we are the last two people alive, right?" Ray asked.

Maggie laughed.

"Oh, there are people around, I'm sure, just not here. What we really need to be thinking about is how friendly they are going to be when we find them."

They had stopped for a moment to consult the atlas, and on impulse, Ray walked over to a snow-covered vehicle. With a single gloved finger, he wrote in the snow on the windshield, "The old woman is in Boulder. Flagg is in Las Vegas."

Maggie was laughing at him when he turned around.

"Nice! *The Stand*, right?"

Ray winked.

"I hope the eminent Mr. Stephen King survived this whole mess, lady. I mean, he lived in Maine, right? There's nothing to blow up in Maine."

"What about 'chowdah' and 'lobstah'?"

"Isn't that more of a Boston thing? Anyway, the guy wrote about the end of the world enough that I'd like to think he was prepared for it," he said.

She grinned at him.

The mood was shattered abruptly a few seconds later when a large raven landed on the roof of the SUV Ray had just written on. It paced back and forth, eyeing them malevolently, cocking its head and blinking its beady eyes. It opened its mouth and *screeched* at them, and then with a series of cries that sounded like the laughter of the *damned*, it flew away into the west. The direction they had just come from.

"*That* was just plain fucking creepy, babe!" Ray muttered, scrubbing the words out with his sleeve.

Maggie didn't say anything. She just looked pale and nodded weakly. With a glance over their shoulders at the black speck flying away, they pulled their cart toward Eagle.

"I actually kinda envy that stupid fucking bird," Ray said a short time later. "Wouldn't it be awesome to be able to fly over all this shit?"

"It would be, but we can't, Ray. We're right down in it with everyone else. We need to figure out soon how we're going to get around Denver as well."

Ray thought again, not for the first time, just how much tougher than him Maggie was. She didn't complain; she just kept going. He wished he was that tough. Her strength gave him strength. If she didn't complain, he couldn't either. They kept up the pace for a long time after that, neither of them speaking, fighting the cold, the cramps, the stress, the exhaustion, and the boredom. They were comfortable with each other and with themselves. They kept walking and pulling the ever-lighter cart full of provisions.

* * *

From the Journal of H. Rayton Townsend
March 29, 2017

I can't believe it has been four-plus months since The Day. It is still winter here in the mountains, even at the end of March. I think tomorrow we will cut north on Highway 131 to begin our roundabout trek past Denver. We can always cut back south once we clear the radiation zone. We are having hot stew tonight, and I wish we had some of Carly's biscuits to go with it. I wonder how they are doing. Someday, I will go back.

* * *

Ray's feet had been bothering him some for the previous two days. Numbness. They limped into an abandoned home up a draw canyon. This had been someone's retreat and had probably set them back a couple million bucks prior to The Day. It had a large river stone fireplace and had been constructed from logs. Looking around, they saw the smashed windows and how all the furnishings had been torn up.

"What a fucking shame," Maggie growled. "God! People *suck!*"

"I know. This place must have been awesome before it all went to shit."

Looters had left their calling cards everywhere, shredded upholstery, graffiti, drawers ripped from custom cabinets and smashed, their contents strewn across the floors. They had looked around carefully outside before coming in here and had seen no recent tracks. Before pulling the cart up to the home, they had attached pine boughs to the rear of it so that they dragged in the powder snow, covering their tracks. No sense in advertising their presence. They had decided to rest a few days, reorganize their gear, and essentially, get their shit together.

They could abandon the cart soon. It had done its job. There was no point in pulling it any farther once everything supply-wise could fit into their packs. They would probably start making better time now that they didn't have to pull it as well. Ray got a small fire going in order to warm up, and it was Maggie's turn to make dinner. Outside, snow was falling heavily again. After he got their sleeping bags and extra blankets unrolled in front of the fireplace, Ray plopped down to take his boots off with joy. The fire was crackling merrily, and he was looking forward to stretching his feet out toward the warmth. Taking his socks off, he noticed his toes were all pruny. He was rubbing them when he noticed something bad. Really, really bad.

With a sick feeling in his gut and a sense of dread, he called Maggie over.

"Babe, can you look at this?" he said quietly.

Something in his tone made her look up immediately, and wiping her hands on a towel, she came right over to where he was sitting. She hissed when she saw the toe. Ray's little toe on his left foot had turned completely black. He had frostbite.

"Oh shit, Ray," she breathed out. "That's frostbite!"

"That's what I was afraid of," he replied. "So now what? What do we do about it?"

"Let me get the pamphlet Carly wrote out," she said, rummaging through their packs.

Ray leaned back on his elbows and sighed. He was terrified.

Maggie was reading for a little while. She was consulting the *Third World Health-Care* book as well.

"Well, my love, it seems that the toe is going to have to come off," she said finally.

"Great! I figured it would be something straightforward like that," he said.

"Well, look at it this way: you'll still have nine little piggies left."

Ray couldn't help it—he laughed. Now that his feet had warmed up, they hurt like hell too.

"Can you do it?"

"I think so," she replied.

"All right, let's do it," he said. "And, lady? Do it *fast*, okay?"

Ray eyed the knife in the boiling pot of water with dread. He was *not* looking forward to this at all. It would sure beat gangrene and blood poisoning, though. He was flying high on Darvocet and had already had a couple shots of brandy as well. He poured a third shot and downed it. What the hell? That was the ticket! He laughed at nothing.

"Feelin' good?" Maggie asked.

"*So* good!" he replied.

"All right! Ready?"

"I don't think you *can* be ready for someone to cut your toe off, Maggie."

"Do you want to lie back and get comfortable?" she asked.

"Sure."

"I'm going to count to five, okay? Don't look."

Maggie ground her teeth. She was preparing to cut the toe off in one quick motion.

Ray had his foot on a *really* nice cutting board they had found in the kitchen. Maggie grasped the boiling blade by the handle and pulled it out of the water.

"In 5 . . . 4 . . . ," she said as she felt Ray tensing up, "and 3 . . ." She cut quickly.

Ray screamed as she cauterized the stump.

He raised his head and saw that the toe was gone.

"No fair!" he mumbled as his head dropped back. "I had two numbers left."

Ray passed out.

They spent the next week in the house, inventorying supplies, repacking their packs, and resting. They had time to clean their weapons, sharpen their blades, make love, and stay warm. Eight days later, they were ready to hit the road again. While losing a toe had hurt, Ray had found that it hadn't hurt nearly as much as he thought it would. After all, he still had nine piggies left and a huge bottle of painkillers. They left the cart behind, and as per their original plan, they had consumed all the canned goods first along with the other heavy food, so now, all they would need to carry was the light-weight stuff, instant beverages and soups, jerky, dehydrated meals, and pouches. It still weighed a lot but would carry them a lot farther than where they now stood. They had multivitamins and water puri-fiers as well.

Ray took one final look at the house where he had lost a toe. He grinned.

"Babe? I am *so* glad we don't have to drag that fucking cart anymore."

"Me too, love," she replied, smiling back. "How's the foot? We gonna make some miles today?"

Ray stamped his left foot down once or twice and winced a little.

"A little sore, but not too bad. The painkillers help," he said. "We should make it to Hot Sulphur Springs by tonight. We'll just have to stop and warm up along the way whenever we have to, change my socks and stuff."

"All right, sir. Just let me know, okay? Don't go all caveman on me and try to tough it out. I don't wanna chop off any more piggies."

"Think we'll find people there?"

"We'll see."

They started walking, and one step followed another. Occasionally, they strapped on their snowshoes to keep going. They stopped occasionally so that they could change socks and warm their feet up. Ray's mind wandered as it often did when he was on the road. He thought about fate, and he thought about the future. He thought about the past. He thought about his family, and hating himself a little bit, he had to concede that their importance had paled and taken a backseat to the life that he was building with this woman. He thought about abstract things, and occasionally, he chuckled at the absurdity of them. Eventually, the walking rhythm came back, and he found himself in almost a Zen state.

Ray had always loved backpacking. The sense that you had everything you needed on your back. The right equipment, the right amount of food, the balance that you eventually attained, both inside and out. Out in the wilds, you eventually realized that you really did have all the things you needed and not the things that society felt you needed. You could let all that other crap go.

He and Maggie told each other stories as they walked in order to pass the time. It seemed there was always something else to discover. Ray liked that a lot. He meditated again on the fact that he not only loved her, he was also in love with her. Every time that realization ocurred, he smiled. It was an amazing affirmation daily when it happened. He had never been in love in his life. He had loved women, but not been in love with them. He had dated them until he left or they left him for someone else. He marveled again at just how messed up the world was. How God had a sense of humor about things, and maybe he *had* done all this just for Ray.

They had fallen into one of those comfortable silences again. Communicating without really communicating. The world was a muffled white place as they entered Hot Sulphur Springs. Maggie was leading at the moment, and her left snowshoe was leaving a long wavy S-shaped line with every step she took. Ray had his head down, thinking, *Another abandoned Colorado town.*

Suddenly, the hair on his neck stood up, and he had the distinct feeling that they were being watched. Maggie stopped suddenly, her nostrils flared, looking around, trying to determine what that feeling was. Sensing threat. A dozen soldiers surrounded them, M-16s almost seeming to float against the background that their camouflage winter uniforms faded into so well. Maggie gasped as she looked up. There was a tense moment when Ray could almost feel the pressure being exerted on triggers. Then it passed as one soldier approached them.

"I would recommend that you lay your rifles down and any other weapons that you may have on you." He gestured to the ground in front of them.

Ray and Maggie laid their rifles in the snow and very slowly, with two fingers, removed the .44 and the 9mm from their waistbands. They put their knives down as well.

"We have been ordered to secure this area, and we have ben playing cat and mouse with an armed band for about the last week. We kind of thought you were them, but then I figured any self-respecting guerilla fighter would probably be carrying more than a single-shot rifle and a .22."

Maggie and Ray just stared at him. He sighed.

"So come with me, and we can get to the bottom of this," he said, gesturing at a nearby building.

Ray and Maggie went with him, with two other soldiers in tow.

"My name is Lieutenant Travis, and you are . . . ? Please have a seat," he said, gesturing at two chairs.

"Maggie Winslow and Ray Townsend," Maggie said.

They both dropped their packs by the doorway and took a seat.

"All right, introductions out of the way, who are you people? Where are you coming from? Where were you heading? We haven't

seen any regular civilians coming out of the mountains in over a
month and a half, so you will, hopefully, satisfy my curiosity."

So slowly they began to talk. They told him just about everything, and since Travis seemed pretty sharp, they didn't leave out
much. Ray filled him in on the Bay Area and California in general
and what they had seen since, and Maggie told him about Seattle and
Portland. They talked about where they were headed, glossed over
how they had met, and didn't say a word about Kyle and Carly's cabin
or the shooting of Toby Carter by the side of the road in Nevada.
They went over their trip through the mountains so far, the fact that
Salt Lake City had survived The Day intact, and the Mormons they
had encountered.

Travis grunted at that and made a few notes.

"You said they were well-armed?" he asked.

"Well, yeah, they all had ARs on their shoulders," Ray replied.

Then Travis asked the strangest question of all.

"Which government do you support?"

Ray and Maggie looked at each other wordlessly, their confusion obvious.

"The . . . United States . . . government?" Ray asked. "How
many are there?"

For some reason, that seemed to satisfy Travis.

"Take them to Loveland. Return their personal effects, no
weapons. Give their medical supplies to Doc and half their food for
redistribution to the camp at large."

Before they left, the other two soldiers had them dump their
packs, exclaiming in delight at the two cartons of cigarettes in Ray's
pack. Those were confiscated, the rest of the ammunition, most of
their food, their trade goods, and all the booze. Their packs weighed
about a third of what they had walking into Hot Sulphur Springs.

They were put into the back of a snowcat and taken out of the
mountains. From there they were transferred to a truck, and from
there they went to a camp in Loveland, Colorado. Ray was completely pissed off. Almost murderously angry, his toe hurt, but above
all, he felt completely helpless. Again. As they were led away, he had
seen Lieutenant Travis admiring his Jud Brennan Hawken before the

door closed. Someday he was going to get even for all this. He was going to get out of this camp too, and someday, people like Travis and his thieving little bitch soldiers were going to be put against a wall and shot. Ray vowed that that was going to happen, even if he had to die doing it.

Loveland

CHAPTER 49

From the Journal of H. Rayton Townsend
April 5, 2017
Loveland, Colorado

Well, we pretty much made it through the Rockies. Pretty impressive, right? We just didn't do it in the way we wanted to or had hoped to. We found people in Hot Sulphur Springs, but they weren't friendly. Because now, now, dear reader, we just so happen to be in another fucking camp! Soldiers stopped us there, disarmed us, and essentially robbed us of everything worth having. They took our food, our medicine, our trade goods, our weapons, essentially just leaving us the things that they didn't want for themselves. It completely pisses me off, and someday, I am going to get even for all this. There will be a reckoning someday, at some point. Mark my words. But not today. Today marks the third time I have now been disarmed, my personal possessions confiscated at gunpoint, and the third time that someone has put me in a camp. This is such bullshit, but I know why all the towns in the mountains were empty now. All the people were sent here. These camps are death traps, and if we had waited around in Santa Rosa initially, I can now see what that would have looked like. There are more graves than I can count outside the wire here. There are about ten thousand other people here as well, and they have been here for months. Sanitation is appalling, there is simply not enough here for everyone, and soldiers guard the perimeter. Leave it to Maggie to look at the bright side of things. She said they could have always just shot us and taken everything anyway. I think if we end up staying here for a long time, we may start wishing that they had.

* * *

The truck backed slowly up to the gate of the camp. Ray saw a double row of fencing stretching into the distance, in both directions, the top posts strung with concertina wire. A large tank, possibly an Abrams, sat to one side. Closest to the gate, an orderly row of tents stood, followed by a mishmash of improvised shelter composed of plywood, plastic sheeting, and other debris, stretching off into the distance. There were military personnel around as well, but not nearly in the numbers that Ray had expected to see after what had been going on in California. Fog covered everything, and the smell of woodsmoke and some undertone of chemicals hung in the air as well.

As he and Maggie jumped down from the tailgate, figures materialized out of the gloom. Thin hungry people began to line up by the gate. Maggie looked at Ray, and he shrugged. They were taken to a tent nearby, where they had to give all their personal information again. They were issued numbers stamped on little plastic wristbands and then released into the camp to find their own accomodations. They wandered for a while, taking it all in, the absolute lack of color, the depression that seemed to saturate everything. It seemed so disorganized and informal. The staffer taking their names had seemed bored and listless and disconnected to everything happening around him. The soldier unlocking the gate waved them through, and once inside, they stood there for a moment, not speaking.

The other camp people had stared at them for a moment, and Ray and Maggie stared back. Ray was immediately struck by the differences between them. Their overall condition was poorer compared to himself and Maggie. The two of them were clean and fit and, up until that afternoon, had been relatively well supplied and equipped. These people had chronic coughs, runny noses, open sores and smelled as if they hadn't had the chance to bathe for months.

"Was there any food on that truck?" a woman asked them as they walked past.

"I don't think so," Maggie replied.

"Oh," she said, turning and walking back into the camp.

Maggie had a death grip on Ray's hand.

"Ray," she whispered, "this is terrible."

"I know," he replied. "We're going to have to watch ourselves and our stuff constantly. Boil our water and try to stay as clean and warm as possible. At least we still have the water purifiers, but I have a feeling that food is going to be real tight, so we may need to improvise."

They kept walking.

"Let's see if we can find someplace to stay, see who is in charge, and find out just what has been going on in here."

Ray wasn't *completely* disarmed. The soldiers in Hot Sulphur Springs had patted them down but not strip-searched them. After reading as much as he had over the winter, he had come across a pretty good idea in one of the books, and there had been plenty of deer's blood available to provide the necessary camouflage for what he and Maggie had done before setting out. They still had their survival kits, with snares, lighters, matches, a little medication, basically a little bit of a lot of stuff, but the Isaac Newton moment came when he got the idea to find an ACE bandage and make it look like the dirtiest, nastiest, infected thing he could find. A large pad inside held a large hunting knife, a Swiss Army knife, and a small first aid kit stocked with some of the most kick-ass drugs they could find while they had scavenged at Lake Alpine. It was taped to his leg like he had suffered a gash in his calf at some point, and then the filthy ACE bandage had been wrapped around the whole package. It basically looked like he had an infected leg wound. The deer's blood really gave it a look of authenticity. Maggie had a similar setup. The idea was that even if someone took their clothing and their boots without actually killing them, they would still have *something* to survive with. After all, who wants a gangrenous, used bandage, right?

The camp was dangerously close to the breaking point. Ten thousand people more or less, all that was left of the original couple hundred thousand or so that had been here. Rows of graves stretched away into the distance beyond the wire. There was not enough food, shelter, water, or anything for the people here. The Army patrolled the perimeter and sometimes came inside to remove the bodies of those who had died in the night. Sanitation was appalling. People were desperate. Tuberculosis, whooping cough, the flu, and other wintertime ailments were rampant. Tents were reserved for the dying, and they were full of the *really* sick people. Food deliveries came twice a day, once in the morning and once at night. It was a first-come, first-served kind of thing, and people lined up for hours before the trucks got there.

They found a place to camp off to the side of the camp, with the fence to their backs. To the east, the camp had once been much larger, and a debris field was there now. Snow-covered plastic, lumber, and who knew what else was scattered to the far side, ending at the fences. Those had been shelters for the others that had died over the winter, now fallen down and buried half in and half out of snowbanks. They unrolled their tarp and sleeping bags and slept that first night rolled up inside, their packs inside with them. Once inside the camp, rolled up in the tarp for the evening, Ray and Maggie had undone their bandages and moved knives to waistbands and redistributed supplies to cargo pockets and packs. They still had about a third of their food remaining and literally hundreds of bouillon cubes so they could make broth if needed.

It didn't take them long to figure everything out. They could stay where they wanted so long as no one had claimed the space before them. No one seemed to be in charge, and there was absolutely nothing going on anywhere. Other than waiting in line for food twice a day, there wasn't a lot to do. Ray and Maggie planned on changing that. They held their own by the gates when the food trucks arrived. They were in simply better physical condition than most that were there. What they received was meager, though, and if they were stuck for an extended period in this place, there was no telling how soon they would start to resemble the others already in the camp.

They relocated away from others as far as they could, within the confines of the fences, and initially, they kept their distance. They preferred to have a good line of sight to anyone who might be approaching them. Between 7:00 a.m. and 5:00 p.m., they foraged in the debris field, gathering and sorting raw materials to construct a shelter. The winter spent building and improvising had sharpened Ray's skills in that area quite a bit. It was a real find the second day there when he came across a shovel blade missing most of its length of handle. He smoothed off the broken, splintered stub and drilled through it with his Swiss Army knife. Then he found a two-by-four with a likely looking length to it and cut a notch from the bottom using the saw attachment. There were plenty of boards around with large nails sticking out, so he found a good one, extracted it, and tapped it through two-by-four and stub and wrapped the whole thing with duct tape tightly. Now he had a working tool.

Even though they were trying to keep their distance from other folks, what they were doing was attracting attention, and it was hard *not* to get to know people. No one had come in from outside for a while, and Ray and Maggie found themselves to be the center of attention by the curious. All sorts of people approached them to find out what they knew, where they had come from, and what they had seen. People were hungry for news, for word from the outside, of how it was all falling together. Most of the folks there were from Denver or the immediate suburbs and had been there pretty much since The Day. They had been evacuated after the bombs went off and had been stuck inside ever since. No one knew anything of the bigger picture. People listened incredulously and disbelievingly at first. Eventually, they just had to accept that they were on their own and that help was not coming.

On the third day, Ray laid out the outline of a rectangle near the fence. He and Maggie had figured they had gathered enough raw materials to begin construction of a more permanent dwelling. The guards didn't seem to care what the people inside the wire did, as long as they stayed inside, so Ray figured he would do what he could to improve their situation. The structure would be about twelve feet by ten, then he started to dig. He wrapped his hands with spare socks to help with the ungainliness of the shovel handle. Most of the soil here seemed to be loose, sandy stuff interspersed with rounded glacier cobbles. He threw them off to the side when he encountered them. He dug down to a depth of four feet, squaring off the sides of the hole, and then he and Maggie lined the walls and floor with loose sheets of fiberboard. Ray had found a few four-by-fours that they would use as support posts for the corners. Ray was able to dig the corners down deeper than four feet to anchor them. Then they lined the big rectangular pit with plastic sheeting that they had carefully cut and trimmed. Ray extracted more nails from loose boards lying around and then began to frame from corner to corner with two-by-fours. He reused the straightened nails and used a cobblestone as a hammer. The walls were constructed from more sheets of fiberboard and plastic sheeting as well as the roof. When the structure was solid, they covered it again with more plastic sheeting, and then Ray began to shovel all the dirt he had excavated back onto the structure to provide additional insulation. It wasn't enough, so he dug another large pit nearby, and eventually, there was an even layer of dirt over the whole thing. It took him and Maggie two days to construct a snug, neat little hut in the corner of the camp. Maggie had been digging another hole behind the hut while Ray had been framing it out, and on the third day, they constructed a privy for sanitation, complete with a seat.

They constructed a hearth near the doorway for cooking out of the cobblestones and a short curved wall behind it to reflect the heat back inside. All the scrap lumber was plentiful, and so they had plenty of firewood to burn. On the fifth day in camp, they got their first neighbors. People had been paying attention, it seemed. So using Ray's notes and ideas and good, hard work, others began to do the

same things that he and Maggie had been doing, and people began
to help one another again. Soon, they had a little neighborhood of
like-minded individuals and more help to scavenge what was there.
The far corner of the camp began to get cleaned up. Maggie went to
the gates one day and raised hell until they were able to get soap. She
came back with bags of it and a huge grin on her face. People began
to pool their resources, and soon they had clean water to wash with
and a large communal area to cook and get cleaned up in. Being able
to be clean, policing the area of garbage, and having warmer, snugger
quarters to sleep in did wonders for people's health and morale just
in a very short time. Besides pooling labor, they began to pool their
food. Larger groups of people contending with others at the gates
in the morning and evening meant a bigger share of the food. Not
everyone had to go at it alone anymore. Large pots of stew bubbled
over fires now, and while no one was getting a lot, no one was getting
shorted either. There were volunteers to get food now, volunteers to
construct new living accomodations, volunteers who boiled water
and filtered it for drinking, and volunteers for laundry.

Of course, no good deed goes unpunished. Their work continued to get noticed by other people, and not neccessarily in a good
way. The camp was of course divided into cliques, with their own
leaders, people that talked a lot and did nothing, or they exploited
others or bullied them or took what they wanted from those too
weak to defend themselves. Ray and Maggie weren't trying to lead
except by example, and they were more interested in helping than
in hurting. This made many who were tired of the status quo begin
to flock to their corner of the camp, eroding the power base in some
areas. As their group grew larger, others looked on in envy or in speculation or in open hostility. Conflict was inevitable.

On the tenth day there, Ray almost killed a man. He had been
taking his turn with the shovel. He carried it everywhere, almost like
a talisman now. He and two others had been digging another *founda-
tion*, for lack of a better word. They had improvised shovels of their
own out of boards and plywood, Ray busting up the tougher patches
with the steel and they scooping it away and out of the sides. He had

been taking a quick break and joking with their two new neighbors when someone called to him from behind.

"Hey! I see you found *my* shovel, man!"

Ray turned slowly and looked behind him, coming to face a tatted-up Latino and a few of his homeboys. They were standing about eight feet away. The two guys digging behind him had stopped and were facing the same way, their faces hard.

"What? This old thing?" Ray asked casually.

"Yeah. I lost it. I want it back now," he said.

"Where did you lose it?" Ray asked.

"Oh," he said, glancing slyly at his crew, "around, man. You know."

The other four guys laughed in a cruel way.

"Well, finders keepers, man. You should take better care of your stuff, you know?" Ray replied evenly, lightly, his heart racing, but he was outwardly calm. He felt like he was stepping outside himself now, watching this situation develop.

"Hey, asshole! Why don't you give him the shovel, man?" one of the guys said.

"Because it's not his," Ray replied.

"Well, he wants it now."

"Or what?" Ray asked, the other guys spreading out to rush him.

"What?"

"You heard me just fine, dickhead."

Their leader took a step forward, and Ray swung the shovel at him, connecting with the entire side of his head. He went down in a crumpled heap, blood pouring from his nose and ears. The others stopped, stunned for a moment. Ray didn't stop there. He knelt on the tatted guy's chest and pulled his Buck Knife out. He slapped him a few times, holding the razor-sharp edge firmly against the skin of his throat, almost drawing blood. He was vaguely aware of some of the other neighbors having gathered around, but his attention was riveted to the other guy's face. His eyes fluttered open, glassy and in shock, and Ray grabbed him by the shirt collar. He put his face almost in the other guy's, and he whispered at great length what he would do to him if he ever saw him again. No one heard what Ray said except the guy on the ground. Finally, Ray stood up, sheathed his knife, picked up the shovel, and looked around. About three dozen people were standing there, facing down the other guy's homeboys.

"Take your guy and go," Ray said. "Don't come back."

He watched as they got the tatted guy on his feet and got him out of there. They didn't come back.

"All right, guys, let's get back to work," Ray said as if nothing had happened.

* * *

From the Journal of H. Rayton Townsend
April 18, 2017
Loveland, Colorado

I haven't had a chance to write lately. All our time and effort go into improving our situation here. I wouldn't say that we are prospering, but by working together with our neighbors, we have managed to hold our own here. Things are hard. We have been here almost two weeks now. First, we had to construct something solid to live in, then we had to address sanitation, cleanliness, and having enough to eat. We have had others attracted by the organization we have tried to impose on the chaos around us, and now, with good neighbors literally dug in on all sides of us, things seem to be stabilizing. I almost killed another man three days ago. Maggie and I didn't discuss it too much, but I can tell it bothers her. I still need to become harder for her and myself. I needed to stand up to those guys; otherwise, what we have been building here would have fallen apart. Such a risk to take over a stupid shovel! It wouldn't have stopped there, though. The shovel would have been the first thing, then it would have been our other gear, our little hut. It wouldn't have ended until they had taken everything. We simply cannot allow others to take from us when we have so little as it is. I am not proud of what I did, but it was necessary. Others have joined us since I did it, and we are stronger now as a group. I keep thinking back to the dream, the one I had the night after we killed Toby Carter. I have had variations of that dream since. Losing her. Sometimes she is not dead, but she looks at me as if not recognizing the man that I am, like we have become strangers. I don't think I could bear to lose her either way, physically or emotionally, and it is a relief to wake up to the reality that they are only bad dreams. It is a comfort to be loved, and to know it, my waking hours are saturated with that love, but at night, the dreams come again, the nightmares, and while I sleep, my brain betrays me, tortures me with the loss of that love. On a brighter note, I have been teaching some of the younger boys to make snares for the rats that are everywhere in camp. When you get right down to it, rats are just ugly squirrels, and so we eat them when we catch them. Every calorie counts, and we need the protein. There are pigeons too, and we have woven together large nets from scraps of rope and cordage that is scattered through the wreckage of the original camp. I have high hopes that we can net some birds soon for the same reasons as the rats. Any form of food will supplement what we can gather as the supply drops. They are dwindling as well, the rations we receive. I have a feeling it won't be long now.

* * *

Ray was walking with another man that had approached him about midmorning. They were touring their little community, and the man was mentally taking notes, Ray could tell. He was one of the "leaders" in the greater camp area and had come to pick Ray's brain and maybe take his measure of him. Ray was a little exasperated these days. It seemed that so many people wanted to talk to him. He just couldn't figure out why that would be so. Apparently, common sense wasn't so common these days. None of the people that wanted to talk to him seemed to have any. If things were filthy, you cleaned them. If water was questionable, you boiled it and filtered it through a cloth if nothing else was available. If chaos consumed an area, then order needed to be restored. If people were stealing, you stopped them and got your stuff back. A group of people with the same goals could accomplish way more than an individual.

The man had asked him another question, and Ray's mind had been wandering. He was smiling, watching a group of five boys returning with almost two dozen pigeons. He gave them a thumbs-up as they ran past with their haul. The nets had worked, then.

"I'm sorry, what was that?" Ray asked absently. "I was somewhere else for a moment there, I apologize."

"I asked how everyone in your part of camp seems to stay so clean," he said.

"Well, we put up a small gravity-fed cistern kind of thing and lined it with plastic sheeting to catch all the snow or rain or drizzle that has been coming down at night. It goes through a filtration system that we built out of alternating layers of sand and charcoal and canvas, and then it drains into garbage cans that we salvaged and scoured out for collection. Then it's just a matter of boiling it and keeping it in a centralized area so that people can clean themselves and their clothing. Some of the water is used for cooking, and a lot of it is used for cleaning. We got some soap when we came in, so it's basically just soap and water, but it works."

The man nodded.

"The important thing is that we work together and everyone does their part. Everyone works, and everyone shares in the results. We look out for one another, pay attention to what others need, and then devise a plan to get there. Sanitation is important, so proper latrines needed to be constructed. No one had enough food on their own, so people decided to pool what they had and devise alternate means of getting more," Ray said, nodding to the boys with the pigeons.

"How is it that you were able to get all this stuff?" he asked, looking around. "Seems to me you people are pretty lucky to have all this."

"Believe me," Ray said, laughing easily, "luck has nothing to do with it. It's hard work and planning and organization. All 'this stuff' is out there, just waiting to be turned into something else."

Ray pointed at the debris fields for emphasis.

"How come none of it has been stolen? How come no one has robbed you people yet?"

"We don't tolerate thieves here," Ray said quietly.

"What about when you go line up for food? I imagine people would be here in a heartbeat to take what you have."

"Well," Ray sighed, "we have volunteers who stay and guard the camp while the others are getting rations. Everyone shares equally in what is brought back."

He nodded to a big man carrying a cudgel who was walking past.

"Security helps people sleep better at night."

"Well, it looks like you have an answer to everything, don't you, mister? You have it all figured out, don't you?" He gave a mean little laugh. "Not everyone is as lucky as you people seem to be or as smug about it."

This was exasperating. Ray had stuff to do. He didn't mind explaining things if people were actively listening and trying to implement a similar setup, but he didn't have time to listen to someone whine about their situation either. Not if they were too stupid or unwilling to do the work themselves.

"I *told* you," he said patiently, "luck has nothing to do with it. It's hard work. You could accomplish the same thing if you wanted to. It just takes a little effort, well, a lot of effort, really."

"I'd be real careful if I were you. Other people are noticing your little commie setup over here, California Man! They might just decide to come on over here and take it all soon. Not everyone believes your little stories either."

Ray stopped walking, a hard look on his face. He had wondered when the next threat was coming. He just hadn't thought it would come from a little weasel like this.

"Are you threatening us?" Ray asked. "Because if you are, you need to realize something. There are ten thousand other people in this camp. Filthy, starving, stupid victims just like you, who keep waiting for *them*, *they* to come help them, that somehow life will go back to being the way it was before The Day. Threats have real meaning now, and no one is coming to help you. You don't know how to do anything useful, so eventually, you will die, just like all the other people that have died so far. You need to learn how to do things, how to build, how to help yourself, because if you don't, you will not survive. If you come take what we have built here, we will fight for it. People are gonna die. If you take it without knowing how to maintain it or keep it going, in a week you will still be a stupid, filthy, starving piece of shit like you are right now. Two weeks ago, this little patch of dirt looked just like the rest of that shit out there. We did all this in two weeks! How long have you been here? Since the beginning? What is your excuse?"

The man started to stutter something, but Ray wasn't having it.

"I SAID SHUT THE FUCK UP AND LISTEN!" he roared. People were turning to see the one-sided conversation, and the little weasel started to wilt under the glares being directed his way.

"If you are going to do something, then do something," Ray hissed. "Bring it! Now get the fuck out of here!"

He turned and ran back to the main part of the camp, with Ray glaring after him. He spat to the side as Maggie joined him.

She slipped her arm around his waist.

"What was that about?" she asked.

"Another dumb son of a bitch who wants a piece of the good life at someone else's expense, of course."

"Of course," she replied. "Do you think there's gonna be trouble?"

"Probably," he sighed. "How about you? Any new gossip? Found out anything?"

"Well, nothing much new, really. I have been talking to the doc and some of the gate guards when they are on duty and I can get away with it. Some are from my part of Missouri. Can you believe that? How in the world they ended up out here in Colorado after The Day is beyond me. Things are falling apart out there, but we kind of gathered that. Soldiers are slipping away in the night, and desertion is rampant. There are only half as many guards left since we came in two weeks ago. Have you noticed?"

Ray nodded.

"It's nice to talk about home, Ray. Some of them are from very near to where I grew up. I don't know any of them, but we went to the same places, hangouts, know some people that I used to know. That kind of thing. Nobody has heard anything from home, though. I am working a few angles to see if they may take us with them when they slip away. It's just a matter of time now, I think. Food is running out. They are starting to think about their own families maybe locked up in a place like this. I have a bad feeling about all this, Ray, like it's all about to go bad."

"When was the last time you felt really good about something, Maggie?"

"This morning," she said, blushing a little.

"Well," he said, clearing his throat with a grin, "besides that."

"All we can do is our best, right?"

"I'm trying, Maggie," he whispered. "I'm trying really hard."

"I know."

He put his arm around her as they walked back to their little hut, talking to folks along the way and keeping spirits up. The pigeons were clean and plucked and ready for the stew later after they were roasted. It would be a little more for dinner at least.

* * *

Five o'clock finally arrived, and Ray and Maggie and thirty others from their group had been waiting by the gate for hours just like everyone else. Evening rations. Only three trucks were pulling up to the gates tonight, and a ripple of dismay went through the crowd behind them. The jostling increased, and a few fistfights broke out. Ray noticed with a chill that there were maybe, at most, forty-five soldiers present. Last night, there had been hundreds. He counted them again and blinked. Where were the rest of them? He bent to whisper in Maggie's ear.

As they looked around, it seemed as if everyone else was focused on the trucks backing up to the gates, with the backup alarms beeping. With a hiss of hydraulic brakes and the taillights flashing one final time, they came to a stop. Soldiers jumped up into the beds and began to unload. Shortly, there were three large piles of crated food on the ground. The captain, the camp commander, jumped up on a tailgate, a bullhorn in hand, to address the crowd.

"Ladies and gentlemen," he began to the now silent crowd, "thank you for your patience this evening. We have received new orders and will be pulling out of here soon, reassigned elsewhere for the duration. It is my duty to inform you that this will be the *last* shipment of food for the camp. Perhaps more will arrive at a later point, but if so, it will be distributed by other agencies than the United States Army. We would like to thank you, for your—"

A brick flew out of the crowd and clipped the side of his head, and he went down suddenly.

An ugly growl was racing through the crowd as a sergeant leaned down to retrieve the bullhorn.

"You did this to us! You brought us here! You made us come here when we didn't want to! Liar!" an old woman shrieked, bending to pick up another rock to throw.

The crowd snarled a little louder.

"I think," Ray started to say as more debris was hurled.

"People, please!" The sergeant was addressing the crowd now. "If I may have your attention."

"It's time to . . ." Ray continued.

"May I have your attention!"

"Get out of the way."

People surged forward, hurling themselves at the gate, as Ray slammed Maggie to the side so they wouldn't be trampled. A human wave hit the chain link, and in short order, the chains holding it closed burst. People were going under and not coming up again. They tried to stay to the side, but the opening was enlarged as more people surged through, and Ray and Maggie were swept along with the crowd. The fence was completely ripped off its support posts just as the soldiers opened fire on the crowd. Thousands surged toward the food and trucks, and thousands more swarmed the skirmish line under. Ray tried to hang on to her hands, but as more and more people came between them, he felt his grip slipping, and Maggie was ripped away from him and swirled away around the corner of a nearby building.

"MAGGIE!" he screamed.

More automatic weapons erupted, and Ray ducked into the closest doorway he could find to escape the crowd. Huddled there, he watched as people were torn apart, shot, and trampled everywhere he looked. Desperate souls hurled themselves on the guards, armed with sticks and rocks and broken glass. They tore them apart when they were finally overrun. The turret gunner on the Abrams opened up with the .50, and blood seemed to mist everywhere as the massive slugs tore through the press. He barely managed to get the hatch down and dogged before the survivors were up on the turret, battering away at the hatches with improvised tools and fists. The tank began to rumble away up the street, and there were still thousands of people in the press. Ray emerged from the doorway and scanned the intersection, looking for her. The tank's main gun began to swivel. Everywhere he looked, it was chaos, and no sign of Maggie. Ray pushed into the crowd now that it was thinning, throwing people out of his way, frantically looking for her everywhere.

"MAGGIE!" he screamed again.

Some of the nearby buildings had caught fire, and smoke was everywhere. The trucks were burning too. People heaved and fought and bit and thrashed over what was left of the food nearby. Just *piles* of people in a heaving, ungainly mass. He was standing there, searching for her, when the main gun of the tank erupted and blew out the entire side of the building he was standing in front of. The concussion and blast wave picked him up and slammed him down into the pavement as bits of brick and metal, rubble, and people rained down around him. He couldn't hear, he couldn't see, and he couldn't breathe for a moment. Gasping in a deep, wracking gulp of air, he sobbed for a moment just at the luxury of air. The world spun slowly, and eventually, he was able to roll over and sit up. The entire intersection was full of smashed people and parts of people and debris. He wiped blood from his eyes, and ears, and nose, and he wasn't sure if it was his own or someone else's. Everything felt strange and unreal.

In the distance, he heard more automatic weapons fire and felt more than heard the main gun erupt again.

He scanned the square one last time. Everything was burning now. He coughed smoke out of his lungs and shuffled past the piles of people fighting over food and back to their hovel. The shelter that he had built with Maggie. Pushing through people, ignoring their questions and concerns. He had to get back. He knew she would be there.

But she wasn't.

Forty-five soldiers never stood a chance against ten thousand starving people. Ray cleaned himself up as best as he could, just knowing that she would be back soon. He packed their remaining belongings into one of the two backpacks. He grabbed two bowls of stew and retired to the hovel to wait. He rolled his sleeping bag and got it into the stuff sack and strapped it to the pack. Then he settled in to wait. Maggie would find him here; she had to. She would come back. They would keep going. Going home. Ray built up the fire and sat there as the long night dragged on and on and into the next morning, but Maggie never came back.

Ray shouldered the pack the next morning. He nodded to a few familiar faces as he walked out of what was left of Camp Loveland. He had to wade over the bodies by the front gate. Some still twitched and moaned. It was horrible. He began his search by looking over the area where he had last seen her. He turned over the body of every woman with long brown hair, but none of them were her. The tank was long gone, the trucks smoldering skeletons of their former selves. The soldiers were dead or had fled, and there were hundreds of people still milling about, unsure of what to do. They all looked dazed and helpless.

He walked eastward toward the plains for two days in a weary, struggling column of people. They fell by the roadside in ones and twos, never to rise again. He turned bodies over in the ditches to see if any of them were *her*, but none were. At the end of the first day, he thought he had seen her far ahead of him, walking, but his frantic shouts never prompted the figure to stop and turn in his direction. He did not have the energy to run and catch up. Ray finally fell into his walking rhythm and just kept going. Thinking his own thoughts and riding the wind in his mind. At the end of his third day of walking, he achieved a kind of self-awareness again and, for a brief moment, clarity of thought. Looking around, he realized that he was walking alone again.

He had lost her, and he didn't know what to do about it. So he kept walking, kept passing bodies on the road, afraid that one of them might be hers. He finally stopped checking. Freezing and alone, he holed up in the ruins of Greeley for the night and fell into a deep and troubled sleep.

Had She Told Him?

CHAPTER 50

Maggie walked the fence line of the camp speculatively. She was watching quietly for the guard change at the gates. For the last few days, she had been carefully cultivating a pair of the guards. Jessica Sims and Angela Adams were from the same county that she was from in Missouri. Their accents had been a dead giveaway. The first time she had overheard them talking, the only thing she could think was, *They're from home!* Of course, she had confronted them immediately and introduced herself. They had been surprised at first, but after asking all the typical questions about restaurants, hangouts, swimming holes, and truck stops, she could tell that they knew she was the real deal.

Maggie wondered how they had ended up guarding a refugee camp in Loveland, Colorado, and carefully, *carefully*, she had been extracting little bits of information and feeling them out about maybe leaving and taking herself and Ray with them. Maggie had a few more things to worry about lately and had had the biggest thing confirmed a little while ago. She couldn't wait to tell Ray. It was a shitty world, but it had its moments. The doc was from her home county as well, along with their CO and two other soldiers she hadn't met yet. Maggie could tell by the way they talked that they were just about done with this situation. She could read between the lines that they had a plan, and she wanted in on that plan, very much so indeed.

She met a new soldier when Angela came on duty for the afternoon. His name was Paul Green. He was maybe one of the biggest guys that she had ever met, not the brightest bulb in the room, but he *was* good-looking, strong, and nice. She could tell Angela had the hots for him. Their National Guard unit had been on a weekend exercise near Omaha on The Day, cooperating with frontline troops and elite forces. The government had snapped them up and sent them to Colorado to distribute supplies and set up the refugee camp at Loveland. Over the winter, out of the original 122 soldiers and officers, only the 6 of them remained. The rest had been picked off in the mountains, died from accidents or camp violence, or had already deserted and tried to make their way back home.

Maggie could tell they were close to a decision just like that, but the camp commander was a real piece of work. He was hard core, draconian, by the book, and the rest of the enlisted men and women stepped lightly around him. Whenever he passed by, the guards would stop talking to people near the gates and look like they were busy, staring off into space. It was frustrating. Maggie wanted to *talk*. The reality was that they couldn't really.

She had been in to see the doc that morning outside the gates of the camp, reminding him about where that little influx of antibiotics and painkillers had come from, and sweetly told him about where she was from and that she was trying to get home too. Doc had grinned at her and shrugged, like he knew exactly what she was getting at, but he had talked about home too. Lieutenant Jill Kelly had popped her head into the room at that point, and Doc had introduced her as well. Jill had been the one to carefully escort her back to the camp, the two women talking on the way.

So now, Maggie was back inside the fence, and after chatting with the gate guards for a few, she went back to their camp, waving to a few people along the way. She was proud of Ray and proud of all they had accomplished since arriving here. At that moment, he was walking with another man, pointing out projects, explaining how things were working in their part of the camp. A lot of people had paid attention to what they were doing, had taken an interest, and had begun cooperating. There was strength in numbers. Now people had at least *something* to eat every day and clean water to drink. They were cleaner and more organized, healthier, and there was a little more hope around than before. Their shelters were warmer, more solid, and things were just *better*. Maggie watched how animated Ray became when he had an idea or a project to share, his enthusiasm running away with him sometimes. She loved him very much, and she hoped that when they got out of here, her family would still be alive to meet him in Missouri.

Ray went from animated and enthusiastic to cold and angry. It was a little scary to watch the transformation sometimes. That asshole must have said something.

"Uh-oh," she murmured, beginning to walk toward the two men around her. The other members of their camp were hefting boards and other things, glaring at the little man now scuttling away with his tail between his legs.

"Hi!" she said brightly to distract him from glaring after the little ferret. "What was that all about?"

"Oh, another dumb son of a bitch who wants a piece of the good life. At someone else's expense, of course," Ray replied.

"Of course," she murmured.

They walked back to their part of camp, Maggie half-listening to what Ray was saying and nodding at the appropriate parts. She was just happy to be with him. She looked around the camp. It wasn't her idea of paradise, but it was going to be what they made of it for as long as they were stuck here.

"I'm doing the best I can, babe," Ray whispered.

"I know, Ray," she replied. "I know you are. That's all we can do, right?"

The afternoon passed with laundry, butchering pigeons unfortunate enough to get inside the wire, communal cooking, water purification, and other chores. Soon, it would be time to go get in line for rations at the front gates. Ray was assigning guards to stay behind and keep watch and designate today's ration crew. There were a few small boys bringing in rats and pigeons to add to the pot, and she grimaced, but food was food at this point, and they needed as many calories as they could get. Besides, keeping the little bastards' number down was probably healthier in the long run for everyone.

Soon it would be time to go wait in line for their evening rations. They needed to line up early and do a little shoving to keep their place in line. There was less food coming in now than there had been just a few weeks before when they had arrived, and every day it got harder to make do with what they had. There had to be some way they could send out foraging parties on their own outside the wire. There just had to be. They waited inside the gates for almost four hours before the trucks approached. There were only three today. *Three* trucks for roughly ten thousand people. Maggie craned her neck, looking for Jill and Angela or Jessica, and didn't see them anywhere. That was odd. She counted the soldiers present. There weren't very many at all. Then all hell broke loose.

She tried to hang on to Ray's hand as the crowd surged and moved around them like a huge unruly beast. People that were right in front of the gates as the rioting began were trampled. Her arm stretched out, more and more people forcing their way in between them, and then it was move or be trampled herself. She was swept through the gates outside, past the trucks, and around the corner, calling Ray's name the entire time. She finally wedged herself into a doorway and watched the crowd stream past. Finally, when it had thinned enough, she began forcing her way back toward where she had last seen him.

She stepped around the corner just in time to watch Ray die. He was standing amid the crowd, searching for her, looking everywhere. She saw the tank's main gun swiveling and pointing into the crowd. Suddenly, the main gun erupted right into the building behind him. As she opened her mouth to scream a warning, the building shattered, and she ducked back behind her own corner just in time to avoid a blood-soaked hail of body parts and debris.

Peeking back around the corner, she didn't see him anymore. Just a rubble-strewn stretch of street full of twitching and dying things that used to be people. The air was choked with dust, and she saw the tank moving up the street into the smoke, people hammering futilely on the hatches with improvised tools, trying desperately to get at the gun crew inside.

"Jesus," she whispered. She was about to go searching through the bodies in the street when a hand seized her upper arm with an iron grip.

Maggie spun to see Jill Kelly, the lieutenant from Missouri, with a finger to her lips, motioning Maggie inside the building. Maggie followed.

"I thought that was you," she whispered.

"My god, Jill! They will kill you if they see you in that uniform."

"I know," she replied. "Come with me. There isn't a lot of time."

The two women went through a doorway and down some stairs inside a musty cellar. There she found Angela, Jessica, Green, Miller, and the doc, Dorance Grey. The whole Missouri squad. They were deeply involved in changing out their camo fatigues and into civilian clothing. They still looked and moved like soldiers, but the obvious signs were disappearing quickly.

"We have had enough of this, Maggie," Jill said quietly, stripping off her uniform and putting on street clothes. "We all discussed it, the others here and the doc., and we're going home. He even wrote out the medical discharge papers so it's official."

Maggie stared at them changing into warm winter clothing and shook her head, stifling a sob.

"Day late and a dollar short," she whispered.

"Do you want to come with us? You and your guy are more than welcome to, and one more makes the job go a little faster."

Jill stared at Maggie, who was now hyperventilating, her head down, her hands on her knees. Suddenly, she ran to the corner and vomited.

"You okay?" Jill asked behind her.

"No. No, I'm not, Jill. I will go with you, though. It's more important than ever now."

Jill nodded uncertainly.

Maggie reached under her collar and squeezed the bear tooth. He was gone, gone, and there was nothing to be done for it. She could cry later, but right now, they needed to *go*.

416

"Good. Here, you are going to need these," she said, handing Maggie an automatic rifle, a belt with a holstered pistol, some webbing with additional magazines, and grenades.

"Jill, I—"

"Just stay close, girl. We're going out low and fast. Don't worry about firing your weapon. We'll train you on that later. If we get in a fight, just stay in the middle with doc, okay?"

Maggie nodded.

"You okay?" Jill asked again, and Maggie took a deep breath, nodding abruptly. "Good."

Jill looked around the cellar at the other five people, who were now changed into civilian clothing. They were all carrying small packs stuffed with useful items. The doc, with his medical kit, winked at Maggie. She felt herself tensing up, just barely holding the tears at bay.

"Just watch me, Maggie. Okay? I know this is hard, but stay right on my ass, and you move when I do, all right?"

Looking around the room, Jill made eye contact with everyone else.

"Are we ready?" she asked.

Everyone nodded.

"All right. Let's *do this*, people! Miller, Green, on point. *Go!*"

They raced up the stairs. Jill, Maggie, and Doc were next, followed by Angela and Jessica.

They exited quickly into the smoke-blanketed street, staying low and moving from cover to cover. They traversed Loveland and had almost made it to the edge of town when two shots rang out ahead. Green stumbled, hopping into view, and slumped against the wall, his teeth gritted.

He cried out.

"*That* really fucking *hurts!*"

The doc moved forward to tend to the leg. Two more shots rang out, and Miller appeared, signing them forward.

"Got 'em, Lieutenant," he said.

"All right! Keep moving, people! We have two miles to the hummer. We can *do* this, people! Go! Go! Go!"

Green was supported on either side by Jessica and Angela, Miller ghosting ahead with Jill, and Doc brought up the rear, carrying Green's weapon and covering their back trail.

They ran and ran and ran. They got the hell out of Loveland.

The next two miles were exhausting, but they made it without incident. What was left of Loveland was burning behind them. Jill and her people had stashed the vehicle three days earlier. It was right where they had left it. Miller climbed inside, manning the twin .50's in the roof turret. Jill got behind the wheel, and Green slumped in the back with Angela and Jessica, fussing over his leg. The doc got back there too. Maggie climbed in on the passenger side, and with a snarl and spitting gravel, they lurched across the field and up onto the roadway. There were full packs in the back with rations, more ammunition, and as many cans of gasoline as they had been able to scrounge. Maggie nodded to herself. It looked like they had been planning this for a while.

She looked sideways at Jill Kelly in profile. One hundred percent focused on the road ahead and grinning. She was short, energetic, her hair was in a blond pageboy cut, and she didn't put up with any shit. Maggie had liked her immediately.

"Are we there yet?" she asked.

Jill looked at her for a moment like she had lost her mind, and then she smiled a wicked grin.

"Why don't we play 'I spy' a little later?" she replied.

"How about some show tunes?" Green asked from the backseat through gritted teeth. The doc was debriding the wound on his leg.

"I have to go to the bathroom!"

"Mom! Green is on my side of the seat!"

"Quiet back there, or I will turn this Humvee right around!" Jill yelled out, then she whooped.

The banter continued for quite a while. Laughing they drove into the twilight, the eastern sky darkening in front of them.

Maggie looked out the window, tears rolling down her cheeks. Had she told him? Had she told him that she loved him? She couldn't remember.

Author's Notes

I used a few lyrics from songs that I like in the course of writing this. The bands that sing them should be listened to...a lot. They are their words after all, and not mine. Music has been gradually getting darker in theme over the last few decades, gradually ramping up to, and I swear, singing about the end of us all. If you listen between the words, the apocalypse is there, waiting for us.

I wrote the kind of book that I have always wanted to read, and did so for myself, before I ever thought of publishing it. Everyone needs a little dark paradise to escape to from time to time, and this one was mine. A sequel will be forthcoming entitled, *Take the Long Way Home.* It's a little scary to let other people into that world. Judge me if you must, but keep in mind that this is my first book. I think with enough practice, I might just get better.

Ed Peden is a real guy by the way. If you are in the market for a used missile base like Harley Earl's, you can find him on www.missilebases.com. If this book does well(ahem) with the way the country is going, I may talk to Ed myself real soon, we'll see.

The Armageddon Plan was, and maybe IS a very real thing. A guy by the name of James Mann wrote about it a bunch of years ago in The Atlantic, and does a much better job of dropping names, and explaining how The Program worked than I ever could. His article is worth a read, and it made me start wondering how that whole process would go down in an election year, especially when the country is as polarized politically as it is right now. Keep that in mind the next time you vote please.

The Iranians have been training with missile gantries on oil tankers in the Persian Gulf since at least 2002. I read about it in the news then, before the story vanished completely. Remember when the news used to actually report on the news? Before fear stifled their first amendment rights and investigative journalism was a worthwhile pursuit? No one can tell me that if the chance presented itself, that the Iranians would refrain from attacking us, just like I wrote about in the book. EMP is a very serious threat to our nation. Ted Koppel recently just wrote a book called *Lights Out*. Read it please, and then think about the world without all of the things that we take for granted.

The world becomes much larger when you remove the means of travelling through it quickly. This is a big story, in a big world. Stop for a moment and think about how far people commute to work every single day. Then imagine having to do it on foot or bicycle. Pretty scary right?

Finally, to the illustrious Stephen King, I hope that it's okay that I borrowed your raven for a few moments. I couldn't resist, I was having a moment, and I truly hope that you would survive and thrive in Maine in the event of a catastrophe. Even if the man in black lured you to New York City, I imagine you might be able to write your way out of it. Somehow.

So that's it. Until next time, be safe, be well, and pay attention to what's going on around you. It might just save your life.

R.T. Hayton
4/12/16

About the Author

R. T. Hayton is a fan of the outdoors. He enjoys hunting, fishing, backpacking, and from time to time, historical reenacting of the French and Indian War period in colonial American history. (It's an excuse to go camping really old-school style.) He is interested in people, politics, history, native artifacts, and travel. He has lived all over the continental United States but currently resides in the Chicago area with his dachshund, Cooper.

This is his first novel.

CPSIA information can be obtained
at www.ICGtesting.com
Printed in the USA
LVOW12s1318011116
511186LV00001B/67/P